Praise for William Wiser's *Disappearances:*

"A compellingly rich and original novel featuring two interlocking story frames. One is a crime documentary centering on the charming and infamous Landru, 'Bluebeard,' who was guillotined in 1922 for murdering ten women and a boy, though none of their bodies were ever found. The other, told in ironic counterpoint by the same fictitious narrator, who was a reporter at the Landru trial, is an American-in-Paris memoir. Its focus is on the narrator's many encounters with Stein, Toklas, and their artist friends, and his erotic adventures in the Parisian demimonde. . . . Full of sharp observation and wit, as polished in style as in narrative technique, the story has a wry and haunting quality that makes one want to read it twice."
— *Publishers Weekly*

"A novel of real literary merit. . . . It has its own kind of haunting mystery and suspense mingled with humor, philosophy, and admirable style. . . . Mr. Wiser does a masterful job with the Misses Stein and Toklas. His Gertrude speaks flawless Steinese. He has made them alive and appealing, evoking the creative electricity at their soirees in the Rue de Fleurus."
— EDMUND FULLER, *The Wall Street Journal*

"One of the most satisfying novels of the last several years. . . . Mr. Wiser's portrait of Paris may be the best in English since Henry Miller's *Tropic of Cancer.*"
— ANATOLE BROYARD, *The New York Times*

DISAPPEARANCES

DISAPPEARANCES

WILLIAM WISER

Carroll & Graf Publishers, Inc.
New York

Copyright © 1980 by William Wiser

This edition is published by arrangement with the author and the author's agent, Curtis Brown Ltd.

First Carroll & Graf edition 1992

Carroll & Graf Publishers, Inc.
260 Fifth Avenue
New York, NY 10001

Library of Congress Cataloging-in-Publication Data

Wiser, William.
    Disappearances / by William Wiser. — 1st Carroll & Graf ed.
      p.   cm.
    ISBN 0-88184-786-0 : $10.95
    I. Title.
  [PS3573.I87D5   1992]
  813'.54—dc20   91-29127
                                                                      CIP

Manufactured in the United States of America

FOR MICHELLE

The author gratefully acknowledges the support of a grant from the National Endowment for the Arts, which helped him complete this novel.

Contents

LIES

One

————————————

CONSIDER THESE BONES. Scattered across a courtroom table in Versailles was less than a kilo of bone fragments, plus a kilo of cinders —perhaps four pounds out of a missing ton of human tissue. Experts declared the calcinated splinters were pieces of tibia, radius, cubitus, and one tooth: they were tagged as such. The cinders contained 5 percent phosphate; the normal amount would have been .5 percent, whatever that meant. A large part of the remaining ash was made up of chicken bones and oyster shells.

I wondered what Cuvier would have made of this pitiful exhibit. From the scantiest skeletal evidence he could flesh out a dinosaur. (I refer to Baron Georges Léopold Chrétien Frédéric Dagobert Cuvier, 1769–1832, a pioneer in the science of comparative anatomy.) He found a way to reconstruct extinct mammals from as little as a fossilized footprint. But this was 1921 and there was no Cuvier to prove to us this pile of ash and broken bone was all that remained of ten women and one young man.

A dapper, bearded dealer in secondhand furniture was on trial. He had spent two and a half years in prison waiting for the bones to be sorted, the ashes analyzed, and the testimony of concierges and sisters-in-law to come in. His own meticulous notebooks appeared to be the only incriminating evidence against him, for he had kept detailed records and accounts concerning the eleven missing persons. He was accused of having invited women to his rented villa at Gambais with the promise of marriage (he was already married, with four children), and there he murdered them by means unknown, dismembered the corpses, then burnt the heads and limbs in his kitchen stove.

Is it any wonder the public took such an interest in the case?

Landru steadfastly maintained his innocence: he admitted only to that which could be proved. Yes, he did invite these women to his villa, in the way of business, for he had agreed to act as their agent in the disposal of furniture and other salable items. If a relationship of an intimate nature was suggested by the court, Landru refused to respond —that was a matter between himself and the lady in question. What, then, became of his clients once the business transaction was terminated? It was no longer his affair. "You will have to ask them," he replied.

At the time I was, almost by accident, a journalist in Paris. I had managed to get a job with a newspaper syndicate called the Channel News Service in the spring of 1919. The syndicate was no syndicate at all, but a man named O'Grady who worked and slept in an office on the rue d'Artois—I was his assistant. Much of what I wrote over a period of three years, under the aegis of O'Grady, had to do with the Landru Affair.

For more years than I care to remember I have been haunted by what I knew and wrote about Henri Désiré Landru. The facts of the case are on file, but mostly forgotten. Perhaps some of the news items I wrote lie yellowing in the morgues of the Manchester *Guardian* and the *Irish Times*—I would not know, I would not want to read them. Nearly fifty years have passed. In those years not one of the victims of Landru was ever proved definitely dead or even possibly alive. Landru's fiancées are missing persons to this day.

I wrote about the case as it unfolded, thus my original scribblings were hastily done. That is the trouble with the news. There will always be some question concerning the truth of what I or any other journalist wrote under the pressure of a deadline. Much of the information behind a news story is inevitably secondhand, then the copy must pass thirdhand through the rewrite of an indifferent or slipshod editor. The truth, of course, is slippery stuff. There can be as much truth in a detective novel as a newspaper account of the same crime. I do not mean to suggest I am writing a novel. Landru would be out of place in a roman policier—and so, for that matter, would I. A celebrated literary lady once said of Landru, "He does not translate."

As for me, she said, "You are completely at home in a world of four corners." (The blunt term "square" had not yet come into vogue.) This famous writer was trying to be gentle but truthful about some stories I had asked her to read. "I do like the one about the man who inherited the guillotine from his father."

That was an essay about Anatole Deibler, the French executioner. "That actually happened."

"You see?" said my friend.

She intimated, and I am obliged to confirm, that I do not possess the gift for fiction. In fact, as O'Grady pointed out, I am not even a competent liar. So be it, as my father used to say.

A young American professor and his wife have come to visit with me for several waning summer days. The professor's inquiries have brought on these memories full flood. I put the words to paper not in the hope or need of literary recognition, but simply for release—release from remembering.

My purpose is to render a factual account of the trial and conviction of the Bluebeard of Gambais. (I am lying already! That is not my purpose.)

Let me begin again: My purpose is to render a factual account of my life from the time of Landru's arrest until his trial and conviction. Peace, my literary friend would say, if she were alive to say it. The man was a monster, c'est tout. But I have no peace. In several oblique ways the monster's life touched mine. We shared at least one obsession.

I grow more skeptical with age. Cuvier proved the Brontosaurus was herbivorous and the Tyrannosaurus was a carnivore but he could have been mistaken: eons have passed since these great beasts fed upon grass, or one another. I am no Cuvier. I reassemble these bones of the missing for reasons of my own. The need to know or believe one knows is a very old and completely human failing. In the Perrault tale of Barbe-Bleue, Fatima, the seventh wife of the chevalier Raoul, is permitted to enter every room of the chateau save one. Of course she will go into that forbidden room. Let sleeping dogs lie is a foolish piece of advice. Besides, I must exorcise a ghost.

Two

MY MOTHER DID NOT come with us. "I cannot bear to see my poor sad devastated country." (My father did not try to convince her to come, for she would have been in the way of his plans.) To me France in February of 1919 was not poor or sad or devastated—perhaps because we went first to Paris. True, there were soldiers about, looking grim, with mud on their boots and something awful in their eyes. The number diminished daily as they were discharged. (Demobilization was the one operation the French performed with speed and efficiency.) The next time you saw them they were civilians looking for work with stiff collars and sober neckties and ribbons in their buttonholes.

The façade of the Madeleine had been chipped by a shell from Big Bertha, and a zeppelin had bombed to rubble a block of the rue de Rivoli. I noticed an occasional Red Cross armband, but the ambulances had been converted into taxis. There was an artillery post on the roof of the Hôtel de Ville. Patriotic posters were peeling or covered over with posters for the comedy *Phi-Phi*. You were asked to give up your seat on the métro to mutilés de la guerre. (My father had no intention of associating with the mutilated, so he did not travel by métro.) There was a shortage of truffles and shellfish. I knew there were casualties groaning in suburban hospitals—some of them American—but we did not see them.

Paris began to stir after the latest siege. Reunited couples filed into the city halls of Paris to be married en masse. Older women were wearing lip rouge for the first time, and the skirt hems of the young approached the knee. None of the new songs mentioned the war. The horror had been pasted over like the posters.

My father and I stayed at a hotel on the rue Saint-Honoré across from the Ministry of Finance. I think we stayed there because Madame S was at the Meurice, not far away. She was my father's Swiss widow, and I suspect she paid the bills. I do know she paid that first night's dinner, with champagne. The meal was festive and expensive but my stomach had not altogether subsided from the voyage. Our cabin was only one deck above steerage and I had been miserably seasick on the *Leopoldina*. My father said it was all in the mind—but he had spent his time with Madame S, in first class. It was good to have terra firma underfoot, and to dine on filet de turbot from a motionless table. Madame S slipped me the money to pay the waiter while my father pretended to calculate exchange rates. I passed the bills to him beneath the tablecloth, enough to include cognac and an after-dinner cigar.

Palais Royale was a pleasant quarter and if not the heart of Paris, only a heartbeat away. The Hôtel des Bons Enfants was not particularly chic and my father frowned upon the view. Our window looked into the windows of the Ministry of Finance. At the ministry it was business as usual, and had probably been so all during the war. The clerks wore green eyeshades and put a rubber thimble on one finger to riffle through dossiers. It was a world of ink pots and wrinkled foreheads. After the bellboy opened the drapes the first night, my father never again glanced in that direction. The chief clerk drank bottled water in his semiprivate cubicle and kept galoshes in a desk drawer. From time to time he came to the window (unaware he was being watched), opened it wide, and struggled for breath, as if he were drowning in his cubicle. I did not know you could drown in that way, in Paris—but the cadavers of suicides fished from the Seine were not all identified as disappointed lovers: many might have drowned in their cubicles first.

When I shared this thought with my father he said, "Possibly," and changed the subject. He had an eye for the ladies, but he did not look out of hotel windows at clerks across the street.

My father spent most of his time at the Meurice, so I walked the streets of Paris alone. For a week I seemed to carry a stone in my stomach, or in my throat, but I was too enchanted by the place to feel homesick for long—yet not quite at home in that extraordinary city. How different the façade here from Baltimore's scrubbed doorsteps, how different the anticipation of what will pass behind the façade.

It was a grey time, midwinter, and Paris is a grey city, the fortress color of metal and stone: a hard place that goes soft in a certain light. The light shifts, and with it the ambience. The sun may break through for no reason from a slit of unexpected heaven, a passing cloud will turn the gun-metal grey to pearl. A sense of elation might lie at the end of an obscure cul-de-sac, or, exploring a new quarter, my heart could shrink at the sudden onset of dark.

That first winter was dark, admittedly. (How much darker were the winters during the war?) Nevertheless a peculiar light filters through the dark, early and late. Paris will show herself when she chooses. There is a dark curtain one afternoon or evening; the curtain becomes a veil, the veil is drawn for an instant (a bearded man lifts his hat to a homely woman on the omnibus—why?) then the dark comes down. Or the grey sky will close in, with clouds low enough to touch, then lift lightly as a pigeon wings its way across the Seine.

The week I still felt the stone in my throat there appeared suddenly in the February rain a mass of white carnations at a stall with a charcoal brazier—red coals to melt stone. Shopgirls, those other flowers, were bundled against the chill on the boulevard des Italiens. Their stark white faces came toward me, just faces, but I could imagine the rest—I knew they were perfumed and pliant under the scarves and fur. I fell in love with their flower faces all at once, then one at a time, and yearned to pluck just one flower out of the rain and cold and warm her at a charcoal brazier of my own.

"You seem to be fogbound," said my father when we met in the lobby or at breakfast.

My father enjoyed a hearty breakfast, English-style, at a late morning hour. I was glad of a hasty croissant and strong coffee with chicory as soon as the first light showed. You would have thought I had a rendezvous, but there was no one out there in the grey to meet me—yet I could hardly wait to get out from under my father's indifferent wing. As soon as he finished breakfast and operated on his fingernails with a pen knife, the adventure was under way. He supplied me with money for lunch and we parted. The city was whispering to me, drawing me on. Anything could happen in a grey city as lovely and mysterious as this. I was open to seduction: eighteen years old, and a virgin.

Impossible to talk with my father about this extraordinary place: as far as we got was to laugh together over a drunk chasing his beret across the pont des Arts. My father had a cultured laugh and an occasional sense of humor. But how could I describe to him the man with glass windowpanes strapped to his back? When the light hit the panes a certain way you could see through the man.

"An optical illusion," said my father.

Of course—but . . .

I suffered alternately from diarrhea and constipation—the common plagues of tourists. My father said it was from the drinking water, so I drank only mineral water: my father drank champagne. I brushed my teeth with l'eau de Vichy; I do not know what he brushed his teeth with. The symptoms persisted: I was a tourist still—or had I caught a touch of typhoid, or Spanish influenza left over from the war? Light-headed and feverish, I bought a thermometer but I did not know what normal was, centigrade. All that I measured was the queer way I felt about Paris. It was all in the mind, as my father said.

Meanwhile I picked up pieces of the Paris jigsaw puzzle, in the streets, pieces I would never be able to put together entirely. I have them still, in my memory's eye, along with another puzzle with only one piece missing.

Once, I could swear, a stone angel holding up a cornice winked at me, and a painted horse's head at the sign of the boucherie-chevaline laughed. Then, when I was about to give a coin to a legless veteran collecting coins in an army helmet I was so startled to see a tattooed arm, a woman's, dangling from a passing taxi (there was a sausage in her hand) that I contributed instead of the intended coin a ten-franc note. I was being seduced, and mocked.

(Intermingled with these scenes, might I have seen Monsieur Frémyet—or Guillet, as Landru called himself then—politely guiding a ladyfriend by the elbow through the Luxembourg Gardens? I think not. Many of those who did claim to see him, including witnesses at his trial, did not really see him. As overwhelmed as I was by the daily spectacle of postwar Paris, my impressions of that period remain lucid and clear. I have an eye for a striking face, and his, I think, would have lingered in my memory. Despite the many published photographs and drawings of Landru, the man was a stranger to me when I first saw him in the courtroom at Versailles.)

My mood tilted extravagantly. At first I felt as buoyant as the street sweeper I saw vault onto the back of an omnibus with his broom. Yet, the display window of a Pompes Funèbres with its coffins tilted to show the crêpe linings and the apprentice stonecutter watering down the dust at the marble works next door depressed me for a day. When I came across a concierge feeding six kittens on a windowsill, I thought of my mother and instantly missed her, then forgot—yet I remember the concierge even as my mother's face fades. A daily mélange of sounds and smells stirred my adolescent blood. My dreams fed on a swirl of images I had taken in, nourished by unaccustomed quantities of wine. I was never drunk, but often close to delirium.

Even a flag could alter my pulse. A flag is so vivid against grey, especially the tricolor. (The war was over—I could afford to be a secondhand patriot inspired by flags.) My father would not have recognized the French flag flying over the Ministry of Finance across the street. Why should he?—he was a true son of the Stars and Stripes. It did not occur to him his wife had taught their son the words to the "Marseillaise." But the anthem I heard in the Parisian streets was a mélange of café conversation and bicycle horns, harmonicas and hurdy-gurdies. A street vendor's wheedling and the oath hurled at me by a fiacre driver were both part of my half-French heritage. In Paris I was aroused as well as comforted to find myself chez moi, to find myself out. It was here, I knew, I would come into my own.

Three

MY FATHER SET OFF for Delmonico's and I the opposite way.
Some streets around the market district of les Halles were still lit by
gas lamp. That end of the rue Saint-Honoré becomes narrow and desolate just before it enters the belly of Paris. (Zola called it that.) I
stopped for a demi of beer at the glassed-in terrace of a dim café. I was
the only customer. There were new waiters in aprons too large for
them, raw-shaven—perhaps soldiers returned from the war, trying on
civilian garb. The waiters paced restlessly between the empty tables,
happy only to have got back from the trenches alive, dead to all else—
if I read their faces right. I sat near the charcoal brazier for the spark
of life as much as the warmth. Outside, the ancient street lamps gave
off that peculiar ringed and jaundiced illumination of another century.
Gas lamps can be picturesque, but my inner eye speculated rather on
Delmonico's, on the avenue de l'Opéra, its named spelled out in white-
hot electric globes. (I had been there once only: Madame S paid.) My
beer tasted of rust.

Solitude had become unbearable. Paris is known for that. The
stone was in my throat again: I suddenly wanted my father to drive up
in a cab and call to me to join him, or them, if Madame S was with
him (and she surely was). But the street was empty, no sign of a cab.
In the shadow of a kiosk I saw what looked like a pregnant policeman.
He had a girl under his cape.

I left the desolate café, abandoned my watery beer in search of stronger stuff, and brighter light. Almost immediately I stepped into the world of the great market. This was the time of night the vast central Halles come alive, illuminated by arc lights and bonfires, populated mostly by hustling market loaders called les forts. (They drank calvados—and marc with breakfast—to keep up their strength.) Produce came in from the provinces by truck and horse cart to be unloaded and displayed under the vast structures of Baltard ironwork. Smoke from the cratewood fires tempered the winter chill, and even through the smoke I could smell the heavy earthy scent of the garden south. This was the open-air vegetable shed, displaying pyramids of tubers, garnished with pale winter greens: a ton of onions rolled by in wheelbarrows; two playful huskies unloaded a wagon of cabbages in a game of toss and catch. An old woman holding a single carrot brought me back to myself. She seemed to contemplate the root with something like nostalgia: it was large and phallic and uncircumcised.

Ahead of me walked a whole treeload of African bananas, two burlesque legs showing beneath the stalks. For no reason I followed the ambulant bananas along an aisle of fruit stalls. In one of the sideshows at that circus of edibles a hawker caught my eye and juggled three lemons for my benefit. The lively repertoire brought me out of my own shallow territory and into the larger night world of the marketplace. I wandered from shed to shed stumbling over crates, dodging the carcasses carried in gunnysacks, crushing bruised and discarded foodstuff underfoot.

Suddenly I was walking through puddles of blood. Strips of beef hung bleeding from hooks, a stray dog was sniffing at the edge of the exhibit until a butcher threw a bone at him. Meat stalls had been erected here where once the city gibbet stood: two hundred years before, a scaffold cast its shadow across the paving stones; before that, the king's condemned were drawn and quartered in this same place.

I stepped from the gutter and made bloody footprints down Pierre Lescot. Again, for no apparent reason or desire, I bought a bottle of champagne in a wine shop near the square des Innocents. As I left the shop a girl stepped out of a shadow and asked, "Tu viens?" Are you coming?

"Where?"

"Chez moi."

She was thin and pretty and not much older than I. Her hair was cut short, in the new fashion: one mèche of hair was plastered to her

forehead in a Spanish curl. She dressed oddly, a girl in women's clothing, in her mother's dress, in costume. She had outlined her eyes with
kohl the way dancers do, and gypsies.

I took a breath. The raucous market din receded, came back again,
as the blood pounded in my ears. Was this to be my initiation?

I had always wanted the first adventure to be with a special girl.
Louise? (I clung to some adolescent notion of love, mingled with my
lust.) Louise had been at Johns Hopkins with me, my uncompleted
freshman year. We had never kissed. Louise was a girl to write letters to.

"Bon," I said, and the market sounds faded again.

The girl touched the bottle of champagne as if for luck and said,
"Ça alors!" She said I was a type who knew what a girl liked. "Comme
tu es galant." Her enthusiasm sounded genuine.

The hotel she used was across from the square but we stopped
first at a fish stall for ice. The poissonnier remarked on the champagne
and wished us santé-bonheur, but at the mention of health my thoughts
turned to disease. My father had warned me about that. Suspecting
my innocence he had discussed tabes dorsalis and other horrors in
Latin, with instructions about washing scrupulously after contact.
"Always carry a cake of strong soap!"

I carried only wine. Never mind. I followed her clicking heels
up a creaking staircase. Despite her thinness there were dimples at the
backs of her knees, a mole below one of the dimples. As soon as we
got to her room she pushed off her shoes and said, "Ouf!" and something about the Pope, or the devil—a street joke in argot I could not
understand. I had started to pour ice into an enamel basin.

"Not there, chéri."

It was a portable bidet. She kept another basin under the bed,
perhaps to bathe her feet in. I emptied the wet newspaper packet into
that, then plunged the green bottle into the crystals of ice. She was
playing with a packet of Tarot cards she had taken from beneath the
pillow. She drew a card from the deck and passed it to me, smiling.
Her smile was queer, the corners of her mouth turned down; it
seemed impossible to smile that way without producing a grimace of
pain. The card depicted two naked lovers standing side by side, fingers
entwined: Les Amants.

We questioned one another while the wine cooled, a polite interrogation between two strangers. How delightful to speak to a pretty girl
in a private language, hers and mine. She was from Lille, she said, a

refugee from the boche. Lille was the place to be from, that year—and a refugee. I did not know then that a girl in her métier sells the present moment only. She had the gift for fiction that I lack: her story was casual and unimportant, so there was no reason for me to disbelieve her. I mention this only because of questions I asked myself later.

Would she go back to Lille now that the war was over?

She half-closed her darkened eyelids as she asked, "What is there to go back to?" There was no nostalgia in her sigh: she was a girl who did not go back.

Since I persisted in my naive questioning, she embroidered further. She had been a cantinière, not far from the front. (There was a romantic wartime song about a cantinière, so that became part of the story.) She served British soldiers at an army cantine behind the lines. (Did she mean cantine, or a maison de tolérance? The British called them Red Lanterns, for enlisted men; Blue Lanterns were utilized by officers.) She asked me if I had been in the war and I said no in a tone of regret (the regretful tone was a lie of my own). I missed the draft by a scant few months when the armistice was announced, or I might have come to France as a doughboy instead of a tourist.

"Bon," she said. Soldiers, she declared—even British soldiers (though they were polite)—were cons.

Con is a foul expression my mother never taught me. I had wanted to be a soldier to impress her, but had barely escaped being a con.

Impossible I could be an American, she insisted. Americans did not speak French. She thought my accent charming. I explained that my mother was French and I had in fact been born in France but my parents took me to America before I was three.

"America," she sighed. "Ah, the Americans." The French are always sentimental about Americans after a war. It was obvious, she went on, I could not be a Frenchman. I was too gentil to be French.

In France you do not say thank you to a compliment but something offhand, like, "You find it so?" She spoke to me as tu and toi but I could not bring myself to tutoyer her in return. I called her vous to maintain our polite distance.

The melting ice smelled of fish. I was nervous and uncertain so I turned the bottle in its bed of ice to do something with my superfluous hands. When I popped the cork the girl cried, "Bravo!" I felt something of a release, and relief. It was a fête after all.

We might have been at a speakeasy, for we drank from teacups. There were no glasses—her gentlemen, she informed me, were not always so chic as to think of wine. She meant it to flatter me but I was put off by the thought of other clients. I was again remembering my father's talk of social disease and my desire became riddled with concern.

"Ah, champagne," she said, with the same happy passion as she had pronounced the word Americans. She drank thirstily, with her feet tucked under her on the bed.

The wine was perfect (I began to think I had planned it as an aphrodisiac): it took immediate effect. We quickly became children—or became children again. Had we not been children all along, pretending to be adults? Yes, she was pretty in a childlike way, the child not altogether obliterated by her profession. I did not know if her eyes were as large and innocent as they appeared to be or if the dark shading only made them seem so. After a time there was an aura around her: her skin and hair glowed in an eerie but attractive way. This no doubt was due to the champagne.

You became blind, I suddenly remembered, or paralytic. There was a diseased man in Baltimore whose nose had come off.

I continued to dwell gloomily on thoughts of la petite vérole (the pox) as my hostess put her cup aside and her cards beneath the pillow. She opened her blouse as casually as a nursing mother and beckoned me to join her on the bed. My focus narrowed. How could two pink nipples staring up at me so fill the room? She leaned luxuriantly backward propped up on her now bare arms. I sat beside her and first, fearfully, put my hand on her shoulder, then caressed the side of her neck, but she winced—"Not there, chéri"—and applied my hand to her breast.

(These thoughts affect me strangely, even now, at my age. I see myself as the young man I was then—a boy, really: a droll naïf studiously contemplating a breast's faint tracery of veins as if reading the map of the universe. I tested the weight of each pendant offering of flesh in turn, a startled buyer at les Halles fondling an unfamiliar and exotic fruit.)

She took the teacup from me so that I would have both hands free to roam where they would. I will swear this (and I am an old man, with an old man's numb hands): I can at this moment feel her nipples erect against my palms.

Then she sat up abruptly. She had remembered something important.

"I am sorry to have to ask for money now, but if I do not, my gentlemen are liable to become distracted and forget."

This sobered me. Her gentlemen. She must have caught my look for she began to stroke me in a way to make me forget her gentlemen. The money, however, was another peril to consider. I wore a money-belt next to my skin, a cautionary gift from Maman.

The girl murmured the sum I was to pay (even as she stroked me), and I was obliged to detach myself from this reassuring embrace, stand, and turn my back to the source of my pleasure. I dug inside my pants to feel for the canvas pockets. It was an ingenious device of hooks and fasteners, a monument to prudence, the bane of pickpockets. My passport was strapped in there as well, pressed against my belly like a truss. Damnable gift! Had my mother thought of this predicament deliberately?

When at last I turned around to present her with the crumpled franc notes I wondered what agony my face revealed. But she ignored my awkward performance and stuffed the money carelessly into her shoe. Immediately she was up from the bed shedding her queer costume. Straps and buttons and buckles gave way until she was slim and pink standing in a puddle of fabric with nothing on. A marvel of nakedness, she glowed. My eyes went to the small patch of hair below her navel. It was like an arrow pointing to a secret place.

"Do you like me a little?"

I said in truth she was lovely. This gave her pleasure and she bestowed her odd off-center smile upon me—she was not without vanity. She, too—for reasons of her own—wanted the encounter to amount to more than a game for pay. The wine accomplished something I could never have done on my own, and turned our transaction into a tryst.

Playfully she unfastened my suspenders. I let my trousers lie where they had fallen, but she stooped and picked them up and folded them across a chair—though she had carelessly left her own garments on the floor. Strangely, the domestic gesture of caring for my clothes aroused me all the more. Or perhaps I simply delighted in the way she moved to do this. Slender as she was, her breasts bobbed enticingly as she bent, her hips and buttocks undulated when she stood. All of this was for me alone. I could have watched her forever, except for my need.

"You are gallant and considerate—you will be gentle, I know."

As blunt as she had been at first, she could be delicate in her sentiments. I assured her I would be gentle, though I did not know what gentleness she expected. My role was still a mystery. It took her only a moment to realize this, but she was not mocking when she called me her débutant charmant, her charming beginner.

She took that implement of mine and played with it shamelessly, as if it were a creature apart from me. She was as delighted as I—or pretended to be, making an O of her mouth, amazed—when the thing sprouted by magic and grew hard. She then positioned me above her. You would not think I could, in my awkward excitement, bear to look into her eyes, but I did. They were the wide grey avid eyes of a cat. Her smile showed only on one side, and her little pink cat's tongue appeared between her lips to wet them. There we lay face to face sharing the same breath, my weight pillowed by her slender body, our flesh touching all the way down.

The setting may have been sordid for all I remember—my thoughts were not. I lay pressed to her, only a moneybelt between us, clinging to her purchased flesh for dear life.

She opened below me like a flower, grasped my penis in a most natural way, and inserted that instrument into her sheath. How unlikely are the mechanics of sexual intercourse: what an unbelievable place to join two beings together. I felt as original inside her as Adam must have felt with Eve—yet, if I could have observed our lovers' tangle from a perch (or, as I see it now, in my mind's eye) I might have laughed aloud. Truly this ridiculous joining may well have been introduced by a serpent—the creature condemned to crawl upon his belly, and sleep coiled upon himself. Nevertheless, I entered an exciting place of exquisite pleasure when I entered her. The fruit of the tree of knowledge is a far subtler fruit than Genesis lets on.

A blooded piece of muscle throbbed inside her: I was astonished to realize that this length of blood and cartilage belonged to me. Since she knew I was an apprentice at fornication, it was reasonable that she whisper to me what might be taken as instruction. She said what I was to do. I did. She wound her legs around me (on the serpent's advice?) to bind us all the more. I drove my flesh recklessly into hers, until I thought I had hurt her, remembering my promise to be gentle —but she only smiled at what must have been a look of alarm in my eyes.

Could she really have said, "C'est bon comme ça," that it felt good—or did I?

She pulled from under me, but never away; she twisted as if to escape my assault, but in the most pleasurable way possible. I felt her smaller pelvis against mine, to the bone it seemed, until she sprang away again, and I pursued her, following her movements, plunging at that moist warm hollow she provided—then again, again, again.

To my horror we came undone, an awkward movement of mine. No matter. She attached us again so swiftly the moment of panic vanished. I kept my eyes open after that, but could not look again into her eyes. Instead, I fixed on a moth-shaped water stain on the wall above her head.

I was out of my mind with wine and delight. Perhaps I said some foolish things—I do not know, I cannot remember—but I do remember thinking a foolish thought. So this is what my father does, what all men do. (Not all, I would find out later.) I pictured my father in this same comically intricate position with Madame S at her hotel, back from Delmonico's. As fearful as I was of being laughed at, I might have laughed at myself at what I felt: I was at the edge of a great letting go, on the brink of a delicious excitement beyond anything until now. (Anticipating a frontier, I considered my passport—and possibly smiled; as I say, I was out of my head—and just past that frontier was a place of madness and bliss.)

"Vas-y," she whispered, for she knew.

I released all. Spasm followed spasm as the liquid essence of life flowed from me to her.

I looked at her then, expecting to find the rapture in her face I felt in mine—or at least the mirror image of my foolish smile—but found instead a grinning skull. My pleasure came to an abrupt end. Her features swam back into focus, and the grin changed to a pained professional smile. She had left our room for a moment, abandoned me, but here she was again. There was a look of suffering in her eyes. The kohl had smudged with our exertions, perspiration turned the Spanish curl into a question mark: she looked more than ever like a child, a wounded child. While we were still joined, she asked me: "Do you believe in the devil?"

"The devil?" Then it was the devil she had joked about, and not the Pope.

Her mood shifted as swiftly as a bird's sudden abrupt flight. She laughed aloud at my puzzled reply and lightly pinched my nose.

"I have slept with him."

I thought she meant with me, that I was a devil of a fellow.

Four

BELIN CAME AWAKE in the fetal position on the door sill of a second-floor apartment at 76, rue de Rochechouart. A woman was singing inside the apartment, softly (for it was just past daybreak), something from an opera. Belin's quarry was still in there. An inspector cannot make an arrest in the middle of the night, on suspicion only, so he had slept against the door. If anyone had gone out at night he would have stumbled over Belin crouched in the doorway.

He went down to the concierge loge to call, but first he stepped into a corner of the courtyard to urinate. When he turned he saw the concierge watching him from a window. She allowed him to use the telephone only after he presented his police card.

"I'm stiff," he said to Commissioner Dautel. "He's in his nest, still. His ladylove is singing to him. Better send somebody."

Dautel sent Brandenperger. Brandenperger brought cigarettes, knowing Belin would have smoked all of his during the vigil. The two inspectors went up and knocked on the door of the apartment. When a woman's voice asked who was there, Belin said, "Delivery. For Monsieur Guillet."

"At this hour?"

"Thought I would drop it off on my way to work."

They could hear voices, then the woman asked: "Where is it from?"

"Les Lions de Faïence."

This was the right answer (their information had been correct), for the bolt was released and the door opened. Before them stood a young lady in a rose-colored dressing gown, her long blond hair in disarray. There was an older man in the room with her, in bathrobe and slippers; he wore his beard long and full, and he was almost completely bald. The two men pushed their way into the room.

"Don't make any trouble. We're from the Mobile Brigade. The commissioner has some questions to ask you."

"What is this?" The young lady sounded more frightened than outraged.

"An affair of the police," said Monsieur Guillet with extraordinary calm. He gave her a significant look, just short of a wink.

Since Monsieur Guillet was himself a police inspector, her puzzled expression was understandable.

"You had better come along too, Madame."

Brandenperger was being polite: she was not Madame but Mademoiselle. While Monsieur dressed, Brandenperger offered cigarettes; Belin took one, but Monsieur Guillet did not smoke. Mademoiselle Segret dressed in the next room, and she was ready soon after her friend. The quartet went downstairs: Belin, Mademoiselle Segret with Monsieur Guillet close behind her, holding her elbow, then Brandenperger. They filed past the window of a startled concierge and into a waiting police van.

IMPORTANT ARREST IN MONTMARTRE

Yesterday the 1st Mobile Brigade received an anonymous tip that led to the arrest of a well-dressed individual, almost completely bald but with a full black beard. This man is believed to have used the science of hypnotism in the service of his evil instincts. He has been sought by more than ten criminal courts throughout France, under the names Dupont, Desjardins, Prunier, Pèrres, Durand, Dumont, Morise, etc.

Once under questioning by the Sûreté, he finally admitted his real name was Henri Nandru, born in Paris, 19th arrondissement, in 1869. Nandru is under suspicion of fraud, theft, and abuse of confidence, all of which he denies without offering

the least explanation, satisfied to answer every question with:
"I have nothing to say to you. Deal with my lawyer."

It would seem however that this odd character would do
better to explain himself more openly, for he will, according to
certain developments, be obliged to answer to charges far more
serious than those he is burdened with so far. He is suspected
of the most heinous crimes.

Let me point out that the newspaper report of Landru's arrest was
essentially true, but studded with incorrect and fanciful detail. Danglure wrote the piece for *le Petit Journal* and scooped every other reporter in Paris, but Danglure was not the keenest or most conscientious
of newspapermen. It is a matter of no consequence that Landru (with
an *L*, not Nandru with an *N*) was arrested in the Opéra district instead of Montmartre: the rue de Rochechouart is close enough to
Montmartre. Landru was wanted by one other criminal court in
France—ten is a gross exaggeration. Danglure did not state definitely
that Landru was a hypnotist, but his statement "believed to have used
the science of hypnotism" came to be believed: from that time on
Landru would be considered a Svengali.

Danglure colored Landru's beard black (and the rest of us applied the same color)—the beard was really a reddish brown, but black-
is closer to blue, as in Bluebeard, and much more suggestively sinister.

Since Landru was a liar and did employ false names, why not
falsify further? Danglure invented the alias Durand; Desjardins was
the name of his news editor, and Morise was his divorced wife's maiden
name.

I knew Danglure from the low-life haunts of French and foreign
reporters in Paris. The first time we talked was over a drink at the
famous bistro across from la Santé prison: A la Bonne Santé. Landru
was to be transferred from la Santé to the prison of Saint Pierre at
Versailles. Reporters invariably gathered at this strategically located
café whenever a notorious inmate of la Santé was due to be transferred
or released. It is a dingy halfway house between prison and Paris, now
crowded with newspapermen intermingled with lawyers in business
suits (instead of black and crimson court robes) and wives and sweet-
hearts of prisoners, waiting for visiting hours to begin. The air was
thick with smoke and talk: a great many cigarette butts littered the
floor along the base of the comptoir. The café windows gave onto the

grim cinder-colored walls of la Santé, directly opposite the medieval prison gate, with an oblique view of the antiquated fortress roof above the walls. La Santé is the ugliest and most depressing structure in Paris.

Danglure was seated at a table beside a woman nursing her baby; he and the woman ignored one another. He was chewing on a stick of réglisse, a French pharmaceutical children suck as a substitute for sweets. There was an empty chair at the table, so I asked, "Permettez-moi?" The nursing mother assured me the chair was free. In no time Danglure had sniffed out my métier and asked me what newspaper I worked for.

"The Channel News Service."

"Never heard of it."

I could not resist thinking the baby at its mother's teat and Danglure sucking his stick of réglisse had the same puckered moon faces, the same self-gratifying air.

At the time, Danglure was not far from retirement. He had been recruited during the war by *le Petit Journal* when younger reporters had been mobilized or were covering the front. The job was insignificant during the war years: newspapers were permitted to print only one page, due to the paper shortage, and even that single page was heavily censored. Danglure covered drunk-and-disorderly arrests, petty scandal, and bicycle thefts. After the war he was kept on, and became a member of that contingent of older reporters who made monotonous rounds of hospitals and commissariats between midnight and dawn, then filed their miscellaneous gleanings and went to bed. Since there are seventy-eight police commissariats in Paris, these competing night reporters divided up the round among themselves: they met at Le Boeuf sur le Toit to exchange and trade off the items each had picked up that night. Big stories never came Danglure's way. He was a specialist in minor faits-divers, the filler items. A lost dog himself, he wrote about lost dogs.

I leaned as far away from Danglure's mortuary smell as I politely could. He claimed that réglisse was an antidote for bad breath: in his case it did not work. Other reporters avoided him, so it was I who waited with him for Landru to appear.

"I'm a night hawk myself," said Danglure, "but I want to get a look at his gueule."

He had to see the man's face, though he had come here on his own time when he should be sleeping. Night work, he warned me, was a leading cause of constipation and divorce. He offered me a drink, but I ended up paying for both. He complained about his editor and his ex-wife. The nursing mother listened in, and nodded as if Danglure had directed his confidences to her. He ordered a second drink (for which I paid, as well) and continued being bitter. *Le Petit Journal* had taken him off the story and put Fauverge on. "But I scooped them all," he assured me, again and again. It was the only triumph of his dreary career. Commissioner Dautel of the First Mobile Brigade had dropped the story in his lap.

I thought of Belin waiting all night to arrest Landru and reflected that reporters, like policemen, spend most of their working time waiting.

Across the street a guard stepped out of his sentry box and policemen began streaming out of the loge door beside the gate. Immediately the newspapermen were scrambling to their feet, a table of drinks was overturned. Even the bartender and waiter and prisoners' wives joined the crowd in the street: I was one of the last to leave the café.

The great prison door gaped open and a ring of gendarmes guarded the section of street where the van must pass. A news photographer was on his knees with a camera at the ready, but the crowd shifted, moving between his camera and the gate. Suddenly the van came through the opening full tilt, and the reporters were obliged to trot after it, down rue de la Glacière as far as the corner, but in vain. The only view any of us had was a swiftly blurred glimpse of a small man seated between two guards.

I looked around to see if Danglure was in sight. He might have noticed Landru's beard was brown, not black. But Danglure was too old and wise a dog to chase after a police van: he had never left the café. Only he and the nursing mother had remained behind. Through the window of A la Bonne Santé I saw him throw back his head to finish off some reporter's abandoned drink.

Five

IT RAINED IN APRIL and the sewers backed up along the rue Saint-Honoré. My father read the English-language daily newspapers, and I read the French.

A certain Madame Collomb had been missing since 1916, and Madame Buisson since 1917. By a remarkable coincidence both women had been engaged to marry an engineer named Frémyet. Frémyet was not an engineer and his name was not Frémyet—he had been arrested under the name Guillet and admitted to having been acquainted with Madame Buisson and Madame Collomb. The police hinted darkly of worse revelations to come.

Clemenceau was very nearly assassinated on the rue Franklin by Emile Cottin, known as Milou. The dollar was at 5F 45 and drifting upward. (It would go to 10F 50 by year's end.) According to *l'Humanité* a mother in Clichy had beaten her idiot son into a coma with a paperweight; a destitute veteran of the Franco-Prussian War had eaten his cat. *L'Aurore* reported the discovery of a three-month-old baby in a trash bin outside the Bourse, still alive. In the yellow press alcoholic husbands did their wives to death with hunting rifles, bayonets, and rat bane.

President Wilson was in Paris for the Peace Conference. This gave my father the idea to promote gold medallions inscribed with

Wilson's head on one side and his Fourteen Points on the other.

The rain turned the metallic roofs and stone sides of buildings from grey to black, and kept me indoors reading *l'Illustration*. Proust had just published *A l'ombre des jeunes filles en fleurs* and I tried to read it, then went looking at pictures in the Louvre where I hoped to meet a young girl in flower. The girl I sought would be as well-bred and delicate and pre-Raphaelite as Louise, but would entertain me in the way of the girl at the square des Innocents. I lingered before a beheading scene by Henri Bellechose—no beautiful thing, despite the painter's name—the execution of Saint Denis: the patron saint of Paris carrying his own head, including the realistically detailed windpipe and severed arteries spurting blood. There were no young girls in flower in that gallery.

My father took Madame S (or Madame S took my father) to see *Phi-Phi* at the Bouffes Parisiens. Chevalier was at the Casino de Paris.

FIVE WOMEN ASSASSINATED BY AN ENGINEER. Frémyet sometimes spelled his name Frémiet. As the list of victims increased, every newspaper in Paris was on the story.

When Frémyet was arrested at his apartment he gave the name Lucien Guillet. This was the name his mistress knew him by. He had also told Mademoiselle Segret (a girl in her twenties, who believed herself engaged to him) that he was born in Roicroi. He told the arresting officers, Belin and Brandenperger, the same. Age, forty-five. (He was fifty—the day of his arrest, April 12, was his fiftieth birthday.) He was also known as Diard, Cuchet, Forest, Alphonse, Petit, Barbezieux, and Dupont as well as Guillet, Frémyet, and Frémiet. His real name was Henri Désiré Landru.

"To lie is easy," said my father when he read the story in the *Paris American,* "but assumed names are a nuisance to remember." My father always used his own name.

Mademoiselle Segret could not believe her fiancé was under arrest, and protested, "But Lucien is himself a police inspector!"

Until this moment Landru had lied or simply refused to speak. Now he smiled and shrugged. "Indeed, gentlemen, I did say that. In order not to reveal my actual profession I suggested to my companion that I worked for the police." He went on to confide to the officers, man to man: "One must never tell a woman precisely what one does for a living."

"What precisely do you do for a living?" asked Commissioner Dautel.

"I am a businessman," replied Landru. "Je m'occupe d'affaires."
My father might have said as much. To this day I do not know
what my father's business was. Yes, he accepted money from women—
including my mother—but he also earned money of his own. He
dressed well. We had a Ford motor car at home, but I think my
mother paid for it. I am not sure why my father decided to come to
France: I had no idea what he meant when he declared he had come to
the old world to sell better plowshares, now that Europe was beating
its swords into plowshares.

At the commissioner's hearing, Landru was confronted with his
criminal record:

CASIER JUDICIAIRE—Landru, Henri Désiré.

21 juillet, 1904: ESCROQUERIE—2 ans prison, 50F d'amende   PARIS
28 mars, 1906: ESCROQUERIE—13 mois prison, 50F d'amende   SENS
27 mai, 1906: ABUS DE CONFIANCE—3 ans prison, 100F d'amende PARIS
20 juillet, 1914: ESCROQUERIE—4 ans de prison, 100F d'amende SENS

This last conviction, in 1914, included the sentence for habitual
criminals to relégation, banishment to a penal colony for life. The
sentence was handed down in the absence of the accused, for Landru
had wisely chosen not to appear in court.

In the course of the hearing Commissioner Dautel had determined
that Mademoiselle Segret was innocent of any criminal association with
her supposed fiancé, and she was allowed to go free. As she left,
Landru, to the astonishment of the First Mobile Brigade, burst into
song. He sang the aria "Adieu, notre petite table" from the opera
Manon.

Six

My mother wrote asking me to look after Papa. (She did not ask Papa to look after me, for which I was grateful.) I had interrupted an unsuccessful freshman year (and an adolescent flirtation with Louise) at Johns Hopkins to come to France. My father considered travel the equivalent of an education. Ostensibly I was my father's interpreter, to help him in his business transactions—"the devil's apprentice," as my mother put it. Her letters to me were in French, but she wrote to my father in English. "Your father's French is all right for Baltimore but not for France." This was true, but it did not prevent him from speaking his American French to the French. I was never called upon to interpret. It did not matter: the French are uncharacteristically tolerant of Americans after a war. If my father failed to make himself understood the first time, he simply repeated the same words in a loud and determined tone. Emphasis, he said, is the secret of speaking any language.

In a weak moment—for he seldom told me any more than I could see for myself—my father stated his reason for coming to France was to sell U.S. typefaces to French printers, on the theory that Europe had exhausted its supply of lead making bullets during the war. A printer friend in Washington who worked on the Congressional Record had given him the idea. As far as I could ascertain he did not take time from his alliance with Madame S to approach a French printer about this project. I was hoping he would get started, for it would give me something to do. He said he was still calculating gross profit minus freight rates less conversion. Another time I reminded him of the requirements of the French alphabet, and he pretended to be discouraged to learn he would have to supply the letters *é, è, ê,* and *ë* as well as just *e.*

Not many wet April days after this, my father gave a well-bred cough to attract my attention, and remarked: "Paris in the spring is giving me congestion of the lungs." True, there was mold on the walls in the WC, and once the floodwaters from a sewer had seeped into the hotel lobby. That same night we were on the Blue Train headed for Cannes. We traveled by wagon-lit, first class, because "One never meets first-class people in second-class." My father spent a part of the evening before bed counting his collection of large colorful French banknotes then current. I did not know what had become of Madame S. Unlike Landru, when my father got what he wanted from a woman it was he who disappeared.

The leading international economists of the day were convening at the Carlton Hotel. We stayed at the Hôtel Gonnet et de la Reine, only a short walk away. The rooms had high ceilings with molded scrollwork and cut-glass chandeliers. The windows were French windows opening onto the sea—except for ours, which opened onto the tennis courts. The only players who used the courts called to one another across the net in Russian. (Lenin was now installed at Moscow and White Russians were fleeing to the south of France.) I was trying to grow a mustache and finish *A l'ombre des jeunes filles en fleurs.* My father tipped his straw boater to the women who strolled the Croisette.

We met John Maynard Keynes, a member of the British treasury delegation to the Peace Conference. In that late spring of 1919 Keynes was not yet known to the general public. My father felt comfortable in the company of men who had theories about money: in no time he was calling him Maynard and discussing Ricardo and Mills and Adam Smith—all of whom my father thought were staying at the Carlton, for the conference. We sat under a parasol at the Carlton boat landing drinking citrons pressés. My father took gin with his, but Mr. Keynes abstained. Contrary to his usual habit, my father paid for the drinks—one could not expect an economist to handle money. When my father presented his design for the Wilson medallion, Mr. Keynes said he hoped none had been struck yet.

"Why is that?"

"The Fourteen Points have got as much chance as a snowball in the nether world."

My father raised an eyebrow. (His hair was greying at the sides, but his eyebrows were impressively black.)

"Orlando has already stalked out of the conference."

The only Orlando my father knew was the Orlando in *As You Like It*. Vittorio Emanuele Orlando was premier of Italy, one of the Big Four at Versailles: he demanded the enactment of the secret treaty of London of 1915. A large portion of Dalmatia was to be ceded to Italy by this agreement, contrary to the letter and spirit of Wilson's Fourteen Points.

"The dogs of war are growling over the bones of peace."

Under the table Mr. Keynes's hand was resting on my knee.

"Can you beat that?" said my father. He was disappointed about the medallion but pleased to have got the word, sub rosa, in time.

I thought Mr. Keynes might have mistaken my knee for his own, so I diplomatically moved my leg when I added sugar to the citron pressé. But he placed his hand on my knee again. He was elaborating on the risk of excessive territorial and reparations demands.

"In twenty years we will have another great war on our hands."

He was right, of course. His book *Economic Consequences of the Peace* made him famous. He had also evolved a theory about deficit spending which he told us about under the parasol. It would revolutionize monetary policy. Potential wealth, he declared, was as valid as apparent wealth and should receive equal consideration in budgetary planning. It was an original idea but I was uneasily preoccupied with the hand on my knee so could not give my full attention to Mr. Keynes's unique approach to economics.

"You are one hundred percent right," said my father, who had practiced deficit spending all his life.

In France, according to the Code Civil, a husband has the right to dispose of his wife's money and property as he thinks best. The Code Civil was written by Napoleon, who held women in low esteem. Upon her marriage a woman relinquishes her adulthood and places herself under the jurisdiction of her husband. She cannot sign her name to a legal document without his consent. (It was for this reason Landru sometimes took the name of his missing fiancée: as her husband, he would sign her property over to himself, then sell it.) For this reason, too, my mother never told my father about the small property she owned near Grasse. She wrote me about this, saying it was my heritage—my only heritage, she added, for my father had contrived to spend most of the money she had brought to America. Now that I was in the neighborhood ("puisque tu es tout près") she thought I might like to inspect my heritage and visit the place of my birth.

Also, I should obtain a duplicate birth certificate at the mairie in Grasse: the original was affixed to my mother's livret de famille. "If you go," she wrote, "go alone. You might tell your father you have gone to get a birth certificate in Grasse. It would be prudent not to mention the little house and olive grove to Papa."

I did as my mother suggested. I told him about the birth certificate but not about the property: this I considered an evasion, not a lie. My father was just as happy to have me out from underfoot. Whatever his intentions (he had met several interesting ladies on the Croisette), my presence cramped his style. I took a bottle of mineral water and the local newspaper, *l'Eclaireur,* on the train.

By now eight women were missing, women whose paths had crossed Landru's. Across from me in the train a touring couple carried the same newspaper.

"Those eyes!" said the woman, indicating a photograph of Landru. The husband made his eyes grow large and stared into his wife's eyes. They burst out laughing.

I ignored them. It was too fine a day to contemplate murder, even as a joke; the vista from the train window was too lovely to ignore. I folded my newspaper away. A toy steam locomotive pulled us through fields of jasmine and newly plowed olive groves. There is no brown like the rich brown earth turned up around the roots of olive trees. The terrain of each farm was set off from the other by a stone wall or cypresses. The vineyard workers were tying up grapevines so that the grapes would not rot on the ground.

The region supplied the parfumeries at Grasse with cultivated blossoms. We lingered at a freight platform in Mouans-Sartoux to load a cargo of roses.

My mind wandered, then paused at the thought of that unlikely bouquet delivered to the sister of the late Madame Collomb. Was she really the late Madame Collomb, or simply Madame Collomb, address unknown? She might still be living on the Riviera and have truly sent the bouquet herself—despite all the stir over her alleged disappearance. But her sister declared it was not like Madame Collomb to send flowers, that Landru must have sent them. Her calling card was attached to the bouquet. Why had she not sent a message with the flowers? Because she is dead, insisted the sister.

But it was too fine a day. (You see how the Landru Affair can become an obsession.) Jasmine was coming into flower and the almond trees were just past blooming, resplendent in their saucy new green. The flower pickers harvested the jasmine petals early while the dew was still on and would weigh extra on the parfumerie scales. You could barely trace the train tracks through the fields of lavender and genêt. Yellow wasps and nectar-drugged bees, disoriented, passed through the train window—frightening the lady across the aisle in a way Landru's photograph had failed to do—then out again, as haphazardly as they had drifted in.

The train eased to a groaning stop below the town of Grasse, in a postcard station of stone and flowers. So this was my birthplace. I tried to feel provençal, a native son—asking myself in which white hospital was I born? But they were tuberculosis clinics now, or clinic-hotels for exiled and consumptive Russians. There were several polished motor cars, chauffeur-driven, on the Jeu de Ballon. I walked under plane trees cut back to the bone, sprouting their limbs that would in summer shade the dusty cafés from the relentless sun.

From the ramparts of the cathedral I could see the Mediterranean, as if it were under my nose. An organist was playing a Bach chorale, so I ventured inside the church, but quickly retreated: there was a funeral under way. The black box was sealed shut, only a corner of it peeking out from a blanket of odorous flowers.

I thought of Madame Collomb's bouquet again, a bouquet supposedly sent from here to Paris, death's calling card attached—her killer's grim subterfuge? My mind still lingered in the newspaper columns, cluttered with criminal indictments and scattered clues. To turn my thoughts from death I went immediately to apply for a birth certificate.

The clerk at the mairie refused to issue the document unless I could prove I was the individual of the name stated, born on the date claimed.

"What proof must I present?"

"Un certificat de naissance."

But how could I produce a birth certificate if no birth certificate could be issued without a birth certificate as proof? A birth certificate, the clerk reminded me, was issued at birth. To obtain a duplicate, one must produce the original. Thus I was obliged to show my birth certificate in order to obtain a birth certificate. I explained that I lived in the United States. My mother had a copy of my birth certificate affixed to her livret de famille.

"Then you are not French?"

"I am half-French. I was born at Grasse."

From his face I could see that to be half-French was worse than not being French at all. All very well to say I was born in Grasse, that my mother was born in Grasse—and her mother, as well—but where was my proof? I showed him my passport. An interesting document, but it was in a foreign language—the clerk did not read English; besides, a passport is not a birth certificate. How did he know I was who I claimed to be and that I was born on that date?

"What if someone were to lose his birth certificate?"

"But you have not lost it."

"It could be lost for all I know. I have never seen it. It is, in any case, unavailable."

I was un cas particulier and only the chief clerk could deal with exceptional cases.

"I would like to see him then."

"He is having an apéritif, I believe. Or playing boules. He might be back after lunch. Or later."

The cathedral bells were tolling, either for the lunch hour or the termination of the funeral service. The clerk began drawing the shutters closed.

That is the way it is in France. I could imagine the sister of Madame Collomb presenting herself before the parquet de Mantes to request the investigation of a missing person. Did Madame have proof that her sister had disappeared? Small wonder the case took three years to come under serious scrutiny. I did not expect my case (un cas particulier) to be resolved any sooner.

Outside, several gentlemen in their shirt sleeves and stiff collars were rolling iron balls in the dust. They measured minuscule distances with a tape when there was a disputed point. One of the players might have been the chief clerk I was seeking but he would not want to be disturbed at so passionate a recreation. Also, it was the lunch hour and the lunch hour is sacred in France.

I made my own lunch of a crêpe soaked in rum and rolled in sugar: with this I drank my mineral water shaded by a statue of Fragonard and his bosomy muse. Fragonard, too, was born in Grasse. Then I hired a diligence (in this case, an unpainted farm wagon with a makeshift canopy) to take me to the village of Ys. Ys is only five kilometers from Grasse, via the Route Napoléon (my driver explained). The little general had traveled this road on his return from exile. The coachman was a local historian, and a philosopher. His philosophy was that great men are permitted to make great mistakes, but a great man—by the very nature of his greatness—will not make the same mistake twice.

"Take this Landru, for instance. Obviously an assassin of the first rank—a formidable criminal, if you will. But by the thorn of a whore's tongue, to kill ten!"

"Ten?"

"And a boy. The latest count." He was sitting on the afternoon edition of *le Petit Niçois;* he pulled it from beneath his buttocks to show me the headline. Then he described to me how Landru would have been dealt with in the days of the kings of France.

"Blind him with a white-hot poker, to begin with. Cut off his ears and tongue and toss those items to the crowd. Feed his tripe to dogs (while he is still living, mind you) and, before he has drawn his final breath, excise his prick-and-sac to be presented to her highness, the queen, for pickling. Meanwhile he would have been attached to four horses, an arm or a leg tied to each, to partition him equally when the horses were whipped and driven in opposite directions."

The driver whacked the rump of the nag that pulled the diligence as if the horse were pulling at one of Landru's limbs.

We traveled during the dead hours between noon and 2 PM, when all of France is at lunch: by the time we arrived, the narrow streets of Ys were empty except for an ancient bearded lady in garden clogs who spoke only the local dialect. She was able to point out my mother's property to the driver (they spoke provençal together) but shook her head sadly and indicated the cemetery as the present dwelling place of all those of that name.

Not so, I wanted to tell her, but could not speak the dialect. My mother was living, and so was I. All of us were dead and buried as far as the old woman was concerned.

My heritage was two irregular hectares of terraced hillside on a southerly slope overlooking Grasse. There was a view of the cemetery as well as of the flowered plain I passed through on the way from Cannes.

"On a clear day," said the coachman, "you can see Corsica." He reminded me the little general was born in Corsica, and we both squinted into the sun's haze searching for Napoleon's ghost from here.

I would have to write my mother that the stone walls supporting the terraces had collapsed. Sheep were grazing on the terraces interspersed with bell-ringing goats and two indifferent dogs.

(Why do I pause along this idyllic byway contemplating broken stone and scattered livestock? None of this had any connection with l'affaire Landru. Yet here are my origins, this is where my story properly begins. I write these words from that same ruined house, now restored—and I will end my story here, in time.)

"The fruit of that tree makes an excellent infusion," said he, guiding me to the place of my birth. The house was of stone—a structure called in provençal a mas—with narrow windows (the glass broken) set against a grove of pine and scrub oak. Its façade was shaded by a luxuriant linden, and this was the tree he referred to. He might have thought I was planning to buy the place, and he the agent for the estate. At the time it never occurred to me I might someday take up residence in this abandoned stone bastion in the Alpes Maritimes.

I entered the house without difficulty: the door had fallen from its hinges. I tried to think how I felt about the empty rooms I passed through—the rooms of my mother's life, and those of my mother's mother—but I felt nothing beyond a fleeting dismay that the beams were rotting. There were bones in the fireplace.

"Sheep," said the coachman, kicking at them.

Shepherds and lovers must have used the place. It was inhabited by a mixture of smells.

On the way back to Grasse the driver recited in detail what the Germans had done to Belgian nuns during the war. His vivid account of these bloody doings so sickened me that I tasted my undigested crêpe again. The war had left ten million dead, said the coachman—he had read the figures in *l'Eclaireur*. One could almost forgive Landru, he offered, when one thought of the Germans.

When I went to the mairie the clerk was gone and the chef du bureau was in his place. My passport was perfectly acceptable as proof of my existence, and I was issued a duplicate of my birth certificate in ink the color of dried blood.

"You must excuse my assistant," said the chef du bureau. "He was naturally suspicious. You claim to be born here, yet you do not speak with the accent of the Midi."

Seven

Monsieur, 45 yrs, alone, without family, possesses 4,000 F, residence, seeks marriage w/woman in similar situation.

MADAME COLLOMB responded to this offer the very day it appeared. She gave her age as thirty-nine. (She was forty-four.) She earned 2,100 francs per year as a secretary in an insurance company. She had put aside 8,000 francs, part of which had been inherited from her late husband. She was a widow, with no children by that marriage, and no family to speak of.

Of course, she did not reveal she had had a lover after the death of her husband. She may or may not have had a child by him—a little girl, said to have been born in Marseille and brought up by nuns in Mentone, or San Remo. (If she had had a lover besides Landru, he was never found. As for the child, I once tried to trace her: I thought she might have been a girl I met at a maison close—but that is another story.) None of this would have been of interest to Landru, neither the lover nor the hypothetical child. The financial statement was correct, and that was what mattered. That Madame Collomb was forty-four and not thirty-nine was a trifling, even amusing, deception. Landru had learned to expect this sort of dissimulation from women of a certain age: deviousness was an element of their coquetry. How childlike they were, and naive—with lowered eyes and flushed cheeks, whispering their little white lies. You pretended to believe them, for what did it matter?

"No family to speak of," however, was misleading in an unfortunate way. Actually Madame Collomb was very close to her mother, brother, and sister. They were protective of her, concerned for her welfare. They considered her innocent and easily led. She wore her heart on her sleeve. They had never approved, for instance, of the lover Bernard.

Landru was annoyed when he learned about the family. They were a hindrance to his plans. Ordinarily this disturbing factor would have been enough to eliminate Madame Collomb from Landru's list of eligible fiancées. He would have filed her correspondence under R.A.F. (rien à faire: nothing to be done, hopeless) and had no more to do with her. But a year's work had gone into the enterprise of wooing her, and he was desperate for money by then.

As Landru might have anticipated, Madame Collomb never quite broke with her family even after he insisted she do so. She deceived him about this. (How awkward families can be, Landru well knew—he had one of his own.) But the appearance of a break satisfied Landru. He no longer had to answer to *them*. On the day after Christmas 1916, Madame Collomb went with him to Gambais. Meanwhile she had secretly promised her mother, brother, and sister to be back in time to spend New Year's Day with them. They were at Bry-sur-Marne for the holidays. She did not show up at Bry-sur-Marne as she had promised. There was no further word from her.

Naturally the family was distraught. Private inquiries came to nothing. The police were informed and the facts of the case noted in a missing persons file, then filed away. In 1916 a great many missing persons files were filed away—it was the year of Verdun. Refugees were pouring into Paris from the northeast. The mother, brother, and sister waited in vain for news of Madame Collomb.

On the first of February Madame Collomb's sister received a gift of mimosa and roses from the Midi. A young man delivered the flowers, there was no message. Madame Collomb's visiting card was attached to the bouquet, and there was a tag that indicated the flowers came from Nice. But Madame Collomb's sister did not for a moment believe her sister would have sent a gift from Nice with her visiting card and no message. She would never have sent flowers, in any case. And the delivery boy who had come to the door—he had the queer smile of a boy playing a prank: he did not even wear a messenger's cap. The mysterious bouquet did nothing to assuage the family's misgivings. Yet no formal investigation of Madame Collomb's disappearance was undertaken until January of 1919—not long after the armistice. It was as if the creaking machinery of state began to function again now that the war was over. In February of that same year a similar dossier came to light. The parquet de la Seine received a demand by Mademoiselle Lacoste to investigate the disappearance of her sister (a sister again!), Madame Buisson, missing since August of 1917. There was a disturbing coincidence concerning the two dossiers. Both women, widows, had been engaged to marry a short, bald, bearded gentleman named Frémyet, an engineer, who had a villa at Gambais. Two fiancées within a year, and both missing.

This remarkable coincidence might have gone unnoticed forever: the two dossiers originated in separate quarters of Paris and were dealt with, routinely, by independent bureaus. However, the mayor of Gambais came upon the first two pieces of an intricate puzzle. He had received two oddly similar letters of inquiry: one, from Mademoiselle Lacoste, asking after her missing sister, Célestine Buisson, supposedly married to an engineer named Frémyet who had taken her to his villa at Gambais for their honeymoon, and not another word since. The other letter was from Madame Collomb's family—the mother, brother, and sister who had been suspicious of Frémyet all along. The mayor advised the Pillot family that no one by the name of Collomb (nor yet of Frémyet) had ever resided at Gambais, and now he was obliged to inform Mademoiselle Lacoste that her sister, Célestine Buisson, had never to his knowledge resided in his area of administration. Further, there was not now nor had there ever been a villa at Gambais registered under the name Frémyet. Mademoiselle Lacoste (wrote the mayor) might be advised to make contact with the family Pillot who had made similar inquiry concerning their daughter and sister, Madame Collomb, also said to be affianced to this same Frémyet, engineer, supposedly residing at Gambais. Perhaps this line of pursuit would render both Mademoiselle Lacoste and the family Pillot satisfied and, he hoped, put all fears to rest. The mayor closed, offering his distinguished and respectful sentiments.

When Mademoiselle Lacoste got in touch with the Pillot family, bearing the letter she had just received from the mayor of Gambais, her fears were not at all put to rest—nor were theirs. The two bereft and bewildered sisters joined forces. It was time for the parquet de Mantes to compare dossiers with the parquet de la Seine.

* * *

On a frigid grey morning in February (the same morning the *Leopoldina* docked at le Havre, the day my father and I arrived in France) Jules Hebbé, a mounted police officer, set off for the village of Gambais to make inquiries concerning the mysterious Monsieur Frémyet. According to the description of the villa supposedly belonging to Monsieur Frémyet, the mayor of Gambais suggested it might be the villa Tric, somewhat remote from the village and seldom occupied: it was owned by a Monsieur Tric who did not himself reside at Gambais, but rented his villa through the services of Monsieur Vallet, the local cobbler.

"Bearded, yes," said the cobbler, "and pays his rent. Dupont's his name, not Frémyet. Never heard of Frémyet. If you want his address, it's rue de Darnetal, Rouen."

From the cobbler's shop Jules Hebbé walked his horse through the streets of the village making casual inquiries as he went along. The butcher barely knew Dupont: "He seldom comes to Gambais, and not much of a meat eater when he comes." Dupont/Frémyet purchased his pittance of groceries at the épicerie.

"Stops in with a lady friend, not always the same lady." The épicier supplied this information, winking behind his wife's back.

Dupont was never seen in the café. "If he drinks," said the barman, "he drinks at home."

Jules Hebbé talked with an old woman coming out of the church. She lived in the neighborhood of the villa Tric, but no one lived nearby. "It's the house nearest the cemetery—there's a wall around it."

Monsieur Dupont?

"A quiet type. He's away a lot, and keeps himself to himself when he's here. He's a nuisance all the same."

"On what account?"

"The smoke," said the old woman, "and the smell."

"What smoke?"

"Always burning something. Black smoke pouring out of his chimney all day sometimes. Winter, summer, the same. And the smell is enough to turn your stomach."

The old woman crossed herself and turned away, perhaps for the dry old sins she had just confessed in church, or perhaps for the confession she had made to Jules Hebbé.

Eight

"THE BUSINESS OF LIVING," my father informed me, "is a full-time pursuit."

He expressed this precept while stretching a rubber band around a roll of banknotes and looking at me as if to ask what *my* full-time pursuits amounted to. "Tennis," I would have had to reply if he had asked. I played tennis with the daughter of the Russian lady at the Hôtel Gonnet et de la Reine from whom he had acquired the banknotes. The daughter was a flushed and robust version of her pale mother: fat, with the face of a fish when she was short of breath—but a consistent winner of games. When we played she called out the score in French instead of Russian, for my sake, and casually demolished me at every set. My father probably thought I should have tried to score in the boudoir instead of on the courts. But there was more than a tennis net (or a chessboard, when it rained) between my young companion and me. I could not tolerate her troutlike expression as she was about to win again, but I had a far more urgent concern than her unattractiveness. I had discovered a rash between my legs.

My father had tucked the roll of bills into his humidor and was coughing discreetly into a handkerchief. He examined the results, then spoke of a fear of his own.

"These Russians are consumptives, every last one. They come to France, you know, for the cure."

He thought—or pretended to think, or wanted me to think—he could have caught tuberculosis from his Russian friend. I did not think that was the case—her daughter said they had fled Russia because of the Bolsheviks. My father was showing the symptoms not of a terminal illness but of a terminal affair. In the pursuit of the business of living he had, for now, got his money's worth. Coughing into a handkerchief was a way of announcing we would be leaving Cannes immediately.

For a moment I forgot my rash and thought of Paris. But we did not go to Paris. We went to Nice, only an hour away. "Nice," declared my father, "is a town with get-up-and-go. It will revive your spirits." It did not.

We stayed at a mustard-colored hotel near the Vieux Port where I fed seagulls bits of croissant I tossed from our balcony. The squawking of these mournful birds seemed to echo my own suppressed outcry: I was dying inside when I had barely begun to live. To dispel my gloom I wrote fanciful letters to the girl I had known at Johns Hopkins. I told her I was a writer of stories. (Louise was the only girl at Johns Hopkins who did not roll her stockings but dressed rather in pre-Raphaelite fashion, and wrote poems.) The stories I intended to write turned into letters to Louise. In secret I examined the progress of my rash: it showed only where my thighs touched and had not yet attacked the genitals. I would waste away from venereal disease, like Maupassant, and die.

Now that I had been baptized (perhaps by fire) and knew the carnal pleasure I was denied, my dreams were a torture. I dreamt always of the same girl—her queer half-smile, and the rest of her aglow —until the dream became a wet dream that momentarily relieved the tension. If relief did not come about of itself I was obliged to retire to the bathrom and alleviate the love cramp by hand. At that time I believed this practice would only increase venereal infection. I was constantly aware of my penis. I wondered if my newly inaugurated instrument of pleasure would rot (like the nose of the man in Baltimore) and come off in my hand.

My father did not often sleep at our hotel, and so was not disturbed by my nocturnal thrashings and frequent trips to the salle de bain. Inevitably he had met a blue-haired divorcée at the Nice Opéra, and spent most of his time in her company. But once he came in when I was on the balcony staring at clouds. He came out to look at what I could possibly be drawn to in the empty sky. Of course he saw nothing: to my eye only did the clouds form parts of female bodies adrift across the baie des Anges. The shapes of breasts and buttocks were immediately perceived, but I could also distinguish the outlines of legs and—as the vaporous contours altered in the wind—watch airborne thighs drift open before they disappeared. My father was unable to make out images in clouds but he could not fail to see the bulge in my trousers that daydreaming led to.

"You must spend more time with the opposite sex. Mingle with the demoiselles on the Promenade des Anglais."

He gave me fifty francs—"if some unexpected expenses should arise"—and slipped a bar of soap into my pocket as I went out.

The soap only reminded me of my folly in Paris, and my rash. Outdoors the clouds turned grey and shapeless; the women around the Vieux Port were long past flowering. One of them approached and murmured to me a service I might enjoy, at a ridiculously low price. Her face was in shadow, but when I looked closely at her I drew back. She was the age of my mother. Her face was a horror of broken nose and smallpox scars, her breath smelled of sour wine. She offered me herself in my mother's same slow southern speech, and tenderly asked, "Tu viens?" I thrust the fifty francs into her hand and fled.

I began going regularly to a sordid bistro patronized by Foreign Legionnaires. They came over on permission from a training camp in Corsica. I would eavesdrop on their blunt conversations: they grunted and swore with a mixture of accents; the only adjectives they knew or used were obscene. They, if anyone, pursued the business of living with all seriousness, which for them meant the pursuit of combat, women, and drink.

The barman supplied the Legionnaires with homemade absinthe, banned in France since the war: this is a toxic concoction brewed from wormwood and anise; it is 80 percent alcohol and tastes like licorice. If it did not kill you, claimed the barman, it would make a man of you. The Legionnaires drank it, they said, against venereal infection. I drank Pernod, a mild counterfeit of absinthe with only half the degree of alcohol. The barman would not sell absinthe to a jeune homme de bonne famille.

My father had been invited on a cruise of the Mediterranean with

Madame d'O. I assumed the invitation did not extend to me: three, in those circumstances, is a crowd. (Anyway, I had suffered from seasickness on the *Leopoldina* while my father sported with his Swiss widow, in first class.)

And now, Madame d'O. What a queer pairing that was. My father's modus operandi was similar to Landru's, but my father—in the tradition of professional men, like lawyers and doctors—did not advertise. Nor did he ever, except in my mother's case, intimate that marriage was under consideration. Also, unlike Landru, my father was inherently incapable of cultivating a woman of modest means. Madame d'O, for example, kept an apartment on the boulevard Victor Hugo in Nice and a seaside residence on the cap d'Antibes. (Her ex-husband had been a successful war profiteer.) In Paris she stopped at the George V at least twice a year to buy frocks and hats, with accessories by the frères Lazar. She was the owner of a Mercedes touring car and part owner (with her ex-husband, I believe) of a race horse. In my presence she referred to my father as vous. "So this," she said when we first met, "is the nephew of our entrepreneur?" My father had removed his wedding band. I heard them tutoyer one another as they set off for the Casino in her Mercedes.

I was on my own. At the bistro near the cathedral I overheard a Legionnaire say he had beaten a girl insensible when he discovered she had infected him. I felt no such resentment against the girl in Paris —far from it: I would have risked hell (or the pox) to be with her again. I learnt from another Legionnaire that the penis dripped pus and to urinate was painful. For a moment my hopes were up, for I had no such dreadful symptoms, but they were dashed again when I heard that nine full weeks was the incubation period. I began to study the calendar as closely as a girl who, after her first misadventure, is concerned about her menstrual period.

The Legionnaires' café was the scene of my only adventure in Nice. It began over an argument about Landru.

"I knew a woman in Algiers claimed she was about to marry Landru, the conasse."

"Conasse," said another, "but a clever one."

A third Legionnaire challenged the first: "It was me she told about Landru. I knew her before you got up her skirts."

Good-naturedly the first threw his absinthe into the face of the third, and the battle was on.

A bottle exploded against the wall beside my table. Suddenly I could not see for the blood in my eye. A gardien de la paix (who had come too late to guard the peace) led me to a nearby aid station. This turned out to be a clinic for maternity cases. As soon as the blood was washed from my face I could see across the corridor into a room where a woman lay half-covered on a table, her legs up, attached to a saddle and stirrup device. She howled like a wounded animal or cursed the name of a man. Her pain made me forget my own while a midwife sewed up my wound, gave me aspirin, then crossed to the delivery room. I was free to go—ignored, in fact, or forgotten. In a daze I followed the midwife. I thought I heard gulls shrieking, but it was the woman fastened to the table. She sucked desperately for breath, drowning in her pain, and when she had breath enough she moaned piteously or screamed the same vile oaths I had so recently heard in the shattered café. I slumped against the door frame, light-headed, as the midwife lifted the sheet. From between the woman's tethered legs an infant's brown skull protruded. I thought I might faint when the midwife took hold of the thing. A creature began to issue forth in a trail of blood and slime. With my remaining strength I staggered out of the place and into the street. The damp night air brought me back to myself: I felt my forehead throbbing. From an open window I heard the first piercing cry of the newborn babe.

When I got back to the hotel my father was just coming in from the Casino. I told him I had got into a brawl with the Foreign Legion.

"There is your war experience," said he, rather proudly. He thought fighting was a foolish waste of a man's life force, but he was pleased I was showing some spunk for a change. "It will look like a dueling scar. Now you can get on with the business of living."

But when? At this pace, stepping gingerly in my father's footsteps, walking in his larger shadow, I would never enter into a life of my own. While my father sat down at the escritoire to count his money (he had won at baccarat, or borrowed from Madame d'O) I fidgeted over the facts of my life so far. Eighteen is not an easy age. I was an innocent bystander and passive voyeur, marking time outside of life. The business of living was under way elsewhere. I could hear the screams of the woman giving birth and I saw again the face of the aging prostitute with its stigmata of smallpox and twisted nose. Even a Legionnaire kicking his fallen mate in the ear mocked my hollow existence.

I had written a lie to Louise about being a writer but now the ambition came to a boil. I did want to be a writer, or thought I did.

(There was much thinking about being a writer in those days, since writing is the last resort of those with nothing better to do.) Suddenly I announced to my father I wanted to go back to Paris (since that was where writers wrote) and write.

"A newspaperman?" he asked.

He did not know or would not approve of the other kind, so I thought why not? and said yes.

"What about your education?" He knew my mother would ask about that.

I reminded my father of his theory that travel was the equivalent of an education.

"True," he mused. "If writing does not work out as expected, well—you can always come home again."

I had approached him at precisely the right moment: his winnings were spread out before us on the desk top. He presented me with five hundred francs (before the Casino could get them back) and said, "So be it."

He told me he would write to H. L. Mencken on my behalf. He did not know H. L. Mencken personally but he was willing to go out of his way to advance my career. Also, my return to Paris would work into his own plans for a Mediterranean cruise with Madame d'O.

While I was packing my father delivered an oration on honesty and thrift. He warned me against sharpsters and schemers of every stripe, and to beware of Parisians in particular. As for feminine companionship, I might want to put myself in the hands of an older woman. Beauty is only skin deep and youth but a passing phase. There is something to be said for maturity and experience. I think my father did not have any great hope of my success with women of any age. He was fond of me in his careless way, though he might have wished I were more like him.

He then referred to Dr. Paul Ehrlich, who had won half a Nobel Prize for the discovery of the Magic Bullet against venereal disease. "Stick-to-itiveness was his forte. He tried six hundred and five times to find a cure for syphilis and discovered salversan on the six-hundred-and-sixth try. That is why it is called 606 today."

Nine

A WORKMAN IN BLUE DENIM attached a bronze plaque to the base of an obelisk: the monument appeared to point an accusing finger at the sky. From the train window I saw an assortment of these newly erected sculptures to the dead. War memorials were being installed in public parks or against the façades of post offices and town halls. Nos Enfants Morts pour la Patrie: Our Sons, Fallen on the Field of Honor.

At the quai in Lyon a vendor sold me a bottle of wine from his pushcart and a cornet of frites in a newspaper. I ate the fried potatoes as the train chugged north and read the oil-stained newsprint around the cornet. Here was another list of the missing, this one greased and crumpled, no bronze plaque (1915–1919) to bear the names. These casualties were women, and one woman's son:

> Cuchet (et Cuchet, fils): Février 1915
> Laborde-Line: Juin 1915
> Guillin: 2 ou 3 août 1915
> Héon: Décembre 1915
> Collomb: 27 décembre 1916
> Babelay: 12 avril 1917
> Buisson: Août 1917
> Jaume: 26 novembre 1917

Marchadier: 13 janvier 1919
Pascal: ?

There were photographs beside the names, like the lonely photographs in lockets, or those stark portraits on tombstones in southern European cemeteries. One woman frowned bitterly (Guillin, I believe); those who smiled, smiled distractedly, and stared into the middle distance. They were elderly or middle-aged, plain-looking (three were as homely as any women I had ever seen), except for one, who was young and pretty (as far as I could tell, through the stain), and seemed as if she had got into the newspaper—and into the bizarre company—by mistake. She stared out of the photograph directly at me.

The Sûreté Générale had traced all ten women. By that I mean they had found out who the women were, but they had not found them. "Landru's fiancées were installed at his villa in Gambais discreetly, without fanfare—and then," according to the newspaper, "were made to disappear."

There was a photograph of the villa at Gambais under the heading "The House of Death" or some such label. Monsieur Tric, the owner, complained that he would never again be able to rent the now infamous property.

"Au contraire," replied the juge d'instruction.

(By now I had unwound the cornet and was reading the complete article.)

The juge d'instruction is a magistrate whose function is much the same as that of a grand jury. He must make a preliminary inquiry—including a formal interrogation of suspects and witnesses—to determine if a crime has been committed, and if so, draw up an indictment. In the Landru case the juge d'instruction was Monsieur Bonin, of the parquet de la Seine. Soon after Landru's arrest he directed Dr. Paul and Monsieur Labussière of the Paris Sûreté to make a personal investigation of the villa Tric and environs. The investigation was to be made in the strictest secrecy; nevertheless, the newspapers—as they inevitably do—got the word. At least a dozen reporters accompanied the investigating authorities on their tour of Gambais. And the residents of that community (for they had got the word as well) had already gathered at the villa Tric.

Danglure was one of the reporters.

"It was a circus," he told me (half a year later, over a glass of Sancerre at the bistro A la Bonne Santé). "I myself poked around in a trunk full of documents. Bills, tickets, receipts—everything. He even kept their baptismal certificates and sugar ration books."

Landru maintained that his clients had simply "gone off" after his business with them had been concluded. But no civilian would have gone off without his ration book, during the war.

"Women's stuff, all over the place. Hairpins, corset hooks, even a curling iron. And intimate garments, if you know what I mean." Danglure's fat hands did an obscene dance. "Souvenirs, you might say, of the rake's progress. Somebody found a football in the shed next to the house."

A football! A Frenchman never throws anything away. The football made me think of Cuchet, fils: the only boy among the missing. Had it been his? Had he been kicking a football around the garden at Gambais, a last bit of pleasure before . . . ?

Then Danglure brought out a single gold earring from his vest pocket. "I snagged this little item when I was browsing through the trunk."

"Wouldn't that be evidence?"

"Evidence! Bordel de Dieu, they've got enough evidence to guillotine the rascal ten times over. I wanted a bit of a souvenir for myself— after all, it was I who introduced the affair to the public. Anyway, it's not even gold, I found out. Landru must have discovered the same thing. All that glitters." And he slipped the earring back into his pocket.

"Was there any sign of blood?" (I had, by then, become a ghoulish member of the public myself.)

"There was a piece of concrete in the cave with bloodstains on it, but Dr. Paul decided it was not human blood. He found some bones in an ash heap outside the house. Not much, only little pieces—all broken and burnt—but *human,* said Dr. Paul. Human, without a doubt. Some of them, anyway. The toe bones and slivers of skull were mixed in with chicken bones and oyster shells."

"Oyster shells?"

"The oysters, my friend, I find significant—don't you?" This he said with a wink and a leer, then wet his tongue in the wine. "Next to the woodshed we dug up what was left of three dogs. By then you couldn't hold the crowd back. All over the place, pulling drawers open, tearing up floorboards. The souvenir hunters were impossible. Lucky I got to that trunk when I did—God only knows what the bastards got away with. I did notice every deuced doorknob in the place was missing by the time the police got the crowd out and the house sealed."

Dr. Paul testified before the juge d'instruction that the bones and teeth were definitely human remains: rib sections, fragments of tibia, radius, cubitus, and cranium. Along with these were the complete skeletal remains of three dogs.

During the hearing Landru was either flippant or mute.

"Look here," said Maître Bonin, "these are human teeth. Look well, Landru. Alors?"

"All I can say, your honor, is that they are in a poor state of preservation."

Yes, he had been acquainted with these women, in a business way. No, he had never proposed marriage. How could he? He was a happily married man, the father of four children.

Landru's oldest son, Maurice, was questioned about the furniture he had helped his father transport.

"My father told me the furniture was his, and I believed him."

It was at this time Landru revealed another facet of his character. His voice became sharp: he was indignant that his family should be brought into the affair.

"When I give an order to one of my children, your honor, he obeys. He does not ask the why and wherefore of my order. That is the way I have brought up my children, sir, and I should hope you have the good sense to do the same!"

The judge, in pursuit until now, recoiled. There was more to this furniture salesman than heretofore suspected. When the judge recovered himself and regained the initiative, he returned to the question of furniture, savings accounts, securities, and personal effects of these several missing individuals.

"I was entrusted with these matters by the ladies in question. After all, I am a dealer in furniture and other salable items."

Did he lead these women to believe he intended marriage?

"Women are inclined to believe whatever they choose."

What, then, became of his clients after his business with them was terminated?

"I have no idea. Why should I have? Having completed my part of the transaction I took no further notice of the customer."

When asked specific questions about individuals on the list of the missing, Landru made no reply, said he did not remember, or stated he did not know. Three dogs? Yes, he had destroyed the animals because he did not want to pay license fees. He had strangled them with his bootstrings.

"The most beautiful death imaginable," declared Landru. "The creatures do not suffer in any way."

Ten

I WAS EIGHTEEN, with all of Paris to myself. The strongest impression of my return was standing on the mossy grille of a streetcorner pissoir, urinating in the easy dreaming way of a reprieved prisoner. No burning or blockage, no sign of disorder. I was as ebullient as a Foreign Legionnaire with permission papers in my pocket and a bottle of absinthe. The sixty-three days had safely passed. I wanted a girl of course.

I could not find the girl for whom I had been a charming débutant. In her place at the square des Innocents was a leather-skinned prostitute with the shoulders of a wrestler, wearing black boots laced to the knee. "Tu viens," she demanded. Her specialty had something to do with whips. She stood with her feet apart blocking the sidewalk: to get around her I would have to step into the gutter, but I did so—I was seeking gentler pleasures.

I asked the fishmonger who had wished us santé-bonheur that night what had become of the thin sweet dark-haired beauty who used to work this side of the square. Yes, he remembered her: Anne, Anna? She rode a bicycle, she told fortunes on the side. But that girl no longer worked this district.

"They come," he said, "they go."

I was staying at the hotel at Palais Royale where the chief clerk at the Ministry across the street still came to the window like a fish drowning in polluted waters. Eventually the expense of the Hôtel des Bons Enfants was more than my diminishing funds would allow. I packed my suitcase and drifted farther along the rue Saint-Honoré—like a moth, closer to the gas lamps—in the direction of les Halles, where I found a desolate hotel called the Sans Souci. Even this squalid corner of Paris pleased me. The city cast its spell, seduced me once again: the very air was an aphrodisiac. A Belgian I had met on the train from Nice had given me an address.

There is something grotesque about a brass door knocker in the shape of a woman's hand. I took the disembodied hand in mine and rapped several times. My own hands were moist, my throat dry. Guiltily I checked to see if my fly was buttoned.

Inside the house I heard a stir, the sound of laughter spilled out of a window above my head. I thought I heard birds chirping from within, finally I heard footsteps.

"Comme vous êtes matinal!"

I was an early bird indeed, appearing at a maison de passe before noon. The madam reminded me of Madame d'O, which may have something to say about distinction. She affected a gold-headed cane (minus the limp that went with it) but was in all other details and dress a reproduction of my father's mistress in Nice, even to the blue-tinted hair.

There were night birds on the staircase, a cageful coming down to breakfast. Three others fluttered in a salon off the reception hall, taking coffee. The three Gratiae in the salon wore gowns as delicately colored and diaphanous as butterfly wings. I was too excited not to stare.

The house, the Belgian had assured me, was one of the best managed in Paris: it drew an exclusive and exacting clientele from the 7th arrondissement. (Until the redoubtable Sphinx, three years later, it was the only three-star maison de passe on the Left Bank.) The Belgian considered the house the equal of One-Two-Two (de la rue de Provence) and the historic Chabanais.

The carpeting underfoot was soft as eiderdown, the corridor perfumed. "Fewer girls than the One-Two-Two," my Belgian confessed, "but of a quality, a quality!" And he touched his thumb to his forefinger in a gesture of perfection. Also, he assured me, the girls were inspected regularly by a physician living on the premises.

"Solange?" repeated the madam, to my inquiry.

I had been hearing the name Solange, a lingering sensual echo, ever since the Belgian recommended her. It was a name full of languid associations in sound: as soothing as soulage, soft in the hidden meanings of lange and linge (and as suggestive of the latter)—even to the thought of langue, though I did not yet know why the word tongue should have occurred to me.

"She may be sleeping."

"Not at all," said one of the Gratiae in the salon. "She is taking chocolate in her room."

The girl who spoke had let down her butterfly wings exposing her breasts to the nipple, a playful performance meant to engage my wide-eyed attention. A bird in the hand, thought I, ready (for that instant) for a change of heart and choice. However—since my train mate had rhapsodized so convincingly about her—Solange had become a password to pure bliss. I was inclined to accept the Belgian's mature judgment in the matter. After all, he had made a fortune dealing in armaments during the war: I could assume he would be as knowledgeable concerning le commerce de la chair fraîche.

The directress indicated the way with her cane, and I followed her into a parlor to await Solange. She looked about her and smiled at the décor, satisfied I would be comforted by the handsome setting; then she withdrew.

The parlor was furnished in the Louis XV style doctors and lawyers choose for their waiting rooms to this day. I was reminded of the lobby of the Hôtel Gonnet et de la Reine. The same four cherubim in plaster held up the corners of the ceiling, their penises defying gravity. One entire wall was devoted to shelves of books with expensive leather bindings. The bindings made me think the library was a collection of leather spines only, but I took one down and opened it: an illustrated treatise on corporal punishment—it was a book after all.

Above the marble fireplace hung a murky oil of a shepherdess being pursued by a satyr, the scene illuminated by flashes of lightning and flashes of lust. The gilt frame was possibly more valuable than the work of art. Also, there was a pastel of a pink lady in her bath, in the style of Degas—except for the gentleman in opera clothes who was peering into the tub.

Idly I picked up objets d'art from the mantelpiece, mostly phallic: one, a fan that opened onto a scene of Oriental erotica; another, the parts of a woman in ivory—a Chinese puzzle I tried to assemble but my fingers were too awkward, and I put them down again. I even looked into the eyepiece of a stereoscope I found on an end table: a very three-dimensional man wearing only garters was penetrating his buxom partner from behind. Why this should have reminded me of the Belgian on the train, I do not know. Perhaps I thought of him waiting here, as I was, for Solange.

(We had shared a table in the dining car and he talked of gunpowder, bayonets, and copulation. I ventured the remark that the armaments business must be slack at the moment, now that the great war was over. He smiled at my naiveté. "There is always a military conflict raging somewhere." He cited the example of civil war in Russia, where he was at present supplying arms to both Reds and Whites.)

I might have looked at more stereoscope slides—my curiosity larger than my repugnance—but that was when Solange made her appearance.

"Bonjour, Monsieur. Comme vous êtes matinal."

She was wearing the same transparent toga as the girls in the coffee room: she was quite young, with heavy breasts and plump legs and the complexion of a milkmaid, even to the sprinkling of freckles across her nose and cheeks and the tops of her breasts. Her forehead was a mass of little girl's ringlets. She had the face of those Parisian angels I had first seen along the rue de Rivoli and become enamored of. She was putting on earrings which she would take off again very soon. I thought of her as a white French doll wrapped in pink gauze, a pillow for a man to lie upon. I greeted her awkwardly, too unnerved to utter anything more than a return bonjour.

No, she was not the girl I expected—neither the girl from the square des Innocents nor the dream nymph I sought in the corridors of the Louvre—but I was so aroused by now (by her ringlets and earrings and freckled breasts) it did not matter what her name or who she was. She extended a milkmaid's arm and I took her hand.

I was the satyr from a bad painting pursuing my own smiling shepherdess—behind us followed a black woman, bearing towels. We went to the assigned room; it had a name—the Blue Room? le Parc aux Cerfs? (there was a daguerreotype of deer copulating)—I forget. The negress lingered for a moment, then left us to ourselves. (It was customary to tip the chambermaid, but I did not know this.) On a stand beside the bed was a silver coffee service for two: the pot was steaming. Solange offered me a cup. She took my refusal graciously, knowing my appetite was sharp for something else.

This time I was prepared with the fee in advance. (The Belgian had advised me of the price, and I carried little more than that amount in my pocket—the ridiculous moneybelt remained in my suitcase at the Sans Souci.) In a charming, coquettish, matter-of-fact way—but her face became shrewder than an angel's should—Solange informed me that for a supplementary sum I might enjoy a spécialité at which she was adept. I had not considered a mouth serviceable in that way, had never dreamed of the variation—but now that I thought of it was obliged to say, "I think not." In any case I did not carry the price of fellatio in my pocket.

I was less shy than with the girl from the square des Innocents, but not much less. I did initiate the preliminary caresses, under her butterfly wings and through the pink gauze, until Solange suggested we might be more comfortable out of our clothes. As for her, she shed her delicate garment with a gesture that resembled a shrug. She reached into the thick halo of ringlets and drew forth two tears of pearl, then put the earrings on the stand beside the coffee service.

At the marble bidet (the Belgian was right: the accommodations were first rate) I submitted to a tender washing. The water spouted from a swan's beak, my genitalia dangling below, gently soaped and rinsed by Solange, naked, on her knees. In some other ambience the ceremony might have been as domestic as a mother washing her babe. For me this reassuring ritual of hygiene turned into an act of hydro-therapeutic foreplay. I grew hard under the caressing stream and manipulative fingers. Had we lingered at the font long enough, the swan would likely have received my seed.

My performance in bed was far less naive than that first fumbling time, but was still no proud feat of sexual engineering. At least there was no barrier of moneybelt between me and my bedmate, and the bed itself was a canopied marvel Madame Pompadour might have made use of: the sheets were scented—with lavender I think—and you stepped into bed from a footstool.

The touchpoints of flesh were familiar now, even though the girl below me offered a larger bounty of flesh. My brief apprenticeship had acquainted me with the essentials of placement, sequence, and flow. Her pink opening did not admit me at the first attempt: there was a constriction that turned her dreamy smile into a grimace. Was it too

early in the day for her to feel something other than blunt intrusion
down there? (I do not mean to suggest my endowments in that area
are exceptionally large. The problem was one of lubrication, and my
inconsiderate haste.) I politely drew back. While I tasted her nipples
with my tongue, an hors d'oeuvre I have always been fond of (hers did
not stiffen, I must admit), she maneuvered around me, sought a jar of
lotion in a drawer, and anointed herself. "Voilà." I was deep inside
her before she could put the jar aside.

My need was too great, my eagerness extreme, after the intolerable
denial of sixty-three days. The eruption came long before I would
have wanted, too soon to allow my pleasure to extend itself in full.

"Voilà," she said again, glad, professionally, to be done with it.

I withdrew with regret.

The French call the moment of orgasm la petite mort. After a little
death there is bound to be a certain tristesse, and soon after my exertions had come to a premature conclusion I was immeasurably depressed. Monsieur Nicolas Restif de la Bretonne, whose writings I later
discovered, has recorded in Latin his version of this phenomenon:
Omnium animal post coitum triste; excepto gallo-gallinaceo, et
scholastico futuente gratis. My knowledge of Latin is slight, but I believe I know what Monsieur Nicolas means to say.

The pleasure in the act of love comes to an end so abruptly. In
time I would learn the difference between desire assuaged and the
banked fire of genuine love, but I would never escape the sadness that
follows even the most satisfying climax. Here there was no daydreaming afterglow (and no champagne) as with the girl at les Halles. I had
produced a little money, then spilled my liquid into Solange, and she
had accepted these two offerings with professional aplomb. Wine had
perhaps made the difference that first time, and a first time is inevitably
an adventure.

Yet, how could the nameless girl of one vagrant night so dominate
my imagination? I thought of her even after this new episode with
another girl. A girl is a girl is a girl—is she not? She is and can provide comfort and release in variable measure, as Solange had dutifully
done. But now that I had lived through my little death the world
looked bleak. The rapture had drained out of me and left behind a
cheerless void.

Solange went to the swan's beak for water and washed herself, then me. I could not blame her for my blue mood. She put her earrings back on but not her toga, and offered me a cigarette. I was obliged to reply, "Je ne fume pas," when it would have seemed so much more mature to accept a cigarette. She was an agreeable creature, and accommodating in every way. That she now resembled a pink fat pillow rather than a French doll was not her fault.

I was about to roll away from her and dress myself when she said, "Tu peux rester un peu, tu sais."

I might stay with her awhile, if I chose, since this was hardly the busy hour at a maison close. I was suddenly overcome by lassitude, contented not to have to dress and go away. Did I mind if she smoked? Not at all. We sat up in Pompadour's bed naked still, like two plucked birds, she with a cigarette between her lips. With her crown of ringlets and child's pouting mouth, she did not appear old enough to smoke a cigarette. (Then I recalled the service she had proposed to render with those innocent lips.) She was, I think, as morose as I—for reasons of her own. My melancholia might also have come from the realization, a moment before entering Solange, that a Belgian dealer in big guns had preceded me. And how many others? I asked myself now. She too might have been brooding about those others, or me, or a place that hurt—there is no earthly way to know what a prostitute thinks. She did not bother to brush away the cold ashes that fell upon her breasts. I contemplated my limp penis, newly washed.

Our episode together had been so brief the coffee was still warm enough to drink. She poured me a cup of it, and passed the cup to my side of the bed. I glanced upward and saw for the first time the full-length mirror, upside down, framed by the flounces of the canopy: patrons could observe their own gymnastics in it, and catch the moment of carnal triumph—but I saw the reverse image of two dazed children chastened by circumstance. She blew smoke rings out of ennui and asked me how I got that scar, out of politesse. I fingered the little V-shaped indentation on my brow as if trying to place that scar among so many others. I told her I had got into a brawl with Foreign Legionnaires in Nice—almost the truth, except for the false modest way I said it.

I asked her where she was from. From Lille, of course—a refugee from the boches. I could have related the rest: she had been a cantinière not far from the front. She did not know I knew the words to that ballad, and the music.

But then, between puffs, apropos of nothing, she revealed how a friend of hers had become a prostitute. She would not ordinarily have told me this, I knew—it did not go with the décor. Her melancholia (and mine) must have prompted the tale.

Shall we call her Ninette, the girl in the story? This was not Solange, you understand, but another—Solange insisted on this.

The girl (Ninette, then) had only the vaguest recollection of her mother, and of her father none at all. The nuns in the home (home is the French word for orphanage) in Mentone told her she was born in Marseille, and the postal orders for Ninette's maintenance came from there. They informed her, as well, that she was of illegitimate birth.

"They need not have told her that," I commented.

"Nuns, my friend, are no less cruel for being brides of Christ."

Ninette had spent most of her childhood in the establishment run by these good sisters: "She came to detest their grim robes and pale pinched humorless faces. Sister Angélique was not angelic at all and Sister Denise had a man's mustache."

Purgatory, however, has an end. When the funds for Ninette's upkeep ceased altogether, the fifteen-year-old child was obliged to leave.

"Fifteen," Solange repeated bitterly. "With no family, and no place to go."

Ninette found her way to Marseille and tried to discover the origin of the postal orders, but this was during the war. More than one mother had disappeared into dossiers and thin air. The abandoned child found temporary solace in the arms of a sailor who kissed away her tears and fed her oursins with chilled wine at a waterfront café. That same night, in the crudest fashion, against the mossy piling at the end of a dock, the sailor rid her of her maidenhead. She stayed with him, for she had no one else. When her sailor-lover's ship sailed, he left Ninette in the care of another sailor—and that sailor did the same.

"Marseille is a dirty town, dirty in ways I would not tell you."

"Have you ever been to Marseille?" I asked Solange, for she seemed to be speaking for herself as well as Ninette.

She ignored the question and went on. When Ninette became sixteen she grew tired of the fleeting tendresses of the French fleet and decided to seek her fortune in the capital. Paris in wartime was not the same city as now. She looked for employment in vain: the principal occupation for a girl of Ninette's age and situation was the ancient profession she had fled in Marseille. To earn a few sous those first

weeks she sold paper carnations in the cafés along the grands boulevards. Men touched her without buying and whispered obscene suggestions concerning other merchandise. One does not eat well selling
paper flowers, is it not so?

"True," said I, but I did not want to hear about it.

I was uneasy with this story: it seemed somehow as familiar as the
one about the cantinière. But Solange went on with the telling; she
had forgotten her audience, she was reciting a litany to herself.

There was a job for a serveuse through an employment agency in
Clichy. Ninette saw the ad in *le Petit Journal* and thought, why not?
Serveuse is an honorable trade, even if it should be in a bistro. She
clipped the ad and took it with her to Clichy.

(I thought of the ads Landru inserted in this same journal, but
his were worded in quite a different way, directed to another kind of
desperation.)

The gentleman at the agency did not present her with a fiche to
fill out. In a fatherly way he asked all the questions himself. Where did
she come from? Did she have family in Paris? Was she alone? She
told him the truth (she had never been spoken to in a fatherly way):
she had no one, she needed a job. His unrelenting gaze made her
uneasy for long moments, but she was relieved to hear him say, "You
shall have it." She could not believe her sudden change of fortune.

"I cannot pay you," said Ninette, but the man informed her, "Your
employer pays my fee."

The job was at Enghien, and he would take her there. He drove a
motor car. How chic, thought the girl: the crowd at Enghien would
be sportif—the racetrack was out there. This was truly her lucky day.

Solange opened her petallike lips and blew out a smoke ring that
floated like a halo above our heads.

"What do you think of Paris?" she suddenly inquired.

"It is," I said, in truth, "the most beautiful ctiy I have ever seen."

"Yes," she replied, then went on with her tale.

It was not a bistro at Enghien, nor a café. There was a house with
a wall around it. As soon as she stepped out of the car and saw the
gate the girl said, "Non!"

Beside me, the plump Solange with her teardrop earrings and
kindergarten ringlets uttered the word "Non!" with all the force and
fright of the girl she told about. (It was a warmish midday in a drape-
shrouded suffocating chamber, yet I felt a chill and covered myself

with the sheet.) The girl at my side erased the last smoke ring with a swift gesture and dropped her spent cigarette into the muddy dregs of my coffee.

"Non!" was of no use; it was too late to say "Non!" Another man came out to help, and the gate closed behind Ninette. The man from the house with the wall around it was called the Trainer. He trained horses and women. "I break them in for others to ride."

Eleven

As my moneybelt flattened I grew light-headed with eating less: even the Sans Souci with its damp plaster and unreliable plumbing was beyond my means. The week Madame d'O's franc notes dwindled to centimes I received an international money order from my mother. Of course I could not go on this way, dependent on my family's irregular largesse. I would have to find a cheap room and a way to earn some money of my own. I found the room first, in a hotel called simply Hôtel, on rue Tiquetonne, off the rue Saint-Denis.

The street was one of the sinuous market arteries running along the periphery of les Halles. It was not officially part of the market network, but the sprawl of wholesalers and handlers had overwhelmed rue Tiquetonne: at night the quarter was also part of the belly of Paris.

By late afternoon the farm carts and camions that could not be accommodated at the Halles Centrales jammed themselves along the side streets all the way to rue Tiquetonne and beyond, to unload fruit and vegetables, cheese and flowers trucked in from the provinces. The drivers and tradesmen and produce dealers employed a rich and colorful profanity during their maneuvers along that narrow thoroughfare, and I quickly acquired a new vocabulary of gros mots. By midnight the sidewalks were piled with crates of tangerines, celery, poireaux, and betteraves: a still life of vegetable color. The ends of my street might be sandbagged with sacks of potatoes, like a garrison town. Strutting huskies (les forts, the strong ones) carried the victuals of Paris on their backs: a crate of dates balanced on a shoulder, the burlap cadaver of a turnip sack flung from a farm wagon, garlands of garlic around the thick neck of a sweating Atlas.

The cafés came alive at night, soon after the sidewalks sprouted their perennial night-blooming produce. Until I learned to sleep through the din of honking taxis and perhaps the wheeze of a bagpipe player from Auvergne beneath my window, I did not close my eyes till dawn, when the garbage carts came rumbling down rue Dussoubs escorted by cleaners walking ahead with great brooms of willow twigs. Then the gutters were washed down with hoses and buckets; a tide of eggshells and orange peel and pigs' blood poured into the sewers. The last sound I might hear was the matinal flute player across the street practicing scales or piping snatches of Pergolesi and Rameau.

After the midnight curtain came down at the Comédie Française, and the theatres and Opéra let out, the new rich from the war and remaining rich from la belle époque and well-heeled café society known as le tout Paris came in taxis and horse cab to eat onion soup and disport themselves and mingle with the stealthy poor foraging in the piles of damaged fruit and discarded légumes.

In those times you could still sound the klaxon of a motor car with impunity, and all the drivers did. Wholesalers and their stock men tried to shout above this and above the strolling customers demanding "Combien?" from stall to stall—even the chickens competed, cackling through their prison slats until sold, and their necks wrung—and winding through this cacophony came the muezzin cry of an ambulant Arab selling honeycakes. The collective breath steamed with commercial heat in the dank night air.

There were four rowdy cafés on rue Tiquetonne, and three cheap but good restaurants. Prostitutes of the rougher sort patrolled the curbs or hovered in hotel doorways. These were workaday beauties with draft-horse derrières and the strong yellow teeth of farm animals, ready to reply to inquiries of "Combien?" in the blunt good-natured street jargon of their sort. Others swam down rue Tiquetonne like predatory fish, feeling for a wallet or a scrotum in the crowd, feeding upon food buyers and les forts. A fierce set of twins from Brittany operated as a duo out of the Café des Amusements; a plain-faced girl with a hinged wooden leg displayed herself regularly at the corner of the rue Française. Even more curious was the dwarf woman of middle years who paced in front of the PTT striking at the knees of passersby with her handbag to call attention to her tiny self.

At first I was greeted with the classic welcome of the quarter: "Tu viens?" in a hoarse whisper of complicity. I would turn each time with an expectant stare and hope to encounter a familiar smile, a Spanish curl, my dark-haired dream who had slept with the devil. But the smiles were invariably large and yellow, or smirking, or sinister (one particular mouth was filled with metal teeth, another with no teeth at all), until I began to recognize the habitués and they me; an implicit wink was shared in our passing: we lived together in the rot and flower of the marketplace.

I shaved off my hopeless mustache. With it went (I hoped) my pretensions, my callowness and naiveté. I was an adolescent with or without mustache, a wide-eyed romantic shy of romance, and especially was I sentimentally enraptured of my piece of Paris, my little part of what I thought was paradise.

There was an enamel pitcher for water in my room, set in a tin basin. (Once a week, I used the public bath two blocks away.) In my memory's eye I will see forever a white pitcher and tin basin in a peculiarly triangular room, like a wedge of brie. The rooms were so shaped because here rue Tiquetonne was intersected by the rue Dussoubs, and the adjoining street had sliced the hotel in this fashion. From my single window five flights up I had an oblique view of angled roofs and protruding chimney pots all the way to the blunt, unfinished towers of Saint Eustache.

I purchased six oblong notebooks bound in red—the same cheap cahiers favored by Proust (and Landru, incidentally). Restif de la Bretonne had stayed at this hotel, Madame Vitrine informed me. Madame Vitrine was my landlady. She declared Monsieur Restif de la Bretonne had lived and worked in the very room she rented to me. I did not know who Restif de la Bretonne was, but immediately went to Gibert's bookstore where I found a copy of his *Monsieur Nicolas,* volume I. I did not go back for volume II: *Monsieur Nicolas* was his autobiography in fourteen volumes. He was an eighteenth-century novelist who was called the Rousseau of the gutter by a critic of his day. He was a great seducer of chambermaids (and died of venereal infection as a result), but like most authors who specialize in their own sexual exploits, he was apt to exaggerate. He wrote a flowery French full of maudlin sentiments, but reverted to Latin when he got to the point. He leads the reader into an intriguing encounter full of erotic possibilities only to shift the text to: mastupraverat, fellaverat, mammaverat, tandem futuerat ingentibus conatibus; postea pluries vitiatam puellam irrumerat. My interest—and that other part of me—flagged. At any rate, Madame Vitrine was mistaken about Restif de la Bretonne: he had actually lived three doors down.

Except for its association with the Rousseau of the gutter, rue Tiquetonne is an undistinguished and mostly overlooked thoroughfare. It serves no discernible purpose and leads nowhere. The same might be said of my life at that point.

The nearest avenue of note is rue Saint-Denis, named for the patron saint of Paris. The martyred Saint Denis was decapitated by the Romans (for reasons unknown), but picked up his head and walked. Frenchmen are much attached to the legend of Saint Denis and painters are fond of illustrating the legend in colorful detail. The street is also known for its large population of prostitutes. Rue Saint-Denis was where I collected my mail at a branch PTT poste restante, also patronized by the prostitutes.

There was a postcard from my father from Naples asking me not to mention Madame d'O when I wrote my mother. I was just to say he was in Italy on business. My mother knew all about my father's business, which was chiefly women, and my father knew she knew, but the three of us pretended it was not so. I might add that my father loved my mother, and she also knew that.

Louise wrote, and sent me poems. Her America sounded very far away, and very American. I wrote her about my encounter with the Foreign Legionnaires in Nice: the episode had grown large. I added color and flourish until it was (as my father suggested) my war story.

By nature and inclination I am an honest individual. Until now I had kept myself from indulging in lies by the mere fact of having nothing much to communicate nor an interested enough companion (or correspondent) to lie to. Earlier I had been caught up in my father's lies: I acquiesced in playing the role of his nephew, believing this prevarication had nothing to do with me since I did not originate it. Lying is an insidious process that grows out of just such careless acquiescence. I was learning. Already I had practiced on Solange, allowing her to believe what she would—to make myself more dashing than I was—without in fact (or so I thought) lying. In my letters to Louise I pushed beyond the stage of passive fabrication: I took the trouble to invent and elaborate. My version of the story about the Foreign Legionnaires was considerably removed from the factual incident. I did not yet consider myself a liar.

Fiction attracted me at the time. I read novels and would like to have written them. In Paris I took up the writing of short stories again, and that may have led me to exercise my imagination in that naive correspondence with Louise, beyond the mundane truth. This, at any rate, was my excuse. A definition of terms soothed my slack conscience. There were social lies, like the kind my father told, in order to put one's best foot forward. The practice seemed harmless enough. All the same, my growing tendency to prevaricate became troubling in more reflective moments: I dissembled in haste and repented at leisure.

(Was conscience, dear Miss Stein, what prevented me from developing a literary imagination?)

My father forwarded a letter he had received from H. L. Mencken, written on the letterhead stationery of a Baltimore funeral parlor. Mr. Mencken had somehow got the idea my father was a cello player he used to eat oysters with. He would be happy to introduce "the kid" to the editor of the Baltimore *Sun,* if ever I decided to come home. The only influential character he knew in Paris was a freewheeling Israelite named Stein, but he did not know the lady personally and personally he would rather spend time with a beer stein. Pray to the Great Bootlegger in the Sky that the plague of teetotalism be not visited upon the enlightened Old World. (His commentary on Prohibition ran on for the length of a page, somewhat crudely put but altogether entertaining.) He invited my father to go oyster eating with him when he got back to Merryland, and closed with his best wishes in German. It was not the kind of letter that would help a young man find newspaper work in Paris, but for some months I carried it around with me in my moneybelt.

Twelve

"IF YOU'RE LOOKING FOR a job as a newsboy you've come to the wrong office."

"No, as a reporter."

His smile was offensive: "Look, lad, you can't just step in off the Champs-Elysées and expect to work for a newspaper."

"Where else would I step in from?"

The office of the *Paris American* was on the Champs-Elysées. The boy at the reception counter was my age, so I resented being called lad. (This was Harry, as I was to discover—and I would learn that his bluster was put on to cover a lack of self-confidence equal to my own.) He was stoutish and jowly, already turning bald in adolescence yet sprouting a ridiculous mustache like the one I had just shaved off.

"Besides," said he, "there's no jobs anyway. They'll tell you the same upstairs."

He meant the editors, upstairs. I would rather have heard this from the editors than be patronized by a cocky nuisance behind the Classified desk.

"I've got a letter from H. L. Mencken."

"They'll tell you upstairs where you can stick that."

I must have flushed or changed expression for he quickly said: "Don't take it so personal. You'll have to get used to that kind of talk if you want to work on a newspaper. You speak French?"

"Oui."

"Anybody can say oui."

I told him I considered the *Paris American* a good newspaper, in French. Then I said, "Ma mère est française."

"You born here?"

"Yes, but I lived in America."

"Can you translate?"

"I don't know."

"Jesus, never say 'I don't know' in the newspaper game. Say yes."

"Yes, then."

"Look. Go see this character." He scribbled a name on a scrap of paper. "A dipsomaniac, a disgrace to the profession. He's looking for a leg man. Don't tell him who sent you."

I didn't know who was sending me. I wanted to ask, and also to find out what a leg man was, but thought it best not to show my ignorance. I left the *Paris American* and walked over to the rue d'Artois.

There was a modiste on the ground floor with cloche hats in the window: the Channel News Service was above the modiste. I am fearful of French elevators. This one was an elaborate cage of ironwork, and operated hydraulically, so I took the stairs. On the door to the office was a flyspecked sign that said, "Clarence O'Grady is IN," and beneath the lettering appeared the same message in French. If you turned the sign over it said, "Clarence O'Grady is OUT," without the flyspecks. I stepped in without knocking. The room smelled nauseatingly sweet and was full of smoke.

"They're coming in the windows," said O'Grady. It was something he always said.

He was fanning the smoke with a folded newspaper: a slender freckled man in suspenders, he was his own barber and had cut his hair into a bristling reddish brush. A thick red mustache was similarly butchered. He smoked aromatic Egyptian cigarettes, which accounted for the smell.

"Clever of you not to take the lift," he said. "What the devil do you want?"

I told him I could translate.

"So can every moneychanger on the boulevard des Capucines. Can you typewrite?"

I was on the way to telling the truth, then remembered Harry's advice.

"Yes, I can."

"Age?"

I started to say eighteen, but said, "Twenty," instead.

His red-rimmed eyes grew so fierce I thought he might throw me out, but I was feeling reckless enough—or desperate enough—to stand fast, standing almost at attention while he assessed me with his relentless stare. His sleeves were rolled, showing an expanse of freckled forearm, but now he rolled them down and fastened the cuffs with rubber bands. He asked my name and advised me to call him O'Grady: "Not Mister, if you please. And not Clarence, mind." We had the same given name.

The smoke had cleared and I saw that the office was not much larger than my own room, but square-shaped instead of triangular, and with two windows instead of one. The walls were covered with newspaper pages from the Manchester *Guardian* and the London *Daily Mail,* with columns of newsprint outlined in red ink. The desk was cluttered with thumbprinted manuscripts and smeary tearsheets, among them a platter of cheese and a volume of Sherlock Holmes. On the wall behind the desk dangled a crank telephone on a flexible lattice, and to the right of it a stopped clock, the word *Dublin* written across its dead face. I noticed a gramophone out of its case on a table between the two windows, with an empty wineglass, not very clean, set upon the gramophone turntable.

"Hark!"

The elevator mechanism had been set in motion.

"She will have a man with her. A lawyer, perhaps, or a notaire."

"I could come back—"

"Stay where you are. I want you in on this." He stuck a cigarette behind my ear, then stood away from me to measure the effect. "Do you carry a pistol? Of course not. Here." He drew a paper knife out of the Sherlock Holmes (it had served as a bookmark) and handed it across the desk. "If Monsieur should forget himself, I want you to step between us."

Was he playing with me? The man's devilish grin made me feel all the more foolish as I put the paper knife—which smelled of cheese —inside my jacket.

The elevator halted: there was the sound of clanking metal as the occupants attempted to open the door. As the sound increased in volume, O'Grady's grin broadened. I knew now why he thought me clever not to have taken the elevator: the security latch on the cage door invariably stuck at this floor. One of the stranded passengers (a contralto voice) shouted, "Au secours!" The rattling of the cage bars grew desperate. With all deliberation and calm, O'Grady clipped a pretied bow tie to his paper collar, then went out into the corridor to free the two frantic prisoners.

Shortly a top-heavy woman in black, partly veiled, burst into the office, voicing her outrage in an operatic way. She was followed by a bald man with hat in hand who seemed to tiptoe after her. O'Grady came in behind, closing the office door, his grin replaced by an expression of sobriety and concern. He was elaborately polite and offered two cane chairs to the visitors. I sat on a stool in the corner, like the dunce I was.

"Vous m'avez trahi!" the woman declared, then tucked her mourning skirts about her and sat. To document the betrayal she accused him of, she plunged into a vast beaded handbag and emerged with a news clipping which she thrust at O'Grady: "You assured me you dealt with the English press, but you have betrayed me to a Paris newspaper."

She played her tragedy in an operatic way: a diva, bosom heaving, she spoke in arias. Her companion turned out to be her business manager, or gérant. He sat with his hat on his knee, a supernumerary throughout.

O'Grady, appearing puzzled, passed the clipping to me. "What do you make of this?"

I was startled that O'Grady would have brought me into the matter, but tried, self-consciously, to read the article while Madame B and her gérant stared at me.

In the spring of 1918 (according to the text, with the lady in question muttering her grievances in counterpoint across the room) Madame B met a gentleman during the intermission of *Faust* at the Paris Opéra. She was not in the habit of conversing with perfect strangers, but Monsieur Forest, one instinctively knew, was a person of good breeding and reliable background. The gentleman was a widower, she a divorcée. They shared a love of good music and other refinements (plaisirs, in the French, was more suggestive). Monsieur Forest was a successful entrepreneur who maintained a thriving business—never specified—in Morocco. Eventually Madame B accompanied Monsieur Forest to Biarritz where they were to be married. In a very delicate and reasonable way Monsieur Forest convinced Madame B to invest in his Moroccan enterprise, which she did, to the extent of 200,000 francs. Soon after he received the money, a telegram arrived addressed to Monsieur Forest, signed, appropriately, Maroc. He showed this urgent message to Madame B, which called for his presence in Morocco at once, and he left Biarritz on the next train. Weeks passed, and Madame B waited in vain for word from her intended. Finally she was obliged to make private inquiries—first in Morocco, then in Paris—to no avail. Monsieur Forest had disappeared from the face of the earth.

I looked up from my reading—Madame B had assumed a pose of prayerful suffering, her veiled face tilted toward the ceiling fan—then returned to the final paragraph.

It was not until April of this year (1919) that Madame B opened a newspaper to discover a photograph of her errant betrothed flanked by police officers. Monsieur Henri Forest turned out to be Monsieur Henri Landru.

When I finished reading I looked up, ill at ease, no more enlightened than before. O'Grady was already offering an explanation to Madame B.

"My assistant" (he meant me, and I could feel Madame B's accusing eyes behind the veil) "must have delivered the typescript to *le Figaro* by mistake. It was meant, I assure you, for dispatch to London. He has only just come to work for us, and this is not his first blunder —but I speak for him and the organization when I offer our sincere apologies."

My mouth may have opened in astonishment, but Madame B was not at all concerned with the guilt or innocence of an underling. "I am considering a libel action," she announced. Her gérant, mute until this moment, ventured a grunt and a sharp nod of assent.

There was an unpleasant pause during which O'Grady lit one of his abominable cigarettes (he did not offer them around) and considered his position. After he exhaled the first sickening draft of smoke he pretended to believe he was not the intended target of Madame B's lawsuit.

"Against *le Figaro,* no doubt."

"No, Monsieur. Against you."

O'Grady contemplated his dilemma with perfect aplomb.

"You would sue *me,*" O'Grady asked, "for what *le Figaro* has published about your misadventure with Landru?"

"It was to *you* I offered my story."

"A true story, of course."

"But of course."

"You would seek damages for libel because of a printed story, true in every respect, that you yourself offered to the press?"

Madame thrust back her shoulders while her gérant whispered something into the veil.

"I hold you responsible for breach of contract and abuse of confidence," said she. Her companion nodded.

"Contract?" O'Grady did something puckish with his freckled forehead as he pretended to search his littered desk for a contract. He shrugged and exhaled the malodorous smoke and launched into legal discourse on the chances of the complainant scoring in court: "Dear lady, a session before the tribunal will do nothing to restore your fortune or your reputation and may, to the contrary, do further injury to both. Remember, your name was never used, only an initial—in court your name would be made public. If friends and acquaintances who have read *le Figaro* divine who Madame B might be, they will, believe me, be more impressed than shocked. Landru has caught the public fancy. Any woman who has been associated with him becomes a celebrity in her own right. You have lost an investment and a fiancé, but you are still alive. You might well have ended up as ten other acquaintances of Landru did: a few charred bones and toenails in a trash heap."

Madame B, who had been majestically enthroned till now, abruptly stood, and her associate with her, like two automatons, the lady agitatedly swinging her beaded purse in nervous little arcs, like a deadly pendulum. I do believe she might have swung it hard against O'Grady's face, but at that moment I stood, and the ridiculous paper knife slid clattering to the floor.

An awed silence fell. We all four stared down at what appeared to be a weapon of assault—it sobered us. Madame B gave a little cry, a last contralto passage before her exit. She made swiftly for the door, followed by her bustling ineffectual confidant.

The room had meanwhile filled with smoke, O'Grady the center of it, a puffing chimneypiece fading almost into a mist, with his grin (unlike Alice's cat) disappearing first, his red hair turning grey as the fog thickened.

"I smelt a swindle from the moment she pranced in," said O'Grady, and I wondered how he could smell anything in this room but cheese and tobacco smoke.

"I don't understand."

"Of course you don't. You are an apprentice liar with much to learn. (Do you know, by the way, that scar on your forehead turns red when you lie?) You were admirable with the knife, however." O'Grady took the wineglass from the gramophone turntable, and found another —as stained as the first—in a file cabinet, along with a bottle of whiskey called John Powers. He poured out two rations and quickly drank his portion down with a shrug, then a shudder. "Anyway," said he, "it was not our dish of tea. That was why I passed the little affair on to my French colleagues, in exchange for one of theirs."

I assumed the "our" included me, and that I was hired.

"Did you see the pawn ticket in her handbag? Of course you didn't. Nor did you notice the gérant's cheap dentures and cracked boots. I'm sure you have no idea why she was wearing black?"

I admitted as much.

"For two reasons: one, to impress upon us the seriousness of her intentions (black is the perfect color for blackmail), and two, it is the only costume of any distinction she owns. She has no money, my boy— not a sou with which to sue: that is why she was *considering* a lawsuit, and not suing straightaway."

"Maybe Landru took her for everything she had."

"If she ever had anything, which I doubt." He poured himself (but not me) another drink, and drank it off. "Did you see the face behind the veil? Landru must have had to close his eyes to press his lips to that pudding." O'Grady shuddered from the thought, or the whiskey. "She came to me (in that same mourning outfit, by the way) simply to establish her story in print—a story published in the upstanding British press—with the thin hope of making a claim for her alleged loss, if she lost anything at all, in case Bluebeard turns out to be solvent (and survives the guillotine) when the courts finish with him, which is not likely."

O'Grady emerged from a cloud of thought and smoke and rolled up a sheaf of newsprint; he removed a rubber band from one cuff and snapped it around the roll: "You'll be amused by this little lady. There's a couple of columns on her, courtesy of our friends at *le Figaro*. Copy it out for me in the King's English, but remember you are writing for the barely literate. We cater to mother hens and their wayward chicks scattered throughout the British Isles. Get the facts straight, mind—leave the embellishments to me. And be back before five or consider yourself cashiered."

Before I left he plucked the cigarette from behind my ear, put it in his mouth, and lit it with the putrid stub of the other.

Thirteen

NOW WHY DID I TELL O'Grady I was twenty instead of eighteen?
I truly believed I was twenty when I said it—at least I felt twenty.
Twenty seemed the right age to be, in O'Grady's eyes, so I made myself
twenty.

I walked past the modiste wondering what O'Grady meant by "an
apprentice liar"—wondering, too, where I could find a typewriter. I
headed back to the *Paris American*.

"Is that you again?" asked Harry.

I told him about my encounter with O'Grady.

"That's him. I'm surprised he only gave you a paper knife as a
weapon. He's got a pistol in his desk. A dueling pistol. Got himself
into a duel back in Dublin and had to run for his life. Never did show
up on the field of honor. He left Ireland in disgrace, and that's why
he's here."

I was learning not to believe everything I heard.

"Unprincipled bastard. I wouldn't have sent you to him only you
looked hard up."

"He asked me if I could typewrite and I said yes."

"Can you?"

"No. But you said to say yes in the newspaper game."

"So I did," said Harry proudly. I had put myself under his wing, followed his advice and thus acknowledged his experience and maturity—how could he help but like me?

He took me to a stark office which might once have been a storeroom, now furnished with two typewriters and a telephone. Behind one of the typewriters sat a girl applying lip rouge with her finger. Harry ignored the girl and the girl ignored Harry. She had a mirror propped against the keyboard of her typewriter but the other machine was free. Harry showed me how to operate the space bar and the shift key, then he tapped out: "The quick brown fox jumped over the lazy dog."

"Now you," said he.

He got up and I sat down and tapped out the same message with the same two fingers. We changed places and he typed: "Now is the time for all good men to come to the aid of the party."

"Now you."

I had the feeling the girl was watching us in the mirror.

After I typed that phrase he typed: "Don't try anything with the girl. She's engaged." Before he left he said, "Anybody that can't learn to typewrite in an afternoon is a damn fool." It sounded like something O'Grady might have said. Later I learned Harry had been O'Grady's leg man before me.

I translated directly onto the typewriter, pecking out the words with two fingers the way Harry showed me. It was painfully slow— the typewriting, not the translation—and the keys kept sticking. The girl ignored me. When she finished rouging her lips she put the mirror in a desk drawer and looked out the window. I was translating the story of a girl who had met Landru on the métro.

The telephone rang. The telephone was on the wall near me and the girl got up to answer it. She said, "No," into the mouthpiece and hung up. When she passed I heard the swish of her silk stockings and was overwhelmed by her perfume.

According to the news item in *le Figaro,* Landru was known to have had relations with 283 women. Two hundred and eighty-three! The French expression was avoir des rapports avec, and I translated this as had relations with. It suggested sexual relations without saying so.

A horsefly came in through the open window and began buzzing around the office. The girl rolled up a copy of the *Paris American* and waited until the fly landed on her desk, then she smashed it. She had

a very pleased look on her face when she smashed the fly and I wanted
to congratulate her.

But I was too shy to speak. I did not know if she was American
like Harry or French like her perfume. She had only spoken one
word and that was *no*. Two hundred and eighty-three women, and I
was alone in a room with only one I would like to have relations with.

Mademoiselle Deschamps then came forward, the last of
the day's witnesses to testify before the examining magistrate,
Monsieur Bonin.

She had met a man in the Paris métro at approximately
10 AM on April 12 who introduced himself as Monsieur Frémyet. He was well dressed, a perfect gentleman—rather distinguished, in fact—and politeness itself. The magistrate inquired
why she had allowed herself to be spoken to by a stranger in
the métro. Mademoiselle Deschamps was slightly disconcerted
by the question, but she went on to state that Monsieur Frémyet possessed a gentlemanly charm that completely disarmed
her. He suggested a rendezvous for the following evening, but
at this the young lady demurred. She did not at first agree to
see him. He walked along with her and spoke poetically of
his little nest in the country [son joli nid dans la verdure],
which was a villa at Gambais. He also spoke of his motor car.
Mademoiselle Deschamps did not know anyone who owned
a motor car. Nor did she know anyone as distinguished as
Monsieur Frémyet. Eventually she did agree to the rendezvous
he proposed. However, for some reason, she was unable to
make an appearance at the agreed-upon evening. She sent
Monsieur Frémyet a pneumatic telegram with her excuses and
suggested perhaps another time.

On April 13, the day she was to have met him, she saw
Monsieur Frémyet's photograph in a newspaper, under another
name. He had been arrested that same morning in connection
with the disappearance of two women, Madame Collomb and
Madame Buisson, missing since 1916 and 1917 respectively.

Mademoiselle Deschamps was one of many women to
have been approached by Landru in this manner, or, more
frequently, by letter after having responded to a classified ad-
vertisement in the Personals column. According to Brigadier

Riboulet, who is in charge of the investigation, Landru had relations with at least 283 women. Of that number ten have completely disappeared since becoming "engaged" to this gentleman.

Though this was but a formal translation from a French newspaper, I think of it as my first piece of journalism. Later that same day O'Grady took the text in hand and splattered it with hieroglyphics in red ink. Eventually he rewrote the piece in his own flamboyant fashion while I watched over his shoulder. He continued, for instance, after "Personals column" with the phrase "meant to attract female victims into Landru's insidious web," and objected to the words "for some reason" as being too vague.

"Can't you think of some specific reason why the girl did not go to the rendezvous?"

I could think of nothing, and all O'Grady could come up with was a monthly female indisposition which of course would not do. At last he decided to leave the phrase in, but altered to "for some undisclosed reason"—unsatisfactory still, but, as he said, "It does add an element of mystery."

O'Grady read the final version aloud, and made several changes in the text as he went along. I had the feeling the story would have changed out of all recognition if he had spent much more time on it. He drank as he worked, and smoked, and hummed to himself at the typewriter.

"We are, in our small way, doing the housewives and shopgirls a favor. Here is an object lesson to ladies impressed by motor cars and country villas—and a warning about meeting strange men on the public transport. It is a cautionary tale with a wholesome shiver down its backside."

O'Grady then set the gramophone turntable to turning, with the wineglass of whiskey on it. The glass went around several revolutions while O'Grady studied the play of reflected light with exceptional concentration.

My lead, WITNESS TELLS OF MEETING LANDRU BEFORE HIS ARREST, was changed to YOUNG LADY HAS NARROW BRUSH WITH SUSPECTED CRIMINAL, which finally became GIRL HAS CLOSE CALL WITH BLUEBEARD OF GAMBAIS. The French, for legal reasons, could not yet refer to Landru as Barbe Bleue, but O'Grady lost no time in tagging the accused man with that infamous title.

There was no photograph to go on, but O'Grady's version of Mademoiselle Deschamps—an elaborate fictional description, including hat and handbag—was very like Solange (without hat and handbag, of course), the girl at the maison close near the Invalides.

The turntable with O'Grady's wineglass on it was beginning to wind down, so he cranked it up again. I now discovered his purpose in placing a glass on a gramophone. The game he played with himself was to snatch the glass of whiskey from the spinning platform without spilling the contents. He succeeded (as he always did, whenever I was present to watch this bizarre test of motor function and sobriety), then tossed the whiskey down with his characteristic shudder of horror.

"This is a feature piece, you understand, and can be artistically tampered with."

The piece was signed not with O'Grady's by-line, nor my own, but was published in the English press under the name "John Powers."

Fourteen

I BOUGHT THE TWIN of O'Grady's coffee mill at a stall in the flea market off the porte de Clignancourt. (My coffee beans and chicory came from the same shop in les Halles where Honoré de Balzac bought his.) For the compact metal filtre that fits over one cup you grind the beans into powder and scoop three teaspoon measures from the little drawer that pulls out of the mill—this, while the water boils on a spirit lamp. I followed O'Grady's formula in this (for I wanted to be like him) and those mornings my room smelled of strong coffee and chicory (but unmixed with the choking aroma of Egyptian cigarettes).

My breakfast was regularly black coffee with a lump of sugar, and bread with cheese or butter. If I left the bread out when I was away, mice chewed holes in the crust, so I bought only enough bread for breakfast and lunch, a loaf called un bâtard, a bastard loaf. On Sundays I ate two croissants. I kept the butter and cheese in a garde-manger in the closet.

After breakfast I wrote for two hours with a mechanical pencil a lady friend gave my father and he gave to me on my sixteenth birthday. (I do not see these pencils anymore: I still have mine, but can no longer find the replacement strips of graphite the instrument feeds upon.)

I was writing stories again, to live up to the lies I wrote Louise. I led her to believe I was a writer, and made a living by my mechanical pencil. So far I was not even a journalist. I did translations for O'Grady and ran errands for him. He passed on to me assorted French news items to rewrite in English, or scraps of gossip concerning the English-speaking colony in Paris, for me to make more of than was there. Sometimes I drew up lists of stock prices on the Paris Bourse, or copied out speeches of French political figures, or did obituaries. When it occurred to him, O'Grady paid me small sums for these services. The pay was niggardly and irregular, and seemed to have no relation to the work performed. Luckily my mother still sent international money orders. Anyway, Paris was cheap and my needs were small.

The stories I wrote were intended for Mr. H. L. Mencken's *American Mercury*. They were mostly romantic variations of the news items I dealt with, in the style of Marcel Proust or in the manner of Nicolas Restif de la Bretonne. Sometimes I wrote the stories in French, for practice, and because I naively believed French was a more literary language than English. Thus my oblong notebooks began to fill with badly written stories, in two languages.

I was still using the typewriter at the *Paris American* for the translations I did for O'Grady. I had no typewriter of my own and was warned not to touch O'Grady's machine. His was an antique, he said. He had bought it from an impoverished writer named Joyce (I thought the writer may have been a woman, but this was the writer's surname, and he was a man) who could never get the hang of it, so wrote by hand. "Lately," said O'Grady, "the impostor has got hold of some money from a lady with a salon who believes in him. Six months ago he pawned his pocket watch and sold me this typewriter, now I hear he dines regularly at Michaud's."

Many of those first feature items I translated, then embellished with O'Grady's collaboration, had to do with Landru. The features went principally to newspapers in London and Birmingham that had no regular correspondent in Paris. O'Grady also sent duplicate copy to Irish newspapers, but they, he claimed, paid far less than his English subscribers. "The English are dotty about two things, and one of them is murder." He did not say what the other thing was.

As soon as Brigadier Riboulet released Landru's letters to the press, O'Grady set me to translating them. The letters I transcribed (three) served as models for all the letters Landru wrote to his 283 correspondents. These model letters were discovered in a wicker trunk that Landru had employed as a filing cabinet for the letters and dossiers of the women who wrote to him. Landru carried a key on his watch chain that unlocked the wicker file. He kept these files in meticulous order, the responses to newspaper ads under *To Be Answered at Once, First Reply,* or *In Reserve.* Other categories were *P.R.* (petits revenus), *S.S.* (sans suite), and *S.F.* (suspect fortune). The hopeless cases—for Landru never threw anything away—were filed under *R.A.F.* (rien à faire), nothing to be done.

Landru wrote an exquisite hand, each character beautifully formed in the classic French lycée manner. O'Grady made this assignment into a special feature I would write and he would edit only marginally. If he approved my "Baltimore prose," I might, he hinted, be rewarded with a by-line.

I wrote about the discovery of the wicker file as if it might have contained a body—but the police were disappointed to discover only letters and dossiers. I described the filing system, and how Landru did variations of the three model letters according to the intensity of the relationship, or to suit the personality of his fiancée of the moment.

Madame,

I have just received your letter of (insert date) and want to thank you for the information you were good enough to send me. Please be assured—no matter how our project turns out—of my absolute discretion, because my proposal is serious and straightforward, and I consider it a point of honor to return your letters the day it pleases you to ask for them.

I lived alone with my mother in the same house where my father started a modest business establishment, which I continued after his death.

My mother's death at the end of 1913 left me completely alone, without family. When the war broke out I was obliged to flee from the north, and now I have established myself in the vicinity of Paris with all I could save from the invasion in the way of linen, furniture, and silver. Also I was able to bring along a good part of my work material, that which was suitable for transport.

There have been mornings in my life when I did not know or care if I would ever see another day's dawn.

Nevertheless, I am once again in excellent health and spirits. Also, I have accumulated a substantial savings through a rather profitable enterprise.

I seek a genuine love, a sharing of feeling, that will lead

to lifelong happiness. I have independent means enough to assure you, on my side, that financial considerations do not enter into my choice of a wife. I seek above all a person of good heart, a good housekeeper—a woman worthy of the name, sincerely affectionate; a sweet, loyal, charming, tender partner.

Naturally I might be inclined to spoil her a little—but oh how I would cherish her if I sensed she had frankly opened her heart to me, without calculation or frivolity, for I have lived so long with a tender-hearted mother who, I believe, formed my own character out of a loving sensibility of her own.

What more can I say, Madame? It is above all for you to let me know what you think of the foregoing, in which I speak with the same frankness you have offered me. . . .

I was at the office of the *Paris American* and the typewriter was beginning to fail, its ribbon practically in shreds. When I looked up from the keyboard the last sentence seemed to disappear into the page. For several paragraphs I had resorted to typing on the lower part of the ribbon, the red half (as if Landru's words were meant for red ink, in the liabilities column of an accounts ledger), but even this expedient failed as the ink faded to a faint pink, then nothing.

There was a fresh ribbon in the desk drawer. The girl in the office, whose name was Irene (this was all I knew about her), watched me attempt to change the ribbon until my clumsiness—not at all a calculated ploy—drew her to my side.

"You'll never get it in that way."

The remark struck me in another context. I thought of myself as being taught again, sexually.

"Like this," said she, and showed me how.

Her voice was crisp and the accent nasal—Midwestern American— and the words fell as hard and flat as typewriter keys against paper. But it was not her voice that concerned me. Her gestures were feline and her manner frank: she stared at me as boldly as a girl on the rue Saint-Denis. Irene did not actually touch the typewriter ribbon, for she had just applied almond paste to her hands. I was further distracted by the smell of almond as she rubbed her hands to dry them—and the nearness of her breasts. One breast did touch my ear, and that was when the ribbon spool escaped my grasp and rolled across the desk. As

I shakily rewound the ribbon I noticed she was reading the page in the typewriter.

I thought she might think I was responsible for the composition, so I said, "It's just a translation. The letter is evidence in a criminal case."

She did something with one eyebrow but did not reply. She continued to look over my shoulder as I worked on the next letter.

Madame,

It is not without a certain confusion I reply to your good letter and to the delicate thought with which you sent me your photograph, for there is always, in effect, a certain curiosity on the part of a man who is able to appreciate other attributes of a delightful person, to recognize her physical charms as well.

Do I need to tell you these charms are, in your case, all to your advantage and cannot but increase my desire to merit your esteem? I have delayed writing you in order to retain for a while longer that photographic proof of your existence which I have received by written communication only (and ordinary delicacy requires that I return it to you, though I do so with obvious regret), but you may rest assured that I would, henceforth, recognize you in a crowd of thousands: that elegant silhouette, the grace and charm rendered by this unforgettable portrait, and I am convinced—no matter how you protest—that if some years have gone by since the photograph was taken, time could not alter that indefinable and captivating expression in your eyes.

I would be delighted to honor your request concerning my own physical appearance, but for many years now I have had no occasion to place myself in front of a photographic lens.

For you I will make an exception, and send the result as soon as the picture is made. But I should warn you that I am physically ordinary and ugly, as most men are.

"I can believe that," said the girl at my shoulder, with a shudder.

. . . The one thing I do promise to bring to the woman who would honor me with her affection is a continuing love, for which I hope to receive her devotion in return. Is not that the substance of perpetual happiness? And, sharing your same point of view, I would suffer horribly at any indication of coldness or disdain. That which you have been so kind as to confide in me sustains the sweet hope that coldness finds no place in your nature. I have nothing to reproach you with. Things stated frankly can never shock—except to shock those silly and pretentious persons who spend their lives chasing chimera—and I can well understand how much easier it is for you to express your desires in a straightforward way while at the same time you cannot bring yourself to speak of that chagrin you hint at so discreetly. You are, I suspect, a fine and loving creature who has been the victim of a cruel unhappiness, but one who must remain silent out of dignity and pride.

It is I, on the contrary, who should be obliged to explain my seemingly belated reply . . . but you have aroused a sweet dream in me, and I anxiously ask myself if each day brings me a little closer to that dream—or farther away.

"Sweet dreams, my foot."

. . . The single enduring affection in my life was the love of my precious mother, and henceforth I seek to replace that love with a woman who is willing to join her loving nature with mine. I suffer from my present solitude, but—like you—I also hesitate before the unknown. I pray that you do not think of me unkindly, and I live for a swiftly following affectionate word from you, assuring me that you have not turned away from your devoted and respectful . . .

"What slop."
"Women fell for it."
"No woman in her right mind—"
"Older women, that is. Widows and divorcées."
Now that I had her interest I showed her the original versions of Landru's letters. "Here's the one he wrote when he got behind in his correspondence and the lady complained about receiving no reply."

Madame,
Your note of (insert date) covered me with confusion by reminding me how uncivil I had been not to answer your letter by return post.
Do I care to confess? Your note gave me pleasure none-

theless, for it was a communication that recalled the gracious correspondent whose image I cannot put from my mind.

Do you chastise me, Madame? Please do not, I beg you. Prove to me you have the forgiving heart of a woman, noble, good, and compassionate—a heart beside which one may loyally plead his defense and be understood. My chagrin increases at this fall from your esteem just when I had begun to hope for a meeting under the subtle influence of that disconcerting physical charm I know you possess as well as the noble and elevated sentiment you express—a dear and lovely friend whom I hope, without restriction or reserve, to make my cherished spouse.

"The dirty liar," said Irene, as if the letter were addressed to her and she had been jilted. A vein in her neck throbbed ominously.

. . . Lately I spend half my week, at least, in a small cottage in the countryside, the locale and environs are ravishing—there lacks only that ray of sunshine which animates all the earth, the gay companion whose enchanting eyes and sparkling words light up and make lovable all things.

Will I ever have the pleasure of seeing you, even for a simple visit?

"Not me, brother!"

. . . I am really indiscreet, but I have an overwhelming desire I dare not express . . . however, I know you will understand; if I suggest a meeting between us it is simply that a discreet talk might—better than all our letters—be a step toward the total happiness and fulfillment I speak of.

I have opened my poor solitary heart to you; do not laugh. A completely open heart is so rare these days.

Please accept, I beg you, my most refined and devoted thoughts . . .

"Merde," said Irene, with an authentic French *r*—though she was, I assumed, American.

I tried to think of some way to hold her interest, now that I had run out of letters from Landru. Perhaps she would ask me about my scar—but of course she did not.

"He had other ways of meeting women," I informed her. "Sometimes he picked up girls or older women in the Luxembourg Gardens or on the métro."

"With that phony line of his?"

"Or he put ads in the matrimonial columns. He used a dozen different names and fifteen addresses."

"The dirty liar."

"Of course he had his greatest successes with lonely middle-aged women who wanted to believe him."

"What about young ones?"

"Those too. He had relations with two hundred and eighty-three women."

"What kind of relations?"

I hesitated. Instead of something clever, I replied: "Business relations. He says."

"Oh yeah?"

Her eyes went flat. I was losing her, so I quickly added: "And, I suppose, the other kind, too."

"Other kind of what?"

"Relations."

Her nostrils flared. "And they went with him, to that villa?"

"In Gambais. Yes. Some of them did."

"Like sheep." Her fists were clenched. I did not know if she was furious with the women or with Landru.

"He promised to marry them."

"Then killed them."

"The police think so. They went with him to the villa in Gambais and that was the last anyone ever saw of them."

"Like sheep," she said again. Her eyes lost focus as she touched her throat with one almond-scented hand. I could almost see her thoughts. Landru was said to have dismembered the cadavers and burnt the limbs and heads in his kitchen stove. Then she became angry again: "You know what I would do to that bastard?"

Just then Classified Harry (as O'Grady called him) came into the office. The girl trembled briefly as if throwing off a dream.

"You here again?" Harry said to me. He looked unhappy.

Irene ignored him and went back to her desk without saying what she would have done to Landru. Harry asked me into the hallway for a word. His fish eyes were almost crossed with anger, his fat face suddenly suspicious and sharp.

"Look," he said, "I got you a job, right?"

"Yes, you did."

"Now it's your turn to do me a favor, right?"

"All right."

"Go get a typewriter of your own."

Fifteen

THE FIRST TIME I went to 27, rue de Fleurus was to ask Miss Gertrude Stein if her Smith Premier typewriter was still for sale. A short thin spinsterish woman with bangs met me at the door. Ordinarily visitors went directly to the pavillon. The woman with bangs resembled the woman I bought bread from: her forearms were powdered with flour just like the baker's wife on rue Tiquetonne. This was not Miss Stein but her companion. I was naive enough to have come to 27, rue de Fleurus without knowing who Miss Stein was.

"If you've come with a letter of introduction would you read it to me? I've been needing dough."

Actually she said "kneading dough" but I misunderstood and thought perhaps that was why the typewriter was for sale. (Americanisms were not out of place here: Miss Stein herself spoke very American English, and one of her favorite expressions was "You bet you.")

I thought of the letter from H. L. Mencken, then thought not. I said I had heard of a typewriter for sale, through Mr. Hickok of the *Brooklyn Eagle* who had heard from Mr. Sherwood Anderson that Miss Stein owned a typewriter she was not satisfied with, and if she was not, I might be.

Miss Toklas did not know anyone in Paris named Hickok, but she knew a Mr. Benedict Hickok in California. "Does he wear a mustache?" she asked. (She may have been conscious of mustaches, for she had a noticeably dark mustache of her own.)

"Yes. But this is Mr. Guy Hickok who manages the Paris office of the *Brooklyn Eagle.*"

"Then probably Gertrude knows him. I know she knows Sherwood but how on earth Sherwood knew about the typewriter I'll never know."

Suddenly a French poet Miss Toklas called Gabriel appeared saying Miss Stein had been stung and asking if there was tincture of iodine in the house.

"Where was she stung?" asked Miss Toklas.

"In the passageway," said the poet, distracted.

We hurried into the passageway between the apartment and a pavillon that served as a sitting room and studio. Miss Stein had been showing her collection of pictures (she always referred to paintings as pictures) to an Italian diplomat and his mistress; as they were leaving the pavillon a wasp had stung Miss Stein.

It affected me strangely to come upon Miss Stein that first time in the courtyard before the pavillon: a massive woman (imposing in her mass; you did not think of her as fat) in heavy clothes too hot for the season; supported on one side by the Italian diplomat, his mistress on the other.

"Where were you stung?" asked Miss Toklas.

But Miss Stein—her head bowed (the only time I ever saw it lowered in that way) so that the knot of hair at the back of her neck was all I saw at first—could not speak. Her face came up sharply when she heard Miss Toklas' voice, but her eyes were closed and tears ran down the great flat planes of her face.

"Where was she stung?" asked Miss Toklas.

The Italian did not speak English, and Gabriel, who spoke English with odd phrasing, said, "On the limb."

"Which limb?" Miss Toklas persisted, but Miss Stein only shook her head and squeezed out more tears.

The poet was possibly amused but tried politely not to show it. The Italian diplomat appeared perplexed and his mistress somewhat desperate over the sagging bulk of their wounded hostess.

"I could send Hélène for a doctor," said Miss Toklas, but Miss Stein shook her head.

I was inclined to agree with Miss Stein: a doctor seemed excessive for a wasp sting. When I was a child my mother told me I should quickly urinate when I had been stung by a bee or a wasp, and apply a little of the urine to the sting and it would be all right, and it always was. But I did not know how to tell Miss Stein this, or Miss Toklas, so I quietly told the poet, in French. He was delighted. He whispered the remedy to Miss Toklas, who gave him a hard look but nevertheless took Miss Stein away from the Italians and led her into the apartment.

We four strangers were left awkwardly together—the poet suppressing a smile, the Italians perplexed, and I wondering if I had come to the right place.

"Some," offered the Italian diplomat, "are more affected by insects than others." He could speak French but not English.

His mistress could speak neither French nor English, but she said something appropriate in Italian. The poet was still trying not to smile.

"The pictures are unusual but nice," said the Italian diplomat, referring to Miss Stein's collection. I believe he thought I was a painter, or an associate of painters, for he offered me his card.

When Miss Stein came back she was smiling. She had a very winning smile and marvelous eyes, wide now with pleasure, and I have always thought how unfortunate I should have seen only the top of Miss Stein's head, then her tear-stricken face the first time we met. Miss Toklas was smiling too, and she did not smile often.

"Miracoloso!" said the Italian diplomat's mistress.

Now that Miss Stein was quite recovered and smiling, the Italian diplomat said, "The pictures are unusual but nice," and offered Miss Stein his card. His mistress said, "Miracoloso!" once more before they left, and as soon as they were gone Miss Stein began to laugh. Her laugh began on a high note like a boy soprano's, then went into the contralto range and even lower, melodious and contagious. We were all laughing. I did not know if we were laughing about Miss Stein's wasp sting or about the Italians who had just left. We were laughing about the Italians, Miss Stein informed us, when she got her breath back.

"Bianca," she said, referring to the Italian diplomat's mistress, "was a model before Count G knew her. She was everybody's mistress and model and even another model's mistress, Kiki, and everybody knew her, Soutine knew her and I know Modigliani knew her and I believe she lived with him one winter during the war. She knows French but pretends not to for her new lover's sake and not to remember Montparnasse during the war. As for Modigliani he is not a painter I know so I don't know if he knew Bianca in the biblical sense or not."

I did not quite follow this revelation, nor catch the humor in it, but I laughed along with everyone else. Miss Stein was a great gossip and knower of people in Paris at that time, and her laughter was irresistible. You laughed when she laughed and tried to think what was funny afterward.

"And who are you?" she asked me suddenly, as if in the middle of laughing together she realized we had not been introduced.

"This is Mr. Hickok," said Miss Toklas. In the excitement and confusion of the wasp sting she had forgotten my name but remembered who sent me.

As for the typewriter, yes, Miss Stein owned a Smith Premier with English keyboard and had thought of selling it and may have mentioned this to Sherwood when he was looking for a typewriter in Paris because the letter *p* sticks (it was surprising how often *p* comes up in a piece of prose) and she could never master the machine nor did she ever learn to typewrite and never will but then Alice came and could typewrite and did.

"Are you a writer?" she asked in that blunt way she asked anything and everything, her eyes searching out the answer in mine.

"Yes."

"We will call you dottore all the same," said she, laughing again in the same contagious way. Then she introduced me soberly to Miss Toklas, her companion, and to Gabriel, the poet, both of whom I had already met, but under distracting circumstances.

"You must come again and tell us what you write."

With this courtly dismissal followed by a warm invitation my début (accidental as it was) at 27, rue de Fleurus was a success. Being asked to return was a mark of acceptance into Miss Stein's charmed circle.

To finish my story of typewriters, I am writing these pages on an ill-used but still sturdy battle-scarred Underwood I bought for fifty francs from the concierge of the Anglo-American Press Club soon after I met Miss Stein. The typewriter had belonged to a British war correspondent who left it at the club as an I.O.U. against his overdue bar bill. I was afraid the correspondent might someday return to the club and want to redeem his typewriter, but the concierge assured me that the correspondent had not long before committed suicide in Cairo.

Sixteen

IF A NEW GIRL came to rue Tiquetonne she might at first whisper to me, "Tu viens?" and touch my arm, then lift her breasts as if offering fruit, fresh fruit, in a passageway of stalls displaying fruit of another kind. She was never the girl I remembered, nor the phantom I thought I was seeking. I had come to realize I would never in any case find her on the marketplace. A strange encounter would not likely occur a second time in these same haunts.

Anyway I wanted a girl who would be mine without money passing between us. The vision of her flashed by from time to time at the window of a trolley or standing on the back platform (fading fast into the distracting traffic of a Parisian street) and I recognized without truly knowing her that she was the girl. In dreams her face was a blank to be filled in at my leisure. Her form was familiar. A dozen times a day I was offered a tantalizing glimpse of her: a Spanish curl in the confusion of a crowd, the backs of her knees as she disappeared into the métro entrance. Her insubstantiality tortured my sleep.

I did not go back to a maison close to relieve my lust. The waiting for something extraordinary thwarted my desire. En attendant, my pillow lost its shape, my sheets were stained. Then I came to believe the girl I sought was Irene, who had been at the *Paris American* all along.

It took me half a week to devise a strategy any tepid suitor would have decided in half a minute: I would wait for her outside the *Paris American* offices and ask her to lunch at a convenient restaurant. The day this encounter was to take place I spent an hour over a Cinzano at a café where the *American* reporters drank, then at noon I stepped outside to keep watch, lingering furtively behind a kiosk plastered with concert posters.

She came out of the office alone, wearing white gloves and silk stockings and a Robin Hood's hat with a feather in it. I was immeasurably depressed to see Harry walking behind her. She ignored him. He followed her all the way to Concorde, and I followed them both. She went into a tea shop on the rue Saint-Florentin and Harry went in behind her. My thought was to wait behind another kiosk to see if they came out together, but I had already carried my folly far enough. I walked on, feeling impotent and ruined.

The damage a Big Bertha had done to the façade of the Madeleine was only just now being repaired. Watching the masons, I remembered that the Great War had raged only a year ago. (It was during the chaos and confusion of war that Landru operated so effectively.) While I was remembering this war I had never seen, the masons put down their tools to unwrap the midday meal. One man bit off the foil cap on a liter bottle of wine. It was one thing to watch men work and another to watch them eat, so I left the scene in a hopelessly vagrant mood.

In the window of the modiste on the ground floor of O'Grady's building were the scattered parts of a mannequin. This was the lunch hour, and the mannequin had been abandoned in a grotesque display of unassembled parts. The bare arms and detached legs left scattered at odd tortured angles appeared so contrary to nature my mood plummeted anew. The creature in parts reminded me of my dilemma: I was trying to piece together a girl of my own from a face, a limb, a feeling.

The sign on the door read: "Clarence O'Grady is IN."

"You look like a toff that just stepped in a turd."

O'Grady was lunching on cheese and a jigger of calvados. The smoke and smell of his Egyptian cigarette were especially poisonous that noon, and I was glad to get away—I left to deliver some mail dispatches to the boat train.

At the gare Saint-Lazare a man was having an epileptic fit in the first-class waiting room. A woman was holding his head in her lap and the rest of him was writhing frantically on the waiting-room floor. "Tenez-lui la langue," said somebody in the crowd, and an employee of the SNCF tried to take hold of the man's tongue.

I did nothing to help, I was only a witness. (This was the story of my day, and my life till then: innocent bystander, passive voyeur.) Landru would have pretended to be a doctor in order to get to know the woman holding the man's head. (He once used that cold-blooded approach to make the acquaintance of a nurse outside a building that had been shelled.)

All that wasted day I would witlessly crisscross Paris—but how different my schedule from Landru's tight horaire. Brigadier Riboulet was decoding Landru's notebooks, and as he did so he fed the leftover data to favored members of the press.

> Mercredi 19 mai 1915: à 9h 30, tabac gare de Lyon, Mlle Lydie; à 10h 30, café place Saint-Georges, Mme B; à 11h 30, métro Lancry, Mlle L; à 2h 30, Concorde nord-sud, Mme L du 15e; à 3h 30, square Tour Saint-Jacques, Mme D; à 5h 30, Mme V; à 8h, Saint-Lazare, Mme L.

All those L's. Was Madame L the same as Madame L du 15e— not likely, at an hour's remove. And he would have had to be particularly careful not to confuse Mademoiselle L with Mademoiselle Lydie, two hours earlier.

That page from his notebook might have been a passage of fiction, or lies: it seemed impossible for one man to meet all those women in scattered parts of Paris—often only an hour between appointments— in a single working day. The notebooks lacked the romance of the letters: Landru saved his lies for his correspondence. All the women behind those initials had appeared to identify themselves while Brigadier Riboulet put together the cross-indexes of the Landru file. Landru considered women a métier just as a prostitute considered men hers. Despite the demanding schedule he had left time out at noon for lunch for the same reason masons repairing the façade of the Madeleine opened sandwiches and wine on the church steps. It was a job, and a man must eat.

Walking through the Luxembourg Gardens I ate an apple I had bought at the buffet counter at the gare Saint-Lazare. How did he remember who B or V or D was and under what alias he was known to her and what he had said to her last? Did Landru ever worry about venereal disease? In spite of his sense of organization and obvious intelligence and fastidious respect for detail—could he be considered sane?

In these formal gardens Landru sometimes made the acquaintance of a prospective fiancée. One such conquest occurred on a park bench, according to the testimony of Madame M.

As an excuse to introduce himself, Landru commented on the droll impudence of the pigeons. Madame M ventured a reply in kind. He called himself Monsieur Barbezieux (pronounced aloud, the name is a pun on beard-and-eyes, Landru's most memorable features). He was a gentleman in every way, fastidious in his dress and exceedingly polite. Later he swindled her of 1,200 francs. Yet, she was not missing. Why had ten "been made to disappear" (according to the indictment) while so many others were alive to tell the tale?

My excuse for stopping at rue de Fleurus again was to ask Miss Stein if she was altogether recovered from the wasp sting, but Miss Toklas' hawklike demeanor and Miss Stein's imposing presence put me off that subterfuge. It was not the thing to ask. Finally I did not have to ask anything.

"Here is Mr. Hickok," said Miss Toklas. She still confused me with Mr. Guy Hickok of the *Brooklyn Eagle*.

"Dottore," said Miss Stein. "The young man who treats stings so originally."

"He is a news editor from Brooklyn," explained Miss Toklas.

"Not I," I confessed. "That's Mr. Hickok. I work for the Channel News Service, and Mr. O'Grady is the editor of that."

"Our first Irish newspaperman," said Miss Stein.

"Mr. O'Grady is Irish, but I'm not. My mother is French and my father American."

Miss Stein said, "If the wife is French and the husband American it is all right, but not the other way around."

"A Spanish and French marriage is not happy either way," said Miss Toklas. "They are better off to have a fling and accept the inevitable without tears."

"Fernande, alas, will weep," said Miss Stein, referring to a Frenchwoman living with a Spanish painter. Then she went on from the specific to the abstract: "Germans marry everybody but the Swiss marry only Swiss. Italians marry Italians but the husband might take a mistress of any nationality. His wife will remain faithful if she has children but if not not."

Not everything Miss Stein said made sense.

"Do you like pictures, Mr. O'Grady?" asked Miss Toklas.

"Of course he likes pictures."

I told them my name again so they would not call me Mr. O'Grady. Later when we became friends Miss Toklas called me Clarence but Miss Stein always called me Dottore.

We went into the studio to look at Miss Stein's pictures.

I knew nothing about paintings then and I have learned little since. My promenades through the Louvre were occasions to examine lovely girls as much as to examine works of art. Miss Stein had an intuitive feeling for pictures and the painters of pictures, and I believe so did Miss Toklas, though her understanding was quieter than Miss Stein's. It is a gift that cannot be forced.

The studio had the air of comfortable clutter yet considerable investment. I first noticed the walls were water-stained and then I noticed the pictures. They were painted by modern painters Miss Stein knew personally. The walls were covered to the ceiling with paintings, but you still saw the water stains.

Even a philistine—and I was one then, perhaps I still am—could not fail to react to these pictures in some way. The Italian diplomat had called them unusual but nice: they were indeed unusual but they were not nice. They may not have been beautiful but they were sensational —by which I mean they acted upon the senses.

"What do you think?" asked Miss Stein.

My first thought was that the painters painted in a great hurry. I still think that, even though these painters later became famous. (If they had taken the time to think about what they were painting they might not have become famous.) I knew that if I said what I thought it would be a philistine's remark, so I pretended to study the pictures more carefully than I thought the painters had.

"The small ones look as if they were painted before the painter felt successful."

"And the large ones?"

"The large ones came later."

"Exactly," said Miss Stein as if she had said it herself.

"He is an original," said Miss Toklas.

I knew enough to say no more. At the moment they were happy to have collected me: I had made an acceptable remark. Though Miss Stein's books are full of remarks and she is remembered for the remarks more than for anything else, she used to say remarks are not literature. I had been permitted the indulgence of a single remark: two remarks would have been too many.

A serving woman came with a tray of chartreuse and three cut-glass liqueur glasses and we sat upon the heavy furniture from a period quite removed from the paintings. Then we drank chartreuse under the skylight while Miss Stein talked. Her voice was lovely to listen to and almost hypnotic on a willing listener like me. She spoke in such an offhand way I did not at first quite understand the shrewd and original things she said. Even her gossip was memorable (but I have forgotten the gossip she offered up that first afternoon). She did not mind being wicked, but she knew when she was being wicked and she was just as capable of being kind. She would ask the most unexpected questions, and not always listen to the answers. She had a large but strictly defined inventory of interests.

"Do you write for this news agency or for yourself?"

I hesitated to lie to this knowing Buddha-like figure, so I replied that I wrote for both, and at the moment I was writing about Landru.

The corners of her mouth turned down. Landru was not in her inventory of interests.

Miss Toklas had less to say. She worked at a piece of lace with miniature needles and occasionally offered a remark in counterpoint to what Miss Stein was saying. I was delighted to find myself in their exceptional company. My long day's unhappy mood turned upward. I knew from the questions Miss Stein asked and the way Miss Toklas nodded at my answers that I had passed some obscure examination. They liked me. My head spun in this rich and decorative setting listening to Miss Stein's rich and decorative remarks. I felt I was being adopted by two intelligent older friends I could be eternally at home with in Paris, like aunts.

When Miss Stein began fanning herself in silence I was perceptive enough to know it was time to go. Miss Toklas showed me to the door while Miss Stein remained seated in that heavy way of hers like the cornerstone of an important structure, fanning herself with a delicate Japanese fan. On the way out Miss Toklas informed me the fan was a work of art collected by Miss Stein's brother Leo, who begged her not to fan with it because of its fragility. (I was reminded of the erotic Japanese fan on the mantelpiece of the maison close near the Invalides—in its way a work of art as well.) I was made to know by Miss Toklas I might come whenever I liked: "Afternoons after five."

Writers and poets came at five and drank grenadine or were

offered pears in Madeira, whereas painters and sculptors came after seven and were invited to dine.

Instead of crossing the park again I took the rue de Vaugirard to the boulevard Saint-Michel, alive with students pouring from the classrooms of the Sorbonne. Some of the girls were accompanied by their dark and intense petits amis; some walked alone with their books and their thoughts. I must have examined every female face and form along the boulevard, but none of the student nymphs was the girl I was searching for.

Then I walked home by way of the rue Saint-Jacques and the two bridges leading in and out of the bird market on the île de la Cité to the square Saint-Jacques. I had spent the day crisscrossing my horizontal city. It is a mistake to traverse Paris with eyes in the gutter as mine had been. There is always a strip of sky above the narrowest street and a dizzying expanse above the parcs and boulevards. But now as I looked up I discovered I stood in the ominous shadow of the tour Saint-Jacques, a medieval tower bristling with gargoyles.

This is where Landru met Madame D at 3h 30.

Seventeen

AT THE END OF summer my father came to Paris with a silver-headed walking stick and a Neapolitan suntan. I met him at the gare de l'Est. He had come by way of Geneva where he made a surprise visit to Madame S, his conquest from the *Leopoldina* and those first days in France. You might have thought Madame S would slam the door in his face, but she did not. In Switzerland my father fell in with a consortium of fellow schemers to build a tunnel under the English Channel: through Madame S he had met influential bankers in Geneva. It would be the opportunity of a lifetime, he told me—this was undoubtedly the age of the motor car. A small toll at either end of the tunnel would bring in a fortune to a man with vision, and capital to invest.

I knew the trip had been successful because my father presented me with a wristwatch Madame S had given him. My father preferred a pocket watch. He thought a wristwatch just the thing for a rising journalist writing timely stuff. "And a most convenient item to pawn," he reminded me, "if it should ever come to that."

We went to lunch at an Italian restaurant on the rue Jean-Jacques Rousseau. My father spoke Italian with as much authority as he spoke French, and as little fluency. The waiter was impressed, but it turned out he did not himself speak Italian. We had tortellini with veal and a bottle of frascati. After a Bel Paese cheese my father unscrewed the handle of his walking stick to show me the drinking glass inside the silver head. The cane was hollow and filled with grappa, like Lautrec's famous cane filled with absinthe. "An excellent ploy for passing through customs undisturbed." We drank grappa as a digestif. My father was always interested in putting something over on the authorities.

I thought he might like to stay with me on the rue Tiquetonne— the bed was quite large enough for two, though I did not know his feelings about father and son sharing the same bed. He came up to see what my room was like, winded by the climb from the street. Dim lights unnerved him, and obscure smells. I think he came more to see if he could find any trace of female companionship—something like the investigating committee appointed by Maître Bonin, juge d'instruction (to search the villa at Gambais for bones, finding mostly hairpins). Sadly, there were no hairpins in my room. It was an austere monk's cell with an Underwood typewriter on the table beside the pitcher and basin. I had tacked newspapers to the wall the way O'Grady had, with columns of newsprint outlined in red: the pieces I had translated into English or assembled from French dailies. My father sniffed the air as if for the perfume of the girl who had been there or for the ghost of the girl to come, but actually he had caught the scent of the WC on the landing.

"A fine garret for a starving poet," he declared. "By the way, where do you bathe?"

I told him about the public bath on rue Tiquetonne, only a short walk away, but I might as well have suggested bathing in the Ganges. He raised one eyebrow and shook his head. That afternoon he booked a room at the hotel where we had stayed the first week in Paris, with electric chandeliers and a private bath.

His remark about starving poets reminded him to ask me if I had money and I told him about my job with the Channel News Service, somewhat exaggerating my responsibilities. Also, I did an occasional free-lance translation for the Paris offices of the *Brooklyn Eagle* and the Chicago *Tribune*.

"And Mother sends money orders."

"The ladies. Their tender hearts and loose purse strings. What should we do without them?"

It was a remark Landru might have uttered in a careless moment, and it was as much as my father would ever say on the subject of women. I knew instinctively not to inquire after Madame S or Madame d'O or a Madame Farfalla he might have met in Pompeii. My father, respecting my own sensibilities, would never have asked me outright if I were still a virgin. That part of a man's life is inviolable. I might have wanted to tell him about my sexual initiation at the square des Innocents or describe chubby cherubic Solange of the Invalides—but I kept these adventures to myself. The soldierly café riot in Nice was acceptable male conversation, but men approach the subject of women in two ways: either they remain silent or they tell lies.

Before we left my room my father emptied his pockets of the loose change and a few crumpled notes in Swiss francs and Italian lira and left them beside my Underwood. He did not intend to stand in a queue at the foreign exchange window and be taken for a tourist. It came to a little over five hundred French francs.

Then we were walking through the Tuileries. The sun was low and the light unreal.

"You seem to take to the way of life here."

He meant Paris, and I said I did.

The concourse was thronged. A light breeze rearranged patterns of sun and shadow. Children played with cork boats at the edge of the bassin as if painted there by Seurat. There were more women strolling about than men. It was the apéritif hour and the men were elsewhere.

Why did Landru never begin a courtship in the Tuileries? The women are perhaps of a social standing he considered out of comfortable reach. The open park, with its wide vistas, is too exposed to the light of day for his kind of secret tryst. Strollers do not so much linger (the benches are stone) as make a leisurely tour from Concorde to the Louvre, or the opposite direction, without pause. The less formal Luxembourg Gardens with its several discreet meeting places was more his style.

"The surface of this city is, I must admit, agreeable to look upon."

"Yes, it is."

"A charming place, in several respects. I hope you are not taken in by its superficial attractions. There is more to a beautiful city than meets the eye."

I agreed. He was speaking of women in his roundabout way, as well as cities.

"There are no beggars to be seen here, as in Rome. The French are the world's great purveyors of perfume, and masters of the trompe l'oeil mural painting."

I knew what he was meaning to say, and hoped it would not lead to a lecture on Ehrlich.

"Every great city," he warned, "has an underside to it."

The tranquil scene at the bassin was transformed by a sudden breeze rippling the surface of the water. Children leaned perilously forward to recover their boats (one sailboat had already capsized): the colors were broken up, it was no longer a composition by Seurat. A woman's white glove floated between the cork boats.

"Well," said my father, somewhat too heartily to sound genuine, "Paris is a very special attraction that has won you over, underside and all. That may be the French in you. Not lonely?"

"I have been. But everybody is sometimes. And I've been lonely other places too." (I was thinking of Nice.)

"I suppose you know your mother has written insisting I get you back home post haste."

"I thought she might."

"Women," he said with a sigh. "No doubt you miss your mother, but I would not like to think you would go home on her account only."

"No."

"Good."

Only a moment ago Paris was sultry and I had wished for rain. Now a pleasant evening cool was coming down—pleasant but disturbing. The light was extraordinary. The pastel colors faded, grey was dominant again—but an airy grey, as if the stone statuary were afloat. Paris is like that, a place of shifting surfaces. The last green of summer tinted the park—not a city green, the green of somewhere else, a country garden. You could sometimes be in Paris but not of it, and sometimes of it but not in it. I was transported to America for a moment.

"You are half American, you know."

"I know."

"You could finish your education and get a start in some sterling enterprise in the USA."

"I would rather stay here."

"So be it," said he.

I was pleased to have his swift consent—and probably his blessing —but somewhat unnerved to have decided. For an instant I was walking the reassuring streets of Baltimore, and I suddenly saw my mother's face in the face of a woman who passed. But just as suddenly I was back in the Tuileries again, relieved that the matter was settled.

Just as relieved was my father, happy to have got that conversation over with. He had done his paternal duty (his last, as it turned out)—for him the subject was closed. He walked gaily on, using his new walking stick as a pointer, indicating here and there a piece of heroic statuary as if he were bidding on it at auction. He was particularly attracted to undraped Greek and Roman goddesses, though the flesh was of stone.

I was flattered to be seen with him. He doffed his hat to the ladies if they were unaccompanied. (This was not the custom in Paris but the ladies seemed not to mind.) With his deeply tanned face and greying hair he had the distinguished appearance of someone quite well known but not easily placed. You might think you knew him from the newspapers, but could not remember what he was famous for. We were of the same height and shared certain physical features, but women's eyes invariably went straight to his instead of mine. I walked in his shadow. I was both proud and jealous of him. His was a confidently masculine presence I had not yet and might never acquire.

Furthermore he was impeccably dressed. His grey suit had been tailored in Rome, his white spats were immaculate. When he removed his hat you could see its expensive silk lining. I was wearing a corduroy jacket with a button missing. I should have polished my shoes before meeting his train. Beside my father I must have appeared insignificant and possibly unkempt. Self-consciously my hand kept straying to the hasty knot in my cheap necktie.

I was still an unfinished product; my father was the real thing.

Eighteen

MADAME VITRINE STOOD just outside my door behind a candle, and by the light of it I saw her scant grey hair bound up in little bits of wire and paper—the paper twists she saved from coffee sacks.

"I could not of course allow her up to your room at this hour."

Her? Madame Vitrine's shadow enlarged against the door of the WC. I attempted to come awake, to understand. I had trained myself to sleep in the early morning hours despite the noise and chaos of the night market.

"She has come with a message about your father."

"What is it? Where is he?"

"At his hotel. They have sent for a doctor."

Madame Vitrine went away with her candle like a sleepwalker. She was as bewildered as I. She too had trained herself to sleep through bedlam.

I dressed and stumbled dangerously down the stairs, for in my haste I had forgotten the electric torch. I expected to find someone waiting in the café with a message, but the messenger had gone. Two sweaty loaders with wet burlap across their shoulders stood at the zinc counter drinking cognac. The café-bar never closed, catering to the market workers, tonight a welcome shelter from the storm.

"Elle est partie," said Georges, the barman, and he indicated the puddle of water where she had stood.

I recognized my father's black British umbrella, rolled shut, hooked on the back of an empty chair near the door. I took the umbrella and went out into the rain, dazed, but awake enough to be cold with fear.

The grey of rue Tiquetonne seemed to melt into the gutters under the steady downpour. Not far ahead of me, against a maze of carts and crates and produce scales, I thought I saw the girl—but she may have been a ghost, wearing a shawl. I tried to run to her but the street was too slippery, then the wind caught in the umbrella bearing me backward while the bright shawl sailed ahead and disappeared. I drew the umbrella shut and plunged through a wet avalanche of lettuce where I had seen her last. I knew she had passed that way. In her wake I heard a series of vulgar suggestions come from a circle of melon vendors warming their hands over a metal drum of blazing cratewood. She was no ghost.

The Hôtel des Bons Enfants, then. At Etienne Marcel I looked for a taxi, but there was none at that bleak wet hour. I saw fish heads in the gutter, cats prowling, their damp fur glistening in the lamplight; then I saw her again. A girl in a Spanish shawl had already got across the flooded street: she was passing a water-filled excavation with a DANGER sign showing in the light of a red lantern. I waded through the brackish backwash of a strangled sewer to shorten the distance between us, but she darted ahead, dodged my company, fled.

Suddenly I was out of the rain cutting a diagonal path through potted ferns and flowers, across a crowded market shed and sheltered for a moment—but in a panic, all the same—then into the bleak obscurity of rue Saint-Honoré. During that briefly illuminated passage under the arc lights I thought I saw fringes of her shawl dripping tears of rain water, then her face, once, in profile—a hollow cheek, one fearful eye—but that was perhaps another girl, yet one with a fear as great as my own.

A drumhead of thunder rolled behind me, then cracked open overhead. The night turned electric blue in a flash of unexpected éclairage: I could see her as clearly as the night we met not far from here over a bottle of champagne—before the black came down again and she and Paris and my memory of her went into shadow. I lost her.

The hotel lobby was empty, no one behind the desk. I have always avoided French elevators but this time took the unmanned lift with no thought of claustrophobia: the deadly slow ascent gave me time to catch my breath but did nothing to ease my heartbeat. A streak of light lay across the hall carpet where the door to my father's room was ajar. I went in. A man wearing an embroidered vest said, "Ah, le fils," relieved. He was the night porter.

An elderly doctor was seated beside a table lamp scribbling a prescription. "Une crise," said he—he did not say what kind of crisis.

Under the bedsheet, covered to the chin, lay my father. He was breathing heavily through the mouth, staring expectantly upward at the unlit electric chandelier. His Italian tan had drained away. He appeared diminished by half, almost unrecognizable, lying pale and rigid under the white sheet.

"So there you are."

He made an effort to sound jaunty and offhand, but the spaces between words gave him away: his voice, like his face, had lost color.

The night porter excused himself and bowed out, anxious to escape the sickroom.

"A close call," intoned the doctor. "An affair of the heart can also be damaging to that organ—" then added dryly, "at our age."

The doctor, an obese character from a Molière comedy, affected the pompous manner characteristic of the French medical profession. Doctors in France do not so much treat illness as pronounce upon it, then affix seals to documents containing these pronouncements, serving in an official capacity between midwife and croque-mort. He signed his prescription with a flourish.

As if each word were painful, my father whispered hoarsely, "Can you get rid of this ass?"

I suspect the doctor understood English or could at least interpret the tone, for he immediately adjusted his stomach, pushed the tubing of an auscultator into his satchel, and heaved himself to his feet. In exchange for the superfluous prescription (it would never be filled) and superfluous advice, I passed him some franc notes from my father's money clip. With an astonishing sleight of hand for a man whose every other movement was ponderous, the doctor caused the notes to disappear, then left us.

When I placed the clip in my father's hand his drained face turned thoughtful: he was trying to remember some other debt.

"The girl," he said.

"The girl who came for me?"

"A gypsy girl. She told my fortune." He was uneasy saying this last, the truth as far as it went. "She may be waiting in the lobby."

He gave me the money to pay her. It was not his habit to offer money to women—rather, the other way around—but this was a girl not a woman, and a pretty one. It was clear what the doctor had meant by an affair of the heart. Also, I recognized the sum of money he gave me.

I took the stairs, the money in my hand. Lights flickered with the thunder that rocked Paris. In the lobby the night porter had put on a blue denim apron over his colorful vest and was mopping rainwater from the tiles.

"Your father's niece, you mean?" The man attempted to keep his face in stone, but his voice betrayed the worldliness of anyone who has ever worked in hotels. No, she had not returned. The puddle he dabbed at with a rag mop was the watery trail I had myself made walking to the elevator.

I went back to the room and told my father the girl had disappeared.

"Strange," he said. "She was a strange little thing."

In a moment the strange girl was forgotten and he began to murmur in a sick dream before sleep. I leaned close to listen, but there was only a broken delirium of half-thoughts mumbled aloud: schemes, enterprises, money, means. The telephone system. Think what a handful of American electricians could accomplish in medieval France. And a master plumber could live like a king. The French did not have popcorn yet—did I know that? Their toilet paper was a scandal.

I sat in the chair where the doctor had sat, and perhaps the fortune-teller before him, taking up my vigil during the storm that raged outside and in. Finally my father slept and both our hearts were calmed. By dawn the storm had blown itself out and he had survived his crisis. I knew he would quit Paris as soon as he could—already there was color in his face again. In his sleep he murmured more than once the name Jeanne. He always pronounced my mother's name in the English way.

LOVE

One

SCARVES, SHAWLS, NECKTIES, NECKS. It is late and I have
consumed more eau de vie than my self-important doctor would consider safe. (Eau de vie, he tells me, will be my death.) In my distorted
memory I see the doctor at the Hôtel des Bons Enfants who was so
fat he had, like Humpty Dumpty, no neck at all. I see the night
porter's prominent Adam's apple working queerly over the word niece.
My head is crowded with images, though all I can truly see from this
window is the linden with half a southern moon caught in its branches.
Four of these branches—in my mind's eye, mind—outline the frame of
a guillotine.

All of this is foolish, and brought on by drink. I will burn these
pages in tomorrow's trash.

Mademoiselle Segret, who lived with Landru at the time of his
arrest, was said to have had (in the newspaper prose of Danglure) a
swanlike neck. I saw her in the witness box and she had a pretty neck
indeed, but not like a swan's. Some of the women my father (and
Landru) knew had necks like puddings.

To trace backward this pattern of neckpieces: in the chill grey
Parisian autumn of '21 (two years after my father's crisis in a hotel
bed) Gabriel, the poet, wore a long red scarf like Aristide Bruant's—

or like the long scarf Isadora Duncan wore the first time I saw her at
La Coupole with her insanely arrogant (or arrogantly insane) Russian
lover, who pulled her to him by the two ends of the scarf as if to kiss
her, but bit her on the neck instead, then leaped up, kicked over a
waiter's tray, and left Miss Duncan to exhibit her tragic white face
to the world—"Why didn't you," O'Grady asked, "interview her?" (he
was putting on his detachable collar with clip-on necktie attached)—
yet caressing the bitten place on her neck with an expression so lascivi-
ous it brought on a stiffening of arousal in this shy apprentice news-
hound four tables away.

(At the present moment my guests, the Flowers—professor and
wife—are evidently making love in the bedroom below mine. Under
the circumstances, above them I mean, even a septuagenarian can
recall tumescence.)

Miss Duncan's neck had thickened and grown slack when I saw
her next, in Nice (where her long scarf caught in the wheel of an open
motor car and broke her neck—but I did not see that).

To return to Gabriel, and the bicycle, I can see him trotting alongside as I pedaled the length of rue Tiquetonne. He held one handlebar
to steady me (I was a beginner) and I was afraid his long red scarf
might catch in the bicycle's wheel. A girl waited in front of the hotel
to know if I would buy the bicycle or not—I already knew I would
buy, hoping it might purchase the girl too (it did). She was not wearing a shawl, and a spit curl was no longer her style, but I knew she
was the messenger and fortune-teller of my father's fate two years
before. Some months before that, as I rid myself of my innocence at
the square des Innocents, the neck of a champagne bottle had stood
erect in a basin of ice and she had asked me to be gentle and please,
chéri, not to caress her neck.

An altogether different chain of events (or cards, if you believe
in them) had brought her to me this time. She was a different creature
now. My father, who had total recall for female friends, would not
have recognized her. Even I was sometimes misled by her lies. Who
was she? My memory of her is a troubling piece of confusion still.

Her name was Anne or Annette or Ninette, and might even have
been Andrea or Andrée. I called her Fleur. A sculptor named Anacréon called her Gitane—gypsy—and that is what she often called
herself. I am sure she was not gypsy, but she did pretend to tell fortunes. Her arrière-grands-parents, she said, had been in the diplomatic
service in Rumania. Gypsies, diplomats?—I questioned her closely.

Then they were not, she conceded. She was born in Spain. Her mother —a gypsy, une vraie—had taught her to tell fortunes. In Spanish? I asked. No, in French. She did not mind if I disbelieved her—what did it matter?—she did not expect to be believed.

The truths and lies of her life were told to me piecemeal, an episode at a time, over the months I knew her; but as I try to assemble the patchwork on a page it still falls to pieces.

She worked as a model, I knew. She had been a prostitute, I swear. (And might still have worked at that nefarious trade—for what, in her words, did it matter?) It all mattered to my literal mind, but I was obliged to suppress my persistent curiosity if I hoped to keep her.

The first night she stayed with me I feared she would ask for money, and she did—but it was for the bicycle. (I had forgotten about the earlier transaction.) By then she had removed her clothes and had nowhere to put the two hundred francs I gave her. She was alternately innocent and sly. She put the francs notes into her shoe, then we made love.

In bed she was a thin starved kitten, both playful and hurt. Later her claws would grow and the game might turn rough, might become vicious. That first night I entered her with my own brutal greed: a nuptial violation she endured with a downturned smile. I used her according to my droit de seigneur. It was all I could do to maintain a seeming-civilized self and not allow my pleasure to feed on her pain.

"There are pieces of me missing." Her smile was indecipherable, the tears were genuine.

Truly some part of her was dead. She could play and satisfy her playmate, his satisfaction her only triumph—for that was the way of the world. Nevertheless, her sigh at the end of our strainings was more than a sigh of relief. I would like to think she did réjouisse—or was vaguely comforted—in that part of her that still lived.

I once asked her if she had ever reached her pleasure's peak, and she replied, "Once upon a time, yes," and I believed her even though "il était une fois" is the way French fairy tales begin. There was in her expression the promise she would with me achieve the same fulfillment.

Still, some large damage had been done. Her life with me did not repair that damage to any extent, though I was not insensitive to her hurt. I was twenty that year, my sap had risen; I yearned to spill, and she was my receptacle.

* * *

The night she consented to stay with me her sleep was ragged and distraught. Though she had curled herself tightly into a satisfying fetus enveloped in my larger frame, she trembled in her sleep. She cried the half-words of a nightmare dialogue aloud.

Once, fully awake, she declared, "I have forgotten how turbulent this quarter is."

The noise from the all-night market disturbed her. Yes, she had been here before, whoever she was.

When next she woke—before dawn, still dark—I came awake at the same moment. Without waiting for her acquiescence I embarked on another invasion of her flesh. She responded sleepily to my eagerness, more amused than aroused.

She might have got up after that, for she could no longer sleep, she said—but I kept her from her clothes. I held her with my hand between her thighs as if to hold that part of her forever. Already I knew how evasive she could be: a night creature come in out of the cold, a cat, a phantom, a lie.

Sated, I thought we might sleep again.

"J'ai peur," she said. She was afraid to sleep now.

"Pourquoi?"

She did not answer. I drifted off still holding her to me, uneasy in my sleep with a vague sense of her wakefulness. I felt a beam of light, even through my closed lids. She had turned on the electric torch and was illuminating the columns of newsprint pinned to the wall. When I opened my eyes I saw a yellow circle of light on a news item about the oldest woman in France (Mademoiselle Chédeville, 104), then another: Carpentier's defeat by Dempsey. The beam traveled from column to column, page to page, from one corner of the room to the other, though the print at the far end of the triangle was too distant to read.

It was no use trying to sleep. Eventually the weak watery light of a Paris dawn filtered through the window. Suddenly she turned off the torch and said, "Will you take them down?"

"The newspapers?"

"Yes."

"Pourquoi?"

But there was never an answer why. I learned finally not to ask pourquoi. She was restless, I could not relax in the aura of her agitation. A strange request, but if she was unhappy with my wall of newsprint, I was unhappy too. I got up and began removing the newspaper pages, careful to put the tacks in a bowl so that she would not step on them in her bare feet. She was up and trembling in the dead light, then gave a sudden cry of joy, like a child. There was money in her shoe.

Two

My recollections come to me out of sequence (in disorder, is what I mean), so I will put them down as they occur. I am moving backward one day from that first meeting with Fleur—assuming it was a first meeting and not a revoir.

Gabriel was walking with me through the market district. He lingered, amused, in front of the exterminator's shop at the intersection of Pierre Lescot and Etienne Marcel. This was a window display I generally took pains to avoid: J.-J. Péru & Fils (or their taxidermist) had stuffed and mounted a collection of rats. The creatures were loathsomely arranged in lifelike posture, staring out at the passerby with fierce bared teeth or, in another tableau, stealthily invading the hollows of a huge artificial cheese. Those rats trapped in the exterminator's foolproof cages appeared deceptively docile. Behind the panorama was a reassuring shelf of J.-J. Péru's poisons and preventives, but this inventory was not nearly so awesome as the colony of rodents itself.

It was a relief to walk on.

"Est-ce que tu savais," Gabriel asked, using the informal tu for the first time, "Marcel Proust has been known to decapitate rats with a miniature guillotine for an evening's amusement?"

I did not know. I knew nothing about Proust at all except that he had written *A l'ombre des jeunes filles en fleur* which I had tried to read but could not finish.

Gabriel's odd English phrasing fluttered in and out of his recital in French, for he liked to practice English but not be confined to it. He was a handsome young man and sometimes affected a cape, but that day was dressed in velveteen poet's garb with a long red scarf around his neck and a white gardenia in his buttonhole.

None of the late afternoon prostitutes said, "Tu viens?" to him as we passed, and this surprised me: he was slim and well proportioned, with the classic Greek features of a sculptor's idealization of the male.

Miss Stein referred to his Raphael look. She once informed me that Gabriel was a very fine poet but his handsome appearance placed the poetic gift in jeopardy. (Miss Stein did not read French poetry. It was Miss Toklas who read Gabriel's poems and told her about them: Miss Stein was more interested in Gabriel's Raphael look.)

Meanwhile the prostitutes ignored Gabriel and Gabriel ignored the prostitutes. It was as if he did not believe in the colorful display ranged along rue Saint-Denis. But he was familiar with the quarter. He mentioned the name of a restaurant where he sometimes came with his copains to eat onion soup in the small hours. I decided his poetry came from some other source than the market district: for him les Halles was a bowl of onion soup.

"They are quite curious about your place of dwelling."

I thought he meant the prostitutes were curious (for my mind was on them) but he was referring to Miss Stein and Miss Toklas. They were curious to know about my room on rue Tiquetonne, and how I lived. I realized they had sent Gabriel to investigate my living accommodations.

He thought my room very nice, but somewhat stark. My father had called it a poet's garret and Gabriel, who was a poet, said it was a monk's cell. He was perhaps too polite to say what he really thought, but I knew he would express himself more openly when he went back to the rue de Fleurus. I noticed he inspected the cushion carefully before he sat down in my only chair. For a moment he searched for an appropriate comment, then said the view over the rooftops was charming; at the same time he inhaled deeply, sniffing the air as my father had done.

While I made coffee he talked about Miss Stein and Miss Toklas in a mélange of English and French.

"Do you recognize l'amour exquis the one feels to the other?"

I said it seemed to me Miss Stein and Miss Toklas got on very well together.

Did I realize truly what their relationship was?

Not altogether, I said. They seemed to be living together as man and wife though they were both women.

"Qui donc est la femme, et qui le mari?"

I told him I did not know which was which or who was who. Only now did I try to imagine Miss Stein's thin lips pressed to Miss Toklas' mustache.

My puzzlement amused him. "Their relationship is more spiritual than physical," he said, but he said it in French.

Miss Toklas and Miss Stein were spiritually attractive ladies, but not physically, so I thought a spiritual relationship was best. But I did not say this to Gabriel, who knew them better than I and was a gossip like Miss Stein, for he might repeat my remark.

Gabriel glanced about the room again in case he had overlooked some treasure in its drab furnishings. His eyes rested on a newspaper page pinned to the wall with a photograph of a sculpture by Landowski of the boxer Georges Carpentier.

"What a handsome animal," he said. The room was redeemed by that single rotogravure.

I had only one cup in the room so Gabriel took his coffee in the cup and I drank mine from a water tumbler. I was afraid the glass would crack from the freshly boiled coffee but Gabriel told me to leave the spoon in it when I poured and it would not crack. Then he told me he was a lover of men not women.

"It is not a sickness as some people think. It is simply another way of loving."

"Yes," I said, "people should love however they please." I was trying to hide my distress. I wished he had not come to my room to discuss this.

"Or whomever."

"Yes."

"It is not always a question of how they please but how they must." (All of this was in French.) "When I see an attractive man it excites me in the same way other men are excited by the sight of an attractive woman."

Gabriel's scarf fell open with a gesture, the two ends dangling apart over his knees: "Have you ever made love to a man?" he asked me.

He was speaking altogether in French now, for these were sentiments too delicate to express in English. He was perfectly at ease discussing his sexual inclinations, balancing his cup on one scarf-covered knee, but I was not.

"No."

"Pas encore?"

"Pas du tout."

"It is nothing against virtue or manliness, you know. You would in no way be corrupted by it. It is like the glass of coffee—you see, it did not crack."

I did not see what a glass of coffee had to do with homosexual love. Gabriel was now talking about Plato and what the *Symposium* had to say on the subject.

"Perhaps you have never really thought about this?"

"No," I admitted.

He then explained that all of Proust's jeunes filles en fleur were really young men, but all I could think of when he mentioned Proust was the author's idle pleasure in cutting off the heads of rats.

"I am obliged to confess I fell in love with you when I first saw you at Miss Stein's."

Gabriel could say this with a shrug and a gesture of helplessness, without spilling his coffee. The confession did nothing for my composure.

My confusion (how apt of the Bible to describe pederasty as confusion) was worse than the time Mr. Keynes placed his hand on my knee. With Mr. Keynes I had only to deal with a stray hand hidden under the table while my father sat conversing with the gentleman—when the conversation was over I could stand and liberate my leg. Here I could not escape the blunt declaration so openly made by a young man my age. I would have to answer the question that hung suspended between us. I could not think of a useful or believable or diplomatic lie, so I told the truth.

"You are a friend," I said. "I do like you." But the verb aimer means more than I wanted to say, so I used vous instead of te. Cautiously I continued with the truth: "I want to keep your friendship."

"And love?"

"If you want to call it that."

"It is that."

"A loving friendship, then."

We were playing with the words amitié and amour.

"With the commitment the term love implies?"

"With the commitment the term friendship implies."

"Do you believe we can remain friends without loving?"

I thought a moment. "I want to be a good friend to you in the only way I know how, even though I am unable to express my friendship in the way you suggest."

Gabriel's heartfelt sigh filled the room as he looked down into the coffee cup. There was a knock on the door. It was Georges from the café-bar downstairs to tell me someone had come to see me about a bicycle. The waiter's interruption was a great relief—to Gabriel, I think, as well as to me.

Gabriel came down with me to share a strange moment of déjà vu. "You are acquainted?" he asked.

The shock of recognition must have showed on my face, but the girl returned my stare with a puzzled look: she might have wondered which of us wanted to buy a wheel.

The girl was known to Gabriel as Anacréon's model, the owner of a bicycle for sale—a bicycle I had examined at Anacréon's studio earlier that day—but known to me from a time earlier still, the female half of a Tarot card called The Lovers.

Three

ALL OF THIS came about because of a stray remark Miss Stein made at lunch.

"Weren't you looking for a wheel?" she asked me. I am certain she used the word wheel instead of bicycle.

Miss Toklas answered for me: "No, Gertrude. He was looking for a typewriter, and that was two years ago."

"I found a typewriter," said I, and I told them the story of my Underwood that had belonged to a British war correspondent who committed suicide in Cairo, though the story was two years old.

"I am glad," said Miss Stein. She was glad about the typewriter not the suicide. "Because I really could not part with mine." She referred to her Smith Premier on which Miss Toklas had typed *The Making of Americans*. "But I know of a dandy wheel for sale."

"Now, Gertrude, why should he want a wheel?"

"A journalist must get about, and he is not of an age nor financially able to own a motor car." Miss Stein owned a Ford motor car of which she was very proud—she had driven it during the war as an ambulance. "The sculptor who is selling his wheel is in need of money and I have every reason to believe it is a dandy wheel."

"We are all in need of money," said Gabriel, who was also at lunch and only the day before had borrowed money from Miss Stein. (Gabriel and I were always invited to the rue de Fleurus together and I did not learn until later that Miss Stein and Miss Toklas assumed we were lovers.)

"I fear he will only spend the money for cocaine," said Miss Toklas.

"He cocaines himself," explained Gabriel in his quaint English.

Lunch was an excellent pâté (made of blackbirds, Miss Stein explained) with cornichons that Miss Toklas had pickled herself, then a cheese omelette with salade verte. Gabriel had brought the wine, a vintage Saint-Emilion. Miss Stein admonished him for spending money on an extravagance, especially since he had bought the wine with money she had lent him yesterday. For dessert we had mousse au chocolat. Miss Stein was fond of chocolate and ate a second serving.

After coffee Miss Stein drove us to Anacréon's atelier in her Ford. (I am not certain this was the Ford automobile Miss Stein had driven as an ambulance. She had bought another Ford after the war, a smaller motor car she called Godiva—but I do not believe the four of us could have arranged ourselves inside tiny Godiva.)

When we drove past the corner of rue Rochechouart and rue de Dunkerque I remarked that here Landru was arrested with his mistress, but nobody heard me over the sound of the motor. The Landru affair was two years old and public interest in the case had waned. Miss Stein had never been interested in Landru. This may have been why nobody heard, or chose to hear, my remark.

For some reason Miss Stein parked the car at Abbesses and we walked to Anvers and took the funiculaire. I think she wanted us to see the view of Paris on the way up. Gabriel, I recall, paid all our fares out of the money he had borrowed from Miss Stein. I have always had a fear of heights and was too uncomfortable in the cable car to enjoy the view or Miss Stein's conversation on the way up.

(There were no painters in the place du Tertre in those days. The square was not quaint but just a square. A legend grew up about the painters of Montmartre and then bad painters set up their easels in the place du Tertre to make it seem quaint. The bad painters are still there but the real painters have disappeared.)

Anacréon's studio was near the Montmartre cemetery. The high atelier windows were begrimed with smoke in mournful patterns of stained glass. The interior of the studio was very much like a cluttered garage, with mewling cats underfoot and a blacksmith's forge at one end. I noticed a string of women's underthings hanging near the forge, the only touch of color.

Anacréon's sculpture of this period reminded me of the sculptor himself, elongated and emaciated. When I looked at his work he followed me from sculpture to sculpture like a tour guide at a museum.

"Look at it with one eye closed for a better impression of the verticals."

I did as he advised.

"The essential in the human form," he declared, "is the bony structure."

Miss Stein explained: "Anacréon does not sculpt more than the essential."

The sculptor had long grey unwashed hair and the dry brittle look of an aging alcoholic. His beret and jacket were powdered with plaster dust, or dandruff. His sculptures were in metal or stone or twisted wire, but he himself was made of something brittle. I shook hands with him with great care in case a piece of him might break off.

He followed me all around the garagelike studio with Gabriel and several of the cats following both of us while Miss Stein and Miss Toklas stood near the dead forge. The sculptured figures were emaciated, with narrow heads like pressed skulls. Everyone seemed to be waiting for me to make some pronouncement on Anacréon's work. The only thing I could think of was that he must have been influenced by working so near to the Montmartre Cemetery, but I could not say that. Finally I came to a bicycle hanging by its front wheel from a hook on the wall. It was a sturdy-looking vehicle. The spokes and fenders were somewhat rusted and the pedal chain would need a greasing.

"How much is it?" I asked.

"But that," said Anacréon, beginning to tremble (it was his way to laugh), "is a bicycle."

The sculptor bent stiffly at the waist, holding himself, trembling, his great yellow teeth showing in a death's head grin. Strange sounds came through his nose. Miss Stein had neglected to tell him I had come to buy a bicycle.

I told him I would like to buy the bicycle, and again he was taken by a seizure of dry laughter.

"Yes," said he, "that is a bicycle," before the tremor took over.

Gabriel saw fit to slap him on the back so that he would not choke. Each time the flat of his hand struck the sculptor little clouds of plaster dust rose from Anacréon's jacket.

Miss Toklas explained that I was looking to buy a secondhand bicycle and Miss Stein added that I was not a collector of art, like herself. Gabriel stood ready to slap Anacréon on the back again, but the sculptor seemed at last to have got control of himself. Nevertheless, from time to time (when he thought of my passing each piece of sculpture without comment, then asking the price of a bicycle) the lunatic grin would take over and he was obliged to hide his teeth behind his hand.

Miss Stein became annoyed with the joke. She took art with ferocious gravity. The Dada movement, before it blended into surrealism, was a constant vexation to her. (Dada originated in Zurich, and Miss Stein's comment was: "Nothing good has ever come out of Switzerland except chocolate bars.") Raoul Haussmann's "l'Esprit de Notre Temps"—which was a dress model's head with gadgets attached —made her truly angry, and when Picabia passed around a toile vierge for his friends to sign and attach photographs to (called l'oil-cacodylate, the salts of an acid used in the treatment of venereal disease) Miss Stein not only did not sign or offer a photograph but did not speak to Picabia again until 1924. (Tristan Tzara attempted to exhibit a bicycle horn at the Salon des Indépendants, to Miss Stein's great displeasure, but she did not sever relations with him over it.) Nothing about the Dada movement interested or amused her. I think this might have been because people made jokes of Miss Stein's work when she was most serious.

"In any case," Anacréon confessed, "it is not my bicycle." The bicycle belonged to his model. It was indeed for sale, but he did not know the price his model would ask.

Miss Stein then said, "My friend is young and poor and beginning to be a journalist. He cannot afford to pay more than two hundred francs."

"I will tell my model this," said Anacréon, and the yellow smile stole over his face again.

His model was away for the afternoon, but if I would be good enough to leave my card he would inform her of my proposition. Frenchmen—even the poorest—carry cards (Landru carried an assortment, a series for each of his pseudonyms), but I had never had cards printed. Instead I tore a page from the redbound notebook I kept in my pocket and wrote out my name and the address of my hotel. The sculptor accepted the torn page with great dignity, but the parchment skin of his face was cracking with the effort to suppress a grin.

"There," said Miss Stein. She took pleasure in a transaction of any kind. "You are on the way to becoming a cyclist."

Miss Stein then discussed sittings and an advance payment on the torso the sculptor was doing of her. One of the sculptures I passed without comment or recognition was of Miss Stein. All of the sculptures in Anacréon's studio were so skeletal it was impossible to find Miss Stein among them.

I have told my story in reverse order, but where is the beginning? Never mind. Gabriel and I are again walking past the exterminator's shop (a display window full of rats) at the intersection of Pierre Lescot and Etienne Marcel. Anacréon's model, the girl I call Fleur, will arrive at the café-bar while Gabriel and I are talking in my room. The sequence is unimportant, Fleur did appear. "Chronology," Miss Stein said (more than once, so that it might be correctly attributed), "is meaningless."

Four

AMONG MY PAPERS (I have been ransacking a steamer trunk, hoping to interest the professor in some trivia from the twenties) I find a news photograph of a family scene on the Sables-d'Olonne. Here is the Deibler family ensemble, rarely photographed, never interviewed by the press.

No one looks happy there beside the Atlantic—men with tops to their bathing costumes, women covered to the knees—posing in frozen attitudes for the family album. Anatole Deibler visited the Sables-d'Olonne every summer, but he was obliged to take his vacation under an assumed name for he was the official executioner of France, known as Monsieur de Paris, guardian and chief operator of that infamous instrument the guillotine.

By its grotesque nature the profession of executioner becomes a family calling. Anatole Deibler's grandfather, Joseph Deibler, was an executioner in Algiers at a time when provinces of France, and even overseas territories, had their own executioners. Grandfather Joseph's son, Louis-Stanislas, married the daughter of the official executioner in Algiers (whose name was Zoë Rasseneux, called Ras-à-neuf, meaning: to shave down to a stub), for executioners were inclined or obliged to marry within the profession. Eventually local executioners were replaced with one single lifetime-appointed national executioner who traveled throughout the republic with his portable guillotine wherever his services were required. When the first of these national executioners died—the famous Roch—the job was inherited by Louis-Stanislas Deibler, who had been a member of the Roch team.

Anatole, the son of Louis-Stanislas, determined early to forsake the family career. He was mocked at school, an outcast in games and humiliated at every turn. Once at the dinner table his father—in the way of a professional man relating an out-of-the-way incident during the working day—described the first execution at which he served as chef d'équipe. The prisoner was so enraged and unmanageable Louis-Stanislas had to knock his head against the paving stone to subdue him: the man was blessedly unconscious when the state exacted its final toll. This tale so shocked young Anatole he swore to himself never to take part in his father's murderous trade.

But Louis-Stanislas intended for his son to follow in the family calling. In the last century young men did as their fathers directed: Anatole Deibler was no exception. At the age of seventeen he became an apprentice executioner as a member of his father's grim corps of public servants. He assisted at his first execution in March of 1882, for the guillotining of Lantz. It was an episode of unrelieved horror, he hated it.

For Anatole Deibler military service was not obligatory (due to his peculiar yet valued function for the state), but he insisted on serving his term in the belief that this might be a way out. Even in the army he was a pariah. His fellow soldiers insulted him openly or refused to serve in his unit. Barracks life became miserable, then impossible, until he was forced, finally, to seek a discharge.

At this point Anatole Deibler accepted his fate. But rather than work at his father's side he went to Algiers and became his grandfather's apprentice. There he assisted—with forbearance if not zeal—at more than fifty executions.

Meanwhile his father began to be affected mentally by the threats and indignities inevitable to the profession. Despite the brutal and brutalizing work, Louis-Stanislas was known to be a loving husband and father, gentle in his family circle, tender-hearted. It was rumored that Monsieur de Paris was actually opposed to capital punishment. (When a newspaperman tried to pin him down concerning these sentiments, and threatened to publish his views on capital punishment, Louis-Stanislas was outraged: "But you're insane. I didn't say that. I'm neither for nor against. Je ne suis rien!")

He was obliged to move his family from the rue Vicq d'Azir because of a bomb threat, but at new lodgings on avenue Michel-Bizot he received the same threat. Neighbors were appalled to have the Deiblers on the same street. No one would rent to him. Finally Louis-Stanislas bought a small brick house at 39, rue de Billancourt, in Auteuil. The Deibler family did not receive; they did not speak to strangers and especially not to journalists. They lived quietly in a quiet neighborhood as anonymously as possible—they could not be evicted because they owned their own house.

When Louis-Stanislas was scheduled to execute Caserio, the anarchist killer of President Carnot, the threats were more vehement than ever. The executioner was called envoyé de Charon and boucher anthropophagique along with other, unprintable, names. For this execution he was obliged to stay overnight in a maison close because hotel keepers, fearing anarchist vengeance, refused to admit him at any legitimate establishment.

For a time he dropped out of sight, and newspapers played up the Missing Executioner, believed kidnapped—or himself executed—but during this time he was at Lourdes, for he was very devout, offering homage to sainte Bernadette.

Once he did come close to being kidnapped, or killed, when he was approached by a man pretending to be a news vendor (hawking, prophetically, *Dernière Heure*) and was grabbed by three men who attempted to force him into a carriage—but he was saved by the very neighbors who had shunned him until then.

In 1894 he was shocked to learn he would have to execute a priest, l'abbé Bruneau. So guilt ridden was he that he asked the good father's blessing before he led him to the guillotine. Following this incident Louis-Stanislas moved ever deeper into a nightmare life. He began to suffer from hemophobia, the neurosis referred to in *Macbeth,* an obsession with blood. He saw visions in carmine, saw himself bespattered with blood from head to foot; he compulsively wrung his imagined-bloody hands in anguish.

(The nightmare turned real at the execution of Hursh, in Nancy, when the convicted man's blood spurted across his waistcoat.)

In June of 1898 when he executed Carrara he screamed to his assistants: "Get water, quickly! I'm covered with blood!" But he was not. His behavior by now could no longer be ignored, the symptoms too obvious to be denied. If he continued to deteriorate in this way, he would go mad. At the urging of his équipe Louis-Stanislas decided to retire.

His final execution was that of Vacher, the shepherd killer (eleven victims), who believed himself a reincarnation of Jack the Ripper. Louis-Stanislas gave up the title of official executioner on New Year's Day of 1899, at which time Anatole was summoned from Algiers to be told he had inherited his father's post as state executioner for all of France. The event was toasted in champagne at the small villa in Auteuil. Anatole Deibler, however reluctantly, accepted the blood-stained mantle bequeathed from father to son. In time he became the most celebrated (if that is the word) executioner in France.

His first presiding execution was at Troyes the fourteenth of January, 1899—that of the ex-mayor of Romilly-Saint-Loup, Jean Damoiseau, sixty-five. The daughter of the man he murdered asked Deibler if she could stand at the foot of the guillotine. He refused.

On the first of February he made his début in Paris. Alfred Peugnez, who killed an old woman and a seven-year-old child, asked him on the way to the guillotine: "Dis, donc, mon vieux, ça fait mal ton outil?" (Tell me, my friend, does it hurt, your tool?)

Anatole Deibler—who despised everything his métier represented —was considered the most skillful and reliable of the long line of executioners in France. (His reputation exceeded that of the Sanson family, executioners until the Revolution, when Charles Henri Sanson dispatched Louis XVI, and his son, Henri, cut off the head of Marie Antoinette.) The new Monsieur de Paris was especially commended for his speed, the sureness of his movements, and the extraordinary precision of the decapitation.

A Frenchman, when he has become secure and successful in his métier, will inevitably want to marry, if he has not already done so. Anatole's first serious love affair was with the daughter of a carpenter known as Père Heurteloup. When Anatole asked for the hand of his daughter in marriage, Père Heurteloup refused because of the stigma attached to Deibler's profession. Deibler—a sensitive man, after all— was deeply wounded by the refusal.

At this critical moment in Anatole's life he took up cycling to distract himself from his gruesome occupation, to escape the shame and odium of it—and to avoid the same nervous disorder which had incapacitated his father. He joined the Société Vélicopédique in Auteuil and there, under an assumed name, attached himself to a set of friends who knew him only as a fellow bicycle enthusiast. Under this pseudonym (do you discern the first slender thread connecting Deibler to Landru?) he met Rosalie Rogis, and fell in love with her. He courted her as someone other than he was.

I wrote two versions of this tale: a straightforward account for O'Grady, with a happy ending, intended for the British Sunday supplements; another version I called "Je ne suis rien" I wrote for myself, full of strained irony and idle conjecture and puns (Deibler and déblayer, to clear away refuse; Peugnez and pugnose; Damoiseau, the damned bird). The ironic link between Deibler and Landru (in addition to the aliases) was a bicycle, which Deibler took up as a sport and Landru as a mode of transport. (Landru's motor car, a four-seater Vermorel, was confiscated by the army in 1914 to be used in the defense of the Marne.)

O'Grady, who was a misogynist and thought marriage a daft and degrading institution, was nevertheless happy with my happy ending.

"So old Rogis relented and let his Rosalie have the rogue?"

"He was fond of Deibler, they had become friends at the cycling club. His daughter was genuinely in love with Deibler so the father forgave him his deception and offered his consent."

"And they live happily ever after?"

"They're still married. I don't know how happy they are."

"They're happy enough to make our readers happy."

O'Grady knew his Sunday supplements.

I showed the other version to Miss Stein and she thought the family history was of particular interest and the wordplay amusing.

"But why do you bring Landru into it?"

"I try to establish a thread. Landru and Deibler were both cyclists, and both made a specialty of death."

"I see no thread in a bicycle." (Or did she say wheel?)

"And I am certain the two men will meet."

"If they are to meet they will meet but that is another story."

Five

"'THEY'RE COMING in the windows," said O'Grady as he cocked one eye at me from beneath the green eyeshade. "Why do you glow so? You must have had a toddy en route."

Fleur's scent was still upon me, he had sniffed us out. But I could never speak of Fleur to him, any more than I could have discussed her with my father. O'Grady believed that any man who lowered himself to love a woman was a fool. He did not have a very high opinion of men, either.

"Today we have a songbird flying in."

He called them songbirds, the women who came to be interviewed, and left the window open to air the room when a songbird was due. O'Grady was idly shuffling through the blurred photographs of Landru's victims—a collection of pictures he referred to as the waxworks—and lingered over one, the single exception to Landru's preference for the homely middle-aged: young and pretty Andrée-Anna Babelay. "If only a songbird could reveal how this lovely got into Bluebeard's gallery of the misbegotten."

Newspaper clippings fluttered against the wall from the breeze, but the fresh air did not entirely overcome the odor of cheese from the platter hidden away in his typewriter case or diminish the sour smell of his célibataire quarters (an army cot and an armoire) on the other side of a muslin curtain.

Until I came to work for Channel News it had been my impression that newsmen went looking for stories, but that was not O'Grady's way. "The best stories inevitably come in through the window." He solicited information by telephone, by pneumatique, and from other newspapers without ever leaving the office. Clarence O'Grady was always IN, and songbirds were forever flying in the window.

"We will need you at hand."

He always said this. As an assistant I did very little assisting at these impromptu interviews, but O'Grady's favorite personage was Sherlock Holmes and like Holmes he wanted an alter ego on the premises. Though he was willing to send his leg man out "to sniff around" on occasion, he considered it demeaning and inherently vulgar to chase a news story or wheedle an interview. "We are essentially eavesdroppers" was his theme. After a session with a songbird he would solicit my impression, then deliver his own observations and conclusions, which were inevitably superior to mine. "She will want an audience," said he. He was convinced a songbird would sing a prettier tune before two men than one.

"She's here." We could hear the grillwork of the elevator rattling as the passenger attempted to open the door. O'Grady sent me out to free her from the cage.

Except for her hat—an extravaganza in peacock feathers chosen especially for this occasion—Laure Bonhoure was everything prim, corseted, and correct. She was precisely on time. (She made certain of the hour as she entered the office by referring to a lady's timepiece pinned to her mannish lapel—one of those fish-eyed watches worn by retired schoolteachers and unmarried librarians.)

She had been a governess in London, so could speak English, and did.

"I have not been asked to testify at the trial," she announced with displeasure.

"The authorities," said O'Grady, "have not been noted for their scrupulousness in this case. Your original report to the police was the first breakthrough in the mystery. Without your keen eye and excellent memory, the Bluebeard of Gambais might still be at large."

A sharp movement of her feathers indicated that Mademoiselle Bonhoure was of the same opinion.

The trial date had been set for November and there had naturally followed a revival of interest in the Landru Affair. O'Grady had made contact with several peripheral figures the trial lawyers had overlooked.

"Yes," agreed Mademoiselle Bonhoure, "they got what they wanted from me, and that was that. Without my help the villain would never have been caught."

"And how did that circumstance come about?"

"As you probably know, or you would not have got in communication with me: it was I who put the finger on Landru."

She had picked up a repertoire of slang from English crime novels.

Laure Bonhoure had been a close friend of Mademoiselle Lacoste, sister to one of the missing fiancées, Madame Buisson. Mademoiselle Bonhoure had met Landru at her friend's house, as Monsieur Frémyet, when he was courting Madame Buisson.

"I never liked him," she declared, the repugnance showing on her unattractive face. "I never trusted him. I was not at all surprised things turned out the way they did."

O'Grady nodded sagely in support of her gift for prediction.

When Madame Buisson disappeared with Monsieur Frémyet and was heard from no more, Mademoiselle Bonhoure made every effort to resist saying "I told you so" to her bereaved friend, the victim's sister. She had had the gravest misgivings all along. The news became worse as the investigation progressed: Monsieur Frémyet was known to have been the fiancé of another missing woman whom the police now claimed he had "caused to disappear."

In a very circuitous and wearying way Mademoiselle Bonhoure began to tell of her unexpected involvement in the case.

"I like an English breakfast," she began, as if this made her all the more exciting in our eyes, "including a boiled egg." She then began to recount her life as governess with an English family, descriptions of the "dear children," the peculiar custom of a rubber bath in the morning and leisurely summers on the Isle of Skye.

O'Grady could not suppress a grunt of impatience, but Mademoiselle Bonhoure was not to be dissuaded from describing her fascinating sojourn in Great Britain. She knew her own mind, and it was far-ranging. No wonder the prosecution had neglected to summon her to the witness stand.

"Well, in April of 1919—"

In April of 1919 Mademoiselle Bonhoure had gone to a chinaware boutique on the rue de Rivoli, the Lions of Faïence—"a very fine shop, incidentally"—to replace a broken eggcup. There was one customer ahead of her, a man at the counter buying a fifty-six-piece set of mock Limoges.

"Poor stuff, I assure you—I was surprised the store would handle such shoddy merchandise."

Mademoiselle Bonhoure had the feeling she knew the man, though she could only see the back of his head. She seemed to recognize the voice. When he turned and she saw him in profile, there was no doubt: in front of her stood the mysterious Monsieur Frémyet!

"That beard, those eyes!" Her face flushed red in the recollection of that moment. "I was positive it was the criminal himself. How brazen of him to appear in public like that! The police, you know, were searching everywhere for him. My heart was beating like mad but I kept my wits about me."

She was a woman who would always have her wits about her. Nonetheless she put a trembling hand to her bosom, tugged nervously at the dangling timepiece, reliving the dramatic heartbeat of the encounter.

I could imagine O'Grady's impatience.

"I turned away so that he would not see my face. I waited until he had completed his purchase, then I followed him out of the store."

Frémyet walked down the rue de Rivoli on the right-hand pavement. She remembered it was the right-hand pavement because the tramway tracks were on that side and she feared he might, at any moment, leap aboard a passing tram. But he did not. He walked nonchalantly on, a man with nothing on his conscience and only the afternoon to kill.

Mademoiselle Bonhoure followed at a discreet distance, matching his pace.

"It was not until he passed Samaritaine he realized he was being followed. It is a feeling one gets, you know. At least it is a feeling a woman gets—especially when she senses a man is following her," insisted Mademoiselle Bonhoure, who had never been followed by a man in her life, "so I suppose men are capable of the same sensation."

Frémyet glanced over one shoulder but directed his gaze to the other side of the street. When they were approaching the place du Châtelet he quickly looked round again. "This time our eyes met. He recognized me!" Her hand went again to her timepiece. Monsieur Frémyet was a ruthless criminal: the vigil had now become dangerous.

He quickened his pace, but Mademoiselle Bonhoure remained steadfastly behind him. She searched the street for an agent de police but, "You can never find a policeman when you need one." At Châtelet there was the usual milling rush-hour crowd, heavy traffic and queues forming for the public transport—but still no policeman.

"Suddenly he was gone! I looked in every direction, I was frantic. But he had disappeared. Pouf! Like Lucifer himself."

Those who believed in Landru also believed in the devil.

"Then I saw him at an omnibus window. The bus was just pulling out. The monster. Do you know what he did when he saw me? He was smiling his horrible smile"—she flushed again, recalling that smile —"then he winked at me!"

O'Grady and I suppressed smiles of our own.

"I went straight to Amélie after that." Amélie was her friend Amélie Lacoste, sister of the missing Madame Buisson. The ladies went immediately to the police. "There was not much to go on, but I did know the name of the chinaware shop. An officer accompanied me to the Lions of Faïence—Dautel, I think was his name—and there we talked with Monsieur Geffy (whom I've deal with for years), the manager (and a gentleman if there ever was one), but it was not he who had served the man I described. That was a clerk named Etcheverry (I've dealt with him too). Monsieur Etcheverry remembered Monsieur Frémyet—one did not easily forget that beard, those eyes— but not the name. Checking back through the sales slips for a fifty-six-piece set of mock Limoges—for I described the dinnerware set in detail—he found the very receipt, but it was in the name Guillet, not Frémyet. Guillet—that was just one of the many names the villain assumed."

That was the end of the trail as far as Mademoiselle Bonhoure was concerned. The police thanked her for her help. There had been some talk of a reward, but Inspector Dautel informed her that no reward had actually been posted. This was a large disappointment. "Not that I wasn't prepared to do my duty as a French citizen, under any cir-cumstances . . ."

Monsieur Guillet had been foolish enough to request that the set of china be delivered to his address. Mademoiselle Bonhoure thought she might go along with the police to identify the man. "I naturally wanted to be in on the kill." Inspector Dautel decided that would not be necessary.

Mademoiselle Bonhoure's story had come to an end, but she was still talking.

"Yes, I am the one who put the finger on him—at considerable risk, I might add. Without me there would be no trial. It is a scandal I have not been asked to testify."

O'Grady assured her there were a good many women ready to testify, with evidence enough to guillotine Landru several times over: she need not fear a lapse of justice.

But Mademoiselle Bonhoure chirped on: "You might mention in the news article that a reward was suggested originally."

Justice was not what she had in mind.

"Ah, yes—the reward. A reward was suggested, as I recall, but suggested by the newspapers. There were several editorials suggesting rewards—that is what editorials are for."

Laure Bonhoure seemed to lose some of her feathers. At that point the interview had come to its logical conclusion: she checked her lapel timepiece and I assumed she was ready to make her adieu.

"I will thank you to spell my name correctly." She spelled Bonhoure aloud for us. "*L'Intransigeant* spelled it Bonheur."

O'Grady assured her we had better marks in spelling than *l'Intransigeant*.

Still she did not leave. That was the trouble with songbirds, O'Grady always said. They will offer a satisfactory solo, then sing encore after encore out of all proportion to the applause.

Mademoiselle Bonhoure continued to comment on l'affaire Landru in the form of footnotes, addenda, and a postscriptum that went on and on. She now began to tell us things we already knew, that everybody knew. She quoted news items we had written ourselves.

She was in the midst of a detailed diagnosis of her friend Mademoiselle Lacoste's perilous state of health and nerves due to the gruesome speculations concerning Landru's macabre style in ridding himself of the corpses of his fiancées when O'Grady interrupted to offer her a cigarette.

She did not herself smoke, but gave her permission for O'Grady to smoke, "By all means."

This was my signal to close the office window, which I did. Presently Mademoiselle Bonhoure was fanning herself with her gloves and referring compulsively to her watch. A coughing spell made it impossible for her to sing on. Eventually, inevitably, the songbird adjusted her feathered crest, made her excuses, and went in search of oxygen.

Six

THERE WAS NO CONTRACT between us, yet I considered her mine.

"Why not bring your clothes here?"

"I have none."

"You must have. Where do you keep your things?"

"What things?"

She owned nothing but a handbag, a Tarot deck, and a distraught lover. She left no other clues of her existence in my queer-shaped room than a sense of wonderment when she was gone.

"Where do you go?"

"I work."

"Where?"

"I am a model. I pose."

"For Anacréon?"

"He does not work now. He has got some money for a war monument and spends it for cocaine."

(Let it alone, I told myself—ask nothing more.)

"Where were you last night?"

"La foire aux modèles."

Every Monday at the intersection of rue de Grande Chaumière

and boulevard Montparnasse (or in winter, in front of the académie de la Grande Chaumière) painters gathered to examine the crop of models. I thought of la foire as a flea market where girls were sold instead of bric-à-brac. I might have bought a girl there myself (but not to paint her) except that I had a girl, or so I thought. (Without agreeing to stay with me, she stayed with me.) A painter would follow his prospective selection into one of the empty rooms of the académie where the girl would undress and he would examine her. If she was to his liking they would probably settle for the standard fifteen francs for three hours—perhaps more, if more was expected of the model than a pose.

"Le foire? At night?"

When I was agitated about her absence for a day (or worse, a night) she might offer a rambling monologue of nonsense (on this occasion accompanied by a cheese) to deceive me or simply to distract.

"I brought you a chèvre but forgot to buy bread—we can eat it with biscottes."

"Where did you get the money?"

"The cheese vendor has a birthmark shaped like a heart, a lucky thing for him, in love." (In love with whom?—who was this cheese vendor?) "Your landlady must be a sorcière with that cast in her eye. There are more black cats on rue Tiquetonne than any street in Paris. They say the Seine will flood in spring because the fish are swimming belly up. Do you know what the mole on the back of my knee means?" And she would show the mole to me, to fix my thoughts on her flesh. "It means I am clairvoyante."

She was clairvoyante enough to know that her lifted skirt would make me want to lift her skirt higher to see more of her than a mole. I could no longer think of the cheese vendor or Anacréon or la foire aux modèles. She moved her legs apart so that I might stare at her thighs.

It was as pointless to ask her who as how many: she was not given to admission, except admission to this place between her legs where a legion of lovers had preceded me. I pushed the skirt above her waist and lifted her by her buttocks to kiss the insides of her thighs.

"Do you like me a little?"

She did not expect an answer: my lips expressed my delight in her. When my trousers were unbuttoned she took hold of the spike of cartilage I intended to fasten her with (nail her to me, to my bed) and laughed at it.

"What a queer machin a man's machin is."

I reached into the tuft and spread her quaint envelope of entry: "No more strange than this pink crevasse of yours."

We played then with words and one another until my machin filled her crevasse and I became a prisoner of my own device.

But when release had come and passion's flood subsided, the flood of questions was restored.

"What was it like with my father?"

"Your father?" She was not given to admissions. "What has your father to do with what we do?"

"You were with him once."

"An old man?"

"He was not old. No older than Anacréon."

"Anacréon? Il est malade, he takes cocaine. He is too far gone"— she took hold of my limp machin—"to get it up."

She could be crude, but even her vulgarity excited me and immediately the limp thing in her hand came alive.

Once, as a variation, she made available to me another and smaller crevasse, saying, "This is the place your friend and his friends use."

Use? With her? "What friend?"

"The one in velveteen with eyelashes like mimosa."

Gabriel. I could not be jealous of a pederast, only jealous of his eyelashes if she preferred them to mine.

I entertained the deception that she belonged to me because she lay crushed below me and my weight was greater, but her ankles were locked at the small of my back: I belonged to her.

Proof of her infidelity were the papillons d'amour (crab lice) that migrated from her pubis to mine and obliged us both to powder ourselves with disinfectant (we powdered one another) for a week. After that I sniffed the air when she came in, trying to smell the man on her, certain she had hurried from some encounter without using the bidet.

"You say you were at la foire but there is no one at la foire at night." (I was back at la foire aux modèles.)

"Personne? I was there."

"With whom?"

"Personne. Your scar turns scarlet when you frown like that. Do

American women wear the same brassières we wear? A pigeon flew into the studio today and broke its wing, the worst kind of malchance."

"Whose studio?"

"Where I posed. I am a model, I must pose."

The word for model is mannequin, a thing placed in any position and anything done to it, limbs arranged to suit its arranger's purpose and pleasure. I pictured her legs apart.

"Listen," she said, an attempt to distract, "if you see a falling star behind the Sacré-Coeur close your eyes and say, 'Que Dieu me protège.'"

"You say you don't believe in God."

"You may pray to the Devil for the same protection but that gentleman exacts a higher price."

Her gentlemen. Those she worked for did not necessarily sculpt or paint.

She pretended to foretell fortune in the shapes of clouds or see calamity in the habits of cats; she could trace the limits of disaster along the edges of wine stains or from the lines in the palm of a hand. "Do not be so superior," she warned if my smile was inappropriate. To ignore the supernatural was a dangerous bêtise of mine: I was naked and vulnerable to the most commonplace (but invisible) horrors. Unlike her, I could not consider a birthmark a blessing or a mole as a sign. To me good luck was having gained this girl, bad luck was having caught crabs from her.

"Beware of an uncaged bird indoors. It could break a wing or worse. The death of a bird means death."

"For whom?"

"If you do not believe me, tant pis. Others know better than you. He was as frightened as I was when the bird broke its wing."

"Who?"

She put cheese in my mouth as if feeding a bird to keep me from repeating who. She searched my pockets for chewing gum, humming the air to a song she knew I liked; she examined my shirt for missing buttons. If she could distract or enchant me in no other way she lured me into the distracting enchantment of bed. If then I tried to speak I received the taste of her tongue and sucked forth her breath only. After that there was no asking, except for bliss—but bliss is a given of coition and comes to an end.

While she dabbed at our intermingled liquids with a cloth I might again become curious but she would manipulate my flaccid machin still wet from its adventure to direct my interest elsewhere. Invariably the thing would turn hard in her tender possession and rise to the occasion, ready to return to its oubliette.

Seven

GABRIEL THOUGHT OF Miss Toklas as a predatory bird because of her sharp features and dangerous look. To me she was a sparrow. True, she had a hawkish profile and an unsettling stare, but the kindergarten bangs (she cut her hair herself, as well as Miss Stein's) made her face into that of a child.

Miss Stein was an owl.

It was slower going to know Miss Toklas, but slowly I began to know her. At first she would talk to me of her difficulties with domestic help, or the problem of typewriting Miss Stein's manuscripts with a broken fingernail, but eventually she permitted me the rare privilege of her kitchen. She began to tell me sly tales about the wives of the famous and guests of secondary importance she sat with while Miss Stein entertained. She never spoke of herself until much later. Once she said to me: "Some day you will remember this time as being worth whatever it was worth for having known Gertrude." Knowing Gertrude Stein was worthwhile indeed, and so was knowing Miss Toklas, but I could not at that time tell Miss Toklas of the girl I knew or anything worthwhile about myself.

Miss Stein liked to walk in the Luxembourg Gardens with Gabriel or with me, never both of us. Later Miss Stein owned a dog she called Basket and walked her dog in the Luxembourg Gardens, but when I

knew her she liked to walk a young man. For a long while Gabriel
was out of favor with Miss Stein because he had been to Natalie
Barney's Greek temple on the rue Jacob and Miss Stein had naturally
heard of it via the grapevine. Miss Stein and Miss Barney pretended
to be friends and ate chocolate cakes together at Rumpelmayer's pâtis-
serie but they did not like one another and were rivals. Eventually
Miss Stein forgave Gabriel his dereliction but for a time she was not at
home to him.

We were walking in the Luxembourg Gardens and Miss Stein
remarked on the sailor blouses the little boys wore and that in a photograph of Lenin as a boy in Russia he wore just such a sailor blouse.
(That was the only thing I ever heard her say about Lenin. During
the Great War Lenin had got safely through Germany in a sealed rail-
way car from Switzerland where he had been in exile, and now he
was back in Russia leading the Bolshevik movement.) Miss Stein did
not talk about politics nor care about them any more than she cared
about what she called newspaper news unless it was gossip and only
incidentally got into the newspapers.

It was during that walk with Miss Stein I received my first and
only instruction in the art of writing. O'Grady had taught me several
lessons in the art of journalism, but that was not the same thing. Miss
Stein was concerned with literature, seriously so, for she loved above
all things to write and to talk about writing. The lesson I refer to took
place I believe in the summer of 1921. (It must have been before I
acquired the bicycle, and Fleur came, for after that my days were
taken by Fleur and my thoughts were of her only.) Anyway it was
summer because the weather was warm enough for us to sit on a park
bench. I see us there now: sparrows and pigeons all around, I beside
Miss Stein and several of my manuscripts on Miss Stein's lap.

(There were special places in the Luxembourg Gardens where
Miss Stein sat with each separate young man. Gabriel told me she
always took him to the circle of benches under the scowling bust of
Paul Verlaine and Hemingway she took to sit in the vicinity of
Stendhal and Flaubert. There was a literary lesson in her choices. She
always took me to sit in the folding chairs around the boat basin or on
the spectators' benches in front of the marionette pavilion when the
marionettes were not playing.)

The sparrows came right up to our bench, to our toes, begging,
looking us straight in the eye, unafraid. Paris was their city, and still
is. There were squirrels too, and with the excuse of the marauding

squirrels and birds Landru often had the opportunity to address a casual remark to a woman on a park bench in this very park. "Audacious little beggars, aren't they?" he might say to a woman much like Miss Stein but certainly not Miss Stein. The woman might venture a reply: "Now that the guns are silent, the birds and squirrels are back."

What park could be more innocent and conducive to pleasantry than the Luxembourg Gardens?

"You are very fond of capitals and commas," said Miss Stein.

"I try to put commas where I would like the reader to pause."

"Yes. But are you certain the reader needs a comma to tell him to pause?"

"I don't know."

"I will tell you then. A reader should read words not commas. You are a reader and do you read commas when you read?"

"I don't know if I notice them when I read."

"There you are," she said, for that explained it.

"What about periods?"

"A period," she said, "is something else."

"And capitals?"

"Capitals were invented by the authorities who decide one word is more important than another. Look at the Germans and what has become of them because of capitalization."

Miss Stein did not like the Germans and she believed much could be explained about Germany through German use of gothic print and capital letters.

Then she told me I was at home in a world with four corners and gently but truthfully told me she did not like any of my stories except the one about the Frenchman who became an executioner because his father and grandfather had been executioners.

"That really happened," I said.

"There you are."

I was still puzzled about periods being something else and Germans being Germans because of capital letters. I thought if I could understand Miss Stein I might learn to be a writer but I was not convinced my stories were as unsuccesful as she said. Young writers are not easily convinced they are not writers born.

(My father and Mr. H. L. Mencken had met in Baltimore and were becoming friends. Eventually I sent my stories to Mr. Mencken, who was a writer and an influence on writers of an entirely different stripe from Miss Stein. He sent them back to me without comment, which is perhaps the kindest thing he could have done.)

After returning my stories to me Miss Stein began to talk about writing and painting and how a writer writes and how a painter paints. I wish now I had listened but I was still hearing what Miss Stein had said about my stories. I was unhappy that afternoon to have discovered she thought I was not the kind of writer, her kind, that I aspired to be.

When she finished talking about my writing and Writing (with a capital letter) we both watched a little boy in a sailor blouse like Lenin's trying to shoo pigeons from an area marked PIÉTONS INTERDITS. The boy's nurse had told him not to walk there because it was forbidden to walk on the grass, and he was concerned that the pigeons ignored the warning.

"Les pigeons sur le gazon, malheur!" he said, shaking one hand downward in that loose French gesture of despair.

Miss Stein repeated what he said in English: "Pigeons on the grass, alas." Later she wrote it (without the comma) and it became a phrase almost as famous as "a rose is a rose is a rose." I had heard the remark at the same time as Miss Stein but I would never have thought to translate it and write it down. This may have been what Miss Stein was trying to tell me that afternoon.

Eight

MADAME VITRINE could not fail to remind me she knew about Fleur.

"I understand your room is now occupied by a second person."

The word personne in French can mean somebody or nobody. Fleur came and went as she would, was there or not, like an apparition. I was obliged to confess that a girl sometimes came to visit me.

Madame Vitrine, for all her outward fussy manner and baleful eye, was not truly concerned with our illicit relationship—how could she be, in that illicit quarter?—but she intended to collect a supplemental rent as long as I harbored a deuxième personne in my room at her hotel. The supplement was only half again the very small rent I paid, and I would have paid far more than that (but did not tell Madame Vitrine this) to keep Fleur with me. Once I had paid the extra rent Madame Vitrine brought two fresh towels to the room instead of one.

I pointed out the two towels to Fleur, a sign that we truly lived together now. But Fleur was not thinking of that.

"What did she say about my papers?"

"Nothing."

"She is obliged to ask for them if I am registered here."

"Then show them to her."

"Perhaps she will not ask." Fleur chewed on a fingernail.

"If she asks, you need only show them to her."

"No."

"Why not?"

"Anyway, I think she will not ask. Why should she ask? I am personne."

"Une deuxième personne," I reminded her.

While Fleur was at the WC on the landing I looked into her handbag—for papers, for I know not what. I may have been looking for letters from a lover. Or money: there was some money, but not much. I found no papers of any kind except the empty wrappers from the sticks of American chewing gum I gave her. But there were no other papers. My curiosity was as relentless as my jealousy. Where did she keep her papers? In France everyone is obliged to carry identification papers. Without papers a person does not legally exist.

"Elle veut en profiter de tout le monde" was Fleur's opinion of Madame Vitrine. She wants to take advantage of everyone for her own profit. Mr. Maynard Keynes made the same statement, the only French phrase he uttered, the day he explained economics to my father: "Les Français veulent en profiter de tout le monde."

Shopkeepers and landlords have that fixed attitude and unique business philosophy I would consider typically French. Since they do not really want to rent or sell, they rent or sell with misgivings and ill grace. They understand they must exchange or serve or conclude a sale in order to make a profit (en profiter, rather), but the profit-making process hurts. A shopkeeper or landlord will sometimes cheat for two centimes when he could with little more effort earn two francs. If a foreigner or tourist accepts this, grudgingly or not, and pays the two centimes (a tax unfairly levied and without legal sanction) he can live in France among the French as agreeably as in a country where business transactions follow the normal course.

At the time I rented my room at Madame Vitrine's hotel I was assured the room was heated. But that was in summer when the room was heated by the sun. It was not until my father came to Paris and remarked that my room was a fine garret for a starving poet that I examined the place with a critical eye.

"Where is your stove?" he asked me.

"I cook on a spirit lamp."

"I mean for heat, not cooking. A spirit lamp will not warm you this winter."

It was a fact I had given no thought to. (I was eighteen at the time, and this was my first independent lodging.) The season had changed from late summer to fall and the winds leaked through the gaps in the windowsills and under the eaves. It was high time to consider the winter.

We went together to confer with Madame Vitrine.

"My son has no heat in his room," my father informed her.

"Ah, yes," said she, meaning yes there was no heat. (If she had meant yes there is heat she would have used the French si, which is a yes that means no.)

"This young man, my son, cannot survive in a room without proper heating."

"Yes," said Madame Vitrine, meaning yes I could not. The cast in her eye seemed to engulf all of her face, and her face became a crystal ball in which we were welcome to seek our fortunes.

"What do you propose to do to heat the room?"

There was a long pause during which Madame Vitrine's very French face became very French again, shrewdly so. Her eyes closed as if to conjure up an image of fire; she spent a silent moment contemplating heat. Eventually she opened her eyes, nodding to herself, having made a large and satisfactory decision. She invited us to follow her to the cave beneath the hotel. "Venez," she said, almost as coquettish as the street girls saying, "Tu viens?"

We descended into a dank tomb below street level. She led the way with an oil lamp and let the yellow light play lovingly over her collection of a lifetime's miscellanea.

How happy Landru would have been at the sight of this accumulation of mostly useless worldly goods. During the war he pretended to be an attic inspector employed by the government to check attics for fire hazard, now that Paris was being bombarded by explosive shells. Householders were eager to allow him to carry off their excess furniture and other inflammable items in order to avoid a fine levied by the pompiers. Landru would then show up with a large cart, pulled by his two sons who served as dray horses, carrying off the salable objects their father contrived to condemn.

We were immediately walled in by great stacks of newspapers which must have represented daily reading matter from as far back as the belle époque (for wartime journals were only one sheet thick due to the paper shortage, and there was no shortage of paper here). Madame Vitrine had kept every issue of the magazine *l'Illustration* ever issued, encased in yearly bundles bound with twine and labeled in descending order: 1918, 1917, 1916, 19 . . . .

She still owned her scarred chopping block split down the middle as if by a bolt of lightning: on it sat a sinister-looking birdcage full of rat bane. (We heard rats, but did not see any.) We did see our three ghostly reflections in a cracked chiffonier mirror—Madame Vitrine smiled into it, as women will, but her smile was broken by the crack. We came upon a collection of shaving mugs and vases de nuit and porcelain bidets that must have leaked or were too chipped to serve. I saw a slop jar full of bits of candles that might someday be melted down to create one full candle, restored.

There was a stack of mattresses, water-stained or with the stuffing oozed out at one end, along with the burst sausages of ruined bolsters like mummies come undone.

It occurred to me the packing cases, all, were shaped like coffins: upon them were piled damaged café tables, then legless chairs stacked upon chairs without backs (the wicker torn open where someone had gone through the seat)—the ranks of broken furniture so like a dress parade of wounded veterans hopelessly scarred (les gueules cassées), or limbs missing in battle, or dead. Buried deeper in this inventory of war and peace and war again was a Franco-Prussian military helmet set upon the headless neck of a dressmaker's mannequin: the rusted musket next to it—from an even earlier war, or revolution—seemed tame and harmless beside the spiked helmet set upon a lifeless figurine.

My father stumbled over a bag of cement turned hard as stone, cursed, and jumped back as if he had stepped upon a corpse.

Here is a sample of French thrift. For some time the café-bar and one lower floor of the hotel had been furnished with electricity (this did not extend to my fifth-floor room, nor to the water closets on the landings), and Madame Vitrine had collected all the used electric bulbs and kept them in a basket, in case there might be a flicker of light left in one of them.

We passed through veils of cobwebs into a separate mausoleum housing sealed steamer trunks Madame Vitrine had confiscated in lieu of rent when precipitate guests departed in the night: they might have contained bodies, or bones. (Landru was a compulsive collector of trunks, full of the gear and garments of the women he collected.) The compartment beyond had been a wine cellar once, and now the racks were laid with empty bottles on their sides the way they had lain when alive and full of wine.

At the last barrier boxes were full of smaller boxes, with even smaller boxes inside these—a final clutter of emptiness, but quite packing full. This was a Frenchwoman's reservoir of hopeless trivia and treasure, a subterranean oubliette where nothing was entirely forgotten, yet nothing allowed to escape.

Next to a pile of warped slats from a dismembered draft-beer tonneau stood an abandoned stove. Madame Vitrine circled it with her lamp so that we might see the black thing in the round. It was a potbellied model that burned either coal briquets or wood.

"Yes," said my father.

It was an apparently sturdy apparatus—no noticeable damage, unlike most all else in this cave—and might serve. Madame Vitrine carefully made her offer. There was a chimney outlet in my room. If I (but she addressed herself to my father, who looked far more prosperous) would agree to purchase a length of stovepipe and pay for the installation I could use this excellent stove to heat my room.

At first my father was perplexed by the inverted French logic behind the offer. But Madame Vitrine chattered on so reasonably and irresistibly right—she had convinced herself of the fairness of the affair, and so convinced us—that my father agreed.

"D'accord," said he. So be it.

Thus the ancient stove was rescued from its dungeon and restored to life. The waiter, Georges, and I carried it from belowground up the narrow stairs to my fifth-floor room—a morning's work, in slow stages. There it was set on a platform of bricks where the floor sagged, at the apex of an isosceles triangle. The chambermaid removed a coating of rust and soot.

The stovepipe was not all that expensive, and the installation by a jack-of-all-trades from the rue de Turbigo cost ten francs and a pourboire of rum. Madame Vitrine further allowed me (my father, rather) to purchase the warped slats from the cave as fuel, and we set a fire as soon as the pipe was attached. It drew beautifully, and warmed my spirit as well as my dwelling space. Restif de la Bretonne might well have stirred its coals in his day. An antique that functions as well as it pleases the eye is a rare treat.

The transaction was a lesson to me, if not to my father. I think my father believed in his heart of hearts he had once again got the better of a woman. But he did not know Madame Vitrine. Indeed, the stove worked far better than any of us had anticipated (and worked beautifully to my advantage in a way I will relate). Not long after my father sailed for the United States, Madame Vitrine found herself obliged to increase my rent. The increase was negligible, a sum carefully calculated not to provoke disagreement yet enough to reward her for the trouble to think of it. I paid, of course, as she knew I would.

"Vous voyez," she explained, "now that the room is heated it is worth more money."

Winter had come without my knowing—but Fleur knew. At first a wet grey fog enshrouded Paris, but I saw Fleur against the grey and forgot to feel the damp chill that penetrated the refrigerated city's walls and paving stones. My room was warm ("le coeur chaud de Paris," she called it: the warm heart of Paris), and Fleur was drawn to warmth.

There were times, I must admit, when she came into my arms only to be warmed. So be it. *Mine* was the wedge-shaped sanctuary she returned to—not Anacréon's hearth, or another. If there were winter, tears to shed (and she did weep, from the cold or from miseries beyond my ken) it was my chest she wept against until my shirt was damp from her tears. She might come suddenly awake at night sobbing, and I was there to calm her with caresses.

I would come awake before she did, alerted when I heard her breath pick up, the little gasps that grew staccato in tune to a frantic heartbeat—but worse, when she ceased to breathe at all, sinking helplessly into the pit of her dream.

"What is it?"

"I don't remember. Nothing. A nightmare. Hold me."

I held her.

"Has the fire gone out?"

The room seemed warm enough to me, the coals carefully banked, but I got up and drew the window shut against the night air, then poked at the coals in the great black stove.

"Warm me."

I came back to her and fed her the heat of my animal self. I inserted myself between her and her dreams, my flesh inside hers, to rekindle a glow that might replace the cold fear of a cauchemar.

Nine

THE FALL CROP of fruit and vegetables colored rue Tiquetonne, but the backdrop was as grey as ever—yet, a faint water-colored sun broke through the open space between rooftops.

"You see?" I said to her. "There's the sun to greet us."

She did not deign to look up, but glanced at me with cool distrust, the corners of her mouth turned down. She was wearing a rust-colored shawl that matched the market harvest. Her hair was long now, and drawn into a knot at the back of her neck: she wore no hat, ever.

"If we must picnic we could picnic in the bois de Boulogne," she said.

"You'll like where we're going better than the bois."

"Where is it?"

"Un joli nid dans la verdure." I would not tell her where. "A lovely nest in the greenwood."

"But where?"

If I had said Gambais she would not have come with me. Despite her dreams or lies of gypsy blood she was a Parisienne in her blood and bones, at ease on the streets of the city—cows and pigs along a country road did not attract her (there were more exotic beasts at the Jardin des Plantes)—the open and exposed countryside was a threat.

"Look into the cards," I teased.

This made her unhappier still. She did not like to be led and she could not tolerate mysteries, except mysteries of her own.

Nevertheless we went downstairs and she waited, twisting the fringes of her shawl, while I carried up the bicycle from Madame Vitrine's cave. (Fleur would never accompany me underground, into a cave or even the métro—nor did she ever, to my knowledge, take the métro herself.) In the street she walked beside but not with me, I pushing the bicycle toward the scent of a bonfire at the corner of rue Dussoubs.

The streets were jammed with ambling shoppers weaving past the pyramids of produce. Impossible to pedal through the maze, so I pushed the bicycle from stall to stall along the gutters slippery with discarded lettuce leaves and spoiled apples. A whole wheel of cheese rolled ahead of us, opening the way for my wheel. Mingled with the wood smoke was a trace of southern spice (or gypsy's scent) in the crisp autumn air.

My blood was up. So delighted was I in this morning's animated panorama I escorted Fleur through my corner of Paris in a lordly way. Her downturned mouth cast no pall over my exhilaration, my enthusiasm seemed to expand beyond every sign of her reluctance to accompany me. I was as young and green that bleak November day as I would ever be—and as happy.

(A short time ago as I sprawled widthwise across the bed she extracted from me a liquid spasm of pleasure, orally—like a servant girl, on her knees—to accommodate my whim or answer my question: "How then does Gabriel do it, with his friends?" If she could with such humility make love to me with her mouth, how could she not share my satisfaction in the prospect ahead?)

When we strolled past J.-J. Péru & Fils I for once was unaffected by the exterminator's sinister nature morte, though Fleur, perversely, paused at the display. At that moment not even J.-J. Péru could have convinced me that rodents crept from the sewers at night or that vermin were secreted in the crevices of my city. But Fleur lingered and looked. She was on more than nodding acquaintance with night creatures: she studied the expressions of trapped rats as if searching for a familiar face.

Fleur ordinarily shopped for us but now took no part in the purchases for our picnic. I bought thin slices of saucisson and a stained paper twist of Spanish olives. Fleur tagged behind offering no comment, mindlessly acquiescent or unwilling to provoke dispute. A net bag dangled from the bicycle handlebar containing two tomatoes, two apples, a Camembert, and a bottle of wine.

We came across a carrot-headed babe asleep against a mountain-side of carrots, a cherub by Raphael, a sight that caused Fleur to smile in spite of herself. I assumed she was reconciled now to the outing, had caught my mood and intended to share my bread and wine and beatitude.

At the rue de Rivoli I pedaled through a convoy of camions from the porte de la Villette where the slaughterhouses were (the truck ahead of us loaded with bones, just bones). Fleur balanced on the crossbar, enfolded in my steering arms, the net bag swinging in front, a long cylinder of bread strapped to the back fender like a stiff tail to our two-headed beast.

I remember we crossed the pont Alexandre III—Fleur's favorite bridge, not mine. I chose that florid span to please her, to wing across the Seine between two winged victories hoping to sustain a notion of flight.

At Invalides we took the train for Houdan—I have the note in my cahier (like Landru, I cling to such trivia): 2 round-trip tickets, Houdan, 9 F. There was a supplement for the bicycle, which traveled in the baggage car, suspended from a hook.

Fleur was instantly unhappy when she heard me ask for the tickets.

"Pourquoi Houdan?"

"I have to visit a place there."

"It is that place, is it not?"

I could not bring myself to say Gambais, nor would she—so we referred to it as l'endroit, the place.

"I must write about the place, so I thought to combine business with pleasure."

I took no pleasure in her expression.

"Besides," I went on, "we both need the country air."

The crease in her forehead deepened. "Someone said that to me once."

"Who?"

Of course she would not say. She would have had to utter a man's name, and she would never speak another man's name aloud in my presence.

She closed her eyes so as not to see him (it would have to be a man) and shook her head no at the image that remained. I was reminded of the same hopeless "no" Solange had cried out when transported to a maison close at Enghien to be made a prostitute. It occurred to me the image was something like the scene Solange had cried out against and that was what bedeviled Fleur's dreams and now cut a crease in her forehead as deep as a scar.

All right, I would say no more about country air. But Fleur's willfulness undercut my good intentions. When we got off the train at Houdan she announced, "I am afraid of this place."

Her reaction was beyond my understanding, and patience. "I knew the train would come to this place," she murmured.

Her logic was exasperating. "Of course it came here. This is our stop."

"I won't go to it."

She meant Gambais. I was annoyed with what I considered an excess of temperament but realized how strange and unexpected were the passions aroused by the subject of Landru. To utter the man's name could set Irene in a rage or fill another young woman with loathing. Miss Stein was jealous of the criminal's notoriety. The subject bored Miss Toklas and consumed Madame Vitrine with curiosity. Fleur knew I wrote newspaper articles about Landru but in a variety of ways made known to me his name was forever taboo between us.

I had thought we would picnic in the vicinity of Houdan, then bicycle to Gambais where I would attempt to inspect the notorious villa—if I could talk my way inside. Even from the outside I might come across some aspect of the scene worth writing about.

("Fat chance," O'Grady had warned me. "The scavengers have been picking the place clean for months.") I could at least look around, attempt to experience the ambience of the place. ("Do so, by all means," O'Grady had urged, "but at your own expense.")

"We'll eat nearby," I announced to Fleur. I was trying to express my wishes in a positive way, as one would with a wayward child.

"I have no appetite."

"Then we'll wait a bit." I was hoping to show firmness and determination. "We'll bicycle first."

"I don't want to move." She shuddered. Fleur would allow any liberty with her body, but her will could not be dominated. I decided she was working herself into a state purposely. I had wanted this to be a perfect day, a special occasion, une fête. Nothing was going right.

(The sun did not, as I promised her, break through the leaden sky.) I should have shown some sympathy for her evident dismay, but I was frustrated beyond understanding.

I had, I told myself, arranged this trip as much for her as for motives of my own. She did need the country air. (We are apt to consider the selflessness of our plans when making plans for others.)

"What do you want to do then?"

"I want to go back."

In a single instant my love lost a large measure of its devotion. She was, I discovered, pigheaded, superstitious, and dumb.

"Listen." This was my last effort: I assumed a majestic calm I did not feel. "We can have a pleasant meal in the woods over there."

"I want to go back."

My face must have blazed up or turned black—I felt its heat as I fumbled for her ticket. I thrust the return ticket into her hand and turned away, expecting her to say, "Wait!"

How little, at twenty, I knew about women. About Fleur I knew nothing at all. ("Female psychology is basic," said O'Grady, "except that it changes from female to female.") My experience with women had been limited to prostitutes, which can leave one with an artificial idea of feminine compliance. The odd bits and pieces of advice from my father formed a crazy quilt of mostly useless information, an outdated repertoire of clever but empty aphorisms.

In my arrogance and naiveté I truly expected Fleur to call out to me—but she did not. I mounted the bicycle with deliberate delay, to give her every opportunity to catch up with me. When she did not appear, I rode away slowly. Were her eyes filled with tears? I dared not look around, I would never know.

Ten

A THIN STREAM of smoke came from somewhere inside the garden and I could see dead roses beyond the open gate. A garde champêtre was urinating against the outside wall.

"Clues," said he when he saw me. "If they found a puddle of piss inside the gate they would bottle it for evidence."

I leaned my bicycle against the wall and casually followed him inside, past the DÉFENSE D'ENTRER sign. Neither he nor the old man tending the fire attempted to bar my way. The old man was frying sausages over a small fire.

"Took away the stove," he explained.

The authorities had hauled off the suspect stove, so now the cooking was done outdoors.

"Think what they would make of these ashes," said the garde champêtre, stirring in the ashes with a stick. He was a purple-faced topheavy peasant in ill-fitting khakis and kepi.

The old man smiled, but his smile had no teeth in it: "You should have seen what they did to my graveyard."

The cemetery was visible from the garden: he was the communal gravedigger, and came by each noon to keep the garde champêtre company. The two men seemed to extend a sly welcome, glad of an audience for a change.

The gravedigger was saying something about "that doctor," but he swallowed his words with his sausage.

"Dr. Paul," said the garde champêtre.

"Yes. The famous expert," said the gravedigger with his hollow smile and a wink at the word célèbre. "Dug up the bones in my bone-yard—all he found was the bones belonged there."

"How would he know the difference?"

"Looking for calcification, he tells me. Looking for certain size, certain type. There's your legitimate bones that belong in an ossuary and illegitimate that don't."

"What's an illegitimate bone?"

The garde champêtre made a foul joke about the bone a man car-ries between his legs, then the gravedigger said: "Illegitimate is a bone somebody put there that shouldn't. Our celebrated expert claims he knows his bones. Knows them backwards and forwards, knows who they came from and when and why. Bones he dug up in my ossuary wouldn't serve. All we had was old bones and what he needed was new, particularly ladies' bones—he can tell a male bone from a fe-male—and female was what he needed." The gravedigger tore into his sausage with vehemence. "Experts. Looking for bodies that didn't belong there. I told the famous expert I knew every square centimeter of my cemetery. Since '89 it was I myself dug every grave in it—I could account for every set of bones under the sod. 'Well,' says he, 'I am au-thorized.' Authorized and baptized. Notarized to inspect underground, see who we bury out here. 'Go to it,' says I. Nothing would do but that he puts a crew gravedigging for him. Nobody asks me naught, in my own graveyard. Amateurs. Dug six or so holes till they hit stone and started to sweat. Once they found out how hard gravedigging is they figured it was foolish to dig the whole place up. They poked around in the ossuary after that. One hole they dug was a fair job. About deep enough for a cesspool. So I later squared it off and that's where the croque-mort put Paulin, a pauper, when he buried him."

The garde champêtre laughed outright and the gravedigger—genial again, riding his success—offered me a sausage.

I had left the picnic with Fleur, but the bread was still strapped to the bicycle fender. We broke bread together and shared the sausages. A liter of vin rouge went around. No glasses, so I made a polite effort not to wipe the mouth of the bottle when it came my turn to drink.

"They were coming down from Paris by the trainload," said the garde champêtre.

"Experts?"

"No, tourists. Sightseers and vandals. Broke the house seals the first week, got in through the windows and stole everything in sight. The so-called experts didn't get here till the place was good and ransacked."

"What about the police?"

"I'm the police," said the garde champêtre. "I'm only one man. The vandals came down by the trainload."

"Scooped up everything that wasn't nailed down," said the gravedigger, "and some that was. Unscrewed the very doorknobs off the doors for souvenirs."

The two old-timers then talked of Landru, when he came to Gambais, before his arrest.

"Quiet type, with a beard shaped like a spade. Different lady friend every time he came to town."

"Quiet, all right," said the garde champêtre. "Now it's the lady friends that're quiet."

They laughed over this. A reference to Landru and his women could always provoke laughter, in male society.

"They say he's got a bigger one than normal," said the gravedigger when the discussion turned to Landru's charms. He pulled down his lower eyelid in an obscene way while the garde champêtre displayed a sausage for our benefit. They cackled together over the sausage's inordinate length.

Banter of this kind was commonplace. Since the trial date had been set, the Landru legend flowered anew. Newspapers were running Landru cartoons and the music hall comedians were making Landru jokes again.

I looked the house over from where we sat: an unremarkable weekend villa with shed attached and a wall around the garden. A summer place, it appeared forlorn now, at summer's end, with a garden of dried stalks and dead leaves and the remains of roses. Here and there the earth was turned up as if a gardener had begun to spade, but then lost heart. You might, from the outside, imagine some mysterious scenario played out behind the wall—but no, not really. So many Frenchmen build walls around their lives and property. A wall is a way of turning one's back.

The gravedigger was saying: "Don't believe everything you read in the newspapers."

"Mon vieux, I saw the smoke myself."

"So did I. I see smoke all the time." The gravedigger indicated the smoke from the cooking fire.

The garde champêtre, on an impulse, poured sausage grease over the smoldering coals. We were obliged to back away from the sudden blaze of spitting flame. A thick black stream of oily smoke billowed upward.

"Smoke like that? That smelled of meat?"

"So they all say—now. Now, every soul within forty kilometers wants to play witness at court. The whole village will troop to Versailles to swear they smelt flesh burning—to get their names in the Paris papers. Did you hear any one of them complain of burning flesh at the time?"

"Who would have thought our quiet gentleman from Paris was roasting his lady friends in the stove?"

"And the stove, mon bon ami. You saw the stove before they hauled it off. Where do you stuff a lady friend's cadaver in a stove that size?"

"He butchered the bodies first, of course."

"Of course. Not a trace of blood to be found—not a trace."

"They found some blood in the cave."

"Dog's blood, according to our celebrated expert Dr. Paul. The cave should have been swimming in blood. Ten women, my friend, *ten*."

"And one young man," I added.

"Carved them into pieces, did he?" the gravedigger went on. "Think of the torso, gentlemen." The gravedigger measured off the middle of his skeletal frame between shoulder and crotch. "Some of them fat women, we are told." With a wink at me he measured off the same area on the thickset garde champêtre. "Not that I believe everything I read in the newspapers."

"He chopped the torsos up, cretin."

"An arm or a leg, yes. I grant you an arm or a leg. Chopped off at the knee or elbow your cooking problem is the same as for that of a gigot of mutton. A head, also. A head I can accept." He took hold of the garde champêtre's head by the ears. "A head is no more problem than a rôti de porc."

"Imbecile." The garde slapped away the gravedigger's blackened hands.

"But the torso, nom de Dieu! Organs, ribs, the fatty matter. Think of the grease involved. Take the breasts and buttocks. Have you considered the lady friends' breasts and buttocks?" The gravedigger pulled his eyelid down in my direction, since the performance was for my benefit. "Try to picture what went on in there." He flipped a thumb at the house behind him. "Do you see Landru at work inside? Our mousy little Parisian cutting off those breasts into slices of saucisson. Then he attacks the fleshy derrière—do you see him carving the ass into stew meat?"

The garde champêtre put a finger to his temple and twisted his fist back and forth, the gesture for insanity.

The gravedigger was not deranged, but when he went on to describe the removal and roasting of female tripe, I began to sicken: I turned away without listening. The garde champêtre, too, had heard enough, and suddenly inquired of me, "You're from the newspapers, n'est-ce pas?"

How did he know? But they both knew, and had known all along. I was flattered to think I looked like a newspaperman instead of a stray tourist down from Paris for the day.

"You will want to see the inside of the villa," offered the gravedigger.

"Entry," the garde champêtre reminded him, "is strictly forbidden."

Nevertheless they both got up, the garde leading the way. I followed them. This was to be a museum tour with two guides. The garde champêtre unlocked the door, saying, "Pourquoi pas? All the world has seen the place. Enter, my friend. Take a look around the morgue."

"Morgue?" echoed the gravedigger. "Where are the bodies then? Take it from somebody who works in the métier—there's got to be bodies before you speak of the dead."

"The bodies," insisted the garde champêtre, "were made to disappear."

"That's what the newspapers tell us."

"That's what the indictment reads."

"Without bodies, my friend, all you've got is missing persons."

Thus we entered the realm of missing persons. A dank sour smell emanated from the open door. The empty rooms and stark staring windows gave the air of a place never lived in, ever. There were no blinds or curtains. Had there ever been?

"No," said the garde. "He never put curtains up."

A dullish stained light filtered through the dirty windowpanes.

My feeling about the place persisted: nothing could have happened here worth shrouding behind blinds. I was reminded of the abandoned house in Ys, near Grasse—my heritage from Maman—empty, desolate even of ghosts.

We left footprints trailing across the grey dust of bare floors. Our footprints might have been the first and last. In the stripped kitchen the garde pointed out a blackened flue where the stove pipe had been: the stove, of course, had been removed by the authorities. Without a hearth the room was neuter (like my own, before I acquired a stove, and a girl). I did not even know the room had been a kitchen until the garde champêtre informed me so.

If I had expected to skulk through the so-called house of death under a sense of menace, I was mistaken. A vague sensation of being watched was my only feeling. It occurred to me Fleur might have come here after all, despite her protests, and was now watching me vindictively through an opaque windowpane. But the eyes I felt on my back were only those of my two guides, checking the reaction of a Parisian journalist to the empty legend on display.

There was only a vacuum to react to. Holes in the scarred plaster might have been where gas jets once burned, or were never installed. No way to know how the villa might once have been furnished, for there were no furnishings nor any trace of them. The place had been thoroughly combed for evidence by the experts, then casually pillaged by everyone else. As the garde had remarked, even the doorknobs were missing.

"Why try the criminal in Versailles?" snorted the garde champêtre. "They should render justice here, where he did his dirty work."

"Because the assizes are held in Versailles," the gravedigger replied dryly.

As we wandered the barren rooms of the villa Tric the two men reminisced grimly about the Gambais of another age, a village of uncommon nightmares.

"In my father's day these affairs were settled out of court."

"You mean Bernard," said the gravedigger, "our half-wit woman chaser."

"Tried to rape a schoolgirl," the garde explained.

"Did rape a schoolgirl," said the gravedigger.

"The town council—fathers, all—took the delinquent to a barn where the doctor awaited him. No more raping schoolgirls after that."

"Would you castrate Landru?" asked the gravedigger slyly.

"Like the animal he is." The garde touched his own genitals for luck and drew the flat of his other hand across his throat: "Then I would assign Deibler to remove his mad dog's head."

The mention of a mad dog reminded the gravedigger of a laundress in Gambais who was bitten by a rabid dog on her way to the public lavoir.

"This happened," said he, "when I was but a child, before Docteur Pasteur's famous vaccine."

"Within a week the laundress contracted the disease and began to convulse. No one could get near her, no one dared. In her madness she fled to the mairie and there tried to bite the mayor."

"Would that she bite our present mayor," said the garde.

"They locked her up in the town hall—for there was no jail here then or now. You could not sleep for her screams. The men of Gambais gathered that night and stormed the mairie armed with clubs and mattresses for shields. In the mayor's very office she was clubbed to the floor and there covered with mattresses. The men pinned her down with their weight, others joined in, piled upon her to smother her. They crushed the life from her wretched body. My father dug the grave she lies in. I could show it to you."

"A good woman, too," remarked the garde champêtre, "before she was bitten by the dog."

"Perhaps Landru was bitten by a dog."

"Would that the dog had torn out his throat."

"He too is said to be a good man, a good father and devoted to his wife."

"Yes, so they say. Meanwhile he butchers ten other would-be wives."

"And one young man," said I.

We were standing outside, having completed our tour of an empty museum and back to our hollow beginning place.

"I hope you have got a story," said the garde champêtre.

"Don't put me in it," said the gravedigger.

I had got a story but not the story I had come for. O'Grady was right about the place: the experts and the populace had got to the story before me and obliterated all sign of it.

We passed the wine bottle a final turn and shook hands across the dead fire.

As I pedaled through the bleak village, farm hounds thirsting for blood howled at me from between the bars of iron gates (why had

the dogs not barked when I cycled by before?). I thought of the towns-
people who would testify against him—Landru was unfortunate in his
witnesses. The gravedigger had told me the villagers believed in witch-
craft until the Great War—and believed in it still, but no longer spoke
openly of witches. The local historians were capable of making substance out of shadows behind blank windowpanes. What tales would
be told in court of smoke and smells and nightmare screams?

There on the station platform at Houdan was the net bag of
lunch, abandoned. Flies buzzed around the ripe Camembert oozing
through its paper wrapping. I took the train—with the day's sad un-
eaten lunch on my lap—back to Paris. The hangover of our lovers'
quarrel ruined whatever pleasure I might have taken in this trip. The
excursion had come to nothing. A lingering sense of evil besieged my
soul, yet I arrived at Invalides without a scrap of evil to report.

Eleven

I WAS PREPARED to greet her with silence (not certain what we had quarreled about, or even if we had quarreled) but she was not there to meet my silence. She may have been in the WC. While I awaited her return I practiced an attitude, but she did not return. In case she should be playing cache-cache with me I pulled open the closet door; I even flipped back the sheet of our ill-made bed: the closet held my yellowing tennis jacket, slack, missing a torso; in bed I found only the streaked trace of her menstrual blood.

Trying to make sense of her absence I glanced at my wrist to record the hour—but I had forgotten to wear my wristwatch in this morning's haste. Nor was it on the night table beside the electric torch where I had left it.

The three following days (and nights, particularly) I dwelt in a wedge-shaped space alone. I did not leave the room, I would not search the streets of the city for her. With the door unlocked, slightly ajar, I waited. I indulged my hurt with self-pity until the wound was made raw. The hurt became jealousy compounded with rage. I began to hate her for her deception and spent my thoughts working at that hate.

Until now I would not have realized (or acknowledged) that her short neck was truly unattractive. And how annoying to contemplate those ankles in a basin of water (when she was cold her circulation was poor) swollen out of all proportion to her slim legs. When she pouted her childish lower lip showed a guttersnipe vulgarity. She chewed chewing gum incessantly. She did not often bathe.

Meanwhile my loneliness was abysmal. I owned two knives now, two forks and two spoons; I had bought a second cup, another wineglass. Because of the solitary sound of my own mastication in an empty room I ate only an occasional biscotte and twice made tea.

I let the fire burn down in my famous stove until I felt chilled, then went to bed. When I could sleep (at night, never) I slept in the milkwater light of a winter afternoon. I drank cognac in bed.

When I was awake the room itself was a mausoleum of rebuke and reminder. I had taken down the hieroglyphics of my trade, stripped the room of my news clippings at her request, and left the walls the way she wanted them, bare. Thus a monk's cell had become a cell at la Santé. The walls were grey with one large stain as if designed by Picasso (a disfigured female face) that did not bear staring at for a three-day retreat.

For those three days I had the same thundering headache and twice suffered inexplicable nosebleed impossible to staunch that left the floor spotted with my blood just as the bed was stained with hers.

Waiting, I planned long cruel speeches terminating our attachment.

"So you're back?" I said aloud in the empty room.

She was contrite, trembling from the cold. She waited for me to take her in my arms and warm her, but I would not. I stood apart, arms crossed like a shield between us, maintaining that severe expression I had practiced in the mirror.

"I'm sorry," I could hear her say. "I was wrong."

But I continued to stand coolly aloof awaiting her explanation. She would confess the theft of my watch. Never mind that, I would say, still waiting. Of course she would not tell me where she had been, with whom she had bedded—very well, I would tell her, in any case, "It's over between us."

She wept—or would have wept, had she been there.

Twelve

IT WAS NOT FLEUR who brought my seclusion to an end but
Georges the barman delivering a pneumatique from Miss Stein. The
pneumatique was an invitation but a pneumatique from Miss Stein
was more in the way of a summons. I was shy of Miss Stein because
of the difference in age and position, but was drawn by her. I would
of course attend her soirée.

Even now, with the pneumatique in my pocket (the hour was
not specified), I lingered uncertainly in the Luxembourg Gardens
afraid of being the first to arrive at her door. Then I saw Gabriel
walking along the rue Guynemer. He was wearing a corduroy jacket
over his shoulders like a cape. Gabriel was too young to carry a walking stick, but he carried one. He was with a young man or I would
have called to him and joined him. They were obviously headed for
27, rue de Fleurus, so I followed.

I was immediately at ease when Miss Toklas met me at the door.
Though many found her hard gaze intimidating, I never did.

"Dottore," she said, and took my hand.

I was late instead of early. The studio was already filled with
guests—not that my tardiness mattered (I am sure neither Miss Stein
nor Miss Toklas took notice of it). Miss Toklas attached me to a
gold-bearded German authority on parasitic worms, and hurried off.

I was too polite to break away from him and so I suffered through a learned discourse on a species of tapeworm that makes its home in the human intestinal wall. To purge myself of the German I searched for Gabriel, a friendly face, but Gabriel and his companion had burrowed into the crowd. Miss Stein's guests aligned themselves in shifting centers to talk, then realigned. The obvious maneuver was to shift circularly in the direction of the circle around Miss Stein herself.

Miss Stein sat in her corner of the studio like the Lipchitz bust of her—a monument carved from a single piece of stone that had never been and would not be shifted. Lipchitz, in fact, was part of the circle closest to Miss Stein. (Anacréon, who had sculpted her less substantially, was not present at the soirée.) Those she permitted to linger nearest her were intimates of long standing, and acolytes. Guests of secondary interest, and wives, entered the charmed circle only long enough to be acknowledged with a word or briefly entertained by a shrewd observation: when Miss Stein was done with them they were led offstage by Miss Toklas to be deposited elsewhere, as the German had been.

My shyness kept me from approaching Miss Stein under these circumstances. I would, I knew, manage a polite exchange with my hostess before the evening's end—meanwhile I kept my place shielded behind the thickset German professor of worms, and from there—in the tradition of journalists always—observed and listened.

Genius was the word I heard most often. Miss Stein was considered—and was, I think—a genius by those who knew her. She bestowed the same title on several of those who bestowed the title on her. Genius, if not in full flower (Braque was there, Picasso was absent), was indeed present in the studio that evening. Perhaps even the German was one, for genius is not always made known by proclamation, but I think his field was too narrow for the term. I sometimes wonder—too late to create an issue of it—if Miss Toklas, sitting quietly at her needlepoint (unpainted, never cast in bronze or carved in stone), was not as much a genius in her way as Miss Stein with her needlepoint of words. Flamboyant reputations are the reputations that endure.

Miss Stein sat beneath the portrait Picasso had painted of her, her favorite of all the famous likenesses. Picasso at the moment was in pursuit of a new mistress—I overheard Miss Stein say—and that was why he was not among the guests. A good many painters did attend Miss Stein's soirée, however, but I did not always recognize them.

Braque was a large man in a small chair. You knew Braque because he looked like a Braque, constructed in cubes, so heavy as to
seem clumsy, but he sat lightly enough in the fragile chair assigned
to him, holding the thin-stemmed wineglass delicately between his
thick fingers. He was talking to Marie Laurencin, the only woman in
the room who wore a hat, a hat that resembled a cloud—he seated, she
standing, a reversal of male-female protocol, but Braque had been
wounded in the war and perhaps needed the support of a chair, however small.

Matisse was there. He did not look like a Matisse. He was a small
bearded man accompanied by (I assumed, but you never knew with
painters) Madame Matisse. His manner was unexpectedly subdued for
a so-called fauve. I must have anticipated something wild—thinking
painters were inevitably as forthright as their pictures (some were,
like Braque and Picasso)—but Matisse in person was colorless and
tame.

There were as well the obscure guests who would become famous
in time for reasons no one—not even Miss Stein, who saw in them
something but did not always know what—could foretell. One of these
was an Indo-Chinese poet who held Miss Stein's attention momentarily.
He was known as Nguyên Ai Quoc, or Nguyên the Patriot, but would
some years later change his name to Ho Chi Minh. I overheard a fragment of his interview with Miss Stein.

"Most recently," he informed her, "I am reading *la Peau de
chagrin.*"

Miss Stein was trying to impress upon him the error and waste
of reading Balzac.

"I have read Mr. Jack London," said the Oriental gentleman, "but
only in translation."

"Then you must learn English. French is literary in a French
sense only, English is international."

He thanked her with a bow lower than is seen in the West, and
presented her with a privately printed volume of his verse. She in
return gave him a copy of John Fox Jr.'s *The Trail of the Lonesome
Pine.* I will never know if either of them ever lifted the cover of the
other's gift.

Then he was passed on to Miss Toklas who passed him on to me,
as soon as the German was passed to an unsuccessful Hungarian
pupil of Matisse. Miss Toklas introduced me as a newspaperman, and

with elaborate courtesy the Asian poet showed an interest in my profession. When I in turn asked him about his own métier he told me he had been trained as a cook at l'école Escoffier.

"So far"—he smiled, mocking himself—"I have been engaged only as a plongeur."

Plongeur means diver, and in this sense means dishwasher in a restaurant.

I was intrigued by this ascetic Oriental transported from Indo-China to the rue de Fleurus. He appeared older than his thirty years, no doubt because of his wisp of Confucian beard. He was exquisitely polite, and deferred to me, his junior—an unfamiliar and flattering experience—throughout the conversation. He did with modesty mention a work he had submitted to the Versailles Conference.

"A poem?"

A neat smile flickered above the wisp. I had misunderstood him. "A memo only. Its unmanageable title is 'Un memoire pour l'autonomie du Peuple Vietnamien.' "

The memorandum had received no noticeable enthusiasm at the conference. He suggested I might like to write about the subject for my "newspaper." Under the sway of his ritual politesse I said I was interested, and even went so far as to take his address (c/o Monsieur Hasfeld's bookshop on the quai Jemmapes, a celebrated rendezvous for revolutionaries), but of course I did not write the newspaper piece on Vietnamese autonomy. I could hear O'Grady say, "What about Irish autonomy, if you're so concerned about the downtrodden?" A pity. In the context of history the world would have been saved much grief and bloodshed if the Versailles Conference had taken up Nguyên the Patriot's memorandum.

Isadora Duncan's brother Raymond was at the party. He had fashioned Miss Stein's sandals, and wore a similar pair beneath his Grecian toga.

He was a neighbor and a constant friend of Miss Stein. She was very pleased with the sandals but often became impatient with their maker and at the soirée took up the defense of psychoanalysis with him, though she did not herself believe in it.

"Psychoanalysis?" he asked the world at large, then answered, "I think not. We must live with our crippled selves and endure the age."

"But will the age endure us?" Miss Stein replied, meaning would she endure Raymond Duncan.

Isadora Duncan, I knew from news reports, was in Moscow, invited by the Bolsheviks to open a dance school there. (She arrived in the midst of riot and famine and came directly back to Paris, accompanied by her dangerously insane Russian lover.)

I met a cellist who was member of a string quartet that played impromptu midnight command performances for an insomniac audience of one, Marcel Proust. The cellist was with Valéry Larbaud, who thoroughly delighted Miss Stein by proposing to translate *The Making of Americans* into French—though that incomprehensible work had not yet been published in English.

I did not meet but overheard others being introduced to the princess of Polignac and the duchess of Clermont-Tonnerre. The duchess had just had her hair cut short and people were admiring her short hair, even Miss Stein—who paid no attention to la mode and wore her hair in the same bun Lipchitz had cast in bronze—and would very soon after have her own hair cut in the same style, by Miss Toklas. Someone said of Miss Stein's clipped hair it made her look like a Roman emperor and someone else said it changed her face from gothic to romanesque. She would wear it in that fashion for the rest of her life.

A British woman with a large diamond brooch took my hand warmly and held onto it while she told she had been the mistress of several of the men present and two of the women. Suddenly I was as lonely with my hand clutched in hers as I had been when alone in my room for three straight days. Could I guess who were the two women? I said I did not think I could.

In all of that diverse company perhaps the most popular guest was a young American cowboy, Gabriel's companion, whom I did meet when I finally reached Gabriel across the studio. The cowboy's name was Vander Clyde, but he—like Nguyên Ai Quoc—would in time change it. Even Miss Stein was taken by him, for she attracted and was attracted by Americans in Paris temporarily lost but soon to find themselves. "He has a radiance," she said to the princess of Polignac, "though an unholy radiance," and asked the princess to bring him to her. I had considered Gabriel the best-looking young man in Paris, but Mr. Clyde surpassed even Gabriel in physical symmetry and natural grace. You could not employ the word handsome to a male so particularly endowed: his face was no less than beautiful, his eyes especially so. He glanced at me only once, when we were introduced, his unswerving sky-blue stare oddly disconcerting, then he blinked once and a cloud passed between us. He could turn his radi-

ance on and off. Only his callused hands suggested the rough rider
from Texas. He was too vaporous and delicately made to associate with
the saddle.

"I worked circuses some," he informed Miss Stein. "Did a tightwire act."

This last may have accounted for his extraordinary grace of movement. His ambition, he revealed, was to work for the cirque Médrano.
At the time he was practicing daily in the bois de Boulogne, on a
length of cable he stretched between two trees: "I've scared the day-
lights out of dudes galloping by on their Sunday ponies."

Miss Stein's rich laughter rolled across the studio and several of
her guests picked it up, though they could not have understood the
cowboy's Texas English.

Gabriel had met him at Magic City, a transvestite bal musette, and
promptly installed the derelict westerner in his flat on the place Saint-
Sulpice. He was teaching him French, and the cowboy could converse
in that language with a clumsy accent (the only thing clumsy about
him) but he spoke to Miss Stein in English. She extended her tête-à-
tête with him for much longer than most new acquaintances were
tolerated. She was completely won over by him when he shyly admitted to having read as a boy *The Trail of the Lonesome Pine.*

I write at some length of this newcomer to Paris (he had arrived,
appropriately, by cattle boat), for he became a celebrated figure within
a few months, the toast of theatrical circles. He was indeed engaged
by the cirque Médrano, and appeared at leading music halls as well.
Gabriel told me about him much later (and I will refer to the cowboy
in another chapter: his apprenticeship, success, and treachery) with
some bitterness and not a little pain. But that night at Miss Stein's
party Gabriel was euphoric, basking in the light cast by his companion,
radiant himself. Gabriel's countenance never failed to register his feelings of the moment: love or lust or disappointment.

The sights and sounds from that evening at Miss Stein's return
to me as if I were there again, listening and watching in that intense
way I had in my twentieth year. I can still hear the wife of Matisse
telling the Indo-Chinese poet how to prepare rabbit with mustard
sauce, and the poet (and patriot) protesting gently that rabbit was not
much eaten in Indo-China. Matisse himself had somehow got locked
into conversation with the same forthright British woman who had
held my hand and told me of her lovers present, and was presumably
telling Matisse the same (she fussed with his collar points), but in

English, which the painter did not understand. An ethereal Italian painter of the futurist school followed the maid who was dressed like a nursing sister from circle to circle serving himself liberally from the hors d'oeuvre tray, as if he had not eaten for some time—and he probably had not. Two rather loud-talking obese Americans known as the Cone Sisters, in bright print dresses that clashed and complemented the paintings on the wall, dominated the opposite end of the studio from Gertrude Stein (they were her cousins from Baltimore, and she disliked them but found them amusing). Marie Laurencin had been drinking glass after glass of the little glasses of eau-de-vie until now she swayed visibly like a tree in the wind, her cloud of a hat slipping down her forehead. Braque noticed her unsteadiness and rose to offer her his chair, and put her into it as gently as one would tuck a babe into its crib—and there she slept, her hat in her lap.

Only the paintings on the walls are blurred, a kaleidoscope of raw colors from which I cannot distinguish any single work—except the portrait of Miss Stein (and Miss Stein representing the portrait by sitting below it)—without a catalogue, for I have a four-cornered mind (as Miss Stein pointed out) when it comes to paintings. But I hear again Miss Stein's unrestrained laughter punctuating the melodic streams of talk and my soul recaptures an impression of humanness, a very civilized and captivating humanness massed in one bright corner of Paris.

For me Matisse is still listening to the lady with the diamond brooch, the futurist pursuing the hors d'oeuvres, the duchess touching her hair obsessively to feel the newly feathered ends, and Braque stands towering over Marie Laurencin as solid as the cornerstone of the Banque de France. In the background I can see Miss Toklas peering out from beneath her bangs to see that everything went well, and everything did, except that the maid had to be sent for more bread (because of the Italian futurist), and even that was well because the amount of bread sent for was Miss Stein's barometer of a party's success.

On the periphery of Miss Stein's inner circle I picked up odd comments.

"As Lacassagne, the French criminologist tells us, 'Societies have the criminals they deserve.' "

"You believe, then, that we deserve Landru?"

"Deserve him? We would not be who we are without him."

"Who is Landru?" asked a puzzled Spaniard beside me and I replied, "A dealer in used furniture, accused of having murdered ten women."

"I am a painter," said he (he was the painter Juan Gris), "and I have been accused of worse."

The man who had quoted Lacassagne suggested Landru was a clown in mufti, and reminded him of a bearded Charlot (Chaplin), but his companion insisted that Landru bore a striking resemblance to Manet. Nguyên Ai Quoc offered up Landru as a by-product of capitalism, while Raymond Duncan, who wore only togas, stated that belts, braces, and celluloid collars created criminals and bureaucrats, and in this case created Landru.

I remember Miss Stein allowed the subject of Landru to continue for a time, a limited time—time enough for her to comment on his character.

"In his case the bureaucrat has carried the bourgeois ethic to its logical conclusion."

She also very generously informed those within her hearing that I was a newspaperman and that I wrote about Landru. Everyone at Miss Stein's gathering was known for something—even if known only as the wife of someone who was known for something—and now by pointing me out as Landru's biographer Miss Stein made me known for something.

Landru's trial was to begin the following week and the topic was a popular one so I was asked questions about the man and his crimes.

"The evidence," said I, "is circumstantial so far."

An American photographer, Man Ray, offered a quote from Thoreau: "Some circumstantial evidence is very strong, as when you find a trout in the milk."

I agreed, citing the discovery that Landru had bought round-trip tickets to Gambais for himself, but one-way tickets for the missing women.

"In that he was simply being French," said Juan Gris.

"Quel type!" said the Rumanian pupil of Matisse, while Man Ray was commenting on Landru's odd physiogomy: "That skull, the sockets of his eyes, the beard—an El Greco manqué."

There would have continued a lively discussion, for the subject of Landru never failed to cause a stir, but Miss Stein was operating her Japanese fan in a significantly agitated way—her impatience went at first unnoticed—and then she swiftly interjected a quote from Balzac: "L'homme c'est rien, l'oeuvre c'est tout," to a burst of laughter, led by herself. Before we realized what had happened the subject under consideration was the music of Eric Satie. I had had my moment center stage (in Landru's shadow) and now the spotlight was turned upon Miss Stein again.

I might have learned something useful about Satie's compositions, but whenever Landru entered my thoughts it was next to impossible to dislodge him. Physically I was a part of the wit and glitter assembled at the rue de Fleurus, but my reverie led me to places underground. I have always associated Landru with something subterranean: the métro stops connecting points of rendezvous, Madame Vitrine's haunted cave, the dark network of sewers leading to the Seine.

At length I shook myself free of these reflections and returned to the surface. Suddenly I was staring at the pictures on the studio walls. I remembered my original puzzlement and shock at seeing them— what had become of my discomposure? The colors had dimmed. It was not just the smoke between me and the canvases (a Danish choreographer had passed around a box of slim cigars and everyone was smoking—even Miss Stein and Miss Toklas—except Miss Laurencin and me), and I understood them no better, yet they now appeared strangely tame. As I squinted at the pictures against the shifting tide and sometimes eccentric posturing of the painters who had painted them, the works became not just acceptable, but—what is worse, from the daring painter's point of view—respectable. The startling accomplishment of a dozen apprentice geniuses was transformed into child's play—with the very children (but with cigars in their mouths) playing here together. I cannot credit Miss Toklas' eau-de-vie with this revised perception (and I smile now over my immature conclusions): to attend a brilliant soirée given by Gertrude Stein, to have just been separated from one's lover, to contemplate the shadow cast by a murderer in absentia against a studio wall hung with pictures was, I decided, the perfect way to study modern art.

I am particularly susceptible to the power of suggestion. Vibrations and echoes from our brief discussion of Landru continued to affect me: I almost felt the man's presence at the party, or expected his imminent arrival at Miss Stein's door. That door, so imposing (with its famous Yale lock, the only one in Paris), suddenly resounded with a thud. Any wonder I was shaken? I alone of the company stared in that direction—was I the only one who heard? I think I expected Satan himself.

The door opened from outside and the maid was standing there with her wicker cage of new-baked loaves. At her feet was slumped what appeared to be a pile of discarded clothing. The garments stirred.

The maid called out to Miss Stein: "He was here, Madame, when I returned." She put down her basket of bread and tried to help the man to his feet.

Suddenly there was a cry from the collapsed figure, a chilling moan not unlike the wail of a Greek tragedian at a moment of crisis. The creature sprawled in the doorway was Anacréon. He half-inserted himself into the studio, on all fours, with the maid pulling at his jacket like a bridle—a scene with any number of comic overtones, especially the stark white clown's face Anacréon displayed, his grotesque gestures: but his face was a dead thing, his expression a mask. Conversation lapsed and our heads turned to see Miss Stein's reaction.

The great lady sat immobile, her brow slightly wrinkled in surprise, yet with that regal self-containment she commonly maintained. Anacréon cried out again. Marie Laurencin was instantly awake asking, "Qui?" against the subdued murmuring around her. Even the Cone Sisters were silenced. The Hungarian student of Matisse went to help the maid: the man crawling into the studio was either deranged or in pain.

The two of them, with Gabriel now, got the disjointed sculptor to his feet. Then Gabriel and the Hungarian bore Anacréon to the waiting Miss Stein, where he slipped from their grasp and collapsed across her sandals. He was whimpering like an animal suffering some awful wound.

"Drunk?" asked the cowboy whispering, and Gabriel replied, "He cocaines himself." Many of the painters knew him. "Bewitched," said Juan Gris audibly. "Bewitched by that gypsy of his."

Miss Stein calmly awaited some word from the sculptor slumped before her. Rivulets of tears ran down his colorless corrugated face; he seemed to support himself at the pedestal of a statue by embracing the stone-graven knees. He buried his wet face in the thick woolen stuff of Miss Stein's skirts.

"Elle m'a abandonné," came the half-smothered words. "My heart has left me. I cannot go on."

The exaggerated statement made a clown of him again, but the pain behind the words was real enough. Was I the only one in the room who knew what he meant?

"His model," declared Lipchitz, "has ruined him."

"A gypsy," explained the Spaniard.

Miss Stein patted the sculptor's shaggy head (as she would later caress the head of Basket, her poodle) murmuring, "There, there," in English, looking about the room with her majestic eyebrows raised as if to ask, What must be done?

Nguyên the Patriot brought Anacréon a glass of eau-de-vie, but stood by in his self-effacing way and was ignored until Miss Toklas took the glass from him and bent down to the weeping man. She touched his shoulder gently and he lifted his head to drink.

"My little one," he babbled, the liquid spilling down the sides of his mouth. "My precious, my life."

I was standing in the rear of the studio, unnoticed, and if I could have disappeared into one of the paintings I would have.

"My heart, my pigeon, my love, my life." His despair was genuine despite the ridiculous sentiments he expressed.

"His gypsy," said Juan Gris.

"She deceives me," he cried, "that is normal. She is young—she will naturally turn away from this ancient carcass." His emaciated body trembled as if in abhorrence of itself. "But my home was her home, the home of my heart."

"What has happened?" asked Miss Stein pointedly.

"She has left me, c'est tout." Anacréon hunched his thin shoulders pitifully—so thin they almost met. "Before, always, she left her clothes behind, and her few trinkets—she would be back, I knew. Now she is gone forever for her clothes are gone. She has taken everything. Gone."

Gone where? I asked myself.

"You will see her again," Miss Stein assured him.

"Never."

"You will."

The broken sculptor lifted his swollen eyes to hers searching for consolation in that shrewd visage: "But she has taken her clothes."

"That has no meaning. Wait. You will see."

Marie Laurencin was now completely awake, and curious: "Did she take anything else?" she asked.

Indifferently, without looking away from Miss Stein, the sculptor muttered, "Money."

"She is a gypsy," said Juan Gris to the studio at large.

"How much?" asked Madame Matisse, curious too.

Anacréon hunched his shoulders again and did not reply.

Miss Stein asked Juan Gris: "Is she truly a gypsy?" but it was the Rumanian student of Matisse who replied: "She says so." He seemed to know her well, he was my age—I immediately feared and despised him.

"Then she will be back," said Miss Stein with the characteristic firmness and finality that made her public statements into precepts.

I felt my face flush with jealousy, rage, and humiliation. In my unstable mental state I wanted to cry out *Never!*—as unhinged, in my way, as Anacréon. She could never have loved that dry old ruin no matter what shameless confessions he spewed forth. (It was his own passion he lamented, not hers—had she not told me herself the old man was impotent?) Anyway, what did these poseurs and eccentrics know of love. I suddenly loathed them all for being hungry witnesses to this scene. I thought I was quite alone with my inner turmoil, but perhaps the very intensity of my expression caused Miss Toklas to seek me out. She came to me and looked into my eyes the way Miss Stein looked into Anacréon's.

Once more Miss Stein intoned, "She will be back." It was a statement of fact that at last convinced the tortured sculptor, or narcotized him. He nodded in a stupor and Miss Stein permitted him to put his head back into the rough comfort of her skirts. She stroked the wire strands of his hair, then—looking out at the rest of us—winked. In a little while the disordered man was asleep and snoring.

Anacréon may have been reassured, but I was not. My thoughts raced ahead of rational possibility, spinning into emptiness. Where was she if she had left him and if she had left him had she left me?

Miss Toklas, possibly to distract me, was saying something about "a favor to Gertrude." I begged her pardon and she was obliged to repeat herself. Would I be so good as to help take the poor soul home?

In my confusion I nodded yes. Gabriel and his cowboy volunteered to accompany me, and the next thing I remember the slender cowboy carried Anacréon's stiffened carcass across his shoulder like a roped calf. Gabriel had found a motor taxi on the boulevard Raspail. Just then, before we could fold the rigid sculptor into the rear seat, the maid ran outside calling, "Attendez!" Anacréon had carried off Miss Stein's cut-glass tumbler, and she pried the antique from his long prehensile fingers before slamming shut the cab door.

We left the cab windows open in case, as the Texan put it, "He might upchuck."

Rain sprayed my face through the open window and the wet cold brought me momentarily to myself. Anacréon was humming in his drugged sleep the song about the cantinière so popular when I first met Fleur at the square des Innocents. The harmless tune the old man grunted renewed my agitation and despair.

"She did not," I declared, "make love with this old man."

I could see the smiles on all their faces (even Anacréon's) without looking at them. I was in a panic, and babbling.

"They may have slept together but they did not make love."

The cowboy, amused, inquired: "Is that some French perversion nobody told me about yet?"

The pont du Châtelet was obscured by the pouring rain but I recognized the watery flicker of theatre lights when we reached the Right Bank. Not far along the boulevard de Sébastopol I asked to get out.

"Bien sûr," agreed Gabriel. He and his friend would see the old man home. Before I fled into the rain I heard the cowboy saying, "Looks like he's the one going to upchuck."

At Etienne Marcel I stumbled over the body of a clochard sleeping under wet newspapers on the métro grating. My tread did not disturb him, I could have been trampling the all but moribund body of Anacréon underfoot.

I took the steep hotel steps two at a time, tasting the sour taste of Miss Stein's soirée at the back of my throat. There was a strip of light beneath the door.

"You are wet," she said when I burst in upon her. She sat on the bed with her feet wrapped in her shawl, playing with the Tarot deck. "Undress and come next to me."

The closet door hung open and I could see a man's Gladstone bag on its side spilling a mass of unfamiliar garments on the bottom shelf. I was out of my wet clothes in an instant. My assault upon her flesh might have been judged a crime had she not responded with a fury equal to my own.

EVIDENCE

One

IN EARLY NOVEMBER 1921, O'Grady handed me a notice clipped from *le Petit Paris*. "Do me this one."

I sat down at O'Grady's heavyweight typewriting machine—permitted to use the antique under his direction—and typed: "Today four sealed boxes were sent by special transport to the Palais de Justice in Versailles."

"Under guard," added O'Grady.

"Today four sealed boxes were sent under guard by special transport to the Palais de Justice in Versailles."

"Too many prepositions," said O'Grady. "Take out 'by special transport' since we already state under armed guard, which is special enough."

I typed a line of *x*'s through "by special transport," then wrote: "They contained the jewelry, papers, and personal effects of the ten assumed victims of Landru."

"Make that 'of the women Landru is accused of murdering.'"

I did as he said with an unexpressed sigh of annoyance. Why did he not simply write the piece himself? Then I noticed how his hands were clutched together, as if in prayer, to keep them from trembling: he was suffering from what he termed his John Powers syndrome.

"Another thing," said O'Grady. "'Jewelry, papers, and personal effects' is too vague. Give D.R. [Dear Reader] specific items of jewelry, papers, and personal effects."

Brigadier Riboulet and Inspector Beloque had investigated the garage in Clichy used by Landru as a depot. The officers had been good enough to distribute a list of their findings to the newspapermen who regularly gathered at La Cage. I found the list in the drawer with O'Grady's dueling pistol, and copied from it: "They contained tooth-paste, letters tied with ribbon, stockings and petticoats, feathered boas, a jacket with an astrakhan collar, ration books, tubes of lip rouge, baptismal certificates, and the identity cards of the women Landru is accused of murdering."

"That's more like it." O'Grady was rubbing his hands together as if he were D.R. himself. "Best to change 'contained' to 'contains,' present tense—give a sense of up-to-the-moment."

I then checked my notes on Dr. Paul's discoveries at Gambais, and added: "One box contains calcinated bone fragments: rib sections, tibia, radius, cubitus, one tooth—all human—along with the skeletal remains of three dogs."

"Capital," said O'Grady. He gazed into the cobwebs hanging from the ceiling fan as if looking for inspiration there. "The bones are good. But perhaps not the dog bones. This is a distraction from the central theme—skip the canines altogether and conclude with the words 'all human.' "

I wrote: "One box contains calcinated bone fragments: rib sections, tibia, radius, cubitus, and one tooth—all human."

"Excellent," said O'Grady. "Grisly. The one tooth is perfect."

I wrote: "Landru's notebooks . . ."

"Infamous notebooks."

"Landru's infamous notebooks were dispatched . . ."

" 'Have been' is more up-to-the-moment than 'were.' "

"Landru's infamous notebooks have been dispatched to Versailles as well."

" 'As well' is a weak termination. Make it 'also under seal,' comma, and continue with another phrase."

"—also under seal, along with 5,000 pages of dossier concerning Brigadier Riboulet's investigation and the interrogation of the accused by Maître Bonin, examining magistrate."

O'Grady stalked from desk to window his hands still clasped in prayer but raised to the level of his mouth now, both thumbnails fixed between his teeth. His copy of *The Memoirs of Sherlock Holmes* lay on the windowsill, and the image of a book may have prompted him to suggest: "After 'five thousand pages of dossier,' mention that this figure equals the number of pages in the complete works of Emile Zola."

"Does it?"

"Who knows? If it doesn't, increase the number of pages in the dossier to equal Zola's output. On second thought better compare the dossier to the work of some less prolific author—I suspect a number of our correspondent editors were failed dons of literature before they resigned themselves to yellow journalism."

"Flaubert, I think, is safer."

"Flaubert, then. Now bring Landru back into the picture."

I wrote: "For two and a half years Landru has been confined to la Santé prison awaiting trial."

O'Grady rattled off several editorial accommodations in rapid sequence: " 'Nearly three years' is better than 'two and a half,' and make it 'languished in prison' rather than 'confined to.' Ah, yes—add 'in a cell,' not just 'la Santé prison.' D.R. is capable of picturing a cell far more easily than an abstract penal institution." He bit off a thumbnail. "You could squeeze 'without bail' between 'prison' and 'awaiting.' Our cousins in the British Isles are unaware the French do not practice this form of usury and will think of it as insult added to injury."

I did as he directed, then wrote: "The trial will begin November 7."

"Flat," he said, "but effective in its sheer simplicity. Make it 'begins' instead of 'will begin,' which gives a sense of up-to-the-moment."

"The trial begins November 7."

Two

I BELIEVE NOW there was nowhere else she could go. I offered her le coeur chaud de Paris—a stove, a hearth—and I see her as she sat on the bed—she always sat on the bed, I on the hard chair tilted against the wall staring dreamily—she, numbly—into the glow beyond the stove's isinglass windows. My room was that impregnable shelter far removed (except when she slept, and dreamt) from whatever haunted her. I do not flatter myself that she stayed with me for love: she was as seduced by glowing coals as by my clumsy caresses; when she left the bed she moved ever closer to the stove, like a cat, or as if she would be consumed in fire—no, she did not love me: whatever love there was was on my side of the lopsided room.

Yet she needed me as much as my heated sanctuary. She might declare, "I feel a chill."

I crossed the overheated room. "You're warm," I said, touching her.

"Dedans," she said, "inside." She cupped her breasts to show me where. Her bitten-down fingernails were a disappointment but the nipples were a roseate enticement to take her hands away and place mine there.

"They're warm."

"Dedans," she said—the cold was inside.

She could have perished in Anacréon's frigid atelier: her circulation, she claimed, did not operate in winter. She put my hand at the approximate place between her breasts to test her heartbeat and I massaged her where her heart must have been or circled her nipples with my tongue till she purred.

Before my wristwatch disappeared (we never spoke of it) she requested me to take her pulse, and now, without a timepiece, she asked me to take my own pulse, and hers, a triangular bond of hands and wrists to measure her erratic throb against my steadier and reliable rhythm. I played with her fingers, tickled her palms. I moved my hand along one smooth flank below the coverlet, past the shawl she had drawn to her lap, until I found the tangle of hair, the crease.

"Where are you going?" she asked like a little girl.

"Dedans," said I.

She was older than me by three years or more, but was a child as well—worldly in demimondaine ways, as naive as I in others. She could inform me how Gabriel and the habitués of Magic City made love. "This they do," she said to me once, brushing my penis with her lips and tongue until that sleeping stalwart was aroused, then took the head into her mouth, then more of it, to suck and seemingly relish sucking as if she had hold of some tasty edible of flesh—but this was an act she regularly performed for my pleasure when her menses made the missionary approach awkward or impractical. Another time she said, "Or this they do," and turned upon her belly and breasts, drew her knees forward half crouching to present to me her underside, buttocks upended in invitation. I had taken her in that position before, slipping into her between the spread thighs, from the rear—but now she reached back and spread the halves of flesh above the customary opening to reveal that other pink flower of folded flesh. By this she meant to show me the only other possible entrée male lovers may enjoy, then anointed her anal cleft and my ready length of cartilage with salve. With Fleur, any game of flesh and fluid I played would, I knew, result in some ultimate delight, so I overcame an initial fastidiousness (the sex, a man's curious flap of it, is blind) and made my cautious way—one millimeter at a time, searching her depth (asking myself questions, some of them comic)—along the narrower passage. Once in, I held my breath—I did not think I could get out again. Fleur, unabashed (except for one brief moment when I first entered her—her moan had a sharp edge to it), moved in my place, tightening and releasing the sphincter or gently revolving her buttocks while I passively sustained my cork in that swaying bottle. Unable to believe the anal cavity left room for climax, I got no release until I worked my uncertain way out again, then abruptly lost my seed—a trace of her blood mixed with my sperm—in the sheets.

No, the rear portal would never adequately serve as my preferred gate to paradise. I could willingly abandon that constricted areaway to those denied the other coupling place. (For a moment I took pity on Gabriel and friends.) Could it be that I—like so many Americans—am but a missionary at heart?

My inexperience amused her, my ignorance was astonishing: children in alleyways, the beasts in the field knew more of copulation than I.

How did Miss Stein and Miss Toklas celebrate their love?

She did not know Miss Stein and Miss Toklas but she knew the famous Moune, had heard of Frida and la grosse Claude, had frequented the bars along the rue Fontaine and the Monocle in Montparnasse. (Moune?—my jealousy stirred anew: sick green was the other color of my passion.)

We coiled together in a way that brought to mind the eternal serpent eating its own tail. I followed her instructions, she tasted of iodine. As much as I sought dominion over that area I could not continue in the smothering embrace of Fleur's thighs or believe Miss Stein and Miss Toklas could link themselves together thus. Anyway, we were not two women making love, or two tapettes, but male and female with our separate and distinct sexual parts meant to fulfill the desire and pursuit of the whole.

"This," said I, sitting up, unsatisfied, "is what the Bible calls confusion."

Fleur shrugged one naked shoulder, smiled, then placed herself in the orthodox pose. She had not been a model (and prostitute?) for nothing.

For all her seeming maturity and erotic accomplishments Fleur was an innocent, in innocent little ways of her own. It was my turn to be amused when she affected an extended little finger when holding a wineglass or teacup, because she had seen this at the cinema and thought the gesture chic. (Meanwhile she might be chewing gum, or gnawing at the fingernails of her free hand.) She had an obsessive need to impress me concerning her origins. On this subject she was voluble but predictably dishonest. One lie contradicted the other. She would run on about Rumanian diplomats one week and claim Spanish gypsy blood the next. I did not point out the inconsistencies. She believed I believed whatever she told me, with a naiveté I found charming at first but exasperating when I tried to trace her recent past.

"I was born in Béziers," she once told me, then forgot she told me and said she was born in Spain. I knew she wanted to convince herself as well as me that she had come from someplace warm—Iberia, the Midi.

At first her father was dead, then he was in Algiers, finally in prison in Montpellier.

"He has a record of three felonies already. A fourth will mean relégation"—she needed to dramatize—"to Devil's Island."

Her father was not just an ordinary gypsy but a Romany prince, or again: not a gypsy at all but a military officer who distinguished himself in the Great War. She had no picture of him, but he wrote her letters—from Nîmes or Madrid or Bucharest—threatening letters, or letters with money in them. "I am afraid of him," she might say, or, "He is a tender-hearted old thing." She never showed me any of the letters. She never spoke of her mother—dead or alive.

Aside from these disparate fantasies, and within the confines of my room, we knew one another so well we might have been married for years, no need of words. I cannot remember anything we ever said of particular import. I learned to keep my thoughts to myself, and my suspicions. Where was she when she was not with me? There was no way to trace her unpredictable passages in and out of my life. So be it. I was determined to suppress my jealousy. I could never altogether accept her vagrant character, but I did manage to accommodate my stolidity to her restlessness. She was not always there when I wanted her—for I wanted her always, and needed her most when she was gone—but I became adept at pretending not to mind. When she went out alone I resisted the impulse to follow her.

Pretense becomes habit and habits accumulate into a style of life—is not any household of two an accumulation of habits?

She made me happy in unexpected ways. She would sew my buttons back, sitting up in bed. She made scrappy meals from whatever caught her eye at the market, but she cooked well on the one burner of our peerless stove. I could not abide those odd cuts of meat the

French are fond of (in this I am truly American), les abbatis: livers, tripe, brains—but she prepared these oddments in so cunning a manner I did not always know I chewed and swallowed the insides of beasts. To celebrate she might purchase two perfect tournedos circled with a strip of bacon fat—to celebrate a full moon, her saint's day—with money of her own (from her father? stolen from beneath Anacréon's pillow when she left him?). Sometimes she would return from one of her mysterious sorties with a tablet of chocolate secreted in her purse, for she knew I loved chocolate, and she slipped it to me with her back turned as if it were contraband smuggled from abroad.

I rejoiced in her child's way of peeling down an artichoke, lingering over the heart, nibbling an individual leaf with her little finger extended, her lips afterward gleaming with vinaigrette. She peeled an apple in the European way, its skin removed in one unbroken spiral which if pressed together accordion style became the reproduction of an apple, emptied—or an orange, its meridians traced by knifepoint, then peeled down like petals. Though she tried to teach me how to do this, my own piece of fruit never came magically apart like hers.

She never spoke of fortunes—hers or mine, past or present—yet I loved to see her Tarot deck spread across the coverlet as she smiled her peculiar downturned smile (or scowled, if the portents were dark—she scowled more than she smiled) over that exotic game of solitaire.

Of my life she knew nothing, and did not ask. I went weekdays into the workaday world: to the Bourse, to gather statistics for a financial dispatch, or to the Bibliothèque Nationale to spend a morning under the multiple domes of the reading room at O'Grady's bidding, or to La Cage in the late afternoon, an unused office at the Préfecture where news reporters gathered for whatever tidbits a news briefing provided. I returned to my hotel excited with the idea Fleur would be waiting there for me, downcast if she was not. Never mind—she would be back, her clothes were here. Waiting, I could drink a hot rum or sip a cognac and wonder at the hour, without a watch. Whatever, I must not ask where or with whom.

When she came awake weeping from a dream, shuddering from some remembered dread, it was useless to inquire, "What is it?"

"Nothing," she would say, or, "It is that I am cold."

Whether she said dedans or not I tried to warm her further, inside, to erase the fearful tremor with my passion until she could breathe freely again.

Once, only half awake, still in her nightmare, she replied, "I lie in my grave and I am cold." True, her pillow was damp with tears, her side of the bed indeed cold—yet she herself was warm and real in my embrace. It was not possible for either of us to sleep after that.

Thus we lived our little mystery by day and at night lay in our separate coffins of thought.

Three

AT VERSAILLES those who had stood in line all night (and many had, wrapped in blankets) were already being admitted. Those spectators allowed to pass into the Palais de Justice were made to leave their picture cameras with a guard: only sketch artists would be permitted to reproduce the scene inside the courtroom. Reporters entered through a side entrance adjoining the prison of Saint Pierre, next door to the palais.

To reach the guard post Harry shoved his sturdier bulk ahead of me while I clung to his coat sleeve, waving our press passes overhead. We were showered with obscene comments on the way. Someone tried to snatch my pass. Odd-shaped pasteboard tubes stared at us as we went by: these were crude periscopes fitted with mirrors a camelot was selling from a booth across the rue Georges Clemenceau. He wore a false beard and disguised himself as Landru to draw attention to his merchandise.

A committee of officers was checking press passes. "There have been forgeries," said a militiaman with a bayonet, so we were obliged to wait in the jostling crowd, our bellies pressed against the wooden barrier, while our passes were taken inside the prison to be verified and made legitimate with a signature.

"There's Colette," said Harry.

The crew of a newsreel service had set up their film camera on a tripod platform outside the palais: the cameraman wore a jaunty checkered cap with eyeshade (there was no sun) and cranked the film reel with élan, but there was nothing to film except the dreary façade of the Palais de Justice and the tops of heads streaming past the lens, the tripod wavering dangerously in the crosscurrents of a human tide, until Madame Willy (the writer Colette) arrived. The cameraman cranked in her direction as she stepped from a private limousine and was acclaimed by the crowd. A militiaman escorted her through the barrier where Harry and I still waited for permission to pass. I was attracted by her smile. She had large excited and exciting eyes, her hair was frizzed in the style of a music hall vedette. When she was led safely out of sight the camera still focused on the spot where she had stood and waved to her admirers.

A regiment of horse guards patrolled the square but could not keep order. I heard someone singing. A chansonnier stood on the steps of the palais hawking the comic lyrics to the latest ballad about Landru. I had got a headache in the press and noise but Harry took obvious pleasure in the scene of confusion around us.

"They say," he shouted in my ear, but did not say who said, "that Princess Georges of Greece is here with a pass signed by the French Foreign minister, but can't get in—there's no room left."

Just as the chansonnier was besieged by rowdies who snatched away his sheet music without paying, scattering a bundle of sheets into the air, Harry and I were admitted to the palais.

The courtroom was smaller than I expected for so celebrated an event. Half the salle was given over to journalists: folding chairs had been set up to accommodate the overflow. Only one aisle was passable. Harry went ahead, and I followed; we were obliged to edge sidewise to our places.

I held my notepad over my eyes to deflect the light. Electric globes were attached to what had once been gas jets in the chandeliers: they cast a relentless glare, as if only under so stark an illumination could the truth be revealed.

Newspaper sketch artists were already at work sketching the familiar faces of Kiki, Chevalier, and Coco Chanel. Harry was in his element: he delighted in sharing the same hard benches with the celebrated. He pointed out Mistinguette to me, his habitually flushed jowls growing redder with pleasure.

Harry had been recruited as an extra reporter for the *Paris Ameri-*

can. He now operated from upstairs instead of in the Classified Department—an opportunity he intended to make the most of.

"Does your alcoholic employer still call me Classified Harry?"

"That's nothing," said I, "he calls me Candide."

"The low-life bastard. He called me Dear Watson when I worked for him."

But in the next moment he was absorbed in the procession of judge and assessors to the bench—O'Grady's insulting nicknames forgotten—and he inscribed in nervous shorthand (which I copied in my own notepad): *President Gilbert, pres. j - assess. maîtres Schuler & Gloria, j's de Trib de V.*

Landru's defense attorney was Maître de Moro Giafferi, the most successful criminal lawyer in France. (Who would pay the defense fee, since Landru claimed he was destitute?) De Moro Giafferi was opposed by Maître Robert Godefroy, advocate general, for the state. The eight members of the jury were a nondescript assembly of mostly bearded gentlemen between the ages of forty-five and fifty-five, Landru's approximate peers. Justice was in the hands of men. Frenchwomen had only got the vote in 1919—in 1921 the legal profession was still closed to them, and they could not sit on juries. The man who was accused of the murder of ten women would be prosecuted, defended, and judged by an all-male tribunal.

Nonetheless, from the public side of the courtroom the spectacle was one of a cinematic matinée reserved for women. O'Grady had predicted the ladies would be out in force, and for that reason (he claimed) he himself would not attend "the cirque d'hiver de Versailles." Many of the women were unescorted, for this was a new age: the old moeurs from before the war had changed and the courtroom crowd was evidence of this change. Beneath the powder and paint their faces were avid: teeth showed along the edge of a smile, there was a predatory brightness of the eyes. The air smelled as much of mint and jasmine as tobacco and perspiration, and I sensed despite my headache a sexual tension in the courtroom that extended to the robed officials seated in the prétoire. We were gathered here, male and female, for reasons that went beyond jurisprudence. Men introduced themselves to unattached women in the easy way of fellow celebrants at a public fête. I too eyed the ladies. A legion of jeunes filles wore the short skirts recently introduced by Liane de Pougy. Instead of corsets they employed the new porte-jarettelles, or garter belts, whose pink elastic fasteners sometimes showed at the top of a stocking when a young beauty leaned forward on the hard court bench.

Harry's eyes were fixed elsewhere.

"From the look of that jury," he declared, "Landru's goose is cooked."

Harry was a professional, a paid witness to an event. Nothing distracted him from the headlines ahead, he had a nose for news.

I found myself depending on Harry for newsworthy names: who was Nancy Cunard, and who the Princess Bibesco? I did not know Sam Mac Vea the jockey from the aviator, Santos-Dumont. Nevertheless, I was greatly intrigued to discover that Prince Youssoupoff was present, the assassin of Rasputin.

A dull formality was under way concerning the election of two jurymen and an alternate assessor. Because of the extraordinary indictment drawn up by the prosecution (eleven murders, not counting lesser charges of fraud, theft, and forgery) the trial was bound to be a long one. It was during this tedious debate on substitute jurymen that Landru, quite unexpectedly, made his entrance.

I had been idly watching the shorthand symbols form beneath Harry's fat fingers when I felt the new presence. I looked up just as Landru came quietly through the small door behind the prisoner's dock, escorted by two guards. The somnolence of a moment before was broken by a rising murmur. The general stir (spectators in the front benches rose to see over the railing, and those behind them were obliged to rise as well) led President Gilbert to rap for order. The disturbance continued, an uninterrupted buzz. A huissier stalked threateningly to the center of the prétoire and militiamen stationed at the exit doors brought their rifles to port arms.

Landru, through all of this, was amazingly at ease. His only visible reaction upon entering the courtroom was a brief grimace of discomfort, for he had come from a dim cell and obscure corridor into a sudden and painful light. He briefly shaded his eyes with his notepad (as I had done) and sat down. He then turned to a page in his cahier and put on his glasses to study what was written there. He might have been alone in his cell with a legal text to study.

We would all report later that he had lost weight, but I had no way of knowing this for I had not seen him at the time of his arrest. To me he appeared comfortable in his clothes—and in every other way: he was wearing the same suit of brown velours he had worn when he was arrested, and it seemed to fit. Deep hollows emphasized his eyes, but he may have been habitually hollow-eyed. His guardians reported that he invariably slept well during the long months in prison. "He gets a better night's sleep than I do," said one of them.

His eyes were restless and observant. I would like to have seen his eyes at closer range: they reminded me, for their dark animation, of Miss Stein's eyes.

Much has been written about Landru's extraordinary eyes. The eyes were said to be the instrument of his power over women. O'Grady, looking for an easy simile, compared his eyes to Svengali's, and I, on another hasty occasion, cited the hypnotic eyes of Rasputin. An examining physician at la Santé prison went so far as to state that Landru's eyes never blinked. I watched him now as he looked up from his cahier into the grey space beyond the windows. He was capable of staring for a considerable time into space, but so am I, and I can report conclusively that Landru's eyelids, like any man's, opened and shut at regular intervals.

An immediate association with news photographs and magazine illustrations made Landru's face as familiar as those of any of the celebrated spectators in the courtroom, yet there was something in Landru's manner and bearing that set him apart, even from celebrity. It occurred to me how much more relaxed was he than any one of his jurors, how much more certain of himself than those of us for whom he was on exhibit. His complete self-composure under our relentless scrutiny increased the sense of insulation between spectator and spectacle. The man was alone. He could not have been more alone had the universe been empty of humankind.

But none of this was in my notes.

Powf shoul & arms. From the fit of his jacket he appeared solidly built, but hardly solid enough to strangle to death (as the prosecution would offer in a lame attempt to explain how he killed) a Mademoiselle Marchadier, for example, who was twice his size. Height: slightly below average—he would have been considered short by American standards. ("We are not concerned with American standards," O'Grady would remind me, and delete.) High-domed forehead, a half-moon of bald pate—hairless parts of his physiognomy made the beard and eyebrows all the more theatrical, but what else could a reporter or sketch artist fix upon? Searching for something original to say about Landru's face, Harry wrote "fan-shaped ears." I did not see that they were noticeably fan-shaped, or any other shape than ear-shaped, but Harry's myopic observation crept into my own copy. We were both a little desperate for something striking to say.

"Would have taken him for a minor clerk at the SNCF," declared Harry.

I was reminded of the chief clerk at the Ministry of Finance gasping for air at his window on the rue Saint-Honoré. Until now Landru had managed to escape the chief clerk's fate (slow death by drowning for the fresh country air—somewhat flavored with smoke—of Gambais). Now however the clerk and Landru shared a similar monotonously confining situation.

But this was a private thought, and reverie did not count with O'Grady. For public consumption Landru's counterpart would have to be Gilles de Rais (or Retz), the fifteenth-century lord of the Breton marshes who was tried by an ecclesiastical court and confessed to the kidnapping, torture, and murder of more than a hundred victims, mostly children. He was the model for Perrault's chevalier Raoul in the story of *Bluebeard*.

Maître Grifon, court clerk, began reading the indictment. There were eighty-eight pages of accusation, something of a record, and Maître Grifon more than once lost his place. Landru was at first as alert as a fox. He was generally attentive, a careful observer when he chose to be, and remarkably patient. He knew how to wait. But as the clerk droned on from page to page of legal prose, Landru became as bored as the rest of us. The clerk would look up each time he turned a page and stare directly at the accused. The first few times he did this, Landru was looking elsewhere, but once when he glanced up his eyes met those of Landru. The rabbit stared into the eyes of the fox. Unable to bear the relentless gaze, Maître Grifon turned quickly back to this text and did not look up again.

At 2:50 PM President Gilbert declared a respite from the interminable reading of the indictment. Landru rose along with everyone else (and presumably with the same relief), took up his notepad—a redbound cahier similar to those in which he had recorded the minutiae of meeting and cultivating his female clientele—and put on his chapeau melon. He then retired as unobtrusively as he had appeared, through the little door behind his chair.

Many of the spectators dared not leave the public benches for fear of losing their places. They had come prepared for the intermission: there were hampers of sandwiches, bottles of mineral water and wine, tucked under the seats. Harry and I stood and stretched. We did not leave because of the impossible bottleneck at the exit door and undoubtedly a crush in the corridor outside the courtroom. A conscientious huissier saw fit to open wide the widows looking into a grey impasse.

At 3 PM the court clerk took up his reading where he had left off. I was less ill at ease during the second session, but my headache throbbed on, in almost perfect rhythm to the measured inflection of the clerk's monotonous delivery.

Having Landru to study was a distraction. The grey-green institutional walls were oppressive, but Landru was much more at home in this green fishbowl than the rest of us. He swam in it, while we gaped and stared. I admired his gestures, graceful and spare. Wrapped in his solitude and silence he was a figure of infinite conjecture. A pity he would be called upon to reply to the charges. The moment he spoke, the spell would be broken: far better if he had never uttered a word at his own trial. As an enigma he had already won the day.

The clerk was reviewing Landru's alleged courtship of Madame. Jaume and now related an episode that conjured up the picture of Landru upon his knees beside his intended at the Sacré-Coeur. According to a statement Madame Jaume made to a witness, Landru was asking heaven to bless their forthcoming union. Laughter rippled through the courtroom. The huissier demanded silence, but sporadic outbursts of giggling and guffaws followed.

When the reading of the indictment had been completed, Landru's attorney interjected a newspaper story from the day before. (Channel News had not originated the story, but we had passed the same dispatch on to our subscribers.) "It would appear," he said, "that the missing Madame Guillin has turned up, alive and well, in Paris."

I watched Landru's face, for he may not have been aware of the published report, but the man in the prisoner's dock barely suppressed a yawn.

The story, as it turned out, was without confirmation, and now Maître de Moro Giafferi enlarged upon this error in reportage: "After careful investigation we have discovered that the Madame Guillin in question is a quite different Madame Guillin—also a widow, and with the same prénom—who, in fact, closely resembles the Madame Guillin mentioned in the indictment."

The court accepted this explanation of a false headline with complacency, but the lawyer paused only the length of a heartbeat before going on:

"However, the so-called mistaken Madame Guillin has also been in correspondence with my client!"

Astonishment, laughter. Landru seemed to shrug imperceptibly.

"My dear colleagues, gentlemen of the press and members of the jury," said Maître de Moro Giafferi in a weary tone, "how this case— if there is one—meanders in a maze of false leads and mistaken identities, unconfirmed dates, disputed figures, confusion, rumor, and outright slander.

"Remember"—he was speaking directly to the jury now—"a court of law must deal with factual testimony alone. Beware of the gossip and innuendo this affair has already aroused. You will hear more of such—far more, no doubt—as the trial proceeds. So far the defendant has been the target of nothing more than unrestrained supposition and accumulated calumny."

President Gilbert allowed the defense attorney's plea and advisory to run its course, without comment from the bench, then ignored its implication (that Landru was merely the victim of rumor and false assumption) by directing the defendant to reply to the indictment.

Landru rose with dignity and poise. His voice was firm and clear as he stated with great calm: "I am innocent of all the charges brought against me."

He remained standing while the sketch artists hastily accomplished their final strokes.

Four

On my way to the hotel I knew without qualm Fleur was waiting. Even now she might be beating two eggs together in a bowl, opening a tin of pâté—as casually as she would later open her legs to me when I desired her. Strangely enough this knowledge was not comforting. She was altogether mine now—no longer a purchase or a gift or a piece of luck—but now that I was certain of her, the certainty was a new vexation. It was as if we had taken vows without my intending to commit my person to hers. Yet she had committed herself to me, as far as her gypsy spirit would allow (her scant patchwork wardrobe interspersed with mine). Indeed, she had come to stay. Even Madame Vitrine—pleased with the increase in rent, reconciled to the two of us in one of her rooms—referred to Fleur as Madame.

I did not go straight home to her but wandered awhile along the mean streets between les Halles and the Seine. Now in bleak November there were still lovers along the riverbank, and an occasional clochard warming his ruined hands over a small blaze of twigs and splinters. I joined the errant homeless in the shadows of the lower quais.

My mood was vagrant. The trip to Versailles and back had left me listless and disappointed. Earlier I had come upon O'Grady incoherent with drink, his eyeshade askew and two horns of red hair protruding through the straps. His dueling pistol was turning round and round on the gramophone instead of a glass—I took it off (it was empty) and put it back in the drawer. I did not think he was despondent or suicidal, only drunk. But I was despondent. I set him straight in his chair and put his eyeshade in place and thought for a moment he might commence to operate, the way a windup toy comes to life when the key is turned, but he only waved helplessly at an untidy stack of pages and left them to me. I completed the day's dispatches and sent them off as they were. This should have made me happy but did not.

Without a father near at hand to model myself upon I had chosen to follow in O'Grady's eccentric footsteps. Would I become another O'Grady in ten years? or (as I watched a clochard suck at his bottle) Danglure in twenty?

The next bateau mouche that passed cast its steering light against the quai and I caught sight of a pale girl crying desperately in her lover's arms. What had he said or done to make her weep (only he, I assumed, could be the source of her misery)—yet clung to her still, and she to him?

I climbed to street level and went looking for a place to drink. At the corner of rue Berger and rue de la Lingerie were situated two squalid bistros diagonally opposite one another. I held my breath as I passed the first: it smelled of merde. This was the only café in Paris where the vidangeurs were welcome, and so it became their own. They were the cesspool cleaners who worked at night with steam pumps and hoses to empty the septic tanks of the city. They patronized the café between night shifts still wearing their stained kerchiefs and foul denims and boots covered with excrement. It was said of them they could no longer smell one another but if a stranger came into their midst he stank.

The café I chose to enter was known to be the gathering place of pimps. An amateur was practicing the accordion and the men in their billed caps (tilted rakishly at the same angle, in the maquereau manner) were throwing centimes at his feet in mock applause. No prostitute was ever seen here. The girls were already at their stations along the curbstones of les Halles or working the maisons de passe throughout the quarter. Their men congregated here until the small hours, then met with the prostitutes at other cafés, each one to his favorite, when the night's receipts were due. As soon as I stepped inside, the accordion wheezed to a halt and all conversation ceased. The same thing would have happened to me at the cesspool cleaners' bistro across the street. I was an outsider. The bartender troubled himself to let me know this by asking, "What is it?" instead of, "What will you have?"

I requested and received a glass of rum, then stood before it in total exile. Eventually a young pimp in a sweater and cap brought his rum next to mine. He slid the glass of rum along the counter with his one good arm: he had cut away the sleeve of his sweater for the other, a miniature withered hand that sprouted directly from his shoulder. The deformed hand appeared to have been attached to him as an afterthought, like the lifeless hand on the door of a maison close.

"Your first time here?' he asked casually enough. His flat face was innocent of all guile, but my insides tightened from the sight of a shrunken hand dangling before my eyes.

"Yes."

"I've seen you with a girl."

I nodded. The talk around us picked up again, but not the accordion. Despite the low hum of scattered conversation I assumed the entire café was tuned to what we were saying.

"Do you know the Pope?"

I thought he might be joking but his question provoked another ominous silence.

"The Pope is in Rome," said I.

There was an undercurrent of laughter in the café, but the pimp beside me did not laugh. His eyes narrowed in the flat face and—did I imagine this?—the dead hand twitched.

When the bartender positioned himself in front of me and the young pimp moved away I had the same sensation I had had at the Foreign Legionnaires' café in Nice: something was about to happen. All that happened was that the bartender took my glass of rum from the zinc counter and poured the contents out behind the bar.

"Compliments," he said, "of the house."

I lingered only a moment, the duration of several suffocating heartbeats, for pride's sake—then abandoned all pride and made my exit.

Five

ON A WINTER MORNING in 1912 Landru's father hanged himself from a tree in the bois de Boulogne. Why this was introduced into the trial I do not recall, but I do remember Landru's statement, as if he were commenting on more than his father's suicide when he said, "The man who cut my father down did not fail to make a profit from his gesture—he sold the rope."

Landru had been an altar boy when he attended school under the Jesuits, rue de Bretonvilliers. He was a competent mechanic with an attraction for motor cars: he worked for a time in a garage, but eventually became involved in a case of fraud when he attempted to open a garage of his own. He was a publicity agent for a time, but failed at that. He became a confidence man, convincing partner after partner to invest in his insolvent enterprises, and was three times convicted of escroquerie, or fraud.

"I made no effort to avoid the law," Landru declared of these indiscretions. "When a complaint was filed I promptly went with my disillusioned client to court. Invariably I was held."

(Laughter.)

He served three prison terms, and because of these three prior convictions he was subject to the penalty of relégation (deportation to a penal colony) if he should be convicted once again. On his fourth summons the conviction was handed down in absentia.

"Naturally," said Landru dryly, "I did not attend."

(Laughter.)

Landru then offered his philosophy of investment: "These people always brought money to me, I did not take it from them. When a proposition works out, the investor thinks his agent a financial genius; when a deal falls through, he is a crook."

Maître Godefroy pointed out that Landru's propositions had a way of falling through every time.

"How do you know that? Naturally those who profited from my efforts did not feel obliged to take me to court."

"Where are they then?"

Landru shrugged. "I assume they have done as I would do—taken their profits and moved on."

"In other words, they have disappeared."

"They moved on."

Despite Landru's request that these ancient affairs be dispensed with, President Gilbert and Maître Godefroy continued to dredge up details of Landru's disreputable past. These episodes had earned for Landru the reputation of récidiviste, or habitual criminal.

But today the spectators had the diverting display of furniture and bric-à-brac assembled overnight, like a flea market, in the prétoire. The court officials maneuvered around this bizarre collection like nimble auctioneers, deftly avoiding a protruding chair leg here, the spokes of a broken umbrella there, occasionally treading on a woman's glove fallen to the floor or stumbling against a rolled-up Persian rug. For the most part the furniture had been ingeniously arranged to take up the least space possible. Chairs of varying sizes were neatly fitted together sitting on one another's seats; armoires and table legs had been interlocked in the way of a Chinese puzzle. The collection represented the former possessions and personal effects of the missing Madame Cuchet, and son.

When a lawyer rummaged through the assortment of combs and corsets, old shoes, stained lampshades, a clock with pendule, a hat rack (hatless), and jewelry boxes (open, empty)—Godefroy was forever ransacking the knacker's heap for an odd piece of evidence to illustrate a point—I thought of Madame Vitrine's cave, until now a symbol of all the collected discard of France. Landru and Madame Vitrine were victims of the same obsession. Landru had filled three garages and the villa at Gambais with such stuff.

Landru had met Madame Cuchet (née Jonard) in 1914. This was before the scheduled hearing at Sens, where Landru would have received his fourth prison sentence had he been so rash as to appear in court. She knew him under the name Diard. She was a widow, with one grown son just under the age of mobilization—my own age and military status at the time, and the age of Landru's eldest son. The son was a problem to Landru, for he and his mother were close. Also, the Jonard family was opposed to her liaison with Landru: her brother-in-law, Friedmann, even ceased speaking to her. Landru lived with Jeanne Cuchet in a two-room flat at place d'Alésia. The concierge testified to this living arrangement, and stated that Madame Cuchet expected to marry Landru.

"A woman's expectations," said Landru, "do not always correspond to reality."

But Madame Cuchet's sister, Valentine, also testified that Landru had convinced Jeanne Cuchet they would be married.

Landru denied he had ever proposed marriage to Jeanne Cuchet.

Valentine Jonard, who was then on the witness stand, repeated with barely controlled fury, "You did! You did!" and screamed at Landru, "Then you killed her!"

The public gallery came to life at this outburst while the trial reporters scribbled the witness' words. Landru, with his usual aplomb, attended Valentine Jonard's hysterical denunciation without recoil—he sat impassive, unmoved. Meanwhile President Gilbert and the huissier made a vain attempt to restore order.

After Madame Cuchet turned over her savings to Landru, her presumed fiancé disappeared. The jilted widow was obliged to suffer the "I told you so" of her embittered family along with the hurt and loss Landru had inflicted upon her. It is a comment on Landru's extraordinary powers of persuasion to learn that Madame Cuchet met her deceiver some months later, and willingly took up with him again. What possible endearments could he have whispered to her, by what means could he have convinced her of his love after having stolen her money and so callously left her? She accompanied Landru, with her son, to his villa at Vernouillet. After August 1915, neither Jeanne Cuchet nor the boy was ever seen again.

"You say you were never her fiancé, but were you her lover?"

"I must draw the veil of privacy over my personal relations with the lady in question."

This was the first time Landru's term "the veil of privacy" would appear in the trial records, and in the evening news—but not the last.

"What became of Madame Cuchet and her son after August of 1915?"

"As far as I know, Madame Cuchet accomplished her intention of traveling to England."

"And her son?"

"They were inseparable. I assume she took him with her."

"But you do not know?"

"After she left Vernouillet I had no further communication from her."

"Nor did anyone else," said Maître Godefroy, pausing to allow the innuendo its full effect. Then he took up the question again: "You never heard from Madame Cuchet or her son in any way or by any means?"

"No I did not."

A witness, Madame Rongine, was called to the stand. Her son had been a close friend to the son of Madame Cuchet. She testified that Landru paid her an unexpected visit, to assure her that Madame Cuchet was quite well but had left for England and was now happily settled there. Her son had always wanted to join the military and had enlisted in the British army.

When asked to reply to Madame Rongine's testimony Landru stated he had never to his knowledge met the witness.

"I apologize to Madame if I do not remember the encounter she speaks of. I have met and known a good many women in the intervening years." (Laughter.) "If we did meet," he went on, "and I told her thus and so, well, it may have been true. I could have had some word from the Cuchets, mère et fils, but I do not recall any communication from them. You must realize this alleged visit took place half a dozen years ago. I cannot be held accountable for a casual statement I might have made to an individual whose name and face are unfamiliar to me, concerning the place of residence of a client with whom I am no longer in contact."

The prosecution took a new line.

"You say you were never engaged to Madame Cuchet and you had no common-law relationship with her—why then did you take the name Cuchet after her departure?"

"At the time, as you know, I was a fugitive from justice." Landru gave a curious inflection to the word justice. "I had papers in the name Cuchet."

"Securities?"

"There may have been. I do not recall."

"Which you cashed."

"Did I?"

"Therefore you assumed the name Cuchet to match the name of registration on the securities."

"It is good of you to answer these questions for me."

(Laughter.)

"But you continued to use the name Cuchet after your trusteeship of the Cuchet account was terminated." Maître Godefroy accented the word trusteeship. "You even introduced yourself to the missing Madame Laborde-Line as Monsieur Cuchet."

A concierge then testified she knew Landru as Monsieur Cuchet when he visited his fiancée, Madame Laborde-Line.

"I believe I did use the name Cuchet on that occasion. I have used a number of names over the years." (Laughter.) "I had taken a villa in the country and I wanted privacy above all. You know how inquisitive country people are."

Even before the last burst of laughter subsided altogether Maître Godefroy went on to make his chilling point: Landru would not have taken Cuchet as an alias had he not known Madame Cuchet and her son were safely removed from the power to challenge or unmask him.

Apparently Landru was discovering he had a gift for theatre, especially a comic gift. He abandoned the image he had created of poise and distance in order to turn verbal duel into music hall repartee. The public was delighted. Maître de Moro Giafferi, however, knew the danger of this tactic: he often tried to intervene, or lead his client into less flippant declarations. The outcome of the trial, he realized, would depend not upon the public (whose laughter was so often at the expense of the advocate general), but on the members of the jury, a solemn assembly, who sat stone-faced during the barrage of quips and witticisms. Unfortunately Landru ignored his attorney's efforts on his behalf. He had tasted success and could not help playing to the gallery.

During the court recess, Harry led me to a lower level of the courthouse, then into a storeroom where binders of court records were arranged along sagging shelves. In the privacy of this forgotten corner we could compare notes and swap the items one or the other of us had missed.

Harry, I learned, possessed a formidable memory for trivial detail. "I have ninety-eight and a half percent total recall," he boasted. I do not know how he calculated the percentage but he did have the ability to repeat whatever passed within his hearing almost word for word.

My French was superior to his, and he often missed a key word or phrase in the testimony. By exchanging notes and observations we managed a patchwork of collaboration. This is common practice among journalists on the same assignment unless they work for rival newspapers competing for circulation. Eventually we came to depend too much upon one another and carried the collaboration too far, but the readership of the *Paris American* and O'Grady's D.R.s on the other side of the channel were not the same, and no one would notice the similarity of our two news reports out of Versailles.

While we were filling in the blanks of one another's notes across an upended packing case, the court clerk, Maître Grifon, suddenly appeared on the stairs. I felt like a truant schoolboy, we were certain to be thrown out. Harry was shuffling together his pages of shorthand ready to make hasty retreat, but Maître Grifon came up to us with such an open and eager expression we both hesitated.

"Do you want to see his cell?"

Of course we did. Did Maître Grifon know we were news reporters? When I think back on this episode, and remember his childish delight as he confided in us, I realize he did not know who we were, or care.

He beckoned with a delicately crooked finger, then straightened the finger and put it to his lips. We followed.

"He is not kept at Saint Pierre, you know."

We did not know. It was assumed Landru's cell was in the prison adjoining the palais. Maître Grifon led us into the hallway, then down another set of stairs into a space no larger than the storeroom we had just left. This was the subterranean cave to the Palais de Justice, its low arched ceiling showing stone in places where the plaster had fallen. The room was empty except for a cane chair placed beside the heavy wooden door to a cachot, with a small barred window cut into the door.

"Voilà."

Maître Grifon first peered through the bars himself as if to be assured this was indeed the place of confinement he had indicated.

Then Harry looked. His froglike eyes protruded all the more, it seemed, as he set about memorizing the scene.

My turn: I stared into a dim space the shape of a loaf, divided into two sections by a full-length grille. A single bulb illuminated Landru's cell, and was burning now inside a cage of its own: it could be switched off only from the outside. The cell was furnished with a narrow cot over which the prisoner had folded a khaki blanket of military hue. I had almost expected the occupant to be sitting there on the edge of his cot, staring back with indignation at our rude intrusion.

"He's in the courtyard of the prison," said Maître Grifon, answering a question I had not asked. "It is his only opportunity for a breath of air."

In the caged-off section beyond (why the division?) was a small table and a cane chair like the one beside the cell door. On the table Landru had arranged his papers at painfully precise right angles to the table edge, his pen and inkwell set like a mark of punctuation between the two stacks. It was the same obsessive way I positioned my own writing equipment. But I had a piece of Paris sky to contemplate from my window, and could take my air whenever I would.

Landru's cell was a replica of the ingenious trap for rodents in the window of J.-J. Péru & Fils.

Six

THERE WAS A PNEUMATIQUE from Louise, the girl I had known in Baltimore. She was in Paris with her parents—would I stop by the Hôtel Lutetia on the boulevard Raspail? Our correspondence had wilted: I did not know she was coming to France.

Louise met me in the lobby, scrubbed and shining, unchanged from when I knew her in college. (She had graduated from Johns Hopkins, and the trip abroad was her graduation gift.) We kissed shyly. Her scent was more like fine soap than the musky perfume I was familiar with in Paris. The American frock was stylishly right for her: the ribbons went with her look of tender innocence.

"You've become so pale," was the first thing she said to me.

"There's not much sun in Paris."

"Do you get enough to eat?" When I laughed, she went on quickly: "Your mother especially asked. Your mother and father want to know how you are and all about what you do over here, and so do I."

She could not fail to notice my V-shaped scar, and I hinted at others, not in sight. Here was my chance to try to make an impression on her romantic sensibility, so I did. I told her I had shown my short stories to Gertrude Stein and I made much of reporting the trial of

Landru for the British press. Louise did not not know who Gertrude
Stein was, or Landru.

I met her parents. We drank American cocktails seated on a
leather-cushioned banquette in the hotel bar.

Mr. Ballantine was a rotund Baltimore politician, pink and hairless like a large adult child. His wife was small and dry with grey
hair done up in little woolen knots, as if she had knitted her own
hairdo. She was wearing lip rouge that had strayed beyond the thin
straight line of her lips. Mr. Ballantine smoked cigars as substantial
looking as himself.

"Do you think it's all right," Mrs. Ballantine asked me, "for a lady
to go to that place?"

Despite having traveled through the Louvre all afternoon, Mrs.
Ballantine had convinced Mr. Ballantine to take her to the Folies-
Bergère that night.

I said I thought it was perfectly all right.

"She wouldn't let me go without her," said Mr. Ballantine with a
wink. "Afraid to let me out alone at night in a wicked city full of
chorines."

Louise smiled indulgently over her parents. She loved and was
a little ashamed of them.

"Do you miss Baltimore?" Louise asked me.

"I haven't been thinking about Baltimore much."

Louise bit her lip in disappointment.

"It's nice over here," said Mrs. Ballantine, "but it's not the same
as home."

"There's no place like home," said Mr. Ballantine absently. He
was pulling French franc notes from his portefeuille, examining the
multicolored bills with amusement. "Well, we're going to a show and
leave you youngsters to yourselves."

Evidently the evening schedule had been rehearsed.

When we sat alone with our sweet iced drinks Louise requested:
"Will you show me your stories?"

"If you like."

"Now?" She expected to go with me to my room.

I knew Louise was more interested in my living quarters than my
stories—there is a universal curiosity about how young men survive
alone. I told her my hotel was in a sordid neighborhood.

"I don't care."

I could not take her there because of Fleur, so I told her the district was dangerous—it would be risky to take a young lady there at night.

She bit her lip again: the risky and sordid was precisely the Paris she wanted to see. She sighed and invited me to look at her snapshots of London and the Lake Country. The snapshots were in her room.

Louise had always been so correct and shy—and tonight, so prim in her ribbons and sensible touring shoes—I was surprised it was she who made the overtures. There was no pretense of showing me photographs. She firmly drew the drapes to shut out the world, then turned the lights out altogether. There was a private bathroom, and she undressed there while I tugged at my buttons and shoelaces in the dark. She would not let me turn on the bedside lamp until we were both beneath the sheets.

"This is wrong, I know."

"No it isn't," I insisted.

She responded to my caresses with more ardor than I would have believed possible. Like her mother, she possessed an excess of energy— or like all Americans, who seem perpetually in motion to European eyes, and with a rugged strength tired Europe can emulate but never match. I felt Louise could, if she wanted, snap me in half between her powerful thighs.

In what darkened corners of Baltimore had this virginal-looking creature acquired her experience? I would never comprehend the ways of women or what they are made of. In a small voice she requested that I withdraw at the critical moment, then guided my index finger to complete its predecessor's work. She knew what she was about, though she blushed in climax and afterwards wept.

I offer my indélicatesses (as Landru referred to his own indiscretions) in the confessional tradition of Nicolas Restif de la Bretonne: a predictable mix of selfishness, braggadocio, and regret. But the truth is, I did not always seek my sexual ease or satisfy my erotic curiosity in the wedge-shaped room. I became suddenly an unfaithful lover to Fleur and, finally, to Harry a disloyal friend.

On the rue de Varenne, near the Italian embassy, was a residential hotel where several *Paris American* employees lived. Harry and Irene had rooms there, but lived apart—though I discovered they were, more or less, engaged to be married. Irene shared a hotel flat of two adjoining rooms with a dull-witted telephone operator who worked at the

Paris American. I was invited to attend a birthday party there, in honor of Irene's twenty-first year, and came late, not particularly eager to attend, with a bottle of cognac wrapped as a gift.

Irene was wearing elegant stockings and a birthday corsage of orchids when she met me, coolly, at the door. I was introduced to Suzanne, the standardiste, and it became evident I had been invited as Suzanne's partner, to complete the mixed foursome of young expatriate newspaper people living in Paris. Harry had assumed Suzanne and I would be a perfect match—our common bond: we were both of mixed nationalities.

"Is your mother French?" I asked.

"No, my father is."

As Gertrude Stein suggested, this combination is less successful than the other way around. Whatever our backgrounds, Suzanne and I were hopelessly incompatible. She was pretty in a dimpled way, with bobbed and tinted tinsel hair. I liked her knees, dimpled too, angled in my direction where we sat together on the sofa, until we attempted to converse; then her knees moved imperceptibly away and I crossed my own.

"Are your parents in Paris?" I asked.

"No, thank God, in Lyon. Where's yours?"

"In America."

Suzanne yawned. She did not cover her mouth when she yawned, but neither did Fleur. However, when Fleur yawned it was like a cat's pink mouth and tongue, but Suzanne's vast empty O intrigued me in no way.

Irene put on an American gramophone record and cheerlessly blew out the candles on a cake. We forced down some cake with wine, then Harry uncorked the bottle of cognac. We drank cognac with another gramophone record. Neither Harry nor I knew how to dance, so Irene and Suzanne danced together.

Harry had given Irene a pair of suede gloves.

"I'll have to take them back." She did not try them on, but decided they were too large just by looking at them.

I did not understand how Irene and Harry could commit themselves even to the thought of marriage. Irene lost no opportunity to show contempt for her fiancé, and Harry, for his part, addressed Irene —if he spoke to her at all—through Suzanne, the telephone operator, as if transmitting his messages through the *Paris American* switchboard.

It was an unhappy celebration. As is common under such circumstances, everyone drank more than he wanted in an attempt to dissipate the cloud of malaise. Harry was an unfortunate drunk: alcohol at first lent him a cocky assurance, the same belligerent manner he had exhibited the day we met. When he went to the window for air he nonchalantly vomited into the rue de Varenne, then returned to the sofa chastened and subdued. In a little while he fell asleep, sitting up, his face a fierce crimson, a crushed portion of birthday cake on his lap.

Irene helped me get Harry to his room, down two flights, a strenuous exercise at the end of a drinking party. When we returned to the flat, Suzanne had already retired to her own bedroom. She did not wait up to say good night.

For a reason unclear to me in my state, Irene wanted to talk before I left.

"What do you think of him?"

"Landru?" My head spun with names and faces.

"Don't be silly. I'm talking about Harry."

"Harry's fine."

"He's an ass."

"Getting drunk doesn't make him an ass."

"You don't know him."

"I work with him. I like him."

"He's so dense."

"It's the way he talks sometimes."

"It's the way he talks all the time."

"Harry's fine."

"No he's not."

I was certain Irene, too, had drunk more than she should have. She began to talk in a way I knew she would never have done in a soberer moment.

"He's a virgin, did you know that?"

"It's none of my business."

"Well he is. He's jealous of you."

"Jealous?"

"Of your experience."

"He's worked longer for newspapers than I have. It was Harry who got me my job."

"Don't be silly. I'm talking about your petite amie."

I did not know that anyone but Gabriel knew about Fleur, I thought the circles I lived in were separate and distinct. In Paris there are worlds within worlds; circles are unexpectedly concentric, arrondissements overlap.

It occurred to me Irene nourished a strong dislike of Harry. Was that why he remained a virgin? I did not see how she could love him if she did not like him, but she did, I now believe, love him. I was at that time (and would be forever) baffled by the ways of love and like.

Irene poured the remaining cognac into our two glasses and I recklessly accepted mine.

"Wouldn't you rather be with your own kind?"

"What kind is that?"

"American."

"I'm American and French."

"Don't you feel American now, with an American?"

I always felt more American in the company of Americans. When I was with Fleur, however, I felt French.

During these unlikely convolutions of thought Irene informed me that this couch where her fiancé had fallen asleep only minutes before could be made into a bed. She made no attempt to lower her voice, or her eyes, when she told me this. We stood—I a little drunkenly, but my acquiescence was not due to this—and accomplished the transformation under her supervision. Then we stripped down in unison, lights ablaze, Suzanne only a bedroom door away.

Irene was stylishly angular in the way of a mannequin formed to display expensive clothes. Naked, she appeared rather too tall and thin: her breasts were small with large brown coronae around the nipples, an unruly puff of pubic hair covered the mons.

She silently assessed my own physical endowments, then took blunt charge of our two nude bodies. She even provided a towel across the sheets and positioned herself on it, then drew me to her. Whatever her experience as a femme du monde, the puckered slit between her thighs had never before been penetrated. I stopped short in surprise. "Never mind that," she said, and then—to exercise her prerogative further—reversed our positions. I found myself buttocks down against the towel in her place while she nonchalantly mounted me.

"Now," she said, with gritty insistence and a grim smile.

Her aggressive modus operandi put me off. The stiffened root I had made ready to force into a bushy crevice only moments ago was but a diminished plant in less than tumescent bloom. Despite the desperate way she clutched at it, the stalk lost all sap and substance to curl lifelessly back upon itself, a bloodless mushroom.

"Merde!" she said with a vehement and authentic French *r*.

The *r* continued ringing in my benumbed brain, jogging my memory of another instance when she had uttered the word merde. I was transported to the barren office of the *Paris American* where I first became intoxicated by Irene's perfume, enamored of her indifference, aroused by the whispered swish of her silk stockings at the thighs. I closed my eyes to concentrate on this earlier image: Irene became smartly clothed again, inaccessibly distant, and I was overcome by a remembered scent—until, lo! my penis remembered with me and rose to the occasion. To our great relief my imagination had accomplished what her insistence had waylaid.

Nevertheless, in the final reckoning, I was no more than a carefully positioned scalpel upthrust for the operation she was determined to perform. When the thin wall of significant tissue gave way she made no outcry: her private smile was unchanged throughout the ordeal, her eyes stared coolly into mine all the while.

It was not so much a petite amie who was betrayed, nor our mutual friend Harry, but I myself who was deceitfully used. I could predict in what terms Irene would relate our encounter to Suzanne, over coffee and croissants. The sound of their rude laughter echoed in my empty skull.

I studied the bloodstains with far more concern than she. Irene simply rolled up the bloody evidence of our enterprise and carried the roll of toweling to a hamper. When she came back she was wrapped in a virginal white kimono drawn tightly at the throat. She brought me my coat even before I had got my shoelaces tied. I was agitated and appalled—sober, but more of an ass than Harry ever was—and certainly as anxious to flee the scene as she was to be rid of me.

Not once during the grim combat d'amour had we caressed or kissed, yet she sent me on my way with a chillingly ironic merci, as if thanking me for a birthday gift. Scorpio was her sign, and I had been properly stung.

I went with my bruised pride to the Lutetia next day, to use and be used by Louise. She was back from a tour of Versailles eager to experience something royally her own other than viewing museum remnants of the royal life. For the remaining three days in Paris she managed to dispatch her parents to the Eiffel Tower, l'Orangerie, and the catacombs—promenades recommended by Baedecker—and a tour of the sewers. The Ballantines were only too willing to be shunted aside to allow their only child her Parisian fling for having graduated.

I was never to know the sight of my coy mistress in the altogether: Louise refused to reveal her comely portions below the neck or above the knee. There was no way to comprehend the source of her shame, for I was assured by an infallible sense of touch how delightfully curved and smoothly made she was—a blind reading by braille, but a sufficiently accurate and pleasantly diverting method for studying the female form. I cannot believe she drew the blinds and extinguished all light to hide a blemish or birthmark. It may have been she was saving the full voluptuous display of herself for her husband, in lieu of a maidenhead, on the wedding night.

When I proposed a hot-water dip together, the vast antique baignoire at the Lutetia did not tempt her: she was, or pretended to be, scandalized. Tant pis. In the luxury of a private bath I privately soaped away the blended juices of our joining and hoped, for Fleur's sake, I was washing the peppermint smell of my American girl down the drain.

Our languorous dallying afternoons came to a not greatly regretted end when the Ballantines embarked for Rome and I could turn my undivided attentions to a petite amie tucked away on the rue Tiquetonne, there to dwell upon, fatuously—as men will do, allowing humiliation to become conquest—three simultaneous affairs successfully conducted in three different corners of Paris, like the separate compartments Landru kept, with women in them.

Seven

"BUT TWO YEARS IN PRISON!" lamented Madame Vitrine, who had a great sympathy for Landru, and a large curiosity about him. "What if the poor man should turn out to be innocent?"

Four thousand Frenchmen had cynically voted for Landru instead of the official candidates in the 1919 national elections: many had come to believe the Landru Affair was a contrivance by the government as a distraction from the shameful treaty signed at Versailles.

A magician onstage at the Théâtre de Variétés offered to make the wives of the men in the audience vanish. There was a trickle of polite laughter as husbands facetiously eyed their wives—the trickle became a roaring torrent when the magician swiftly turned his back, then faced the audience with a newly sprouted beard that transformed him into Landru.

Editorials asked why Landru should be persecuted for allegedly doing away with eleven persons when Kaiser Wilhelm—responsible for the massacre of ten million—went free.

Georges the barman had a theory. He shared it with me across the zinc counter.

"There is more than one Landru. There has to be."

Meanwhile Landru was said to have made a noose of his bedding and tried to hang himself in his cell. A prison guard claimed it was a

simulated act. Landru, whose own father had committed suicide in
this way, commented: "If the guard thinks hanging is a simulated
act, let him put his own head in a noose."

Madame Vitrine, my venerable landlady, was so drawn to the
proceedings at Versailles she kept an extensive scrapbook of clippings
about Landru—including one I had written and presented to her, in
English, which she could not read, but was delighted to add to her
collection.

Knowing I was a correspondent at the trial, she appeared one
morning at my door, in place of the chambermaid, with fresh towels
over her arm as an excuse to knock, an envelope in her other hand.
She placed the envelope in my hand but did not let go of it until
she said with great intensity: "You must promise to deliver it to him
personally."

Fleur sat upon the bed with her feet wrapped in a shawl, languidly
applying lacquer to her fingernails. She ignored and was ignored by
Madame Vitrine.

On the envelope was written the name, in unsteady but elegant
lycée script: *Monsieur Henri Désiré Landru.*

"I do not know him personally," I said. "I only write about him."

"You will find a way."

Landru received from forty to sixty letters a day, from women. I
was curious about what Madame Vitrine had written, but would not
for the world have violated the wax seal she had placed upon the flap.

When Madame Vitrine left I wanted Fleur, her face averted, to
ask me about the envelope. Of course she knew, so why should she
ask? Fleur was the only soul in Paris who was unaware of the trial
at Versailles: she would not pronounce Landru's name, or hear one
word of his crimes.

Eight

"I stand accused. The state has brought an indictment against me. But these women you speak of accuse me of nothing."

"You forget," said President Gilbert, "you have placed them in a position where they cannot."

"I think the accusation is vague about what position I have placed them in, and I say that I placed them in no position at all."

Landru's suggestive hesitation each time he pronounced the word position aroused the expected outburst of laughter.

Madame Guillin appeared in Landru's carnet under the code name Crozatier, a reference to the rue Crozatier where she lived. A concierge identified Landru as Monsieur Petit, the name Madame Guillin knew him by. Madame Guillin had inherited 22,000 francs from her employer, for whom she had given long and faithful service as governess to his children. In addition to this sum, she had invested in bonds and she owned some jewelry. After her disappearance the jewelry had been sold and two bonds were cashed at the Banque de France under Madame Guillin's falsified signature. A handwriting expert was called to the stand.

Maître de Moro Giafferi commented sotto voce, but loud enough to be heard by the jury and the press: "God preserve us from handwriting experts!"

The expert stated the forgery had been committed by Landru's hand.

A bank teller identified Landru as the man who had cashed the bonds, but his testimony was incomplete. He could not remember the date, seven years ago, and was puzzled when Landru declared he had redeemed the securities, but the transaction had not taken place at the teller's window at the Banque de France, but in Landru's apartment—that is, the apartment rented in the name of Monsieur Petit—at 45, rue des Ternes.

"I do remember Monsieur Petit," said the witness, referring to Landru, "but I have forgotten the circumstances."

"I gave him fifty francs," said Landru. "He should remember that."

The concierge claimed to have been a confidante of Madame Guillin. She related a strange conversation between herself and Madame Guillin after the latter had returned from a visit to Vernouillet.

"Monsieur Petit was very devoted to her, she told me—a perfect gentleman, an ideal fiancé." Then she talked about an odd incident that occurred during her visit: she opened a locked door one day—for the key had been left in it—and found a collection of women's clothing piled upon a bed. Naturally she asked Monsieur Petit about the clothing, and he replied, " 'That was my mother's room before she died, the clothing is hers—and I have kept the room as it was, a shrine to her memory.' "

(Laughter. Witness puzzled, wondering what is funny.)

"God preserve us from concierges," said Maître de Moro Giafferi, sotto voce.

"I always wondered what became of Madame Guillin," said the witness, looking sadly into the middle distance. It was a damaging remark, and I wondered if the statement—and the look of condolence that went with it—had been rehearsed in the attorney general's office.

But Landru rose to the remark: "I myself have been sought for a good many years. It is only three years since the search for Madame Guillin was begun. Seek and ye shall find."

Annoyed, possibly aroused by the biblical exhortation, Maître Godefroy bellowed the ominous warning: "You speak facetiously, Landru, for one who risks his head each time he jokes."

"I regret, Maître—since it is a question of my head—not to have more than one to offer you."

(Laughter, cries of "Bravo!")

* * *

That evening on the late train to Paris, Harry beside me (his brief-case across his lap, mine across mine), we put together the meandering tale of Madame Guillin—her small inheritance, her jewelry and bonds, and the dapper bearded mysterious stranger in her life: Monsieur Petit.

When I got to Channel News, O'Grady was taking a sponge bath in one of those inflated rubber tubs the British carry with them to the Continent. He had vomited all over himself after an excess of whiskey and cheese.

"Write it up, write it up!" he said drunkenly, spraying a trail of suds in the direction of his typewriter.

I had never seen him naked. He looked ridiculous sitting there, his eyeshade on, his pale freckled knees sticking up like islands in a dirty sea.

The room smelled of vomit so I wrote quickly, anxious to go.

"Do me one on the Unknown Soldier."

"Who is that?"

"If I knew, he wouldn't be unknown."

There was a note scribbled on O'Grady's fingerprinted notepad about an unidentified corpse—"known but to God"—buried that day at Arlington Cemetery, with full military honors.

Following this item was another, from Mayence: "Naturalized German (no mention previous nationality) claimed knew André Cuchet during the war. Boy was deserter from British unit."

The second scrap of news excited me more than the first: it seemed to confirm Landru's assertion that Madame Cuchet's son had left France to join the British army.

". . . German (no name) met Cuchet, Gelsenkirchen, 1918. Cuchet intended to flee to Switzerland wearing uniform American soldier. Killed in bombing raid before he could reach frontier . . . or so our informant (anon.) declares."

I juxtaposed the two notes, one in one hand, one in the other. My training under O'Grady lent me some of the master's own sense of skulduggery.

"What if I combined these two stories?"

"You mean," asked O'Grady, "turning André Cuchet into the Unknown Soldier?"

"Or turning the Unknown Soldier into André Cuchet. What if,

say, Cuchet had been recovered by an American burial patrol, and out of thousands of scattered unidentified dead—"

O'Grady held his bar of soap aloft, sober enough to stop me short: "You may make light of the deaths of ten foolish middle-aged ladies, and you are free to turn their murderer into a clown, but never—my dear Candide—never trifle with the dignity of a patriotic death."

I tapped out two independent stories from the scant details O'Grady had left me: one of rumor and mystery, one of mystery and death. You would not have known them apart.

The dresses, kerchiefs, corsets, and underclothing of Madame Guillin were still on display in the prétoire on November 12, 1921—the faint odor of mildew and mothballs intermingled in the stagnant air. The assizes at Versailles had not quite done with Madame Guillin, even if Landru had. The third anniversary of the armistice dominated the headlines, but Landru shared the front pages with blurred photographs of military parades.

President Gilbert wanted to know why Landru abandoned his villa at Vernouillet after Madame Guillin's disappearance.

"The lease had expired. I enjoy privacy." (Laughter.) "I decided to take a villa elsewhere, and settled on Gambais."

"Because of the dearth of neighbors, no doubt," interjected Maître Godefroy.

"That was part of the consideration, yes." Landru's face showed an innocent candor. "I have just said I enjoy privacy. Also the villa at Gambais was half the rent."

(Laughter.)

"And had a wall around it?"

"That, yes."

"Neighbors would not likely see or hear anything that went on behind that wall?"

"Probably not. I was never interested in entertaining my neighbors." (Laughter.) "Also, I wanted a lodging for my family eventually. The villa appealed to me for a number of reasons, and I even considered buying it at one point."

The unspoken question wafted through the salle like the overwhelming odor of mothballs: with which widow's money?

"Your first purchase after renting the villa was a stove and three hundred kilos of coal."

There was a murmur from the spectators, but I did not share their assumption: the warmth of his love nest is a man's all-important concern.

"The place was humid, having been for some time without a tenant. There was no fireplace. As a matter of fact, a good part of the coal was stolen soon after I bought it."

"Did you file a complaint?"

"I thought it prudent not to enter into relations with the police at that time."

When the laughter ceased Landru lost all interest in the questioning and remained mute. While a dreary series of witnesses, blinking from the overbright courtroom lights after being released from the darkened salle d'attente, filed by to confirm the purchase of a stove, fuel, saw blades, and mutton chops—this last by the local butcher, who obviously bore a grudge—Landru sat motionless in his self-induced catatonia, a turtle half drawn into its shell, with partially closed eyes, perhaps listening, possibly asleep.

In the somnolent press section was passed from hand to hand, aisle by aisle, a cartoon done by one of the sketch artists present. A woman's feet protruded from an oven, with the caption: "Henri believes a woman's place is in the kitchen."

Nine

SHE CRACKED OPEN her Tarot and riffled together the two halves with a smile so private I inserted my knee between her thighs, jealous (cards were her way to close me out, or kill an afternoon)—but she ignored the provocation and dealt herself a divinatory hand.

For once, to distract her, I asked: "What does that mean?" pointing to the Tower, struck by flame, two figures falling from it to their doom.

"It is not a game," was all she would say, impatient with me.

Her smile turned down as this sequence turned up: the Three of Cups, the Ace of Wands, and the World (upside down)—but soon after that she seemed unreasonably pleased to see the Fool headed nonchalantly for a precipice.

I was intrigued by a youth contemplating a harvest of stars—the Seven of Pentacles—and above all by the fierce bearded Devil holding a pair of nude lovers in chains. The young man with his seven blooming stars may have held some meaning for me, but it was the Devil I asked about.

"Of no concern," said she, apparently accustomed to the Devil's presence.

"Which, then, are the good cards, and which ones are bad?"

"The cards are not good or bad, they just are."

She had read them to her satisfaction, or had given up in annoyance, for she scooped the cards together, all but the Hierophant—a pope enthroned before his acolytes, two crossed keys at his feet—which slipped from her grasp, then that card too was sealed into her Tarot and the deck thrust under her pillow.

I complained that she had seen what the heavens had in store for her while I was left in the dark.

"Do not mock." She pushed my nudging knee away.

"At least tell me my future."

"I can tell your future without cards. Your fate is to have what you want and not know what it is that you want or what you have until you are old and at the end of it."

This she said in such swift clipped French it took me a moment to put the words together. I made no reply. Her opinion of me was never uplifting, her commitment to me the only flattery she ever offered. For as long as she stayed with me that made me a man, like my father, but when I most felt the achievement of a man's estate she could topple my self-esteem with a word.

The grey Sunday gave no further promise of a spread of cards, or thighs, so I proposed an outing. The bruised sky had come down so low I felt I could touch it from the window: if we did not take the air soon, the air would turn to water.

It was a cheerless promenade. Shadows lay across the market streets, an unnatural layer of dark, hours before darkness was due. Only the arrogant dwarf—the only fille de joie in sight—stood her ground before the shuttered PTT. Here and there a café window was yellow with a poisonous light where perhaps a single patron clung disconsolately to his coffee, his back turned to the street. There was no sanctuary indoors or out.

At rue Rambuteau we would have been glad of any shelter, for the menacing sky suddenly broke open with a doomsday crack, then dumped a hailstorm of frozen pellets upon us. We ran through the bouncing stinging hailstones toward Saint-Eustache, and found a motor taxi parked beside the cathedral. The driver had thrown open the door even before we reached his cab: "Entrez," he cried, "entrez!"

We plunged into the taxi—not to drive anywhere, for the driver was unable to see beyond the windshield—but to shake ourselves dry and share for a moment the cabman's immobilized chariot.

"Merde de merde," said the driver, a red kerchief about his neck like a rooster's crop. "Now we have to sit through this merde."

He made extensive use of the term merde, in every possible grammatical modification.

"The emmerdeurs cannot sling enough merde down here but must emmerder us from on high!" He flung his hand at the hailstorm. "This merde that merde and the other—ah, yes, and these newspaper shits practicing their shitmanship on the public, with their shitting criminals and criminal shits like this shit of a killer of shit-brained women!" He rattled a damp copy of *l'Oeuvre* across the back of the seat: Landru dominated the front page, flanked by his guardians. "Why this shitty little emmerdeur instead of another? We are swimming in this shit shat daily upon us by the shit-making courts with their shit-eating lawyers trying to shit higher than their own asses."

Fleur was elsewhere, freeing her hair from the wet kerchief, shaking the hailstones from it. By her manner I sensed she found nothing comic in the cabman's monologue.

Suddenly the sleet turned to rain—"Not enough to shit hailstones on our heads, the hail turns to more shit!"—and a common impulse drove us from the cab back into the wet world (we were soaked through in an instant) to try the side entrance to Saint-Eustache. The cathedral was open to us, but empty in this unholy season.

An alabaster Christ saw us in, hung from the stones in sublime torture, his agony illuminated by a dozen tapers burning on the spiked candelabra. The draft from the door I held open for Fleur blew out two candles: two prayers indifferently extinguished by the weather. Fleur took the two smoking tapers from their spikes and relit them from another flame as if to restore the blessing they represented—but no, she had taken them for a purpose of her own: handed one to me, kept the other for herself.

"Are they not for the dead?" I mumbled in protest, but she did not reply or had not heard.

We made a wet trail across the stones of a vast darkened sanctuary, stolen candles illuminating the hollow stares of sculpted saints whose marble toes were worn away by the kisses of the faithful.

A gilded secular Joan of Arc barred our way—we had no business here—with a plaster sword above our heads like the blade of a guillotine. We sidestepped her, unafraid. Next thing I knew, Fleur had slipped behind the curtains of a confessional—for no religious reason, merely to reduce the scale of our enclosure—and I went in after her, but found a grille between us.

"Am I the priest," I asked, "or the sinner?"

"Have you a place to sit?"

"Yes, with a cushion on it."

"I am obliged to kneel. Anyway, women cannot be priests."

"My side smells of garlic."

"Mine of merde."

I thought this a reference to our merdicious cabman, but Fleur did not laugh—though I was inclined to. I thought of Landru kneeling beside Madame Jaume at the Sacré-Coeur, offering a facetious prayer to God to bless their union, and the thought sobered me, but then I asked in my own facetious way: "Tell me, my child, what sins you have committed."

"Sins? I have done things, things have been done to me. I do not believe in sins."

"What things?"

"Things."

"Tell me."

"I did whatever I did with no conscience or regret."

I could see her face by the glow of the candles, eyes without kohl and ringed with sleeplessness, a sad visage sectioned by the grillwork.

"And the things done to you?"

"I don't remember."

"You do."

"No."

"I am your priest."

"You are my fornicator. Listen, I knew a man who would have married me and I did not care if he married me or not, only that he keep me."

"Anacréon?"

"Don't be bête. What does it matter who?"

"But who?"

"A man. I found out things about him—that is the trouble with knowing."

"What did you know?"

"I just knew. And he knew that I knew—he could not keep me after that. I was afraid."

"Afraid of what?"

"Of him, to stay with him. But afraid to leave—so I stayed. He would have to do something about me, tu comprends?"

I said yes, without truly understanding.

"He would have to kill me."

I could not see her face when she said this.

"But you are alive and talking to me."

"So you say, and so I am."

"You say he would have to kill you."

"He would, and he did."

"Je ne comprends pas."

"A priest understands everything. It rained. When he went for wood I dug myself out and pedaled back to Paris in the rain."

A thread ran through the fabric of her tale that I knew to be genuine, but I could not follow the thread.

"Je ne comprends pas."

"You are bête. Enough. It is not a game."

It was a game at the beginning but had somewhere turned to matters of life and death. She ended in a fit of coughing then stepped from our sarcophagus into the larger tomb of the stone cathedral. We replaced the tapers on their spikes—still lit, no harm done—but would they survive the next courant d'air from outside?

At home we stripped ourselves of the wet vestments and naked drank hot rum from a shared bowl. I fed her bits of biscuit like communion wafers, warning her—playful still—I had not exacted penance. Would she play violated nun to my renegade priest?

"One does not ask permission to rape."

True. With her compliance there was no rape—but the blunt thrust of my attack might have passed for that.

Ten

I CAUGHT GABRIEL'S EYE. He smiled and waved extravagantly from the public section of the courtroom, self-consciously flaunting the presence of a lovely young girl at his side. It was unusual for Gabriel to be in the company of a woman, anywhere, except with Miss Stein, in the Luxembourg Gardens. I learned that he had got passes to the Palais de Justice through the intercession of Jean Cocteau. Oddly enough, the theatre set—to the disadvantage of political figures, even royalty—had weighty influence over the judicial authorities who issued laissez-passer for the Landru trial.

Overnight the furniture and wardrobe of Madame Guillin had been removed from the prétoire: the personal effects of Madame Collomb were displayed in their place. It was Madame Collomb's disappearance, followed by the relentless inquiries of her family, which finally set in motion the ponderous machinery of justice. During the summary of Madame Collomb's relations with Landru, Harry made the only original comment I have ever heard him utter: "He kept killing the same woman." Maître Godefroy read aloud the list of items from Madame Collomb's cluttered life: among her bonnets and belts, stays and stockings, was a breviary in which her name was inscribed, along with documents of so personal a nature she could not possibly have left them in the hands of her furniture dealer—a letter, for example, from the mysterious Bernard.

Maître de Moro Giafferi seized upon this: "Monsieur Bernard?" asked the defense attorney with heavy sarcasm, "or Monsieur Bernard Bernard?"

Who was Bernard, other name unknown? The one intriguing aspect of Madame Collomb's past was that she had taken a lover prior to Landru.

"My client," declared Maître de Moro Giafferi, "was not the only person with a secret life."

The defense attorney made much of the mystery of Bernard. Witnesses gave conflicting testimony concerning the obscure lover, and not even Madame Collomb's family members knew for certain if a child, a girl, was born of this shadowy union. The unconfirmed birth was said to have taken place at a hospital in Marseille, the child taken to an orphanage in Mentone, or San Remo, to be brought up by nuns.

(The story Solange once told me was so similar it might have been the history of this girl—but a tale told by a prostitute is not meant to be believed. Still, there might be something in this enigmatic coincidence. Solange, a prostitute in a maison close at Invalides, would be the same age as a daughter born to Madame Collomb—if Madame Collomb had given birth to a daughter.)

The hospital in Marseille was never named, the nuns in Mentone (or San Remo) never identified.

"It is not only the defendant who is unable to explain the whereabouts of certain persons encountered in the distant past."

At the time of her meeting with Landru, Madame Collomb claimed to be thirty-nine. Actually she was forty-four.

"I wouldn't have believed it," said Landru.

(Laughter.)

Maître Godefroy asked Landru the meaning of his notation 4h du soir, following the name Collomb in his cahier.

"I don't remember why I noted that."

"Doesn't it appear significant that the date on which you wrote 4h du soir behind the name Collomb was the last day Madame Collomb was seen alive?"

Landru insisted he found no meaning or relevance in the time or date he had inscribed in his cahier.

A red-bound notebook found on Landru's person—along with

similar notebooks discovered among the letters and papers in his wicker file—was the centerpiece of evidence in the attorney general's case. Over the two years Landru was kept at la Santé prison, Brigadier Riboulet worked at deciphering the miniature script and abbreviated notations in these notebooks. The brigadier's tedious assignment may not have been so uncongenial a task: he went about his work with diligence and devotion (and was promoted to the rank of chief inspector for his pains)—it was the same kind of devoir a graduate of the French lycée would find familiar.

From time to time the brigadier would feed the reporters at La Cage (where police briefings to newspapermen took place) bits and pieces, scraps and fragments from the infamous notebooks, a series of hors d'oeuvres before the main course. I carried these undigested items back to O'Grady, who savored and sniffed at them with more than passing interest, for O'Grady was a crossword puzzle fan. Working out the ciphers and initials recorded by an ingenious criminal suited O'Grady's temperament. He would ponder these small mysteries at his littered desk, muttering amiably to himself, testing his powers of deduction, a Sherlock Holmes manqué.

What, for instance, did the numbers 1 through 7 represent? These single ciphers were sprinkled throughout the notebooks, accompanied by figures that obviously referred to sums expended or received (centimes separated from francs by the traditional indication of a comma), followed by an abbreviated entry that apparently recorded place and date. O'Grady—though Brigadier Riboulet must already have done so —guessed that the single ciphers represented Landru and his family: this would account for numbers 1 through 6, for Landru had a wife and four children. Number 1 would be Landru himself. In his own ménage he exercised the rule of first person. He was a patriarch, in the biblical sense. Second to himself was his wife—number 2 of course. He loved her unreservedly, no doubt of it, and hoped to protect her from the public humiliation of his arrest and trial. Faithless in the way of the world, Landru was rigidly faithful to the Frenchman's idea of love of family and domestic continuity. At any rate, Madame Landru's assigned code was quickly ascertained: the sums that were consigned to 2 matched the expenditures it would take to run a French household (at bare subsistence level, the level at which the Landru family lived) during the war years.

Brigadier Riboulet personally traced numbers 3, 4, 5, and 6 by interviewing members of Landru's family. O'Grady chose the easier way: he assumed the following numbers would be assigned to the children in chronological order of age, then published this theory as fact, some time before Riboulet's painstaking efforts confirmed the guess.

All of this spadework was being done for purposes of prosecution, but the revelations might have been used as sympathetic evidence for the defense. There was something unusually touching about Landru's family feeling. In February of 1918, for instance, Landru reimbursed his children for the price of admission to a neighborhood cinema: $65 \times 4 = 2F$ 60. Most of the family sums entered were petty, even pitiable. The hard-pressed father was sometimes reduced to borrowing money from his son Maurice (number 4), who worked in a garage, a poorly paid apprentice. Maurice must have been about my own age. Landru was scrupulous about repayment—just as my father had been about small sums he borrowed from me—presumably an attempt (by both fathers) to teach their sons a lesson in economic husbandry.

Landru's women were indicated in several ways. He might jot down an initial, an abbreviation or, frequently, an address or métro stop in Paris. Thus Madame Guillin was Crozatier because she lived on impasse Crozatier in the 12th arrondissement. For a time the police, and newspapers, were baffled by the term Brésil. This code name appeared in Landru's notebooks for the year 1915. My guess was that the reference might correspond to the place du Brésil, in the 17th, but O'Grady thought not.

"You give our meticulous Bluebeard credit for an intelligence he does not in fact possess."

"How so?"

"The women have mostly been assigned code names that correspond to their addresses in Paris. There is one notable exception."

"Mademoiselle Marchadier."

"Exactly. Mademoiselle Marchadier, by general agreement, is Havre, for she was born in le Havre."

I followed the pattern of O'Grady's reasoning, but replied: "None of the missing women was born in Brazil."

"Examine the list carefully."

I did so, and said: "Only Madame Laborde-Line was born outside of France, in Buenos Aires."

"Exactly."

"But Buenos Aires is in Argentina."

"Exactly."

"I see. Landru thought Buenos Aires is the capital of Brazil."

"Capital, my dear Candide." He meant my reasoning was capital. "I have not abandoned all hope that you will learn someday that a straight line is not always the shortest distance between two points."

When Landru, at the trial, was confronted with this unraveling of his tangled notes, he announced: "It is all a game of names and numbers for which you have made up your own set of rules."

"Who is she?" asked Harry, for a change—he knew by sight everyone worth knowing at the trial, and Gabriel's fascinating companion appeared to be worth knowing. I said I did not know. We contrived to join Gabriel during the intermission, and were introduced to Barbette—for that was her stage name—who was in the theatre. The lovely young creature on Gabriel's arm attracted a murmur of approval as we four passed through the corridor where court officials lounged and gossiped and stroked the pleated bibs at their throats like Daumier caricatures. Harry—flushed and blustering, impressed by the company of the beautiful girl—promised to show Barbette the cell where Landru was kept.

We made our way single file to the lower level leading to Landru's cage. The girl was sandwiched between Harry and Gabriel, apparently delighted to have three male admirers—but I could not help wondering at Gabriel's interest in a member of the opposite sex.

In the subterranean light below, Harry gallantly took Barbette's elbow to lead her directly to the barred window in the cell door. I would have been annoyed in Gabriel's place, but he relinquished the girl willingly, with a smile.

"Here's Bluebeard's lair," said Harry proudly, as if he were the criminal's keeper.

"That's a nice tight calaboose," said Barbette, but her voice was the unsettling voice of a man.

It took me a moment, in the dim light, to recognize the features of Vander Clyde under an elaborate wig. Gabriel's young lady was the cowboy in transvestite attire.

"Back home we string the dude up first and ask questions later."

All femininity fell away and one false breast was deflated as the cowboy drew a silk scarf from his bosom. He made a hangman's knot of it, to demonstrate Landru's fate if he had been caught in Texas.

Harry had swiftly drawn his hand from Barbette's elbow and was now rubbing it as if he had been burned.

* * *

Did the number 5 refer to his son Charles? A shadow crossed Landru's face.

Maître Grifon was called to read from the police deposition given by Charles Landru in which Charles admitted his father had sent him to deliver a bouquet of mimosa and roses to Madame Collomb's sister, pretending to be a delivery boy. The flowers bore Madame Collomb's visiting card (no message or signature) and were supposedly sent from the Midi. Actually they were purchased at a flower stall in les Halles. In his deposition Charles reported: "I thought Papa was playing a joke."

At any reference to his family, Landru became wary. When he refused to comment on the statement given by his son, Maître Godefroy expressed the threat—vague, but legally feasible—that Charles be brought into court to testify.

"Jamais!" Landru exploded. He was frantic, as well as indignant. "My son knows nothing of these matters." The droll witticisms were done, the gallery playing was over. Landru's features turned rigid, he wet his lips with his tongue. "Charles did as I told him, as any well-bred son would do."

"Why then did you have flowers sent by way of your son to Madame Collomb's sister?"

Angered beyond the ability to control his voice, Landru made no reply. Maître Godefroy had scored: the response was obvious.

Eleven

THE DOOR KNOCKER was the same, the touch of it familiar: a detached female hand that tapped out its disembodied message on a brass plate. But this time I noticed the brass plate was unpolished. A few moments after I rapped I heard the click of a peephole flipped open; then I felt, rather than saw, the pupil of an eye at the other end. The madam would have to determine if I were a client (regular or occasional), a police officer, a pimp, an enraged brother seeking his runaway sister, a criminal, a madman. After a longish interval the door was opened to me.

My expectation prefigured the same madam of imposing bosom who once reminded me of Madame d'O in Nice—but if Madame X was the same brothel keeper who greeted me two years ago, she had diminished in stature and bosom. Only the gold-headed cane was exactly as I remembered: the scepter of office wielded by the potentate of a small kingdom.

The aging lady appeared in full evening regalia (it was late afternoon): a sleeveless gown, somewhat outmoded, with beaded straps and a careful arrangement of plumes sprouting from one bare shoulder. The gown was too large for her—or she was too small for the gown. She looked ill under her paint and feathers. Incongruously, a pair of grandmotherly spectacles dangled from a black ribbon beneath her several withered chins. She drew the eyeglasses to her face, to examine me more closely than a peephole in the door allowed.

"Monsieur?"

"Je cherche," I began uncertainly, "une jeune fille."

I hardly knew why I had come, before I expressed this quaint request. Stung by O'Grady's insinuations, impelled by an ambition I did not know I possessed, intrigued by the mystery of Bernard, I wanted to do a story about a missing daughter. Before I could pronounce the name of the girl I sought, Madame X showed her artificial teeth in an equally artificial smile.

"She is here," she said.

"Solange?"

"The very one."

She plucked at my sleeve to draw me inside—an unseemly gesture for the proprietress of the most distinguished maison close in the district of the Invalides.

The corridor was brightly lit but I could not fail to perceive a filament of spiderweb between the brilliant prisms of a chandelier. I peered into the small dining salon that opened off the reception hall. There my memory's eye was prepared to repeat the vision of three lovely Gratiae eyeing me over their breakfast chocolate. Breakfast, of course, had passed many hours before. Did they nap or bathe or lacquer their nails in the long interval between breakfast and champagne? My memory—unlike Harry's marvelous machine—was dreamily visual, a storehouse of accumulated images. I saw because I wanted, in my adolescent way, to see three beauties as they had been that summer morn, their breasts visible in nests of gauze, bodies lounging fixed in time like statuary.

I presumed Madame X would escort me to the parlor where I had examined the spurious artwork on the walls and fingered the erotic playthings on the mantelpiece, that first time—and now again—to await the appearance of Solange. But Madame X limped ahead of me tapping her cane on the chessboard pattern of tiles to a bar at the end of the corridor.

"Albert!" she called, but the barman did not appear. She called again but only an echo of her "Albert!" replied. "I don't know where he has gone to. Young men of today—I do not include you, Monsieur— are all so slack and negligent. The folly of war, the chaos that follows when war is done. Truly, ils sont d'une génération perdue."

By now I realized the establishment was not as it once had been.

There had been some large mistake—on my part, if not on hers. The bottles ranged along the mirrored shelf were empty, all.

She took my sleeve again—as if it might occur to me to leave, and thus to prevent my going—then led me to her study, a small office tucked beneath the great winding oak staircase, windowless but dustily elegant. There was no more room inside than inside Landru's cell. I was obliged to lower my head so as not to scrape the trompe l'oeil ceiling. She sat me down on one of the uncomfortable Louis XV chairs and herself before an antique escritoire overflowing with pencil stubs and bits of paper that might have been chewed by mice. The Oriental rug underfoot was too large for the room, and a good part of it lay rolled against the opposite wall.

Madame X sighed from the effort of seating herself, then fumbled through the scraps of paper and envelopes for a bottle of Hollands. She brought forth two tumblers that might have come from O'Grady's desk drawer, sticky from prior use. She poured a generous portion for me, but took only a splash of the liquid for herself.

I wished her health and happiness. She sighed at the words santé-bonheur, then drank her gin down neat.

"An ambassador once kissed this hand," and she showed me it, beringed, the wrist heavy with bracelets. "I cannot of course tell you the nation he represented—only that it remains a kingdom, not a republic—for discretion, chez nous, has forever been the second commandment."

"What is the first?" I asked, though I knew it.

She had forgotten she was speaking of commandments and spoke of Russians: "They bring with them a festive ambience. I mistakenly stocked vodka for them, but they drink only champagne, and, yes, they do break the glasses—there is a great sweeping up afterward." She paused, and inclined her head as if listening for the sound of broken glass. "Tourgeniev once kissed this hand," she said, and lifted the hand to me until I felt obliged to take it and touch my lips lightly to the yellow flesh between two swollen veins. She withdrew her hand, pleased, and looked at it as if she might see the imprint of my lips, Tourgeniev's, the ambassador's.

She wistfully licked the rim of her empty tumbler and looked off to the place where the excess rug was rolled. She spoke more to herself than to me:

"I started with three girls, just three—but of a quality." She kissed the tips of her fingers then threw the phantom kiss into the void. "Of a rare quality unheard of in the hurly-burly of today's frantic rendez-vous, cheap meetings at train stations, lovemaking à la chaîne." Her mouth went ugly with disgust. "But my first three—not even the Pope has a better eye than I for a leg, a waist, the back of a neck. You would be surprised to know how many men are fond of the backs of necks."

I was not surprised, but pretended to be.

"We have never exceeded sixteen girls, three chambermaids, and a barman. I once engaged a dwarf as doorman and dressed him in a miniature copy of the porter's uniform at the Ritz—with pourboires he was earning more than the headwaiter at Maxim's—but he was in-discreet and had to be dismissed. My girls have always been of a quality, my house une maison réputée. Never more than sixteen girls. To those who speak of efficiency and scale, I reply, 'I do not offer a way station or a bazaar—mine is an intimate club for gentlemen away from home.' Take the Chabanais," she said, meaning I could have it, and all its works, "with sixty pensionnaires! What gentleman of breeding would avail himself of that crowded bagnio? A pit for ani-mals, à mon avis. An asylum of vice, not a house of pleasure!"

The indignation throbbed at the veins of her temples. She paused to dab at her eyes with the backs of her hands.

"Here, always, we stress the leisurely pace. There is time for re-flection, un petit verre, to make one's choice at ease and to enjoy that choice at length, at length.

"When one of my girls drinks champagne with her client it is Dom Pérignon, jamais de l'eau gazeuse, with a little color, a deceit practiced at the One-Two-Two." She smiled the smile of one who knows such things and is pained to pass them on. "That is why the celebrities come to us, my friend: the entrepreneurs, sportsmen, literary gentlemen, ministers of state—and, I can assure you, without naming names—a full ambassador, incognito of course."

"Of course." I had finished my gin at the leisurely pace she in-voked. Even without my wristwatch I could feel the lateness of the hour. Soon the stream of clients would begin. I did not want to disturb her reverie but ventured the question all the same: "Is Solange still here?"

"But of course." She was disappointed in me. She drew the spectacles to her eyes to make certain she had not been mistaken in her judgment of me. "My girls stay with me always."

"Could I see her?"

"But of course, Monsieur. She is yours—that is, if she is not otherwise engaged."

I had neither seen nor heard any activity so far. I assumed I would be granted my rendezvous.

"But let me call the girls together for you." She rose with an effort, and I placed her cane in her hand. "That way you may examine what other delicacies we have to offer." She took a set of keys from a pigeonhole in the escritoire. "Do not, my friend, be forever bound to a name and souvenir out of the past. The memory of pleasure cannot be as much relied upon as pleasure at hand."

As we stepped out of the smothering soundproof cubicle, the reception hall seemed full of echoes. I thought I heard the Gratiae somewhere laughing at me.

We stood before the parlor door, and I wondered: why should that chamber of solitary foreplay be locked? I was uneasy under the cobwebbed illumination in the hallway, disturbed by the jangling of keys, the distant creaking of parquet under invisible weight. She handed the key ring to me as if offering the formality of uncorking a wine to the gentleman at her side.

I inserted key after key into the aperture—an exploratory sexual act, sans succès—until at last the right key came round, and the lock turned. Darkness within, for the blind had been drawn—for years, it would seem, from the close odor. Unidentified objects lay under the blue-white sheets. I tried to make out what they were, at the same time as I examined the obscure motives for my coming here. What had I expected to learn from Solange that I could fit into newspaper columns? How could a prostitute's tale of entrapment have any bearing on the trial at Versailles? Would Landru's missing ladies, all, be assembled here when the light came on?

Light came on, flickering, for Madame X was walking from candelabrum to candelabrum gaily striking matches as she walked. The antique pieces I saw in my mind's eye were hidden under dustcovers. Even the paintings were covered, and the mirrors draped, so that I could see neither the pink nude in her bath nor myself reflected anywhere herein. I was welcome to guess at what lay beneath the coverings. A shape I took to be the stereoscope might still offer the vision of a gartered couple cohabiting canine fashion.

Madame X drew me inside by my sleeve. She went suddenly to

the doorway, brisky flipped her cane under one bare arm, then clapped loudly three times.

"Au choix, Mesdemoiselles!" she called out triumphantly. Then she returned to stand beside me during the inspection.

Indeed, I heard the bare footsteps on the stairs in answer to the summons. Whatever light garments the girls wore from their rooms would be cast aside at the door, hung upon pegs along the wall in the corridor, for the girls would appear smiling, completely in the nude, for inspection.

"A pity," she said, as the girls began to gather (for they did, in her eye and mine, appear), "Solange seems to be missing."

I had witnessed the ritual of au choix in other houses much like this, and for a moment I shared the hallucination of a living tableau of filles de joie assembled for selection. The girls lined up before me, arms intertwined about one another's shoulders in harmonious order of height. The last to arrive—no, she was not Solange—knelt at the end of the line to accomplish the perfect descending order.

Truly, for an instant, I saw them. Even that momentary mirage of female anatomy—the enticingly bare breasts, slim waists waiting to be encircled, the coquettish pelvic mounds garlanded with pubic wreaths —aroused in me the inevitable heat.

Before the troupe of naked phantoms vanished, I believed in them enough to listen for someone to say Solange was napping, or engaged with another gentleman—would I wait? would I choose another?— but apparitions do not speak. When the vision passed and we stood alone among the blue-white dustcovers I bluntly asked: "What happened to her?"

"Are you certain, Monsieur, you met her here?"

Twelve

NUMBERS 1 THROUGH 6 were accounted for by Landru himself and members of his family.

"Who, then," I asked O'Grady, "was number 7?"

"Elementary, my dear Candide. Number 7 is none other than Landru's mistress, Miss Segret."

The crowd had increased threefold, making passage to and from the courtroom all the more chaotic. Huissiers served as ushers: an extra row of folding chairs had been assembled along one aisle, a new set of spectators was packed together at the rear of the salle, standing. Mademoiselle Fernande Segret—Landru's mistress at the time of his arrest—was scheduled to testify.

Landru was already onstage, and one could only guess at his emotional state for he sat as placid as ever, apparently indifferent to the sensation aroused by the announced appearance of his mistress. Again, as at the beginning of the procès, the accused was in cool command of himself while his audience was all astir.

Mademoiselle Segret was called to the stand. After a hushed interval she stepped from behind the jury box that led from the small dark room where witnesses awaited the huissier's summons. She blinked, as all the witnesses did, from the harsh light overhead—even as Landru had done that first day. She was indifferently pretty, dressed with all modesty in a tailored suit and simple white blouse, with a hat matching the quiet plaid of her suit. She clung to her handkerchief as if it were a lifeline, passing it from one hand to the other. As soon as she had recovered from the light's assault, she lifted her head, at first to stare shyly into a sea of expectant faces, then into the prisoner's dock where her eyes fixed on those of Landru. It was then that she fainted.

Her collapse was genuine, and complete: by the time a huissier got to her—along with a gallant juror—she had crumpled to the floor of the prétoire with an audible thud. In the ensuing pandemonium Landru was on his feet, as were most of the spectators. Even Maître Godefroy was moved. The little plaid hat had rolled in his direction: he recovered it and swiftly followed after the two men who carried Mademoiselle Segret from the scene.

Fernande Segret did return to testify, this time in some control of herself and with a change of hankerchief. She was permitted to testify seated to one side of the railing that circumscribed the witness stand, whereas witnesses customarily stood at the railing during testimony. She was cautious, sometimes hesitant, but the statements she made rang true and unforced. At one point she wept, but then recovered herself and plunged on in her small but clear lyric soprano.

"I was on a bus bound for the Galeries Lafayette when a friend pointed out to me I was being stared at by a gentleman across the aisle. We were three young girls on the bus together, but the man, this man, was obviously staring at me."

(Mademoiselle Segret was careful to keep her eyes cast downward so that Landru was out of her range of vision, but Landru, leaning forward, was staring at the witness as avidly as he must have done that day on the bus.)

"He invited me—all three of us, I mean, but I knew he especially invited me—to tea. He introduced himself as Lucien Guillet, from Roicroi."

After tea Landru managed to speak with Mademoiselle Segret in private and suggested a meeting between the two of them, to which she agreed.

Maître de Moro Giafferi asked Mademoiselle Segret if she had any other attachment at the time of this meeting, and she acknowledged yes, she was engaged to a young man, a soldier at the front. She said this with simple candor. Then the defense attorney asked pointedly: "Yet you agreed to meet Monsieur Guillet alone, once you had disembarrassed yourself of your friends?"

"I did," she replied, seeking no indulgence for her action.

In her defense, Maître Godefroy pointed out that the engagement between Mademoiselle Segret and her fiancé had all but come to an end: she had not received any communication from him in months—but Maître de Moro Giafferi retorted: "It was not always convenient for our young men under fire to write love letters."

A point for the defense was scored: Mademoiselle Segret had been guilty of infidelity, but she so readily admitted to her alienation of affection—a human frailty, a woman's way—that her moment of weakness was forgiven and the point obscured. At her first private meeting with the older man she became hopelessly enamored of him, and quite simply gave up any thought of her previous fiancé.

"Did Landru—Monsieur Guillet—propose marriage?"

"He did."

"And you accepted him?"

"Yes."

Landru's face remained impassive, but his whole being seemed concentrated on the young lady seated beside the witness stand.

When Fernande Segret's fiancé returned from the war and again asked her to marry him, she would no longer consider his offer. (In a rare gesture—or perhaps psychological ploy—Landru generously insisted she weigh her decision. She did not waver in her choice.)

Naturally the mother was distraught. She had all along opposed her daughter's relationship with Monsieur Guillet—she had even taken the trouble to investigate the man's background: the municipality of Roicroi had no record of Monsieur Guillet's ever having resided there.

The same evening she received the damning information from Roicroi she confronted the middle-aged suitor, in the presence of her daughter, with the fruit of her investigation.

"You have misled us," she stated. "Are you a German spy, an adventurer—or what?"

Landru received her accusation with a sigh. His name, he admitted, was indeed false, but he was obliged professionally to employ an alias. He was in truth a police officer—a detective employed by the Sûreté.

"Did you believe this statement?" asked President Gilbert.

"I believed everything Lucien ever told me."

Landru was Lucien to her, and would always be. Each of her soft-spoken statements earned a murmur of sympathy, her integrity as a witness was established beyond any doubt.

She moved into his flat on the rue Rochechouart, where Landru had installed Madame Pascal only a short time before. In this case Landru had nothing to gain from the liaison but the devotion and affection of Fernande Segret. The two lovers were fond of music: Landru encouraged Fernande's musical education in several ways, and bore part of the expense for her singing lessons. He was liberal with household money, and little gifts—not extravagantly so, but thoughtful concerning the wishes of his mistress, and considerate always. Landru was an opera lover: they attended the Paris Opéra as often as possible.

"Puccini and Massenet were his favorites—and mine."

This recalled the incident of Landru singing the aria from *Manon:* "Adieu, notre petite table," when he and Fernande Segret were separated at police headquarters.

Maître de Moro Giafferi then asked a question I would have considered hazardous under the circumstances: "Did Landru ever invite you to his villa at Gambais?"

"More than once," responded the witness. Her description of the visits to Gambais turned that haunted manse into a domestic country house any one of the jurors or judges might have enjoyed on his own holidays. Lucien and Fernande quit Paris on Friday evenings and returned from Gambais on Sunday afternoons. The two lovers delighted in the countryside: they cultivated the rose bushes in season and kept a cozy fire in bad weather. "I was happy," she said. "We were happy."

At this point Maître Godefroy broke in: "And the stove," he asked, "did you cook on it?"

"Of course. I prepared omelettes, cutlets for two—the simple dishes Lucien preferred."

"Did you use the oven?" persisted the attorney for the state.

"Yes."

"You must have noticed that it had been much used."

Mademoiselle Segret had not followed the insinuation behind Maître Godefroy's statement, and in all innocence said, "Yes."

Immediately Maître de Moro Giafferi came to the aid of the witnes, and summed up for her: "The stove, then, was a stove like any other."

She shrugged helplessly and opened her hands, which was all the reply the defense attorney required.

But Maître Godefroy would not let the image of the stove pass away so easily.

"Was it you who took out the ashes?"

The witness was truly perplexed: "Yes, it was I."

"Did you find anything unusual about them?"

She knew now what he meant to imply, and flushed, saying, "I found nothing."

When Landru was asked by the President if he had any comment to make on the testimony of the witness he replied in a voice too muted to be clearly heard: "Nothing."

Mademoiselle Segret quivered visibly at the sound of his voice, but she did not turn.

Thirteen

THE ASHES IN THE STOVE were cold, so she must have been out since morning. I felt only a moment's fleeting unease. The bits of cut hair beside the basin where she had attended to her coiffure were reassuring, as were the bitten-off morsels of fingernail in the bidet, her fingerprints on the mirror. I was certain of her, the room contained her odor: nevertheless I checked the armoire. Her dresses hung undisturbed beside my trousers, her musky underthings were folded on the shelf beside my tennis whites.

I restored the fire and settled in with a bottle of wine to wait. In a little while I was hungry, and agitated: there was only the dried heel of a cheese in the garde-manger, and no bread, so I went out. Instead of seeking bread I looked for her.

Illogically I began my search at Saint-Eustache, wandering its stone aisles populated now with weekday worshipers. I even drew aside the curtain of the same confessional we had appropriated one tempestuous Sunday. A pale intense young lady—not Fleur—knelt beside the grille, too absorbed in her inventory of sins to notice my intrusion.

Outside the cathedral I scanned the notices stuck to one wall beneath the warning DÉFENSE D'AFFICHER (Post No Bills). I distractedly considered the Help Wanted for maid of all work, announcements of lost terriers, flat for rent, sewing machine repairs, and piano lessons.

She was not there when I got back. I had forgotten to buy bread. I ate tinned sardines with dry biscottes and went to bed, my appetite unappeased. Automatically my hand glided beneath her pillow. The Tarot deck was missing, but that could mean anything—she kept her cards with her always.

Fourteen

"ASSASSIN!" SCREAMED Madame Crèvecoeur retreating from the witness stand. She stumbled against a heap of mattresses piled in the prétoire—a comic waddling figure, like so many who had come here to speak for the missing, all the more absurd in her black crêpe and veil. She had dressed in ostentatious mourning for her departed friend, Mademoiselle Marchadier.

"Then show me, my good woman, the body."

Landru's bark was listless, there was no bite behind it. After two weeks of dueling verbally with court officials and concierges, Landru was showing strain. (He was in any case never to be the same following the heartfelt confessions of Mademoiselle Segret.) He performed with wit and sarcasm only occasionally, sometimes at the most unlikely moment, like an old trouper abruptly aroused from a dream.

More than one hundred witnesses had already been called, most repeating the same phrases, many eager to perform themselves, several hurling insults at the accused, or cries of "Murderer!" Landru was weary of them. He was winding down—as were the judges and attorneys, as were we all.

Madame Crèvecoeur's dog had been destroyed along with Mademoiselle Marchadier's two pets: she had wept theatrically (even her handkerchief was black) when describing her loss to the court. Landru had strangled the three animals, supposedly at the bidding of Mademoiselle Marchadier—"Jamais, jamais, jamais!" moaned Madame Crèvecoeur—then cremated them in his garden.

Mademoiselle Marchadier had been a prostitute since puberty. When Landru met her she was managing a maison de tolérance, a house of casual rendezvous catering mostly to soldiers and sailors on leave. From all reports she was the fat good-humored prostitute with a heart of gold. She had always aspired to a house of her own, a dream she finally realized on the rue Saint-Jacques. A heart of gold is not a madam's most important asset: the venture failed, she was in debt and obliged to sell the furnishings of the house to pay her creditors. It was an ad for the sale of beds that delivered her into Landru's hands.

One original element in the Marchadier episode was that Landru had this time purchased two round-trip tickets to Gambais instead of a round-trip ticket for himself and a single one-way passage for his guest.

When asked why he had been so generous with Mademoiselle Marchadier (4F 90 instead of 3F 90), Landru replied from a great distance: "I don't know."

I shared that great distance with him. Though we were both visibly present in the courtroom—Landru vividly so—the outcome of the trial was of no further interest to either of us. Henceforth Landru would depend upon his lawyer to answer for him, as I would depend upon Harry for my notes. I joined Landru in a state of torpor and indifference.

Once, I can swear—when the mattresses were being carried out by two stagehands—Landru directed his gaze straight at me. Our eyes met and held for as uncomfortable an interval as I have ever endured.

During the recess I asked Harry: "Has he ever stared at you?"

"Who?"

"Landru."

"Of course not. Why should he?"

The shadow of the guillotine hung over Landru. I too had been cast from the Tower into a downward spiral of the damned.

The Gambais stove was on display. It was tied round with a rope bristling with legal seals: several of the openings were wired shut, but the oven door had been left ominously open.

Meanwhile Monsieur Beyle, director of the Judicial Identity Bureau, lectured at length on his work with the identification files of known criminals. He expounded on the Bertillon system of criminal investigation based on classification of skeletal and other characteristics. Landru had been thus classified and could be so identified.

The open stove yawned before us.

Next the toxicologists Kling and Kohn-Abrest reported on the infinite possibilities of homicide by poisoning, but their joint communication was theoretical in nature since there were no cadavers upon which postmortem examination could be made.

Only the squat homely kitchen stove, symbol of hearth and home, kept our attention for any time.

At last Dr. Paul came forward to report on his experiments with Landru's stove. He had burnt sheeps' heads in the oven to test its efficiency.

"It takes thirty-eight minutes to consume an emptied head, one hour and a half to burn to cinders a completed head with brain, eyes, wool, and tongue intact."

"And they went with him," I could hear Irene saying, *"like sheep."*

"We must assume that the midsection was disposed of in some manner other than incineration. Neither the thorax nor the pelvis could be accommodated in an oven of this size, and intestines take the devil's own time to burn."

But the Devil (as Landru, or any of us, could have replied) has all the time in the world.

"I would rule out disintegration of the torsos in an acid solution: this process requires considerable equipment, such as a receptacle of sufficient depth and capable of resisting the corrosive agent. No such receptacle was found on or near the premises. Acids, even in the most concentrated form, as with sulphuric acid, cannot completely consume every particle of human tissue. Gallstones, for example, will still turn up in the residual sludge."

"We are relieved to know you found no gallstones at Gambais," interrupted Maître de Moro Giafferi. "Pray tell us what you did find."

Dr. Paul, a médecin légiste of renown, was accustomed to the impatience and sarcasm of defense attorneys.

"What I did find," said he, moving from the trussed-up stove to a table laden with specimens collected from Landru's garden, "was a heap of bone and ash containing two hundred and fifty-six fragments identifiable as parts of human radius, cubitus, tibia, and teeth." From an apothecary scale on the table Dr. Paul took a substance which he brought to one side of his nose, like a pinch of snuff. "These ashes taken from the garden at the villa Tric contain five percent calcium phosphate, an element in the composition of skeletal matter—an unusually high percentage when one considers that five-tenths of one percent would be normal."

"When one considers the large quantity of chicken bones and oyster shells in the ash heap," said the defense attorney mimicking Dr. Paul's tone of voice, "the percentage, on the contrary, seems unusually low."

Before the doctor could reply to this, Maître de Moro Giafferi had picked up a minuscule particle of bone and was squinting hard at it through his pince-nez: "You are qualified, then, to take a sliver of something like this and tell us it was once a woman's shinbone?"

"Not every fragment is so precisely identifiable. But a piece of bone once identified as tibia can then be proven to be female tibia."

"Thank you, doctor," said the attorney for the defense, replacing the item among its fellows with mock fastidiousness, so that it would not go astray. He then asked Dr. Paul: "Did you find any trace of blood in the villa where this monstrous carnage is assumed to have taken place?"

The médecin légiste was obliged to reveal no trace of human blood was found—a fact the defense attorney already knew before asking, but that did not prevent him from affecting a theatrical astonishment.

"I believe," said Dr. Paul, "the remarkable absence of blood can be explained."

"Do explain, I pray you."

"According to the time schedule recorded by the accused, Landru invariably returned to Gambais alone following a prior sojourn in the company of one of the missing women. It is altogether possible and very likely that the victim expired after garroting or strangulation, which is bloodless, or by administration of a toxic substance (as suggested by Messieurs Kling and Kohn-Abrest), after which the body was left in the villa while the murderer returned to Paris. During this interval of some forty-eight hours a corpse will undergo the metabolic changes known as rigor mortis, livor mortis, and algor mortis, and the thrombocytes—platelets active in the clotting of blood—will have advanced coagulation to the degree that only negligible bleeding is likely to occur during subsequent dismemberment."

The astonishment of Maître de Moro Giafferi now knew no bounds: "You mean to assure us a so-called murderer would walk away from the corpse intending to return in several days' time to dispose of his deed which any casual passerby could have discovered in his absence?"

"Or hidden," said Dr. Paul. "He may have placed the body in a temporary grave. A witness has in fact testified that one of the missing women, Mademoiselle Babelay, was seen digging a shallow trench beside the garden wall. The young lady may have thought she was preparing the soil for the rose bushes now planted there. She would have had no way of knowing she dug her own expedient grave. Her killer would return later to unearth his victim and cause the incriminating remains to disappear."

Fifteen

WITH THE AID OF eau-de-vie I slept.

At first she lay beside me still, her living body pressed to mine, asleep. Again we walked the fearful streets together, unaware—or spun airily along Parisian boulevards on the very bicycle that first brought her to me. I dreamed I made love to her as hungrily as ever, and came awake wet from my solitary passion.

But night is long and the dreams soon turned malignant. The artery of the Seine ran blood at sunset. From the pont des Arts I saw a headless corpse borne along nude with the tide's floating sewage and a scattered Tarot, her talisman. There was a metal drum exuding fumes in Madame Vitrine's cave into which I dared myself to look, and looked: a mass of suppurating flesh half-dissolved in acid, one hand intact, nails bitten to the quick. I stumbled upon a grave in the Tuileries where she lay half buried, the rain washing the mud from her face, her breasts and belly gradually exposed.

In the despondency of daylight I could have carried my nightmare to the préfet de police but knew how foolish that would be. A missing person—who? Personne. I could see one agent winking at another, then pretend to take official note of my complaint.

I searched for her among the prostitutes along the curb. I waited. At night I slept with her in dreams but always, when I awoke, she was missing still.

Sixteen

I THOUGHT OF Anacréon who had come weeping to Miss Stein in the midst of a party and had gone away comforted by a promise spoken with such finality it became gospel. Did I seek the same comforting promise: "You will see her again, she will be back"? I was willing to tell Miss Stein everything. How many confessions she must have heard from troubled members of her entourage. I went in a mist—the weather matched my state of mind—but Gabriel had got there ahead of me. In spite of the mist and a thin cold rain he was out walking with Miss Stein.

"He has had a falling out with a friend," said Miss Toklas, wiping her hands on an apron. "I thought the friend might have been you."

Gabriel had been so far from my thoughts I could not imagine what she meant. Then I saw myself as Miss Stein and Miss Toklas must have seen me, as Gabriel's lover. I do not know if my face turned red from embarrassment. She thought I had come to tell my side of the story of the falling out.

"It has nothing to do with me," said I.

"Come into the kitchen," she advised. I was standing in the doorway, my head wet from the long walk in the wet mist, looking no doubt as dismayed as I felt.

In the kitchen a meal was under way. A copper vessel shaped like a coffin was set upon two burners of the stove. While I talked Miss Toklas, wearing one glove, neatly popped open several oyster shells with a blunt knife.

"I have been living with a girl for some months," I blurted out.

"A girl," she said, surprised. "We thought something else, Gertrude and I."

"No," I said, "it has nothing to do with Gabriel."

"I see," she said, and opened more oysters.

I told her about Fleur, though not everything. Miss Stein and Miss Toklas had long been curious about how I lived, and with whom, and had asked Gabriel about me. Gabriel had hinted that we were lovers, he and I, and I could not bear to be thought of with Gabriel in that way. So I confessed to Miss Toklas—my head bowed, my eyes on the oysters—how I had met Fleur (not the first time, nor did I tell about my father) and that she had come to live with me and we had been living together since summer.

"Since summer," she repeated. The time we had been together meant much to me, but Miss Toklas' tone reminded me that summer was only a few months ago.

"It all began that day we went to Anacréon's studio together, and I bought a bicycle from her."

She smiled. "The bicycle I do remember."

"She's left me before . . ."

"I see," she said, and began to tell me a story of her own with her back turned as she opened the oysters so that I did not see her expression.

"You have been fortunate to meet someone and stay since summer with that person, but the other thing is both harder and easier to do, and more fortunate still." She did not say what the other thing was, but I knew. "When it is right it is natural and what is natural seems easy but at the same time difficult to maintain." She spoke in the same style as Miss Stein and I could hear Miss Stein saying much the same thing and in the same way to Gabriel at this moment—though not telling the same story. "I was a year with a friend from California before I met Gertrude."

Now that her back was turned I could look up, but not at the back of Miss Toklas' head. I looked around the kitchen. In the sink was a burlap sack like Dr. Paul's sack of ashes at the trial, only this sack was wet and from time to time it seemed to stir. While Miss

Toklas spoke and opened oysters I stared at the sack wondering if it moved or if I only imagined that it moved.

"Our being together my friend and I was as easy and natural as my being with Gertrude, but of course not the same. This friend was a woman, for as you know I am attracted to women and some women to me—and one man, yes, but that is another story. I was for a year attracted by that friend and my friend and I assumed our attachment would last forever. It did not last and could not have lasted, but where is the loss? (I do not mean to say you have no feeling of loss at the moment. You do. That is inevitable.) Ours was a natural attraction and our attachment seemed right but after a year not right and finally impossible to maintain. The feeling I had and have for Gertrude was and is quite different. When I first met Gertrude I not only assumed our attachment would last, but knew. It has and it will."

She had taken four oyster plates from a shelf with indented hollows for six oysters each, then placed the opened oysters on the plates where the shells matched perfectly the hollows.

"Today is Thanksgiving in America and Gertrude is very fond of Thanksgiving but I could not find a turkey anywhere in Paris."

Again, I was certain, the burlap sack moved.

"Here we are both telling love stories without once using the word love. That is perfectly all right, for the word love is too easily said and does not always mean what is meant. On the ship that brought me to France I met a commodore and although men are not usually attracted to me, he was. He sent a letter to my hotel in Paris. I read the letter three times and each time I read it I became upset with his use of the word love until finally the word love leaped off the page and meant nothing. What could have been a turning point for me was not, and I have never regretted this. I took the letter with me to the Tuileries where I walked every day in those days and that day tore the letter into very small pieces and threw the pieces into the basin where the children sail their boats. The next day I met Gertrude and everything changed. It was all right about the letter and only natural that I should have destroyed it. When I met Gertrude I knew the feeling I had for her was different from how I felt about the commodore and my California friend—oh altogether different from how I felt about the commodore—and what I felt now was perfect and right. I loved Gertrude immediately and love her at this instant and will love her for all time."

Miss Toklas used the word love with complete aplomb, and now paused. She was waiting for me to say the same, that I was in love with the girl I had lived with since summer. But I could not speak the word love with the same equanimity, so I said nothing. It was as if Miss Stein were there with us saying, "You see?"

"Have you spoken to Anacréon about this girl?"

I said I had not.

"Go to him then. After all, she has been with him longer than she has been with you—though for another reason, surely. Talk with Anacréon, you owe him that. Besides, he may know something you do not."

Miss Toklas had got all of the oysters into their hollows on the four plates. Steam was beginning to rattle the lid of the coffin-shaped casserole, and Miss Toklas moved to the sink where she unwound the cord that bound the sinister burlap sack. She took out two living lobsters grasping them fearlessly at the backs behind the claws, then held the two squirming beasts out and away from her tiny form for me to admire.

"There is not a single turkey in all of Paris," she said, "so these fellows will have to do."

She plunged the lobsters one at a time into the boiling water in the copper vessel. It occurred to me they may have cried out in agony as they were scalded to death, for my mind had taken a peculiar turn. I would go to Anacréon, but I did not relish an encounter with the heartbroken sculptor. Still, I could not linger any longer here. From the four plates of oysters I knew that she and Miss Stein were having guests, and I did not want to be there when the guests arrived.

On the rue de Fleurus two people were getting out of a horse cab in the rain. They were Picasso and his wife of that period, Fernande. They did not notice me as we passed and I heard them disputing virulently, calling one another foul names in French.

"Prick!" she called out gaily from beneath her wet hat.

"Cunt!" shrieked the little Spaniard at his wife.

Anacréon's studio smelled of fish too, and cat. In the dark, lit only by a single lamp, the sculptor knelt beside a mean pallet of old clothes and a burst pillow upon the floor. Cats came slinking out of their shadowy cachettes and toolbox couches behind the elongated metal-work figurines. Anacréon was spooning fish soup to a sickly boy with shaved head who half-reclined on the pallet like someone wounded in a battle, weak from loss of blood. The boldest of the cats came forward to sniff at me and glide between my legs. Their mewling added to the mournful sound of rain beating against the high-banked atelier windows.

The boy had stopped eating when I came in. His face was the same color as the yellow-grey liquid Anacréon fed him. Like the old man, he had no teeth in front. His eyes were both fierce and frightened at the same time.

"He is afraid," said Anacréon.

"Of me?"

"Of anyone. Your look of innocence does not deceive him. Behind that face you could be as cruel and unloving as the others."

I stood back and let the cats nuzzle me while Anacréon continued to urge the boy to eat.

"There is curry in it," he said to the boy, or to me, "for strength."

The boy resumed sipping at the spoon, but warily, still watching me. He drew a guarded fist up to his chest, not an aggressive fist but as if his hand had closed and swollen into that shape. He seemed content as long as I did not move forward, like an animal certain of only a limited terrain.

"Abandoned," said Anacréon. He spoke the word abandonné with passion. "His mother and stepfather beat him, then left him. He hid in the closet of their empty flat until the concierge found him there. He would not come out, she took me to him. I am known in the quarter as someone who takes in stray cats."

Anacréon looked up at me when he said this last. He was referring to Fleur.

The boy could not have been older than ten, but in his pitiful condition—propped upon one spindly arm among the scattered bolts and metal shavings on the studio floor—he could have been any age, old or young.

He had been a backward child, Anacréon informed me, from birth. Though he understood words and would sometimes respond to command, he could not speak. In the beginning the mother had been devoted to her stunted son. She refused to relinquish the child to a hospital that took retarded children, determined to care for him herself despite the poverty they lived in. Her husband was a common laborer, often out of work. He found a job with a construction crew doing illicit work on Sundays, for the crew was not part of the construction syndicate. One Sunday as they were demolishing a warehouse part of the wall fell upon him and crushed him to death. The workers were not, of course, insured.

"The ways of a woman are strange," said Anacréon, shaking his pale death's head over the thought. "I tell you, this was at one time a good woman, une brave femme."

He considered aloud: perhaps her spirit was crushed when the crumbling wall crushed her husband. A soul can be as thoroughly crushed as a body, he assured me. For months she was despondent—and why not? She might have considered taking her own life, but there was the boy to care for and love.

"Have you ever considered taking your own life?" Anacréon asked me suddenly.

I shook my head no, and he regarded me with sour distaste.

One day the woman brightened and began to manifest a growing joy, for she had found a lover. She took up with a character in the quarter named Bonnat, known as Bon-à-rien. Anacréon could understand her weakness: anyone, in a desperate moment, might take up with a good-for-nothing.

"We of the quarter thought of Bonnat as a harmless café clown: the mother had done herself no service to attach herself to him—but where was the loss? How surprising to discover the clown was a devil in disguise. Soon Bonnat arranged for cronies at the café to visit him at home, to bed his new wife—figurez-vous cela!—and pay him for these favors, as one would pay a pimp. Finally he sent her into the streets, openly, to support him in this way."

The husband-pimp could not abide his idiot stepson. Like a living conscience the child would stare at his new father for hours and never speak.

"Who can long endure the silent relentless stare of an innocent child?"

The child could not speak, but he could—the sculptor assured me—scream. The concierge took it upon herself to tell the mother her child was being abused while she was out of the house. The mother was indignant. Here is the strange part: she was outraged not at the brutality inflicted on her son—but at the meddling concierge. What business did the concierge have to involve herself in the personal affairs of the tenants?

"Regardez," said Anacréon. He ceased feeding the boy long enough to point out the raw gap in his gums where several front teeth were missing. "This was the mother's work, not Bonnat's."

Then he lowered the blanket to show me the purplish corded welts across and below the protruding rib cage. The boy allowed himself to be thus displayed, though his fierce eyes stared accusingly at me all the while. I began to feel sensitive in the places where I saw the boy's bruises, the hips and waist—the nausea mounting from there.

"The concierge came first to me. What could the city of Paris do for him more than I? I am known as a ramasseur de chats perdus, a gatherer of stray cats."

Anacréon turned away from me and attended to the boy's nourishment: "So you too have been abandoned?" His pronunciation of the word abandonné was altogether different now.

I could not, in the presence of this boy, explain myself or discuss my loss.

"Do not look so uneasy, my friend. Yes, I took her in, another stray cat. I forgive you, believe me—you are forgiven everything. I found her in the gutter, vous savez? Of all things, she was tied with a rope to a bicycle. Yes, the bicycle you saw here—she tied herself to it so it would not be taken from her. The bicycle was all she possessed and she was sleeping under the pont du Carrousel like a clochard."

He paused to let me picture this.

"Her hair was full of lice—I cut it, as I did his." The boy's shaven skull was yellow in the lamplight. "I treated her sores with ointment, bought medicine for her cough. Like him, she could not speak of her horror. What had been done to her I did not know."

"Do you know now?"

"In time she could speak, but not of that. I fed her. She became pretty again, as she must have been all along. I will tell you something: she slept on this same pallet, never with me. I bought clothes for her— nothing elegant, but in the bright colors she preferred—for a young girl must dress. When her hair grew out the coquette in her came forth. She modeled for me, and for others. She did not sleep with me, I tell you this in confidence. I do not really care. I loved her as a daughter, vous savez?"

"Do you know where she has gone?"

"I knew she would leave me, it is only natural. She had begun to blossom. I am too old for what she sought in that way. She slept with painters, men she met in bars—she sometimes took money for this. Always she came back to me. The others did not matter, vous savez?"

"Do you know where she is?"

"She was a strange little thing," said Anacréon—my father's very words, but now in French. "I never knew where she came from or where she went when she was not with me." He took more broth for the boy. "I have other cats to care for now."

"Do you—"

"Do you know how the concierge found this one? She saw the mother and Bonnat get into a cab with their two valises—there was money now that the woman was a whore, and they could afford to flee by cab. The boy was not with them. The concierge knew they had left for good, but she could not enter their flat without a passkey as much as she wanted to. It is against the law to violate private domain until the police are called. She did not want to call the police, for if the boy was there they would take him. The boy must surely be in the flat—she did not see him get into the cab. Maybe he had run away! She waited a day and a night—the mother and Bonnat had not returned. Think of the horror of that day and night for him: he had been locked into the flat, with the blinds drawn, and in the dark he had sought a darker place still and a place to close himself in all the more by hiding in an empty closet. There he crouched for all those hours waiting, clutching his hand in a fist as he does now. The concierge found the flat stripped of anything of value or use, abandoned, except for an un-cooked chicken left behind on the table. That was what they had left him. A raw chicken!"

I averted my eyes.

"He would not come out of the closet and she did not want to call the police. The city of Paris can do nothing for an abandoned child, so she came to me. Together we coaxed him finally into the light. He was in the desperate condition I described to you. What passes inside his head I do not know. Of that he cannot speak.

"To look at me you would not think it, but I have a certain strength. I carried him here and he has been with me ever since. I carried him on my back and he held to my neck with one hand in a fist, a fist he would not release—just as my other cat would not at first unfasten the rope that bound her to the bicycle."

"Do you know anyone she might have . . ."

"No one. You must ask elsewhere. There are painters she knew who might know—but I do not know them. I closed my eyes to all of that. Ask the pimps of your arrondissement. She was a whore for a time—did you know that? She obtained cocaine for me from a certain pimp, but I do not know who. I stay away from that canaille."

The cats had gone back into shadow except for one restless tom playing with a loose feather escaped from the boy's ruined pillow. Anacréon did not know, it was certain: he closed his eyes to all of that, he had other cats to care for now. The boy had finished all of the soup, and the sculptor sighed with great satisfaction.

"It was a long time before the boy would open his fist to show me." Anacréon opened his own withered claw as the boy had done for him. "It will surprise you to know what he carries so guardedly. He has in his hand four broken teeth."

Seventeen

THREE ALIENISTS were called together to pronounce upon Landru's mental capacity to perform an act of murder.

Dr. Roques de Fursac spoke of a blow on the head Landru suffered as a child, but could find no resulting psychosis from this distant childhood incident. Dr. Roubinovitch confirmed the possibility that a blow to the head could be traumatic and might result in a psychiatric disorder, but—other than a characteristic mélancolie brought on by his lengthy incarceration—the individual under observation showed no sign of incapacitating nervous disorder.

Supporting the diagnoses of his two colleagues, Dr. Vallon summed up the committee report by declaring the prisoner quick of mind, alert, possessed of accurate memory, completely aware of his actions and the consequences thereof. Therefore he, as senior physician, could in all conscience sign the report declaring Henri Désiré Landru entirely responsible and completely sane.

"Merci," said Landru, bowing sarcastically from his perch. "This is the first kind thing anyone has said of me here."

(Laughter.)

A member of the jury raised his hand and was recognized. In France jurymen are permitted to take active part in courtroom interrogation, and he had a question to put to Dr. Vallon.

"Did you discover any disordered or obsessive sexual tendencies in the subject?"

The question was an indication of the concerns and considerations of the jury, and one that aroused the courtroom and amused Landru.

"None whatsoever."

(Extended raillery from the public benches.)

"—no record of wanton cruelty, or what has been called sadism, say, in his childhood?"

Dr. Roubinovitch recalled that Landru as a young boy trapped and destroyed cats, for their skins, which he sold to a pharmacist who specialized in the application of cat fur in the treatment of rheumatism: "But in my opinion the cats were killed for financial gain—there was no pleasure involved."

Maître Godefroy offered a gratuitous: "We know this side of him."

When Dr. Roques de Fursac concluded that no part of the symptomatology of the sadist was apparent in Landru's makeup, the other two alienists nodded sagely, simultaneously.

President Gilbert took advantage of the discussion to ask (perhaps inspired by a reading of Du Maurier's *Trilby*) if a criminal act could be committed by hypnosis.

"As Dr. Charcot maintained," Dr. Vallon maintained in his stead, "crime by hypnosis does not exist."

That was not exactly what President Gilbert meant.

"If you mean, can the victim be hypnotized, then done away with in a helpless state of unconsciousness—yes, of course. A soporific added to an apéritif would serve the same purpose."

As the three doctors filed out, carrying their satchels of self-importance with them, I saw Sem, the caricaturist, sketching the alienists as the three wise monkeys.

I worked distractedly in my empty room on a long translation from *la Revue Hebdomadaire*: "La Gloire de Georges Carpentier," by the young poet François Mauriac. From that dreary exercise I moved on to the Bibliothèque Nationale, ten minutes' walk away, to pore over the faded print of dullish tomes doing insignificant research for O'Grady. The library, like the courtroom at Versailles, was another institutional aquarium stocked with drowning fish, their mouths agape: only the pilot fish in grey jackets (the page boys) swam freely through that aquatic institution, winnowing the requested volumes from some vast underwater source, the archives at the ocean floor. That afternoon I received a book meant for the reader in the next cubicle, and my neighbor received mine.

"Are you a musician?" I asked, for the book was from the music collection.

She was young and not pretty, even with a smile. The chapped skin was not her fault, but unfortunate. A pair of owlish spectacles doubled the size of her eyes.

She was not a musician but a student of music history at the Sorbonne. We exchanged volumes: hers devoted to sixteenth-century Italian castrati, mine on Egyptian funerary practices. (This research assignment was, I suspect, merely to help O'Grady complete one of his interminable crossword puzzles.) When we finished brooding over our books I impulsively asked her to take coffee with me. Her ready acceptance gave me no pleasure—I immediately wished I could rescind the invitation.

In any case, we did not take coffee. I knew a hotel in the neighborhood of the Bourse where stockbrokers took their secretaries. I took her there. The rooms were windowless—ideal, thought I, for committing adultery or murder—and let for a short time only, since stockbrokers are notoriously hurried and brisk about every endeavor.

The marquis de Sade might best understand the compulsion of any such encounter. We turned our backs to one another to undress. She took off everything but her porte-jarretelles, then allowed me to remove that last elastic piece of modesty—and her ridiculous eyeglasses—in bed. I climbed over her in my stockinged feet and saw in her blind eyes an appeal for solace, but by then I had already mounted her and was burrowing my greedy way inside without the slightest preliminary caress.

We made use of one another (but I, chiefly, of her) for no more than two minutes of the twenty we spent in the windowless rented space. Afterward, while she sat astraddle the bidet to perform a precautionary ablution, I took leave of her without knowing her name, or she mine.

From the quais of the Right Bank I scanned the water for evidence of drownings and contemplated my dismal thudding heartbeat. How could lovers continue to kiss beside the Seine, and clochards on its banks build their little fires of hope?

Eighteen

SOMEONE WAS EMERGING from the underground tunnel behind me, eyes fixed on my back. When I turned there was only the word MERDE mocking me, painted by a graffitist against the tiled wall of the métro, the word so carefully inscribed and writ so large it might have expressed the general and anonymous viewpoint from below depths. The several intersecting streets at Etienne Marcel were empty. The display window of J.-J. Péru & Fils illuminated the way.

As I stepped into the familiar shadows beyond the lighted window a figure moved up beside me.

"Viens," he said, using the familiar form.

I stopped, for he now pressed close. It was the young pimp with a deformed hand from the bar on the rue de la Lingerie. The atrophied member, no arm to it, dangled in my face; one mummified finger indicated the direction I was to take. He wore a leather glove on his good hand. To further convince me to accompany him, he opened the glove: in his hand was a wristwatch.

"Yours?"

I nodded miserably. He put the watch into his pocket where it clinked against coins, or a knife. My breath did not come easily as I followed him to a meat storage plant on the rue Dussoubs. The painted wooden horse's head signified a horsemeat butcher. My escort rolled up

the corrugated iron shutter whose lettering announced: BONIFACE & CIE.
I had passed this boucherie chevaline a hundred times, but was trembling now as I stepped inside.

(The following transcript is offered as a kind of deposition based
on notes I made nearly fifty years ago, notes meant to serve as ground-
work for an essay, never written—along with whatever conversation I
can recall from my audience with the so-called Pope. This is, I know,
feeble evidence of a phantom encounter one November eve in 1921.

(According to Harry, the Pope was a Parisian representative of
la Fraternité du Corse—the Corsican Brotherhood, a secret society of
criminals—but I do not think the Pope I met, if Pope he was, belonged
to any organization but his own. Gabriel's knowledge of him was
scantier still—more rumor than substance: a procurer called the Pope
was said to supply Proust, and other notable homosexuals, with
elevator boys and sailors. O'Grady had written about the Pope for
British weeklies as the evil genius behind black-market meat during
the war years, and of the attempted assassination of Clemenceau in
1919—and sundry outrages—but O'Grady admitted he had created his
stories out of whole cloth.

(Although I had never seen the Pope before, nor would I ever
again, I will assume the base of his criminal activities—whatever these
were beyond the maintenance of prostitution in the les Halles district—
was that boucherie chevaline on the rue Dussoubs. The Pope who had
summoned me—Pope Boniface, or le Pape du Premier—was not the
Pope of popular imagination nor the same Pope sworn to by witnesses
with less to lose than I.)

The pimp brought the iron door rattling down behind us. I was
perspiring, though the place was cooled by ice packed in straw. From
great hooks along the white-tiled walls hung the butchered carcasses of
horses, split neatly down the middle, heads removed. The floor was
covered with bloodstained sawdust which must have accounted for the
acrid odor underfoot. The light was intolerable. Naked electric globes
cast every detail of the scene into the sharp focus of a crude and
bloody tableau, real and surreal at once.

The halved carcasses had been scooped hollow of intestines, the
tripe tossed into bins and barrels or sorted and arranged in enamel trays.
Discarded parts overflowed a series of poubelles and tin pails—but the
testicles (frivolités, a delicacy) were kept. One bin contained nothing
but heaps of detached hooves, to be boiled down into gelatin. The
manes and tails filled a large wicker packing case, destined, no doubt,

for paintbrushes; the blood, stocked in demijohns, would be congealed into blood sausage or drunk warm by consumptives as a fortifiant. The heads were nowhere in sight.

There was a back room where four men played belote across a butcher's block. As soon as the pimp and I entered, all but one of the players abandoned the game. The grey-haired man who remained seated nodded by way of greeting: the only one of the four I could have sworn he could not be was he.

The others left us, but the pimp remained. He leaned against the door as if to hold it shut with his weight while the grey-haired man gathered in the cards and invited me to sit. He spoke quietly with the southern accent I had become accustomed to in Cannes and Nice, the remembered rhythms and inflections of my mother's speech. His appearance was deceiving: he might have been any one of the patient jurors at the Landru trial, a bourgeois gentleman of unquestioned loyalty to income, family, and nation, in that order—a man who minded his own business and beseeched his neighbor to do the same.

The sharp smell had followed us into the room, or had remained on the bottoms of my shoes. I was relieved to face so disarming a monster, but frightened enough to need suddenly to urinate. Sitting down at the butcher's block did nothing to put me at my ease.

To look around would have betrayed my fear: I sensed rather than saw, out of the corner of one eye, the racks of knives and cleavers and meat saws appropriate to the place. I found no reassurance in the sight of a gramophone exactly like O'Grady's, because of a buggy whip lying across the turntable—and beside it, another sinister juxtaposition, the bat's wing edge of a black umbrella stretched open to dry.

Yet my host's bland face offered no threat: there was no sign of the Corsican buccaneer, no trace of the white slaver. His visage was pale instead of swarthy, with a network of broken veins in the cheeks like tiny red and blue threads discernible in bank notes, and in stockbrokers' faces. A scarlet rash erupted from the lower part of his neck; the backs of his hands had been attacked by the same infection: the skin was peeling there as if from sunburn, but he did not appear to be a man who sunned himself. I was reminded of Marat—another gentleman from underground—hiding from his enemies in the sewers of Paris where he caught the skin disease that confined him thereafter to his bath, until Charlotte Corday ended his torment and his life.

He wore a neatly pressed business suit of dark blue—somewhat incomplete without col and cravate (his neckwear hung from a knob on the back of his chair), the jacket open as far as the vertical stripes of his suspenders. He was at home here in the company of butchers, and inclined to take his ease. Had I glanced behind the wooden block I might have discovered he was wearing the same carpet slippers Madame Vitrine wore in her hotel, or had at least loosened the shoelaces binding his swollen feet. His grey eyes had the tired look of a man who has seen too much that day, and for many days before. Otherwise, he appeared to be in excellent spirits and prepared for a pleasantly casual business chat. He smiled broadly enough for me to catch an occasional glimpse of Corsican gold.

"Are you acquainted with Mirabelle?" was his first roundabout question.

I said that I did not know the name.

"She posts herself at the corner of your street and the rue Française."

Of course he would know my street—he knew everything about me.

"Is Mirabelle the prostitute with only one leg?"

"The very one. A favorite with les forts. They claim a one-legged chicken [une poule à une patte] brings luck."

Since I was a stranger to his world (though he knew all about mine), the approach to a subject of mutual interest would naturally be circumspect.

He must have made some sign to the pimp, for that young man brought us two small glasses in his good hand and a bottle of emerald-green liqueur wedged in his armpit. It was absinthe, from Corsica— the beverage forbidden in France for the past seven years. The Pope poured, then held his glass aloft to wish us both bonne chance. Nothing is forbidden to the Pope.

"Your petite amie, did she bring you good luck?" He was amiable enough asking this, and did not await or expect an answer. "She was a strange little thing."

To that familiar phrase he drank, and so did I. The unexpected bitter strength of the drink brought tears to my eyes.

"To go, she said, to Béziers." He was talking aloud to himself, chuckling over what he said. "To see her father. Her father, soi-disant. Her lies were so transparent I was amused. 'Go,' said I, and teased her about going by bicycle. She knew I would give her money, and I did. She has many fathers, not all of them in Béziers."

Béziers, then. For a moment I could believe she was in Béziers, out of the Pope's reach, in the arms of a father, so-called.

"She did not leave Paris," he intoned.

I realized he was speaking of an earlier instance. Enlightened, remembering money I had found in her purse, I confessed what he already knew: "She was with me."

"Of course. With my indulgence—with my blessing. She was with you, and others."

I nodded.

"You agree? You knew of her predilections, her unrest."

There was no further need to agree. He poured, replacing the droplets of emerald I had consumed, then resumed shuffling the belote deck in his diseased hands.

"A bicycle. Cards depicting the mysteries. The mania to show herself to painters—to *painters,* when one calculates the difference in pay." For a moment his tired eyes fluttered shut, then flashed open along with a smile. "Une poule sur une bicyclette. She was, after all, a whore." For prostitute he used the cruder term poule, to lend weight to this unhappy admission.

He had begun a soliloquy that required no response from me. Dumbly I sat listening, as fixed as the horn on the gramophone, emitting no sound.

"We are not beasts," he said suddenly, as if challenging an opinion I had expressed. "Enticement? Beatings? Murder? A whore is in far greater danger from the marauding sharks of Paris than from her familiar maquereau. Alone, she is prey to the most vicious savagery. Coercion, force? Why should there be, when so many willingly seek us out? Among the lower orders—the criminal types, the reckless independents—there is a measure of violence, yes. But not here. Not in the premier arrondissement."

As if to convince me of this, he poured again—though I had not touched the last refill, fearful now of the toxic green. I reflected on how horses were treated here, and wondered about poules.

"She was free to choose. She still is, despite whatever claims a soi-disant father, or lover, might make. When a girl takes no protector it can be disruptive to the milieu, but she did not make a choice, and I said so be it. We are not beasts. She was free to model if she so desired: it was a sickness with her. She was a creature of impulse. When she asked for cocaine I obtained the drug for her at no profit to myself: it

was for her father, soi-disant." He smiled privately. "It makes me smile
even now to think of her lies. She could always make me smile. By
now you must have realized: she was a favorite of mine, this strange
little thing. Un cas particulier. I too was a father to her, soi-disant—
vous comprenez? She told my fortune once, she cut my hair. She presented me with a Swiss watch—did you know? When she did not go
to Béziers but to Montmartre and from Montmartre to a hotel here
in les Halles I said to myself, why not? She has chosen a protector at
long last. So be it, she is free to choose. We are not beasts. Nevertheless.
She had been badly frightened or badly hurt before she came to me—
some other time, some other arrondissement—so I said to myself, I will
keep a sharp eye on this English boy."

"American."

"Yes. I will watch him. There are déséquilibrés and criminal types
who would slice a petite amie to ribbons. Why? Pure bestial pleasure.
I did not think that of you. Not then, not now. I have confidence in
you, and wish you to have confidence in me. She has disappeared. Did
she bring you luck? I do not think you brought her any."

As amiable as ever, he spread several cards face down across the
wooden block as if inviting me to choose a card, any card. There was
no menace in his gesture, only mild impatience as he tapped each card
in turn, then suddenly asked, "Where is she?"

I recoiled in astonishment. I had expected to be told by him where
she was.

My startled reaction must have appeared to him genuine, for he
asked gently, "You do not know?"

"No, I do not."

He sighed (but believed me), scooped in the cards again, and
asked: "Do you know why she left you?"

"Not even that."

"What a strange little thing she was. Un cas particulier. I can tell
you only this: she was for a time at the hôpital Salpêtrière. No, not injured in any apparent way, no discernible malady. There is a doctor
there who occupies himself with nervous disorders and the déséquilibrés. I do not believe in this man's foolishness any more than I believe in the cards, but it was to him she went with her unhappiness. He
was as disappointed as you, and I, that she succeeded in an evasion.
After three days of telling Dr. Blanchard her dreams and lies she disappeared."

It was my turn to believe him, and I did.

"And if she did not come to you directly then, she will not come at all."

Confused, demoralized, I recklessly drank again and felt at the first taste to have tumbled from a high place into deep water and dark. My ears ached from the plunge.

I heard myself saying, "She was unable to sleep"—the words resounding in my damaged ears.

"She will sleep now."

"—or if she slept, she was terrified by dreams."

"I too dream. Would you think it?"

"Dreams about death."

"Even that."

"Her own death."

"That too. That is, I dreamed she had died. And now she is dead."

"She is missing."

"I have no evidence." He put down the cards and opened his empty hands to the unblemished underside. "But I know she is dead."

"You say she was at the hospital. And now she has disappeared."

"If she were alive I would have found her. Or she would be with you." He picked up his glass, but left the other hand open, empty. "Do you ever dream of death?"

In a dream I had seen her lying in her grave, but I would not confess this to him.

"No," I said.

"You will."

He was as solemn in his pronouncements as Miss Stein in hers, and as certain. I did not say I did not believe him but he saw my distracted eye move from his empty hand to make a tour of the butcher's tools.

"He calls himself an alienist," said the Pope. "For three days the good doctor listened to her lies and inquired about the dreams and convinced himself the lies were true. A doctor of this kind is invariably a charlatan. But he believes in his own lies so is likely to believe in the lies of others. How can he discern between lies and dreams when he is a liar and dreamer himself? Talk with him if you must. Look for her in the streets. Ask for her at the morgue."

I would.

With the glass at his lips he threw back his head as if to gargle, then let the absinthe seep through him. The effect brought forth a sigh. He began to talk again of Mirabelle, the one-legged prostitute; my thoughts, however, were no longer at the boucherie chevaline but wandering the late night streets where I listened for a familiar voice to ask, "Tu viens?"

"—her protector, you see, is himself incomplete." He was speaking of the young pimp, who took no personal offense at this reference—but rather blushed with pleasure. "The deformed limb is diametrically opposite hers. Have you read Plato? Do you know the *Symposium*? I find something consistent with life and eternally uplifting in the idea of the desire and pursuit of the whole. You see why I consider these two beings perfectly matched?"

He paused to hear whether I agreed with him or not, but I had not read the *Symposium* so could not reply.

"But I keep you from your search. Yes, by all means, talk with Blanchard. And I hope I have been of some assistance."

He did not offer the empty hand to me, and I was relieved not to have to show it obeisance. The pimp went ahead of me through the chamber of slaughtered horses where one of the card players—transformed into a butcher, wearing a blood-smeared apron—sawed through a haunch of animal with an instrument shaped like a lyre.

"It is yours," said the pimp. He attached my watch to the wrist of his shriveled stub. "Take it."

I did so with teeth clamped shut, trying not to touch the dead flesh as I unhooked the wristwatch, hearing him praise its quality: "It keeps good time," before the shutter rattled down behind me.

Nineteen

WHEN MAÎTRE GODEFROY asked for the death penalty there was no public outcry. The crowd, despite its persistent sympathy for Landru, would have been disappointed or outraged if the attorney general had not called for the guillotine.

The courtroom was filled beyond capacity. The heat had been extinguished to lessen the sense of suffocation: spectators were seated on the inside window ledges as well as packed standing against the rear wall. Among these last it was said that Desforneaux, Deibler's assistant executioner, was one. (Deibler could not of course appear himself at a trial for the capital offense of murder.) I searched the eager faces for one that revealed a predatory and professional avidity, but could not guess at the identity of the celebrated member of Deibler's équipe, the man who would inherit the guillotine when Deibler retired. Nor could Harry point him out. Public executioners have given up the medieval black hood for less sinister means of anonymity.

Seats were being sold by scalpers for fifty francs the first row, twenty-five francs farther back. I wondered what bribes those on the window ledges had paid, mostly young women flexing their bare knees above their rolled stockings as they swung their legs. Some of these ladies, and others, winked or blew kisses in Landru's direction while the relentless Godefroy spun out his grim summing up.

The prosecutor was engaged in comparing the accused with a long line of bloodthirsty killers from Jacques l'éventreur (Jack the Ripper) to Tropmann and Pranzini. None, he declared, was as merciless and calculating as the man who now sat in the prisoner's dock.

Landru, all the while, sat abstractedly distant, unaware of either vituperation from the prétoire or kisses launched from the public benches.

"There is," explained Maître Godefroy, "no other recourse in justice"—then lowered his head in regret for having to cite this single expedient—"but to end the life of the man who so inhumanly has ended the lives of ten women."

And one young man, thought I.

Harry, when he had jotted down the shorthand digest of Godefroy's rationale, sat back against the bench and silently applauded with his fat pink hands.

Maître de Moro Giafferi was as distinguished in bearing and tirelessly eloquent as his predecessor. He immediately dealt with Maître Godefroy's demand for capital punishment.

" 'Death!' cries our attorney general. To satisfy the living, to console the bereaved of these women who have disappeared, we will cut off the head of the last man to have had knowledge of their affairs."

Repeating the chant he had intoned throughout the trial—gossip, hearsay, innuendo—the defense attorney attempted to establish the basis for a far different trial "to succeed this farce" in which Landru would sue a series of concierges for defamation.

He then brought to light the law which requires a passage of thirty years before heirs are permitted to take possession of the estate of a missing person: "Thirty years," insisted the defense attorney, allowing the significance of that period of time to extend itself for several heavy seconds. "The law states that a missing person is not necessarily a deceased person."

On this obscure turn of legal interpretation the defense intended to base its plea.

At that point Maître de Moro Giafferi lowered his voice to a still audible yet intimate whisper.

"Landru has been brought to justice on more than one occasion for crimes that are not at issue here. I know this man." (Landru turned from him, unwilling to submit to a mutual acquaintance.) "Despite whatever infractions of the law he has committed—and for these he will be punished—he is incapable of taking human life. The crime of murder is as abhorrent to his nature as it is to yours or mine!"

From his look, Landru could at that moment have murdered his attorney.

"Along with these chatty concierges reciting their old wives' tales, we have been privileged to hear the testimony of experts, soi-disant."

He dismissed the expert testimony by citing a trial based on the discovery of a skeleton found in the garden of the accused. "It sounds familiar, does it not?" The skeleton was assumed to be that of a victim of assault resulting in death. Experts identified the injuries to the skull as fatal. This may well have been true, but the trial did not run to its normal conclusion. "The skeleton, Messieurs,"—he was addressing the jury now—"turned out to be that of a chimpanzee!"

(Laughter.)

"Indeed, as we have admitted—with regret for whatever passion among pet lovers the deed has aroused—the accused did assassinate Mademoiselle Marchadier's dogs."

(Extended laughter, but not from the jury box.)

"As for the cahiers Brigadier Riboulet has so patiently interpreted for us—"

I did not think it wise to refer so lightly to the notebooks. Here was tangible and damaging evidence against Landru; and the defense attorney could not so jocularly discredit those grim notes in Landru's hand as he had mocked the evidence of the experts. His tactic was to ask the members of the jury if they themselves could account for a date, an initial, or a cipher jotted down in haste many years before— but I could not believe the jury would discount Landru's notebooks on Maître de Moro Giafferi's inconsequential argument.

Again, the lawyer lowered his voice and altered the tone of his discourse.

"Evidently ten women have disappeared. Among the hundreds of women my client has known, ten have not been accounted for. Ten women are missing every day in this vast city. Dozens are missing weekly, hundreds have vanished into thin air over the same period those ten are said to have disappeared. We cannot always explain the reasons behind a woman's disappearance, and it is not my place—nor my client's responsibility—to do so. A woman has a mind of her own. If she intends to exchange one life for another, she is free to choose."

The Pope's words came back to me: she was free to choose, we are not beasts.

"—a woman might choose to take up a new life in another city, or a foreign place—a fresh scene far removed from a stultifying past, or possibly burdensome debts. She can choose to be missing simply by changing arrondissements. A change of name, a change of address, and she is another person. Has she fled a dull husband, an insistent creditor, a disappointment in love? All we are permitted to say is that she is among the missing, she has disappeared.

"Messieurs," he addressed the jury again, "have you ever strolled the quarter of les Halles after dark? If so, you will have remarked on the extensive range of produce on display, including produce in the form of living flesh. Or have you chanced to pass at night the place Pigalle, the place de la Madeleine—or explored the streets bordering the gare Saint-Lazare? There, too, le commerce de la chair fraîche is in flagrant evidence. I intend no insult to your sensibilities, I mean no offense. I do not suggest you would have sought these places out for the purchased intimacy offered there—only that you have knowledge of these places, as we all do. Passing through those parts of our fair city, when darkness falls, you will perforce encounter a legion of missing women. These women have chosen the obscurity of night in which to practice their ancient profession. They are the missing. They have disappeared from the light of day, shed name and origin, abandoned all family ties and social acceptance and are missing by choice, for expedience or for shame. Messieurs, these women I speak of will remain missing until circumstances force them to enter la Salpêtrière or their bodies turn up at the morgue!

"No, gentlemen, I do not mean to cast aspersions (though aspersions aplenty have been cast at my client) on the good women we list today as missing and in thirty years are permitted to assume deceased. I make no conjectures concerning their whereabouts, nor do I offer any advice to the police in their efforts to trace these missing persons. I leave the realm of conjecture to my distinguished colleague, who has conjectured an indictment for murder out of chicken bones and dogs' bodies and the cryptic scribblings we have pored over during this lengthy procès.

"Nevertheless, recall if you will and consider a moment the case of Mademoiselle Marchadier. Has this woman not been missing, so to speak, for the larger part of her life? Here is ample cause for conjecture if ever there was cause. Mademoiselle Marchadier was—to put it as gently as possible—une fille de joie for as long as her age and figure made that role possible. In her middle years she became the madam of a house of ill fame—a house that subsequently failed, though I was not aware that so flourishing an enterprise could fail" (Laughter.) "and was in the process of liquidating her bankrupt establishment when she made the acquaintance of the accused. Landru was to purchase from her, or sell for her, the very beds and mattresses we saw heaped here in the prétoire.

"Yes, gentlemen, I refer to the nefarious traffic in women simply because we have been exposed to its actual stock in trade, the beds in which prostitutes entertained their clientele. Mademoiselle Marchadier was an acknowledged procuress, a shadowy figure in the white slave trade, and my client—because of a transaction in mattresses—is held accountable for her whereabouts.

"But I do not conjecture on whatever connection there may be between the inhuman traffic in women as prostitutes, and this case of missing persons set before us. I do not know where Mademoiselle Marchadier has—this time—disappeared to. Nor does my client know —nor will anyone likely ever know. Dear God, it is not for me, it is not for the accused, to make appear those who have disappeared!"

Maître de Moro Giafferi now addressed himself to the judges, the jurors, the audience at large:

"In my final plea for justice I want only to remind you that the accused is, in any event, a condemned man. Landru has been tried and convicted of fraud on three separate occasions. His third conviction resulted in condemnation—in absentia, since he failed to appear in court—to seclusion in perpetuity.

"This man we have mocked and vilified for twenty-one ignoble days has, when all is said and done, no life left to him but that of a prisoner in the hellish confinement of Devil's Island—a punishment, I might add, generally considered worse than death itself."

The attorney suggested to the jury how they might in all justice respond to the forty-eight articles put to them by the President.

"Is Landru responsible for the disappearance of the ten women and one young man named in the indictment? No, he is not. You may cry out in all truth that Landru is a criminal. He has defrauded certain of these missing women—and others, besides. Landru has repeatedly broken the law. He has lied and cheated and forged for personal gain. Yes, and he will be punished for these infringements of the law. But a murderer? That this man we have observed and listened to for twenty-one days did put to death in cold blood some eleven missing persons, that he cut their bodies into bits and burned them in his stove—jamais, Messieurs, jamais! There is only one reasonable and just answer to these forty-eight articles: to each a firm and unqualified no!"

The defense attorney was given water. I would have liked some myself. After a brief statement by President Gilbert, the jury retired.

The commotion was general, and unrestrained. By now the huissiers made no attempt to suppress the uproar, for this crowd was like no other ever assembled at the Palais de Justice in Versailles.

The hubbub continued throughout adjournment while we awaited the verdict (no one dared to leave the courtroom) in an atmosphere of disorder and celebration. Picnic hampers were brought forth from beneath benches and chairs, bottles of wine and beer were uncorked. The diners broke off chunks of bread and passed the loaves along. A bookmaker circulated openly taking wagers on the outcome of the jurors' deliberations.

Cocteau sat with the transvestite cowboy Vander Clyde, but Gabriel was nowhere in sight. I could now understand Gabriel's distress (Cocteau openly flaunted his affection for the extravagant beauty known now as Barbette), and why he had gone to Miss Stein for comfort. In the press section a reporter from *l'Illustration* shared his flask of American rye whiskey with Danglure, the scorned and scruffy colleague he would not ordinarily have nodded to. The same flask in fact was passed along from reporter to reporter until it reached Harry, who feared a drink might make him miss his deadline, but I drank deep and gratefully.

After that I lapsed into a state bordering sleep, though uncomfortably conscious all the while, until I heard the huissier's sharp cry and was aware the officers of the court, clerks, and attorneys had reassembled in the same places they had quit at the instant of adjournment, and I saw, swimming toward me through the murky green of the courtroom, a pale and unperturbed visage, the figure of Landru. The jurors filed in at 9:25 and President Gilbert requested the reading of the indictment with the jury's verdict now affixed to each article. The sound of chief clerk Grifon's voice seemed to answer from underwater.

Yes.

The accused did forcibly deprive Madame Cuchet of life in a manner known only to himself, and did in a like manner take the life of her son, Cuchet, André. Madame Guillin, yes. Madame Collomb, yes. The accused is found guilty of the crime of murder against Madame Jaume, Madame Pascal, Madame Buisson, Madame Laborde-Line, Madame Héon, and Mademoiselle Marchadier. The unbroken sequence of response—oui, oui, oui—fell like hammer blows upon the ear. Spectators murmured quietly at each repeated oui, but may not have heard, as I did—or reflected upon the significance of—the non that followed articles 27 and 28, for there was no pause or inflection of voice to indicate the single exception in the case of Andrée-Anna Babelay. The jury had been as troubled as I about the young and pretty mistress Landru had taken—with nothing to be gained by her death—who nevertheless had disappeared. In every newspaper report but mine (even Harry failed to record this single instance of dissent) Landru was declared guilty on every count.

The calm following the final unequivocal oui was as unnerving as the earlier confusion and noise. President Gilbert turned to Landru and asked the now convicted man if he would care to reply to the verdict as so rendered. Landru was completely unmoved and undiminished by the overwhelming judgment passed upon him—or so he appeared to us, and that is what we wrote. He directed his statement, soberly and with all respect, to President Gilbert.

"The court has made a great mistake, your honor. I have never killed a single living soul. That is my last word."

LAST WORDS

One

————————

THE PROFESSOR is waiting for me, with his packet of nose tissues and a German tape recorder. I have just come from Grasse, where I had consultations with Malsain and Hameçon, my doctor and lawyer respectively. Naturally the professor, my house guest, offered to drive me into Grasse in the automobile he has leased for his sabbatical in France. I declined his offer with thanks. One of my consultations had to do with him, and I would have felt uncomfortable in his company. (Besides, he has too few occasions here to be alone with his young wife.) As soon as I returned—by bus from Grasse, on foot these last few meters from Ys—I caught a glimpse of the professor working at his notes on the lower terrace of my garden, far from the linden tree to which it seems he is allergic.

The French are a pessimistic race: neither Malsain nor Hameçon offered me much succor. Dr. Malsain tells me time is short, but there will be no pain (and there is none, for which I am grateful). Maître Hameçon is doubtful I can legally bequeath my property to an unborn infant—even though I am an American, and the child will be an American citizen—unless I give up my residence in France. "Time is short," I told him, passing on Malsain's word.

"And what if there should be a miscarriage?" he reminded me. "Or if the baby should be born dead?"

The French, as I say, are a pessimistic race.

I have never placed much confidence in lawyers, and trust doctors even less. Perhaps I can outwit or outwait both these astute professionals. There was a doctor in Switzerland, Dr. Berne in Genève (or was it Dr. Genève in Berne?) who gave me only two years to survive, and that was five years ago. Dr. Malsain here in Grasse granted me a stay of six months, unaware of the original sentence. The six months are up. "You will feel a gradual letting go," said Berne, and Malsain described the process as "a steady wasting away." Are we not wasting away from the moment of birth, and letting go all along?

As for lawyers, well—you know what they are.

Despite the scientific assurance of a painless release, I have taken the precaution of stocking a supply of multicolored capsules—some obtained by prescription, others by less direct means. Also, I have inherited O'Grady's ridiculous dueling pistol, but have no intention of using it. I fear the antique mechanism would fail at the critical moment, as it did for him. Nevertheless I keep the pistol oiled and my pills in a cool dry place.

My narcotics are stored in the wine cellar. They were put away in a vintage year, and I trust they will age gracefully and remain potent. I am speaking of pills, not wine.

(I will tell you something about wine. In 1953 I put away an ordinary table wine produced by a cooperative in the Var. The bottles were carefully washed, the corks boiled, then the filled bottles sealed with wax. Now, ten years later, my wine is exceptionally palatable. These are ordinary wines of Provence I refer to. Let me assure you my taste has not yet been affected by infirmity.)

I cannot feel the unpaved road beneath my feet. The doctors were right about this: first, a numbness in the extremities. Since I have begun to feel so little sensation below the knees, I carry a cane (sent to me by Miss Toklas) to help me keep my balance. The cane is made of ash, and Georges Braque once struck an auctioneer over the head with it. Braque gave the cane to Gertrude Stein during her last illness. For reasons of her own (I think she had quarreled with Braque) Miss Toklas did not return the cane to Braque after Miss Stein's death, but sent it to me.

When I told this story to the professor he became so excited he stopped the tape. He wants to buy the cane for a library in Lubbock, Texas. There it would be exhibited under glass, like Lautrec's cane, which is on display at the Jeu de Paume museum. "I still have need of it," I told him, but he insisted he would replace mine with a far better cane: "—and make you a really attractive offer for this one, sir." I have put him off. He has no understanding of sentiment and is single-minded in his pursuit. As soon as I walk out to the terrace to join him, he will, before greeting me, look first at my cane with those handsome covetous eyes.

(I wonder what became of my father's cane. My father returned from Italy with it: the handle unscrewed to become a drinking vessel, and he had filled the hollow walking stick with grappa. No need to speak of my father's cane to the professor: he is interested only in artifacts of some institutional worth.)

"Is that you, Vernon?"

The professor's wife, calling from the kitchen, has mistaken me for her husband. I tell her it is only I, then make a stop at the water closet a few paces from the main house. (The toilet is a primitive installation my young Texas visitors see fit to spray with deodorizer and have stocked with rolls of American toilet tissue.) She has heard my shuffling footsteps on the gravel footpath, and now awaits an end to the tumult of flushing and my reappearance to inform me that today is the Fourth of July.

"Back home," she says, "we make a big to-do."

"Here too, but the French do not celebrate until the Fourteenth." I pray she does not think me sarcastic.

Mrs. Flowers is an open-faced Texas beauty not yet out of her twenties, with long slim suntanned legs. Her pregnancy does not prevent her from wearing shorts. She carries the six months' protuberance with the athletic grace of those who learn to swim at an early age.

"Vernon was just asking about you. He hopes you're not too pooped to do another tape?"

She is preparing a quiche lorraine out of a French cookbook written by an American. (Miss Toklas wrote a cookbook too, but not a French one.) I hear the professor sneezing some distance away. I will take him a whisky and some ice, and a porto for me. His wife offers to carry the apéritifs on a tray, but I can manage the bottles quite easily in a market basket. The professor has a notebook full of questions to ask me, until time for lunch.

En route to sniff the air, I feast my eyes. I have never ceased to love this place, and will leave it with regret. The smells are overpowering, the greens ever greener, this my final summer here. Every stone holding my terraces together is familiar to me. The stone walls were put in by the Romans, I'm told, but the olive trees were planted by the Gauls. The professor has placed our deck chairs in the olive grove as far from the terrace of jasmine as possible. His name is Flowers, but he is allergic to them.

Two

Dear Dottore,

I write to warn you a professor and wife are headed your way. They are texans but not the kind from the cinema except for long legs. He is a dottore too, but in american literature (or american lit as he calls it) and is wanting tenure at some university in Texas. Why anyone with a doctorate or not would want tenure in Texas is beyond my imagination but that is what he wants.

His doctoral dissertation is about Gertrude and he says he wants to go on from there. Where to? I asked but he did not specify. He was here in Paris raking through cold ashes forty years old. Naturally he has picked up some gossip. I wanted to put a stop to it but he has charm and you know how I am about americans with charm who want to talk about Gertrude. He has a recording machine with him he will want you to talk into but beware he doesn't charm you into saying more than you intend to say. I talked so much I may have let a word slip that would be best left unsaid but it is too late now so I must ask you to beware.

He says he wants to get at the essential Gertrude but that is what they all say. I told him what I tell everyone but it never seems to be enough. As Gertrude used to say, it is all there. But not to them and the truth bores them. I told him if the truth is repeated often enough of course it is boring but you can still tell the truth yet express it in an original way. I want to do exactly that, he replied. He says there were too many blank places in his dissertation. I said don't ask me to fill up your blanks for you. He considers that first work merely a springboard. To what? I asked but he did not say. He has left me a copy of his dissertation to read so I am reading it and it is a very slack springboard. Perhaps the book he intends to write will be less professor and more Gertrude.

We used reels of recording tape and I must have told him everything worth telling in those several afternoons but he still wants more. They all do. He is coming to you for more so beware. He dug up some slander Hemingway or somebody spread that it was I who said what Gertrude said before she died, then said she said it. I very nearly sent him packing. But he has charm and very nice eyes and managed to calm me the way steers calm a bull in the arena. I was calm but still angry about Hemingway's innuendo and may have sounded confused on the tape or said something regrettable.

If he asks you and he will this is how I remember it and the way I want it remembered. Just before they took her into the operating room Gertrude asked me, What is the answer? I was too moved to speak so she spoke for me and said, In that case what is the question?

I wish now I had never repeated Gertrude's last words to any of them. What she said was just between the two of us after all. But she was a genius and if the world wants to hold that genius up to the light I must share whatever she wrote and did and said with the world. The professors want tenure but I have Gertrude to think of. It is for her and her work I talk at all. Otherwise I would not give this professor or any of them the time of day.

One thing I did not tell this one or anyone and never will is how the Autobiography came to be written. He knows you proofread and tinkered with the typescript when I was too ill to and that is all he knows or anyone knows but us. I know he will ask you about the Autobiography for he thinks he is onto something that will turn into a springboard. His book he says will not just cover well-trodden ground but take off in new directions. It is the new directions I am worried about.

He will ask you if I had anything to do with the writing of the Autobiography for he has been to everyone with his microphone and has collected tapes and tapes of innuendo along with who-knows-what else. You remember that pamphlet the Jolases and other enemies of Gertrude published when the Autobiography became such a success?

Well Gertrude's enemies are still at work. If you tell the professor anything about The Autobiography of Alice B. Toklas tell him Gertrude wrote every last word and the only thing I ever suggested was that she drop the B from Alice B.

Remember it was always Gertrude's idea to write the Autobiography so essentially she did write it. The words are Gertrude's words and the book is more Gertrude than me so in that sense she did write it. The established truth is the truth as far as I am concerned. It is the truth in an original way and the way Gertrude would have wanted it told.

The university where the professor teaches has an oil well on the campus. He has been provided with travelers checks and recording tapes and a year's sabbatical in which to research and write his book. The university has given him carte blanche to buy memorabilia for the library. Like most Americans and above all texans when they have money in their pockets they will spend it. That is perfectly alright with me. Texas money is not real money but make-believe dollars that no one really loses by the spending of so I sold him some napkins and a thimble. Everything was supposed to go to Yale and everything literary did but you know how the Steins have been about Gertrude's pictures and my allowance and who would have thought anybody would buy napkins? They are embossed with GS for Gertrude Stein and the motif a rose is a rose is a rose printed in a circle around her initials. He intends to call his book A Circle of Roses and I said the title is fine but be sure the circle is a true circle and does not take off in some oblique direction. He paid three hundred and seventy-five dollars for the thimble. It was not even Gertrude's but mine but what is the difference? I sold the napkins for one hundred and twenty-five dollars each. They are paper and I have stacks more which is like having money in the bank. I no longer use them when I serve tea but save them for the professors.

Remember how I always talked with the wives while Gertrude talked with the husbands? Now I talk only with the husbands. He has charm and energy and she has energy but I did not get to know her well enough to know if she has charm. They are on the way to you in a little german car they rented in Paris. They took me to Maxim's in it and I wonder where they put their legs.

I have made arrangements at Père Lachaise to be buried next to Gertrude when the time comes. Meanwhile I continue on alone.

As ever,
ALICE

Three

What is the question?

"Could you tell me, sir, about your visit with Gertrude at Bilignin?"

His use of the prénom amuses me. I am sir to him, yet Miss Stein —who makes no protest from Père Lachaise—is Gertrude, as if the living should be treated with formality but the dead, by the fact of their disappearance, have become familiars.

"I was there in the summer of 1932. I never went again. The war broke out—World War II, that is—and I went to live in Switzerland while Miss Stein and Miss Toklas spent the war years in Bilignin. The stone farmhouse is very much like this house, but the view is of the Rhône instead of the Mediterranean. Miss Stein loved a view, but always sat with her back to it."

"Isn't that in the Autobiography? That Miss Stein always sat with her back to the view?"

What perfect teeth Americans have: a modish blond mustache contributes to his smile.

"It is indeed. Sorry. I am wasting your tape on what is common knowledge."

"Not at all, sir. I'm glad the subject came up—the Autobiography, that is. Wasn't '32, when you were there, the year the Autobiography was written?"

He has charm, as Miss Toklas remarked, but it is a calculated charm. Unlike his wife, whose smile is a natural endowment (a pity Miss Toklas could not have got to know her), his own might have been acquired professionally, perhaps learnt at a university. The smile will take him far, but he will become less charming the farther it takes him.

"It was."

"I understand you were of considerable help in the preparation of that work for publication."

"My assistance, such as it was, was limited to checking the typescript for minor errors. The only other occasion when Miss Stein made use of my limited abilities was when she attempted to write a roman policier." The revolving spools of tape are seductive to watch and incline me to run on. "Detective novels are a harmless form of fiction, but of no lasting significance. I spent a time in limbo—or in purgatory, if you will—translating French detective stories into English, and vice versa. It is like writing pornography for a living, which I have also done. I fear Miss Stein was tempted to elevate the form into literature, as Dostoievski has managed to do, but Miss Stein did not succeed. At any rate, she was inspired to write a detective novel called *Blood on the Living-Room Floor*."

I expect the professor to join me in a smile over the naiveté of this title, but he chews on his mustache instead.

"I know," says he, with a trace of bitterness. "We made a substantial offer for the manuscript of that work, but it went to the Beinecke Collection at Yale."

"Yes, it remains in manuscript. The book was not likely to be published, in English or any other language, but as a favor to Miss Stein I did a translation into French. That version is called *Du sang parterre au salon*."

This also fails to amuse the professor, but he is suddenly eager to know if I have a copy of the translation.

"I may have."

"Even a carbon."

"It would be a rather tattered carbon, if I still have it. I gave the original, of course, to Miss Stein."

"No matter. We would be interested in your copy. We—that is, the university library at Lubbock—might make you an attractive offer for it."

"Would you not want to read it before making an offer?"

"That, yes, too. I mean, of course."

"I will look for it. If I do find my copy I would be pleased to present it to your collection, gratis."

"Gratis? I, well—that's great. But the offer still stands, if you should reconsider."

"You might yourself reconsider, once you have read it."

I have succeeded in restoring his smile but am unsuccessful in distracting him from the Autobiography. He wonders—since I admit to helping Miss Stein with her roman policier—if I have contributed in some way to the preparation of *The Autobiography of Alice B. Toklas.* In other words, he wishes to know if I have written all or parts of it myself.

I can in truth reply, "Not one word."

For a moment he plays with the push buttons on his clever German recording device. He is uneasy about approaching the inevitable next question, since I have been rather sharp in denying my own collaboration. He recrosses his long legs, at the knees now instead of the ankles, and jiggles his drink to make the ice cube spin.

I take the opportunity to muse aloud and let the professor record what he will.

"If fate had not interfered, as it so often does, Miss Stein might have chosen this region in which to buy a home, instead of Bilignin. She and Miss Toklas were en route for Grasse in the Ford motor car they called Godiva, looking for a prospective property. They had driven down the valley of the Rhône and were so enchanted with the setting they got on the wrong road and ended up in Avignon instead of Grasse. So they remained under the spell of the Rhône and never got to this equally enchanting corner of the world."

He feels a guest's obligation to ask me the conventional question: "How did you happen to settle here, sir?"

"This place was a ruin when I inherited it from my mother, who died in 1922—of the same malady, by the way, that killed Miss Stein in 1946: cancer of the stomach. I did not restore the place until 1949 when I came to live here permanently. I have been restoring the house ever since. The house in fact grows younger while its owner ages and cracks."

The professor dismisses my alleged deterioration with a polite smile and a twitch of one shoulder. Youth can never completely accept the inevitability of old age and its concomitant ruin.

"Miss Stein spent her summers at Bilignin, or whenever Paris became intolerable to her. When it became not only intolerable but impossible, she went to Bilignin to stay indefinitely."

"You mean, sir, when she fled the Germans?"

"Fled is hardly the word. Miss Stein had never cared for Germans and might not receive them—except for Kahnweiler, the art dealer, and an occasional eccentric German collector—but she did not flee them in the sense you imply. Let us say she chose not to remain in her beloved Paris overrun with a people she so strongly disliked. The ambience would no longer be the same. So Miss Stein and Miss Toklas closed the apartment on the rue de Fleurus, stored the paintings, and moved to Bilignin. It was a déménagement, not flight. If she had intended to flee the Germans she would have returned to America—or gone to Switzerland, as I did."

He slyly mentions that Bilignin was in Unoccupied France, was it not?

"No place was unoccupied if it was occupied by Miss Stein. It was also occupied by spies, Nazi sympathizers or outright Fascists, and collaborationists of every stripe—a dangerous region for an American in residence, and all the more dangerous for Gertrude Stein, who was Jewish. In Bilignin Miss Stein and Miss Toklas lived from day to day under suspended sentence of death."

"Were you in touch with her during this period?"

"In a clandestine way, yes."

"I wonder, sir, if any of your correspondence from that period still survives."

"I am afraid not."

He is disappointed, for he was prepared to make another offer. I have not been altogether truthful in my reply, but I consider those few rare messages beginning "Dear Dottore" (a formula greeting later taken up by Miss Toklas) inviolable.

"I went to Switzerland to escape the war. I might have stayed on, as Miss Stein and Miss Toklas did, with far less risk—I was born in France, with the advantage of anonymity as camouflage which Miss Stein did not have—but I am not made of the same stuff as Miss Stein and Miss Toklas. I fled. Of course I am antimilitary, but it was not just that. I realize that war, like any other plague—or cancer—does not ask for approval or dissent. You are a worm in the path of a natural force: it rolls over you and marches on. So I betook myself to Switzerland out of its path."

I am certain he does not regret the wasted tape (it can be reused, in any case) but as for the wasted time his shoulder twitches with what might be called impatience, or a polite dismissal of my claims to cowardice. Ostensibly he is being the patient young scholar while I play the rôle of the garrulous old man. His German tape machine suggests a phrase.

"The German war machine, it was called. My newspaper editor said the Germans were a machine-tooled nationality and would be the first to evolve into robots, but he did not live to see the evolution. Inevitably the Germans found a leader shrewd enough or demented enough to reiterate their myths in such a way that the submerged Teutonic barbarism burst to the surface. Such leaders appear from time to time in any country, but the Germans are particularly susceptible to this kind of appeal and are capable of being led on the most unimaginable crusades to commit the most unthinkable crimes."

A flower-scented breeze stirs in our direction simultaneously with the appearance of the professor's wife, who has just stepped outdoors. He is sneezing again. I fear my vagrant line of thought has carried me far beyond the tame literary souvenirs my interlocutor intends to record and classify. I must bear in mind that these young Texans have but a few weeks of summer to spend with me. They expect to be in Paris well ahead of time for Mrs. Flowers' accouchement: she is to be delivered of her baby at the American Hospital in Neuilly. (When they first arrived I naively suggested that Mrs. Flowers might want to make use of our picturesque little clinique in Grasse, which would allow the prospective parents to stay on much longer, but the professor made inquiries and discovered that maternity cases there are handled by a midwife instead of an obstetrician.)

Time is short, therefore, for them as well as for me. I will miss them—even him, despite his dismaying academic ambitions. His single-mindedness is almost endearing.

My uncertain vision takes in the blurred sight of Mrs. Flowers undoing the chic kerchief that kept her golden hair out of the quiche. As motor function diminishes, eyesight also fails. She is calling something to us, with her hands cupped to her pretty mouth.

"In a minute, honey," he bellows in reply. She has called us to lunch.

Honey. How apt that term of endearment for a wife who is honey-colored, honey-smelling, honey-smooth. Women of today, at least this variety, exceed in beauty the movie stars they once emulated. All imperfection has been bred out of them, and they seem to find mates of equal physical excellence. I pause to remember the tangle of unwashed hair worn by a girl I once loved—the bitten-down fingernails, a cold sore (the last time I saw her) in the corner of her mouth. These are blemishes a faculty wife—or a film vedette—will never be guilty of.

I must confess an indiscretion unforgivable in a host. My bedroom is directly above theirs: I hear them move about the room, I know the sound of the springs. They whisper in the night. I sometimes imagine the tall slender Flowers—these two perfect specimens, freed of their casual summer costume—entwined.

She walks with assurance across the dining terrace, then down the primitive stone steps, proudly bearing the rounded pouch of a babe to be. I watch her dimly, the sun in my eyes, as she moves against the olive trees and intervening cypresses. She has not come as far as our deck chairs, but sits a little way off (half leans, half sits) against a stone wall some ancient Gallic agriculteur put there, as if for that purpose. She does not intend to intrude on her husband's colloquy, but she has approached close enough to assure us (only one hand cupped to her lips for this): "There's no rush."

But time is short—and the professor's tape has just run out. The machine ceases to operate while he changes the spools, but my thoughts continue to revolve.

How close the Germans came to taking her that first time. (I am thinking of Paris, for I cannot forget the relentless Aryan lust for her.) The wooer made the first tentative moves toward capture: the probes with cannonade, flesh wounds inflicted by zeppelin and propaganda leaflets scattered like billets-doux—all means of breaking down her resistance. The sexual parallel is apt, when we think of Paris as she.

But Paris resisted. She barely escaped the assault everyone considered inevitable. A hastily arranged and clumsily managed defense— so believably French, with taxicabs—intervened. Then the gallant Americans came galloping to the rescue.

Consider the frustrated ravisher, nursing his grievance for twenty years. He bides his time but will have his revenge. There were no taxicabs at the Marne, and Americans were latecomers that second time. Pimps were in charge of France, and Paris opened her thighs. A madman could hardly believe the highborn beauty had fallen into his hands: his frustration this time was that Paris could be raped but not seduced. Then, when his lovely captive was to be set free he did what any barbarian would do: he ordered Paris to be burnt. A queer necessity it is to burn one's mistress after using her.

Why do I rage so against the Germans? Miss Stein, by extraction, was German—and so, on my father's side, am I.

"I knew a man," I begin, for the tape is turning again, "who was a great seducer of women—a criminal type. An incredibly cold-blooded seducer he was, and very cunning at his seductions. You might think so successful a Don Juan was handsome and tall, but Landru was neither. He was said to have had relations with two hundred and eighty-three women over a period of four years."

"Interesting," is the professor's comment. This is what visitors to Miss Stein's studio used to say when the paintings on the walls either repulsed or baffled them.

"He courted these two hundred and eighty-three women in a way to bring their dreams to life, by flattery, lovemaking, the promise of marriage—though he was already married, the father of four children. They believed in him, the sentimental ladies, for if they did not believe in him they could believe in nothing. A peculiar kind of parasite, he fed upon their misplaced faith. He took everything from them: their earthly goods, their hopes, their love—in several instances their lives. He was brought to trial for murder, convicted, and condemned to the guillotine. It was claimed he dismembered the bodies and burnt them in his stove."

The professor has taken a small cylinder from his pocket and holds it under his nose. He sniffs discreetly from each nostril in turn. I can smell the menthol through the scent of jasmine: the inhalator is to prevent him from sneezing.

"When did this happen?" he asks me, trying to show interest in a subject far removed from his research.

"During the war, and just after. The First War, that is."

The inhalator has returned to the pocket of his jeans, one end of his mustache has been disarranged by it. The smile returns (with only half a mustache). He may be smiling because he enjoys the excellent view of his perfect wife and can contemplate parenthood with pleasure while his elderly host rambles on.

At last the shoulder twitches and he says: "But about your contact with Gertrude, sir—during the Second World War."

The abrupt reminder of our previous subject of discussion does not disturb me. I am as relieved as he is to abandon Landru for Miss Stein.

"As I mentioned, we kept in touch. She could seldom get a message out of France, but I was able to communicate with her through friends affiliated with the underground. Her news was domestic and mostly tranquil. Isolated from her circle she reverted to a form of peasantry—Miss Stein was often compared to a peasant, or a Roman general. Miss Toklas kept a scrappy garden, Miss Stein continued to write (albeit in a vacuum). They were obliged to deal with the black market to survive: they hid and hoarded out of necessity—we all did. Miss Toklas is an excellent cook, as you know. . . ."

None of this, I realize, is particularly new or interesting to him. He has lit a cigarette out of boredom and despite a vow to give up smoking because of his allergy. His wife has looked up in time to observe the first puff of smoke, and frowns (as nearly as her photogenic face can frown). He is careful to avoid looking in her direction.

"I myself was living in almost privileged circumstances as the guest of a Swiss lady who had known my father. She had had money all her life, and knew the uses of that commodity. She was not only generous with her fortune but exceptionally considerate in the way the French call serviable. As soon as I informed her that two dear friends living in France were about to be arrested, possibly sent to a concentration camp, she immediately arranged for Miss Stein and Miss Toklas to be harbored in Switzerland. (The mayor of Bilignin got word to Miss Stein that local German officials had made inquiries about her.) My Swiss hostess found a comfortable residence in Geneva —with a view of Lac Léman—for the celebrated refugees. Through well-placed connections at three embassies she managed to obtain the necessary documents: a laissez-passer, means of transport, Swiss residence permit, currency (French banknotes and Swiss gold)—all of this, and the hopes of a number of us, were put at Miss Stein's disposal.

"At first she said she would come, but then she said she would not. The second decision was irrevocable. Miss Stein and Miss Toklas remained in France till war's end. Furthermore, they were never arrested. I have always and will forever admire this moment and this gesture among all the moments and gestures in Gertrude Stein's remarkable life."

This anecdote has vastly improved the professor's disposition. He inhales with pleasure over an item, finally, he can use. I will not diminish the pleasure of his cigarette and this useful information by adding that the decision to remain in France was made by Miss Toklas.

"Great," says he.

Professor Flowers is using a pencil and pad for the first time (I assumed the work was to be written by tape), occasionally flipping his cigarette ash into a patch of lavender. He now looks up at me with the expression one of his own students might assume on the occasion of inquiring about a grade—for he is struggling with the form in which to place his springboard question.

"Sir, the question has arisen"—he recrosses his long legs, at the knees now instead of the ankles—"among certain literary specialists in the U.S., and Paris—" A wasp has fallen into his whisky, and is drowning there; he fishes it out with a twisted end of his handkerchief. "Critical authorities, that is, on the Steinian oeuvre. I mean, people who have tracked down sources, verified dates, compared drafts, and are really knowledgeable about every significant aspect of anything Gertrude ever wrote . . ."

His wife is pulling petals from a daisy. Does she ask questions of it? I entertain the dark premonition that the Flowers—ideal as they appear together, in all outward harmony—will not remain together in the same garden. He will go far, and she will go elsewhere. Her shoulders are hunched in the way of a creature about to leave the earth, yet she—with the earth's own mystery bulging at her waist—is the truly earthbound being among us.

"What bothers them, and me, is a large question concerning the Autobiography. I'll tell you, sir, frankly, a thesis has evolved—not explicit as yet, a shadow of a doubt, so to speak—but the hint, as it were, is turning into a premise . . ."

I glance beyond the childlike delight in Mrs. Flowers' face to the brooding cypresses that mark our local cemetery. My thoughts have run a morbid course all morning. The cypresses are turning brown and have lost certain of their limbs: they too are dying of some irreversible blight. I have only recently reserved a little space surrounded by those diseased sentinels, a plot of ground, or what the French call une concession à perpétuité.

The reference to Madame S has reminded me of my father, who suffered his second, and final, heart attack in 1924. The obituary stated that death took place at Johns Hopkins Hospital, but a distinguished society matron with considerable influence at the Baltimore *Sun* managed to suppress the information that my father's body was removed from her bedchamber.

"What it boils down to," continues the professor, "is that some of us—and I include myself—are beginning to believe Alice wrote *The Autobiography of Alice B. Toklas,* and not Gertrude."

Four

The steel is forged in the presence of Deibler for a blade 37 centimeters wide, 1 centimeter thick, and weighing 32 kilos (half the weight of an average man). The blade is beveled at a 45-degree angle and drops at a speed of 4 meters per second from the top of the scaffold to the wooden stock, or lunette. Since the length of fall is only 4m 50, this means the blade functions for a fleeting 1.125 seconds.

"Men are hypnotized by statistics," said Miss Stein, who could never remember the recommended air pressure for Godiva's tires.

Lunette in the plural means eyeglasses, but in the singular refers to the hole for the head in a wooden stock, where the neck of a condemned man is fixed in place before the blade falls. Landru made a pun of this word. His sight was failing those last months in prison and when a guard suggested he apply for new glasses, Landru replied, "Never mind. Deibler will provide."

"Lunette is also the word for the seat of a water closet," said the plainspoken Miss Toklas.

The condemned man is pushed forward (hands tied behind his back, to effect a slight curvature of the spine) onto the bascule, something like a child's seesaw, so that he falls helplessly forward. The first assistant adjusts the head in the lower half-moon of the lunette by pulling at the hair with a jerk. (The condemned man is not entirely without resources at this point: Pantin, the murderer, bit the hand of the first assistant before he could withdraw.) The head now lies in the opening of the lower half of the stock, and the assistant pulls the toggle bolt 35 centimeters above the fixed section, which releases the wooden block that makes a full moon of the two halves. The condemned man is bound face down by an immobile wooden yoke.

We were at Bilignin, my one and only visit there. Miss Toklas was doing embroidery at the time, squinting close at the threaded pattern because her eyes were failing. She sympathized with Landru and his troubled eyesight—she thought his pun was apt.

Miss Stein was soaking her feet in a basin of cold water and brushing the flies from her legs with a Japanese fan. Her ankles swelled with the heat, and that was a particularly hot summer, plagued with flies and wasps. We were in the kitchen, the coolest room in the farmhouse, enjoying whatever breeze drifted across the valley of the Rhône.

"One can admire the bull in a bullfight," said Miss Stein, "for there is nothing on his conscience and the ritual of his death is truly aesthetic. Can you say the same of Landru? But read his execution to us. If it is gruesome, Alice will stop listening."

"I will listen," said Miss Toklas, "but I will not hear it."

"Alice is a listener with perfect pitch," said Miss Stein. "She hears the words she wants to hear and can hear through the flatness if it is flat to a natural rhythm the author meant all along."

"I hear the same rhythm anybody hears," said Miss Toklas, "but I listen to it differently."

Gertrude Stein treated us to her extraordinary laugh.

"You may not believe this, Dottore, but Alice is writing a book."

"I do believe it," said I.

"For years I have been saying Alice you should write your autobiography and call it My Life with the Great or Wives of Geniuses I Have Sat With or something with my name in the title and think of the money we would make. Last week I said it seems to me you are never going to get around to writing your book. The way to begin, I reminded her, is to begin."

"So I began," said Miss Toklas.

"Shall we tell him our scheme, lovey?" asked Miss Stein as she mischievously splashed a little water from the basin across the tops of Miss Toklas' shoes.

"What scheme?" Miss Toklas continued to squint into her embroidery.

Without waiting for Miss Toklas to agree, Miss Stein said: "We are going to put my name to Alice's book because my name is known and Alice's isn't."

Miss Toklas bent down and dabbed at the water on her shoes with a dish towel. "We are going to put your name to it," she said, "because it is your book. The words and rhythms are yours. You uttered them, and I am merely putting them down on paper."

"Alice has a keen sense of what the public at large wants to read. We intend to make money."

"I don't know about money but Gertrude is right, I know what readers read. For years I have sat with wives and listened to them. Wives are readers and I know what wives want to read. They want to read gossip. Gossip pleases them more than anything and that is what I am writing."

"Alice remembers everything that ever happened and when and to whom if not always why."

"The why is not as important in a book of gossip as the what and when and to whom."

"If she doesn't remember she asks me and I remember for her."

"Between us we remember everything," affirmed Miss Toklas.

"You bet you," said Miss Stein.

Miss Toklas rubbed her eyes and said, "I have been hindered by migraine."

"She will not wear her glasses."

"I wear them but they are what give me migraine. The typewriting goes well enough but I cannot always read what is typewritten. Gertrude will not proofread the typescript for me. She says it is too tedious."

"It is."

"Perhaps I could help."

"Would you?"

"Willingly."

"I told you he would," said Miss Stein, drying her feet with a towel embroidered with a circle of roses. They had meant all along to ask me to proofread. Miss Toklas thanked me and explained how far she had got and what I might do to help while Miss Stein sat with her great bare feet and swollen ankles resting on the cool kitchen tiles.

That evening we dined on a dish Miss Toklas called oiseaux sans têtes.

After dinner I suggested I might begin proofreading the autobiography Miss Toklas was writing but Miss Stein said, "No. Finish reading the execution to us. I like gossip when it is spoken but not written and I like murder when it is written but not spoken. I am not one of the wives Alice is talking about."

"Of course you are not," said Miss Toklas. "That is exactly why I must write the book and not you."

Five

I PRETEND TO NAP. It is an opportunity to allow the tape machine
a respite, and to offer the professor's wife a piece of the afternoon
alone with her husband. (I never nap, sleep is elusive enough at night.)
The window volets are open wide and through the somnolent summer
sounds—a slight breeze stirs the leaves of the linden, a fly is trapped
inside my light fixture—I can hear them talking quietly in the room
below.

"He knows more than he's willing to say."

"What is he willing to say?"

"Only that he helped proofread the manuscript."

"What did you expect?"

"He knows Alice wrote it. I know he knows."

"Maybe Gertrude Stein wrote it after all. Like, say, if Shakespeare
really did write Shakespeare."

He sighs. I can almost see the shoulder twitch with annoyance
or disappointment or whatever. I feel sorry for him—and sorry for the
wife to have to deal with his thwarted ambition. I wish I might in all
conscience utter some provocative revelation into the German recording apparatus. I would truly like to present the professor with a notable literary footnote (other than the one he insists upon), something
from which he might spring to the eminence he seeks.

I have riffled the pages of my mind's inventory and find nothing pertinent to offer. At lunch he spoke of Ernest Hemingway and was further disappointed to learn I had never met the man and could shed no light on that writer's curiously ambivalent relationship with Miss Stein.

"He's hipped on some murder trial from back in the twenties."

"Why don't you just let him talk."

"Time is short, honey."

Yes. It is also true, my being "hipped." Time and again I come back to the devilish conundrum Landru has left behind. These children of the sixties cannot know how important to me is that dated episode and distant mystery.

For a time I listen to their lowered voices. They have ceased to speak of me—or of the present, or the past—and refer to their own affairs, and the future. The future is of no interest to me, the strain of eavesdropping no longer worth the trouble. I return to my obituary page in *Nice-Matin*. I have a weakness for obituaries. I know none of these departed citizens of the Alpes-Maritimes, yet I check their names and ages as if for some clue to my own down-winding existence on this earth.

How different my life would have been if one afternoon I had dared speak to the attractive secretary in the office of the *Paris American*. No happier, but different. Irene is dead. She lived with Harry for many years, then married him. "Because of her image," said Harry, but to me she confessed it was "to simplify the damned paperwork." Paperwork in France is no small matter—but hardly, I think, a matter worth getting married over. Still, society does impose so many subtle and not so subtle sanctions on an unmarried couple, to conform is possibly the only way to ease the pressure.

Irene would know about social convention. She was its foremost arbiter, at first from the pages of the *Paris American,* and when that newspaper failed, with a column syndicated in the United States called *Speaking Personally*. She was wise enough not to speak personally to her vast audience of women, but to speak generally on every possible crisis from puberty to menopause.

I was Harry's best man at the wedding in the American Church in Paris. After the reception I accompanied them to the boat train at the gare du Nord and the newlyweds quarreled bitterly in the cab. They went to Wales for the honeymoon, but even before that holiday was over Harry was back, alone, asking if he might sleep over at my place for a few days. They quarreled from then on, lived alternately together or apart, perhaps loved but certainly disliked one another—yet never divorced. Irene died in a motor car accident, driving to Deauville with another man. (Her death reminds me of Isadora Duncan's end, so much in character: Miss Duncan's long trailing scarf caught in the wheel of an open limousine and strangled her to death on the Promenade des Anglais in Nice. Her life was no longer a life since the earlier tragic deaths of her two children, trapped in a motor car a careless chauffeur left unattended which tipped and rolled into the Seine.) Harry and Irene had no children.

I still receive letters from Harry, full of obscure facts and trivial detail he accumulates in his reservoir of total recall. I must tell the professor about him: he may be able to contribute a rose to *A Circle of Roses*. Harry now lives in a retirement village in Arizona.

. . . or if Louise had come to Paris earlier? Louise, too, is a survivor. It is pointless to contemplate how we might have survived together. She wed a Washington attorney who became successful politically but then died a dreadful death in a country club fire. There were no children. Louise continues our correspondence of half a century, but no longer sends me poems. Her wistful and witty letters are a pleasure to read—so much more poetic than her poems ever were.

When I think of the lawyer who left Louise a widow I wonder about the Maîtres Gilbert, Godefroy, and de Moro Giafferi. Dead they must be, but I remain in the dark about their disappearances, for I read no other French newspaper than *Nice-Matin*. Occasionally I come across a copy of the Paris *Herald-Tribune,* with a more international obituary page, or I read the column called Milestones in *Time* magazine.

In *Time* I learned of the deaths of Braque and Matisse, but Anacréon's death went unrecorded. He was bludgeoned to death by one of the young strays he had rescued from the streets, and cared for—one of his stray cats turned wild—perhaps the same wounded creature I saw one night at the atelier being tenderly fed a yellow fish soup by Anacréon's hand.

The last time I saw Gabriel was in Cannes, he a handsome thirty-ish, summering at the Carlton under the patronage of an elderly literary figure, a member of the Académie Française—"I am kept," as Gabriel put it, "like a caged bird." We sat beneath a parasol on the Carlton pier where I had sat with my father and Maynard Keynes so many years before. Gabriel told me about the great love of his life, Barbette.

"It was I who discovered him, you know—an ignorant ten-franc tapette from Texas. I took him in when he had nothing and knew no one. I devoted myself to him. I made him what he was."

Gabriel would accompany the cowboy to the bois de Boulogne and sit cross-legged in a pile of leaves while his discovery practiced on the tightwire for hours. ("I developed hemmorhoids because of him.") They went together to the Louvre to study the art of costume through the ages. Gabriel found oils and ointments to soften the cowboy's calluses and lighten his Texas tan. Barbette's act was perhaps the most original in all of Paris.

"I was with him in the dressing room an hour before curtain time—the cosmetics alone took the whole of a valise. I personally applied the rice powder and lip rouge, the kohl to his eyelids—I even perfumed his armpits and groin. The costume—which I designed—was an intricately sewn body sheath of rhinestones and ostrich feathers—can you believe the feathers he wore, *feathers,* weighed twelve kilos?—a costume far more extravagant than anything ever presented at the Folies-Bergère."

I had seen Barbette perform at the cirque Médrano, and again at the Théâtre Lyrique, and had written about him and his act. It was impossible to believe the graceful apparition dancing across a music-hall tightwire was anything but a magnificently costumed young woman glowing in the spotlight. Even when one knew—as I did, and many who returned for repeat performances—there was still a general frisson, the shock of awakening from a dream, at the moment of revelation. The unnatural transformation never failed to create a stir when the lovely performer threw off his wig and shed his feathers to stand before us bowing, breathless, his bulging sex covered by a codpiece in sequins.

"His real name was Vander Clyde, you know. Impossible. I called him Barbette, baptized him so to speak, for it was all my idea—I created him." Gabriel had put all his poetry into that creation, and left his poems unwritten. "Do you think he ever showed that much gratitude?" Gabriel snapped together a mobile thumb and one slender finger. "The paeans written about him in the journals went to his head like champagne." (I had written one myself.) "Cocteau took him up, introduced him into circles of light beyond the footlights, flattered and fawned over him—so he left me." Gabriel's dark eyelashes had turned moist, twenty years after the fact, but then he brightened and dabbed at his eyes with the back of his hand. "He left Cocteau, too— but that is Cocteau's story."

I would have stayed on awhile with Gabriel but his académicien arrived, a pink-faced septuagenarian with dyed sideburns. Gabriel murmured in English, "He's insane jealous, dear friend," then with a wink and his beautiful flatteur's smile, said, "I would not want him to think we were lovers." I stood and shook the gentleman's pink hand, said au revoir to Gabriel (but I would never see him again), and went on my way.

Barbette suffered a crippling fall from the high wire, and was unable to continue his music hall act. (Gertrude Stein told me this, she had heard it from Cocteau.) He limped home to Texas and settled there under his American name, and died in Round Rock, a small town outside Austin where he was born and had been a cowboy.

I have made of my bedroom-study a slapdash restoration of the Channel News Service, as I remember it. O'Grady's desk is now my own, on it my antique Underwood. (I do not know what became of O'Grady's own typewriting machine, sold to him by Mr. Joyce: there is a mystery some professor might want to solve.) His volumes of Sherlock Holmes are intermingled with my books on the shelves below the window, his gramophone (which still operates, but I have no discs for it) is on a stand beside my bed. There are no newspaper clippings attached to the wall, but his clock hangs there, the hands perpetually shackled at 4h 20, the word *Dublin* written across its face. I keep O'Grady's dueling pistol in the same desk drawer where he used to keep it. I must investigate those drawers in case there is something (besides a derringer) which might interest the professor. I have promised him the carbon of *Du sang parterre dans le salon,* a small recompense for his otherwise fruitless efforts at scavenging here. Miss Stein's lamentable detective novel might afford the professor some amusement—though I have yet to discover in him a sense of humor.

We like to think we are masters of our fates. O'Grady must have meant to use the pistol on himself, for it was found in his hand when he died, a cartridge in the firing chamber. O'Grady died in 1922, the year Landru was executed. The two modistes from the shop downstairs heard him cry out, and found him sprawling in the hallway (under the placard: "Clarence O'Grady is IN"), dizzy, incoherent, shouting in what they took to be Breton but must have been Gaelic. They got him into the elevator, but he lapsed into a coma and they were unable to extricate his body on the ground floor. O'Grady smelled of whiskey and they assumed he was drunk. He died in a diabetic coma at the bottom of the elevator cage, a fallen bird.

In the presence of an indifferent official from the British embassy, I signed papers that transferred the mortal remains of Clarence O'Grady to my care. I thought his wish might have been to lie beneath the soil of Ireland: somehow his references to Erin grew large in my inventory of remarks he had made during our association. In my sentimental fancy I assumed I was sending him home. It should have occurred to me his references to the old sod were invariably sarcastic. But I was trying to create a Clarence O'Grady to match my already shifting memory of him—as we invariably do, when resurrecting the dead. My romantic intentions were doomed from the beginning.

That part of Ireland known as the Irish Free State had only just come into being in January of 1922. When the sealed coffin containing O'Grady's body arrived at the port of Dublin, a newly investitured official would not accept the accompanying documents signed by the British embassy. O'Grady had of course traveled on a British passport —since that was the only document available to the Irish before their independence—and was returning to Ireland by His Majesty's permission. No matter that the Irish Free State had no diplomatic establishment in Paris; no matter that Clarence O'Grady was Irish born (and his dying words, whatever they might have been, were in Gaelic) —no matter: his body was sent back to France.

I was young, and determined—I tried again. Three times the errant coffin made the trip by ferry from Cherbourg, and was three times turned back. The corpse might be floating in limbo still, a missing dispatch from Channel News, but I did finally come to my senses when I thought I heard O'Grady chuckling from afar: how he would have relished my quixotic undertaking for the joke it was. He might in fact have wanted to remain in perpetual exile on the Irish Sea, if funds had been available to keep his restless remains afloat. The expense was beyond my slender means.

I began to deal with the French authorities. Here was an officialdom I could understand: a hierarchy of traditional fonctionnaires— mature, susceptible to bribes. A gratuity equal to a quarter of the cost for one of O'Grady's aller-retours from Cherbourg to Dublin was enough to purchase permission for the cadaver to remain in France. O'Grady now lies in the Père Lachaise, halfway between Gertrude Stein's grave and the stone that reads *Ici Repose Colette.*

I go no more to the Père Lachaise, I no longer visit Paris. The city is too distant in both time and space. I have never been in an aeroplane, and the trip by couchette on the chemin de fer is a long night's nightmare from here. For the length of the journey you are closed into a crypt with five other unknowns.

Anyway, what is left for me there? The last time I went to les Halles it was a gaping hole, like an open grave. They have torn out the stalls and sheds and dug an enormous pit where my beloved marketplace thrived. This disembowelment is equivalent to a careless abortion on the belly of Paris. I will not live to see the final indignity. The newspapers inform me a skyscraper will be erected there, with underground parking.

But I must turn from idle regrets and grim memories to the time still left to me. I have my garden, and a view of the introverted Mediterranean—I intend to pass from this scene with some tranquillity of mind.

I was looking for something before my thoughts went astray— what was it?

I can hear the professor and his wife moving about below. The bedsprings play a familiar tune: they are lying upon the bed.

The fetus has manifested life inside her.

"Feel," she says to him; then, after a pause, "Not there, silly."

This makes me smile. I can so well understand the professor's impulse to continue his caress beyond her simple request. In a moment they will, with a shared sigh and quickened breath, take of the pleasure he has provoked. A baby stirs within its envelope, a husband fondles his wife—these signs of life are more than my swelling heart can contain. I weep.

Six

I HAVE BEEN RUMMAGING in the drawers of O'Grady's desk and I find a photograph of Deibler the executioner in bathing costume (with his family, at les Sables-d'Olonne), a pneumatique from Louise inviting me to meet her at the Lutetia, a letter from H. L. Mencken to my father, and another letter—still sealed, never delivered—from Madame Vitrine to Landru.

Also I have come across Nguyên the Patriot's "Un memoire pour l'autonomie du Peuple Vietnamien," a list of celebrities (in Harry's shorthand) attending Landru's trial, a telegram from Miss Toklas informing me of Gertrude Stein's death, a receipt for a secondhand bicycle I sold in 1922.

There is this, too, to burn, along with so many other clippings, letters, memoranda:

DID ANDRÉE-ANNA ENTER BLUEBEARD'S FORBIDDEN ROOM?
Versailles—14 Nov. 1921

One of Landru's most repeated quips was the remark: "Those you call 'my fiancées' knew what they were doing. Besides"—and here he paused—"they were all over twenty-one."

Indeed Landru did specialize in women in their middle years, or older, but the one remarkable exception was young and pretty Andrée-Anna Babelay. Only nineteen when she became "engaged" to the distinguished Sire de Gambais (thirty years her elder), Andrée-Anna has been missing since April of 1917. Today the trial of Henri Désiré Landru took an unusual and unexpected turn. Instead of the usual clutter of furniture and other articles stacked pell-mell beneath the judge's bench, there were only the personal documents of Andrée-Anna Babelay: an identity card, a birth certificate, a photograph of her family in Rumanian costume, etc.—a packet of papers and a few trinkets to attest to the fact that Andrée-Anna Babelay ever existed at all.

President Gilbert led the questioning. He asked Landru how he came to meet the girl.

"I found her crying in the métro, your honor. As a person of some feeling, I naturally asked her what the matter was. She said she was without a job, and had no place to go."

At this point President Gilbert reminded Landru that Andrée-Anna was employed by Mme Alexandrine Vidal, cartomanne (fortune-teller), as maid-of-all-work at 12, rue de Belleville.

"Nevertheless," replied Landru, "that is what she told me. Her tears, I assure you, were genuine. I felt sorry for her, and offered her a room I kept on the rue de Maubeuge."

(The concierge at 20, rue de Maubeuge testified that the girl was in fact installed at that address. Her tenant, Monsieur Guillet—for that was the name Landru used, for that address —had told her Andrée-Anna was his niece.)

On 11 March Andrée-Anna asked her mother for a family photograph showing her grandparents in Rumanian costume. She was proud of her exotic origins and wanted to impress Landru with this background.

On 29 March Landru took the girl to Gambais on the advice of a doctor. Landru did not remember the doctor, or his diagnosis—only that Andrée-Anna was in need of rest and fresh air.

Why, asked President Gilbert (referring to Landru's notes of that period), did Landru see fit to purchase a one-way ticket for his guest and a round-trip ticket for himself?

"I could only leave her there to breathe the good country air."

A knowing murmur rippled through the courtroom.

Neighbors testified they saw her gardening at the villa, and bicycling on the road that ran past the cemetery. After 12 April she was seen no more. Yet Landru was still at Gambais: Monsieur Vallet informed the court that Landru bought two cords of wood at twenty-three francs each (this expense is noted in Landru's cahier: 2 stères de bois, 46F 50) and that he returned to Paris on April 12.

"I was not in Gambais on April twelfth," said Landru, and he stated he could not have returned to Gambais by bicycle because the métro did not permit bicycles aboard the trains.

"Then please explain the notation 4h du soir (4 PM). The prosecution claims it is the hour Andrée-Anna was murdered."

"But that is the prosecution speaking, and has become an idée fixe of Maître Godefroy. Let me state simply that these little numbers in my carnet mean nothing at all."

"Therefore, you maintain that Andrée-Anna Babelay was no longer at Gambais the twelfth of April. How and when did she leave?"

Landru did not answer this question, but instead asked one of his own: "But who, really, can prove I jotted down these notes and numbers at Gambais? The prosecution has got it in its head that I committed certain crimes, and everything it finds in my notebooks is made to fit the mold of this hypothesis. We are seeking the truth here, n'est-ce pas? Seek it then, without arrière-pensée."

This speech, delivered with more than Landru's customary flair, caused a sensation in the courtroom.

President Gilbert persisted in his line of inquiry concerning the departure of Andrée-Anna from Gambais.

"I brought her back to Paris—I no longer recall when, or by what means—and she found another job. Voilà tout. I never saw her again—any more than the police who tried to trace her"

"Why would this young girl leave her personal documents —including her carte d'identité—in your possession?"

"She left them with me saying, 'I want to leave some im

portant papers with you for safekeeping.' She was a careless child, and inclined to lose things. I think the idea of leaving her papers with me came to her when she opened a chest I kept in the villa, full of papers."

President Gilbert snatched at this: "Full of the papers of your other house guests at Gambais?"

For the first time Landru seemed taken aback. Without answering President Gilbert's barbed question, he went on: "Since I was holding other papers, I might as well do her the same service. She owed me a sum of money. I might hold these documents as collateral for the debt. She never came back for them because she never paid me what she owed me."

"In any case, you haven't answered what I asked. It is a strange and troubling coincidence that you hold all these personal papers of women who have disappeared under mysterious circumstances."

"Andrée-Anna left my house in Gambais, Monsieur le Président, under no other circumstances than that she wanted to leave. I am not responsible for the disappearance of anyone!"

"All the same, she owed you money. You didn't seek after her?"

"How could I search for a missing female in the city of Paris. You know very well how difficult *that* is."

A roar of laughter erupted in the public section of the courtroom.

Landru then assumed an air of martyrdom: "I trusted her —and I was wrong. There you have the whole story."

In France, members of the jury are permitted to direct questions to witnesses and to the accused. M. Jacques Martin (farmer) put the following question to Landru: "Why, sir, did you take into your lodgings on rue de Maubeuge a young lady you did not know?"

Landru "As I said, out of generosity—out of a sense of humanity. And you see how I was treated!"

This brought on further laughter.

The juror persisted: "Why didn't you ask Mademoiselle Babelay her address when you took her in?"

"I did not want to show a vulgar curiosity that would seem offensive to her. I waited for her to tell me that."

Maître Godefroy, the prosecutor, then joined in: "Your hospitality was indeed large."

Landru: "Not at all, your honor: only a room two meters fifty."

Again, laughter.

The prosecutor, angered at the comic turn Landru had introduced, stepped forward to remind him of the seriousness of the matter: "Take care, Landru—even if you mock the court, show some respect when one of your judges questions you!"

Landru very politely replied: "I have respect for every one of the jurors and intended no mockery in answering the question addressed to me."

Godefroy then took up the questioning: "When did you realize this young lady had opened the chest where you kept on deposit all these documents?"

"One day when I came into the room I saw the chest had been moved. I knew then someone had looked inside."

There was a pause. Maître Godefroy did not immediately follow with another question, but rather allowed the silence to weigh heavily in the suddenly stilled courtroom. At this moment one could not help but be reminded of the Charles Perrault fairy tale, *Bluebeard*. Fatima, the seventh wife of the chevalier Raoul, is permitted access to every room in the chateau save one. Her curiosity gets the better of her: she peeks into the forbidden chamber to discover Bluebeard's gruesome secret.

"And so," said Maître Godefroy, nodding his head as if in final understanding, "Mademoiselle Babelay—from whom you had nothing to gain but silence—must suffer the fate of the others."

"No!" Landru was instantly on his feet. "I had nothing to do with this girl's disappearance! You ask me where she went, and I can only tell you the truth: I do not know." He struck a dramatic pose, leaning slightly forward, one hand extended to the jury box: "Gentlemen, the court declares I am responsible for the young lady's disappearance. Then let the court prove to you I am responsible. It is not up to me to prove my innocence. No, this is not a case of 'le mur de la vie privée'" (the wall around one's private life, which Landru frequently cites as a reason not to answer questions dealing with his personal relations with the missing women). "I offered this girl sanctuary when she was in difficulties. I allowed her to live in my room in Paris when she was desperate, and at my villa in Gambais when her health was poor. I have admitted to you I did indeed know Andrée-Anna Babelay—but what more can I say? She disappeared. The police do not know where she has gone. Neither do I. Believe me, I truly do not know what became of Andrée-Anna Babelay when she left me. I have nothing more to say at this point!"

Landru sat down abruptly. The courtroom was in a fever of agitation. The murmuring became disruptive and the President called for order.

Madame Vidal, the fortune-teller who was Andrée-Anna's last known employer, gave the following testimony: "On the eleventh of March Andrée-Anna told me she had met a gentleman 'of a certain age.' Well, it did not surprise me. She was a pretty thing, and she made attachments easily. She was 'engaged' to a soldier for a time. But she considered him a common type—Andrée-Anna always looked higher than her own station. Not that I blamed her. She was too pretty to accept being a servant all her life. And she did her work well, I'll say that for her. But I was disappointed to hear her fiancé was a middle-aged man. Andrée-Anna was only nineteen at the time, and I felt something of a mother's responsibility. Anyway, her fiancé had lent her a valise. He wanted to pack her off immediately. No, I did not approve—but what could I do? She packed up her few pitiful belongings. She left me the next day."

Madame Vidal was pressed with questions from the President and Maître de Moro Giafferi, but she complained of poor memory.

"I am not asking you about the future," said Maître de Moro Giafferi, "but the past."

There was a burst of laughter in the courtroom, and the fortune-teller flushed. The sarcasm had made her all the more flustered—but she recovered herself when asked about Andrée-Anna's character:

"She was a very lighthearted person, gay—she loved life.

A sweet little thing, truly—and easily attached to men, as I said."

The President pointed out Landru, and asked: "Was she 'attached' to this man?"

"I don't know if Andrée-Anna spoke to me of this gentleman or another." She studied Landru carefully. "I'm not at all sure. My memory is not good, you know. I can't remember if I ever saw this gentleman or not. I have the impression—" and here she hesitated, then burst out: "it wasn't this gentleman at all."

Andrée-Anna Babelay had no money, no furniture, nothing that would interest Landru except her youth and beauty. It is well known that Landru was attracted to young and beautiful women, as in the case of Fernande Segret, from whom he had nothing to gain.

Did Landru's innocent young mistress pry into her lover's affairs, and was her fate ealed when she discovered his dreadful secret?

Seven

AT THE END of the nineteenth century Dr. Jean-Martin Charcot, known for his research in locomotor ataxia (deterioration of the nervous system in advanced syphilis), became chief physician at la Salpêtrière. There he created the first neurological laboratory—assisted by a young interne from Austria, Dr. Sigmund Freud—for the study of the female insane, and treatment of selected cases by hypnosis.

Two centuries earlier la Salpêtrière had been converted from a gunpowder works on the left bank of the Seine to become the vast Hôpital-Général under the patronage of Louis XIV. Originally the hospice was designed to house indigent females and provide a reformatory for prostitutes, but the complex grew to include a prison for women and underground confinement for the insane. Inmates of the workhouse and reformatory slept four to a bed, or on the floor, but private quarters of some luxury were reserved for the errant or wanton daughters of those who could afford to pay a daily pension. These girls were said to be folles de leurs corps (crazed in their bodies, sexually depraved) and could be committed by their families for a term of confinement rather than shut away in a nunnery for life.

In the Age of Reason it was believed that only women were subject to madness. The term hystérie came to mean a nervous disease of hysterical women, a mental derangement associated with the female nature: women possessed of demons, doomed to fits and convulsions and incurable folie. Those who were adjudged totally insane (not just of their bodies) were chained by the neck or an ankle to iron rings permanently imbedded in the stone walls of the underground oubliettes. Some of these unfortunates existed for years squatting chained in their own filth, sharing their dungeons with vermin and rats, occasionally fed scraps of black bread through the bars of their cages. At intervals one of these creatures might be unchained and brought into the light for some inquisitive doctor to experiment upon. She would be near-drowned in freezing water, or copiously bled, and the results noted.

By 1921 la Salpêtrière was a city of courts within courts and untended formal gardens hidden behind the gare d'Austerlitz. It was to this place I went in search of Fleur.

I found my way to the center of the complex: a domed chapel at the hub of a series of interlocking courts. Here, despite the overcast sky and unsettling wind, a man stood behind a tripod, his head beneath a black hood, taking a photograph of hospital patients ranged alongside the chapel wall. The sad adolescent girls endured the picture taking with smiles as weak as the light through the bare trees. They were dressed in wrinkled white hospital gowns with sweaters or shawls thrown over their shoulders, their faces pale or pained, leaves blowing against their legs. One of the girls sat crouched in a wheelchair, half her face enshrouded in bandages. Instead of staring into the photographer's black box she seemed to be watching me through holes in the gauze wound around her head.

I got to the courtyard beyond, the site of a piece of history and nightmare. At the beginning of the French Revolution a band of Septembriseurs incited by Marat held a drumhead trial here, accompanied by a cloudburst and barrels of confiscated wine. Aroused by constant drink and frenzied lust, they dragged the youngest inmates from the cells of the workhouse and reformatory—girls as young as fourteen—to undergo trial by rapine and torture. There was no guillotine to render justice on the spot, so the mob fell upon the helpless girls with clubs and daggers. They were raped and raped again, ten or twenty times in turn, and then their sexual parts mutilated with pikes and burning torches. The wet cobblestones ran red with blood and wine. Thus, with the cry liberté-égalité-fraternité ringing in the streets, began the Terror.

I asked a hurried nursing sister the way to the Pavillon Charcot.

* * *

Dr. Blanchard was possessed of the attractive grey at the temples and the cultured voice so reassuring to patients, along with the godlike assurance so characteristic of doctors. He received me in the same office, as he pointed out, that Dr. Charcot once used. The desk and furnishings had been kept exactly as the great medical pioneer had left them. Since I had telephoned ahead, Dr. Blanchard had the chart open before him on the desk.

"There is some question of the patient's name."

"She had no papers—she might have used any name."

"As a matter of fact she used the name of the girl with whom she pathologically identified, Andrée-Anna Babelay."

To hear the name spoken aloud outside a courtroom affected me strangely. It was as if someone had placed a photographic negative over another (one that I carried in my mind's eye) and the outlines matched. From my reaction he could see I recognized the name, and he went on to describe the patient.

"Dark hair, grey eyes, weight: 52 kilos, mole behind left knee . . ."

I nodded.

He went so far as to give me her temperature on admittance, and blood pressure—as if I might recognize her from these medical statistics.

"You say you are not a relative, but a journalist. Obviously you take a personal interest in this case. I have no reason to frustrate your newspaper investigation—I have always been extremely cooperative with newspapermen—but medical ethics prevent me from discussing a patient's illness or revealing any confidence that passes between patient and doctor."

The old jealousy made a knot in my abdomen: what had she told him that she could never tell me?

"But I can confirm what you probably know already. The girl disappeared from her ward. We made every attempt to find her within the hospital grounds, but without success. Beyond the precincts of la Salpêtrière we have no jurisdiction."

"Were the police notified?"

"As a formality only, for she was a voluntary admission and under no constraint to remain at la Salpêtrière. To the police she is just another missing person to add to their overflowing files. Technically she could have been charged with the theft of hospital property, for she was wearing a hospital gown when she made her évasion. At the time"

—and here he leaned back, contented with himself—"I saw no reason to add to her misfortune by provoking a criminal charge."

I acknowledged his humane gesture.

"I am perhaps indiscreet to reveal as much, but surely you are familiar with her malheurs. She was tormented by nightmare, she believed she was the victim of a murder."

I nodded.

"I interpret that recurrent dream as an overwhelming manifestation of the death wish. I inform you of my diagnosis as a precaution (in the unlikely event you should find her alive) against the suicide I fear has already taken place. She could not have got far in her hospital gown, unobserved, and I must assume she intended to get only as far as the Seine."

"She might have found other clothes."

"Possibly," said he, a weariness in his voice. I could believe whatever I chose.

Impulsively I asked, "What if she really were Andrée-Anna Babelay?"

He offered me the patronizing smile of a doctor tolerating the bêtises of a layman.

"That obsessive belief was unfortunately the source of her disorder."

At his own suggestion (missing patients all too often turn up there) he made an appointment for me at the morgue, calling from a prototype telephone consistent with the Charcot décor.

A cutting wind from the Seine did not prevent me from lingering through the lunch hour at the Jardin des Plantes. Although there were several cafés along the boulevard de l'Hôpital, I had no appetite: I sat half-paralyzed with cold and misery. Opposite my bench was a notice posted on a tree: *Perdu, Chat*—a tenderly described lost cat, gone astray somewhere in this garden of caged jungle cats. Farther along the allée Cuvier (named for that great assembler of prehistoric bones) I watched a walrus with a slime-green sheen doze fitfully in his cement tank, his fins crossed in resignation, moaning unhappily in his imprisoned sleep. I would never sleep again—fitfully, or at all—until I crossed to the quai on the opposite bank to rummage, like Cuvier, among the dead.

From a queerly illuminated slate sky a thin rain fell across the pont d'Austerlitz. I dared not look into the swirling black water below the bridge. I found the Institut Médico-Légal tucked innocently behind a children's park on the quai de la Rapée. Its architect had attempted a modest institutional façade, but for all the apparent discretion the small building sat perched in grim solitude, as substantial in its aspect as the Bourse or the Bibliothèque Nationale.

The clerk-concierge had me sit a moment beside a bust of Pasteur until an attendant arrived. The attendant was an adolescent boy with wet hair like straw parted down the middle, an apprentice croque-mort afflicted with puberty's pustules across his broad forehead and in the hollows of his cheeks. A partly eaten sandwich protruded from the pocket of his smock.

"Show him Sleeping Beauty," said the clerk. I was made to understand this was the only unidentified corpse available that fit Dr. Blanchard's description.

The boy shuffled ahead of me in his queer green rubber boots (why boots?) alternately fingering his pimples and the portion of bread in his pocket. We went down a circular metal staircase into a glassed-in anteroom where a woman attendant in the same grey smock as the boy sat at a table sorting items from a beaded purse. As we passed she looked up at us but said nothing, then scooped her treasure into a manila envelope. The purse, I noted, was not Fleur's.

We stepped into a brightly lit chamber of echoes—we were, I assumed, below water level here—the tiled walls lined with refrigerator doors, a dissection table in the center of the room, and drains at the four corners. I had been prepared for the smell, but not altogether prepared: no amount of formaldehyde or carbolic acid could quite overcome the sweetly sickening under-odor of human putrefaction.

"She's still a bit damp," said the boy, pulling open one of the refrigerator doors.

The body rolled out on a sliding platform.

The white marble face above the rubberized coverlet was as lovely as anything at the Louvre. Her features were in complete repose, not even the cotton wads in her delicate nostrils could spoil the symmetry. The colorless lips were parted in a beginning smile—you could see the upper edge of her perfect teeth. Her face was encircled by a halo of dark wet hair, the expression was one of celestial peace. She was beautiful, so beautiful I held my breath at the sight, but she was not Fleur.

"La belle au bois dormant," said the adolescent, "and not a mark on her."

He flipped away the rubber sheet. Her body now lay naked and white under the probing light. There was a pile of folded clothing in a canvas pouch at her feet. She was a gracefully formed young woman of some twenty years, her body so splendid it made my throat ache.

"The one you're looking for?"

I avoided his eyes and shook my head no, still staring, unable to break away from the naked spectacle of beauty and mystery.

Who was she, and how had she come to be drowned? Her smile belied all that was ugly and evil in life, her tranquil expression offered mute evidence of a need to sleep one night untroubled in the all-embracing river tide.

Here was the dream creature I had pursued during long promenades through the streets of Paris, down the corridors of the Louvre. This was the girl I had written simpleminded stories about and made love to when I made love to myself and longed to love truly before I stumbled upon my stray gypsy love one night at les Halles.

The attendant may have misread my expression, or he was simply overcome by a boy's obscene impulse, for he suddenly reached down to the dead girl and spread her thighs apart. One filthy hand still grasped her knee while the other made as if to caress her sex when I snatched at his arm and spun him around.

"Laissez-la tranquille!"

He responded to my shrill anger with hurt and puzzlement.

"She's dead," he explained.

Eight

IT IS THE Fourth of July. My young Americans have bought two bottles of Moët & Chandon to accompany the chili con carne, a Texas-Mexican specialty prepared by Mrs. Flowers. We are enjoying a late festive supper on the open dining terrace under a spectacular panoply of stars.

"We drink beer with chili back home, but Vernon thought champagne would be more fun."

"Decidedly."

The first bottle of wine has been consumed, and the professor is gently rotating the second in its bed of crushed ice. The ice is from the fish market in Grasse, a reminder of the fishmonger's ice for champagne to celebrate another occasion, in another age. I predict we will all three be pleasantly intoxicated by midnight.

"I shouldn't," says the professor's wife once again. "Because of the baby. But it's just too good."

The professor pours a child's token portion into his wife's fluted glass, then fills mine and his almost to overflowing.

"You say you sold the Channel News Service after your friend passed away?"

He has been indulging me by asking questions about my life instead of Miss Stein's.

"I sold only a list of subscribing newspapers in England and Ireland. By that time there was little else to sell."

Despite the letting go and wasting away, my taste buds remain intact: the wine is truly delicious.

"And then came the war."

"World War II, yes. I went to Switzerland. After that, in the fifties, I worked for that alphabetical bureaucracy, UNESCO, in Geneva, and later for NATO, in Brussels, but I could never settle into a niche in the organizational superstructure."

The professor assures me I would not, in that case, care for academic life.

"God, no." The faculty wife wrinkles her pretty nose.

"When I was a young man—" I pause to listen for a sigh from my young guests, but they are too polite to sigh. "I saw a fonctionnaire gasping for breath out the window of the French Ministry of Finance, and have never forgotten his look of desperation. At NATO and UNESCO I learned it was not lack of oxygen he suffered from."

The professor has changed from blue denim to white, for the occasion, and his wife wears an attractive frock I assume was designed as a maternity garment, a perfect copy of the high-waisted Empire mode.

"Did you ever go back to the United States?" he asks, while she, on the strength of the wine, ventures: "—or want to get married?"

I answer with a single negative to both.

"I'm very grateful for the manuscript you gave me."

Earlier this evening I presented him with my copy of *Du sang parterre dans le salon,* and he was genuinely moved—but not to the extent of wanting to read it.

"And remember," he reminds me, "the money's there if you change your mind."

He pours more wine. I am tempted to believe champagne is being poured for ulterior reasons, but must try to think better of him than that. He pursues no indelicate inquiry about Miss Stein, so I will assume he has truly taken a holiday from his sabbatical task.

We turn to the stars. The provençal sky in midsummer is too often obscured by haze, but tonight the heavens are revealed in clear and certain splendor. I am able to point out to Mrs. Flowers the constellation that corresponds to her birth sign: the four stars of third magnitude that comprise Libra. It is pleasing to be able to instruct her in something the professor knows nothing about. Nor can he locate his own Scorpio, so I do it for him, pointing at angry red Antares with

Braque's cane, but the professor is looking at the cane instead of the stars.

"What is your sign?" asks Mrs. Flowers.

For that we must stand and look beyond the tops of the cypresses to the northern horizon where a dim cluster known as Cancer glows.

"I could never believe in playing cards or crystal balls to reveal to us what lies ahead, or explain the past, but I sometimes think the heavens spell out a message for us, writ quite large, if we could only read it."

"Do you believe in astrology?" asks Mrs. Flowers.

"I suppose not. I don't know what I believe, or mean to say. I fear the wine is speaking for me."

They join me in a round of polite laughter and we return to our garden chairs and champagne. I delight in watching the professor's wife as she eases herself gracefully into the chaise longue, conscious of the quaint burden she bears along with herself.

It has long occurred to me my little circle in Paris brought no children to the world. We were a barren lot. O'Grady was a misogynist and a solitary, Anacréon (according to Fleur) was impotent. I would guess Harry and Irene never felt congenial enough to consider parenthood, and Gabriel was a member of that sex that does not reproduce itself.

"Sir, did you ever think at the time to buy art work from the painters Gertrude knew?"

I feel free to say, "I never thought their work was worth anything."

We laugh together, then share the last of the wine. The professor's reference to the large circle around Miss Stein reminds me that her friends, at least, included several sets of indifferent parents. A shadow, however, is cast over the children conceived out of artistic temperament. I think of Isadora Duncan's children trapped in a limousine that tumbled into the Seine. I remember the unhappy progeny of Mr. James Joyce. Although I am not a father I consider with dismay Picasso's unfatherly denial of his own son. Mrs. Flowers will make a happier mother than Zelda Fitzgerald, and the professor a more conscientious father than Hemingway.

Miss Stein and Miss Toklas were once upon a time godparents to Hemingway's firstborn—but nothing ever came of that. As Miss Stein commented: when the flowers of friendship fade, friendship fades. Flowers, circles. I am reminded of the title of the professor's book,

A Circle of Roses. Circles and circles, some of them concentric. But there is no continuity in a circle.

The notion to leave this house to an unborn babe—everything I have, as little as it is—is the last foolish wish in a lifetime of foolish wishes. My own life has produced neither art nor issue. I can think of no one else I would want to continue on here, so I permit myself one last sentimental indulgence.

Another senile conceit of mine: I would like the child to be a girl. I have from the first thought of the infant as she. It does not really matter, but my imagination creates her so.

Nine

Landru's charm, in the end, won everyone over to him. The petition to President Millerand was signed by several French notables, by all the jurors, and even by members of the families of the victims. But Landru himself would not sign the petition for reprieve. "Jamais un homme comme moi ne demande ni grace ni pitié."

Miss Stein translated this aloud: "Never would a man like me ask for clemency or pity."

"You have to admire his fortitude," said Miss Toklas.

"I cannot and will not," said Miss Stein, "but I do admire his style."

On the twenty-fourth of February Millerand rejected the final appeal of Maître de Moro Giafferi: the execution was set for dawn of the following day.

Press passes were not issued until the night before the execution, to prevent duplication. Called a coupe-fil (wire cutter), the card admitting witnesses to the execution bore a violet band running from corner to corner in the style of a French condolence card.

Deibler had received his official blue envelope, with the

seal of the place Vendôme. Ordinarily he would have immediately reserved places for himself, his crew and equipment on the train to Versailles, but this time he had been advised to keep word of the execution secret for as long as possible, so he sent the guillotine to Versailles in a discreetly unmarked horse-drawn carriage.

Naturally the event was known in advance to the café and sporting crowd—le tout Paris (for this was Landru's faithful public)—and the night hawks of the theatre set, with their instinct for sensation, began to flock to Versailles long before the arrival of La Veuve (the guillotine).

At four in the morning of the twenty-fifth of February, M. Ducrocq, director of the police judiciaire, and Commissioner Guillaume, along with Judge Bonin and Brigadier (soon to be Inspector) Riboulet, traveled to Versailles in a black limousine. Brigadier Riboulet carried a bar of chocolate in his pocket for the condemned man.

"I like that touch," said Miss Stein, inordinately fond of chocolate herself.

The carriage with the guillotine arrived at Saint Pierre prison later than planned. The dread instrument had been dispatched at 2 AM, but the carriage was stopped on the rue de Rivoli by an overzealous agent de police. He noticed one of the taillights was out.

Miss Stein yawned.

"I could pass over the details."

"The details," she said, "are what you have written."

"Do the details become gruesome?" asked Miss Toklas.

Miss Stein explained that she always advised Alice not to watch the horses during a bullfight, a cruel but necessary spectacle. "Alice loves horses and should not see them injured in that way."

I decided to summarize my essay on the execution in a way to satisfy Miss Stein's love of gossip but not offend the sensibilities of Miss Toklas.

Meanwhile I revisited Versailles via the mind's eye, on my own, and throughout this reenactment only half-heard the version I read aloud to the ladies.

The streets of Versailles were already crowded when the police limousine turned into the rue Georges Clemenceau. Harry identified the occupants for us: we were gathered at a café opposite the gates of Saint Pierre prison, a group of journalists who had made the café their headquarters since midnight.

The crowd was pushed back as far as the boulevard du Roi, and more spectators were arriving all the while. There were barriers around the place of execution, and within the temporary wooden fence Deibler's assistants bolted together their sinister machine by lantern light. The assistants wore blue workmen's tunics for the dirty work of assembling the scaffold, but would change into dark suits for the execution. Monsieur Anatole Deibler was already dressed in dark grey, a color favored by undertakers, with his black chapeau melon fixed low on his forehead. He carried a level in his hand, and would call out the gradient to his first assistant, Desforneaux, as together they calculated the angle of decline.

Deibler was a technician of the guillotine as well as its chief operator. He had made constant adjustments to the original design. It was he who thought of adding rubber cousinets on each side of the lunette to smother the sound of the blade, and he had done away with the elevated platform so that the condemned did not have to climb those dreadful last ten steps.

After the police limousine was let through, the last vehicle to pass the police barrier was an early morning trolley car full of workmen on their way to jobs. The men pushed to the windows on the side of the trolley that gave onto the place of execution. The trolley passed through the forbidden zone at mourning pace while the men stared numbly at the stark scene illuminated by lanterns. As soon as the trolley car got past, the wooden balustrade was reerected.

Harry and I had come down by taxi with the Reuters man and a French reporter. We shared a café table with the scruffy Danglure: he, watchful for any stray drink that might come his way, the others checking periodically through the steamed-up window to note the progress of Deibler's crew.

The French reporter gave me a list of the parts of the guillotine (numbered during transport, for easy assembly): le socle, le cadre, les arcs-boutants, les cales, la bassine, la boîte à lames, la bascule—being placed at that very moment—la glissière, le panier—

"A basket?"

"Filled with bran."

I got the picture, and said, "I understand."

("A basket?" asked Miss Toklas, but I hurried on.)

The Reuters man had been reviewing highlights of the trial to which only Harry made reply, challenging Reuters on insignificant details of testimony and procedure. Danglure had lost or forgotten his cheap dentures and kept muttering through his spittle: "I just want to see his gueule one more time." He complained of being denied a pass. If I had not thought it cowardly I would have gladly given him mine.

A steadily replenished line of taxis disgorged passengers before the café, then sped back to Paris for a fresh load. Our newspaper outpost was crowded now with le tout Paris, women in capes and dancing slippers, their escorts in tenue de soirée—for they had come directly from their nightclubs to this obscure bistro in Versailles. The café society drank champagne, until the patron ran out of it, then cognac, until that too was exhausted. I sat in a private pit of misery, inside the larger pit, my hands clasped around a hot rum toddy. Harry, with the intention of keeping a cool head, had passed his cognac on to Danglure.

All of the troops from the Versailles garrison were on duty that night. They were reinforced by the gendarmerie of the capital. Police were everywhere. Mounted patrolmen blocked the rue Georges Clemenceau, but the side streets were packed with humanity. Adolescent boys had contrived to climb the lamp posts and were now scrambling into the trees surrounding the square, but they were discovered in short order by the roving patrols, and ignominiously hauled down.

As dawn approached, our private outpost was invaded by a troop of gendarmes. They had orders to close the café, which was too near the site of execution. Danglure moaned: we were turned out. Upstairs the officers found four ladies in bed. "We are trying to sleep, Messieurs!" A gendarme bluntly flung away the coverlet: the occupants were fully dressed, in evening attire—only the threat of arrest could remove them from the premises.

Other stowaways were found hiding in the water closet, behind beer tonneaux in the cave, and in the cabine de téléphone. An officer was obliged to escort the bistro keeper from room to room as he drew the windows closed, then shuttered and locked the café.

Danglure attempted to talk his way past the contingent of guards at the barrier, but was turned back, still whining about having scooped them all. Harry and I were allowed to pass, and we joined the growing circle of newsmen and officials gathered around the scaffold. I stood trembling inside from some personal agony as well as the dawn chill. No one spoke. The gas lamps had been turned off and the light from the lanterns cast oddly angled shadows against the prison wall. As the lamps were moved about, I saw a guillotine enlarged, then two, three guillotines together, altering shape—the next moment nothing, then heads—the bobbing heads of assistants scrambling over the scaffold (they moved so fast, they worked so fiercely), then Deibler's head alone, monstrous and detached. In the dark I felt for my own head. It was in place, numb with cold and fear.

At 5h the guillotine was assembled to Deibler's exacting satisfaction, ten meters to the left of the prison gate. Deibler, in his mournful garb, stepped away from the machine, removed the ladder and propped it against the wall well away from his chef-d'oeuvre. He then went through the prison gate.

Landru was awakened at 5h 25. This information was given to the press by Maître Navière de Treuil, assistant to the defense attorney.

A priest was at hand, l'abbé Loisel, vicar of Notre Dame de Versailles. When Landru came awake the priest's words to him were: "Have courage."

"Naturally I shall have courage. Haven't I already shown that I have courage?"

He addressed this last remark to the officials who stood around him in the narrow cell. He looked each man full in the face and said, "Gentlemen, I am at your disposition. Would you be so good as to pass me my clothes?"

Landru proceeded to his toilet as if he were alone. He had always been fastidious about his personal appearance, and had customarily made a complete change of linen before each rendezvous with his fiancée of the moment.

During this time he ignored the assembly of dignitaries, including his lawyer, Maître de Moro Giafferi. The shirt he put on had the collar cut away. If he noticed this ominous alteration he did not comment.

Landru was about to put on his shoes, but a guard informed him this would not be necessary. Landru shrugged. It was then that Brigadier Riboulet stepped forward and offered his old adversary a bar of chocolate. For a moment Landru fixed Riboulet with a look of polite irony. "Je vous remercie," he said, and he accepted the chocolate. He ate it with unnerving aplomb.

Judge Bonin, with his clerk, was on hand to receive any confession in extremis Landru might decide to make. The substitut délégué stepped forward and asked: "Do you have anything you might wish to say at this time?"

Landru examined the man carefully: "To whom have I the honor of speaking?"

"I am Monsieur Beguin, the substitut délégué of the parquet général."

Landru bowed slightly, acknowledging the man and his title, then said, "What would you like me to say? I am innocent, as I have maintained all along. This will not be the first time you have executed an innocent man."

Monsieur Beguin stepped back.

At that point l'abbé Loisel asked Landru if he would like to hear Mass, for a chapel had been set up in the storeroom adjoining Landru's cell, but Landru replied: "I would gladly oblige you, but I assume all is ready." He turned to Deibler and his two assistants. "I do not want to detain these gentlemen."

The first assistant, Henri Desforneaux, asked Landru to place his wrists together behind his back.

"Must you bind me?" asked Landru.

Desforneaux turned to his chief for confirmation, and Deibler spoke for the first time: "I'm afraid it's the rule."

Deibler and Landru exchanged a frank regard: two men observing one another with mutual respect. Had they not, both, been obliged by fate to follow bizarre paths and accept onerous work?

"Very well, then." Landru did as he was requested. He held himself erect and surveyed the gathering with stoic calm as Desforneaux bound his hands with a leather thong.

Landru bade the assembled officials adieu, and to his defense attorney, Maître de Moro Giafferi, made his final statement: "I regret, Maître, I gave you so difficult a case to defend."

"Were those his last words?" asked Miss Stein, who was always interested in last words.

"As far as I know."

"A pity they were not more memorable."

As dawn broke, a large horse-drawn van appeared from the prison courtyard and backed up within a few meters of the guillotine. Attendants pulled two wicker baskets from the van. They placed the round container in front of the machine, and the larger coffin-shaped basket beside the platform. The baskets each contained a layer of bran.

The great wooden gates of the prison yard had been left open.

Harry brought a stopwatch out of the pocket of his raincoat and showed it to me. I nodded at his foresight. As soon as the three swiftly moving figures appeared at the gate, Harry pressed the timer.

By the pale streak of light across the February sky I could make out the shrunken figure and waxen visage of Landru between two guards. So much reduced from his courtroom presence, so much less vivid—with only an instant left to live, he seemed no longer alive.

The mounted police along the length of the barrier raised their swords as Landru was half-carried, half-dragged the short distance to the guillotine. I could see where the shirt had been slashed open at the neck. The condemned man wore cheap prison trousers, but no socks or shoes: I heard his bare feet slap against the cold cobblestone. As he was rushed past the line of soldiers with their sabers drawn, his knees seemed not to function.

I try to recall the thoughts that must have overwhelmed me at the sight of this man moving inexorably to his death. His legend had so dominated my young Paris life until now—but I do not know that I felt pity or fear or disgust, certainly not a sense of justice—vengeance for Fleur, for anyone—only a stunned awe, a stupor that prevented me from thinking anything. I had put my press pass between my lips, and was chewing on it.

Harry's stopwatch ticked in the deadly calm. Landru drew back and stiffened at the dreadful sight of the instrument made ready for him, but that moment of hesitation was fleeting. The guards bore him forward, then thrust his body onto the poised bascule, which tilted immediately with his weight yet seemed to fall in slow motion.

At this instant reflex action will cause the head to be drawn into the shoulders, but the assistant standing beside the lunette took hold of Landru's hair and jerked the head into the slot. Instantly the wooden yoke meant to hold the head fixed in place fell into position. I could discern no lapse of time between the fall of the yoke and the release of the blade. I saw and heard nothing: the blade fell of itself.

Landru's head dropped into the basket. The forward assistant lifted the hinged yoke and a great spurt of blood gushed out of the severed neck splattering Deibler's trousers. The headless body was rolled into the wicker coffin. An aide standing in front of the machine seized the basket containing the head and tilted the contents into the larger basket, then two hasty pallbearers shoved the wicker coffin into the waiting van.

"Twenty-six seconds," said Harry, thrusting his stopwatch in my face. The Reuters man made a note of the time: 6h 04. Suddenly I made out the toothless triumphant grin of Danglure among the faces that swam before my eyes: he had squirmed through the police line after all, and had succeeded in being in at the kill.

I felt faint, glad for once to be supported by the reassuring bulk of Harry, flanked by Reuters on the other side. At the far end of the circle a man with a ribbon in his buttonhole had turned and was vomiting between the forelegs of a gendarme's horse.

The funeral van was already rattling through a narrow passage-way cleared along the boulevard that led to the Cimetière des Gonards outside Versailles. There the mutilated body was to be interred—along with Landru's grim secret, and mine.

FINE WORKS OF FICTION
AVAILABLE IN QUALITY
PAPERBACK EDITIONS FROM
CARROLL & GRAF

☐ Asch, Sholem/THE APOSTLE	$10.95
☐ Asch, Sholem/THE NAZARENE	$10.95
☐ Asch, Sholem/THREE CITIES	$10.50
☐ Balzac, Honoré de/CESAR BIROTTEAU	$8.95
☐ Balzac, Honoré de/THE LILY OF THE VALLEY	$9.95
☐ Bellaman, Henry/KINGS ROW	$8.95
☐ Bernanos, George/DIARY OF A COUNTRY PRIEST	$7.95
☐ Blasco Ibañez, Vicente/THE FOUR HORSEMEN OF THE APOCALYPSE	$8.95
☐ Borges, Jorge Luis, et al./THE BOOK OF FANTASY	$10.95
☐ Brand, Christianna/GREEN FOR DANGER	$8.95
☐ Céline, Louis-Ferdinand/CASTLE TO CASTLE	$8.95
☐ Chekhov, Anton/LATE BLOOMING FLOWERS	$8.95
☐ Conrad, Joseph/EASTERN SKIES, WESTERN SEAS	$12.95
☐ Conrad, Joseph/SEA STORIES	$8.95
☐ Conrad, Joseph & Ford Madox Ford/ ROMANCE	$8.95
☐ Delbanco, Nicholas/GROUP PORTRAIT	$10.95
☐ de Maupassant, Guy/THE DARK SIDE	$8.95
☐ de Poncins, Gontran/KABLOONA	$9.95
☐ Dos Passos, John/THREE SOLDIERS	$9.95
☐ Durrell, Laurence/THE BLACK BOOK	$8.95
☐ Feuchtwanger, Lion/JEW SUSS	$8.95
☐ Feuchtwanger, Lion/THE OPPERMANNS	$8.95
☐ Fitzgerald, Penelope/THE BEGINNING OF SPRING	$8.95
☐ Fitzgerald, Penelope/INNOCENCE	$7.95
☐ Fitzgerald, Penelope/OFFSHORE	$7.95
☐ Flaubert, Gustave/NOVEMBER	$7.95
☐ Fuchs, Daniel/SUMMER IN WILLIAMSBURG	$8.95
☐ Gold, Michael/JEWS WITHOUT MONEY	$7.95
☐ Gorky, Maxim/THE LIFE OF A USELESS MAN	$10.95
☐ Greenberg & Waugh (eds.)/THE NEW ADVENTURES OF SHERLOCK HOLMES	$8.95
☐ Hamsun, Knut/MYSTERIES	$8.95
☐ Higgins, George V./TWO COMPLETE NOVELS	$11.95
☐ Hugo, Victor/NINETY-THREE	$8.95
☐ Huxley, Aldous/ANTIC HAY	$10.95
☐ Huxley, Aldous/CROME YELLOW	$10.95
☐ Huxley, Aldous/EYELESS IN GAZA	$9.95
☐ Jackson, Charles/THE LOST WEEKEND	$7.95
☐ James, Henry/GREAT SHORT NOVELS	$11.95
☐ Jones, Richard/THE MAMMOTH BOOK OF MURDER	$8.95
☐ Just, Ward/THE CONGRESSMAN WHO LOVED FLAUBERT	$8.95
☐ Macaulay, Rose/CREWE TRAIN	$8.95
☐ Macaulay, Rose/DANGEROUS AGES	$8.95

☐ Maugham, W. Somerset/THE EXPLORER $10.95
☐ Mauriac, François/VIPER'S TANGLE $8.95
☐ Mauriac, François/THE DESERT OF LOVE $6.95
☐ Mauriac, François/FLESH AND BLOOD $8.95
☐ McElroy, Joseph/LOOKOUT CARTRIDGE $9.95
☐ McElroy, Joseph/THE LETTER LEFT TO ME $6.95
☐ McElroy, Joseph/A SMUGGLER'S BIBLE $9.50
☐ Mitford, Nancy/DON'T TELL ALFRED $7.95
☐ Moorcock, Michael/THE BROTHEL IN ROSENSTRASSE $6.95
☐ Munro, H.H./THE NOVELS AND PLAYS OF SAKI $8.95
☐ Neider, Charles (ed.)/GREAT SHORT STORIES $11.95
☐ Neider, Charles (ed.)/SHORT NOVELS
   OF THE MASTERS $12.95
☐ O'Faolain, Julia/THE OBEDIENT WIFE $7.95
☐ O'Faolain, Julia/NO COUNTRY FOR YOUNG MEN $8.95
☐ O'Faolain, Julia/WOMEN IN THE WALL $8.95
☐ Olinto, Antonio/THE WATER HOUSE $8.95
☐ O'Mara, Lesley/GREAT CAT TALES $9.95
☐ Pronzini & Greenberg (eds.)/THE MAMMOTH BOOK OF
   PRIVATE EYE NOVELS $8.95
☐ Rhys, Jean/AFTER LEAVING MR. MACKENZIE $8.95
☐ Rhys, Jean/QUARTET $7.95
☐ Sand, George/MARIANNE $7.95
☐ Scott, Evelyn/THE WAVE $9.95
☐ Settle, Mary Lee/CHARLEY BLAND $8.95
☐ Singer, I.J./THE BROTHERS ASHKENAZI $9.95
☐ Taylor, Elizabeth/IN A SUMMER SEASON $8.95
☐ Thornton, Louise et al./TOUCHING FIRE $9.95
☐ Tolstoy, Leo/TALES OF COURAGE AND CONFLICT $11.95
☐ Wassermann, Jacob/CASPAR HAUSER $9.95
☐ Weldon, Fay/LETTERS TO ALICE $6.95
☐ Werfel, Franz/THE FORTY DAYS OF MUSA DAGH $13.95
☐ West, Rebecca/THE RETURN OF THE SOLDIER $8.95
☐ Wharton, Edith/THE STORIES OF EDITH
   WHARTON $10.95